DEADLY LIES

KYLIE HATFIELD SERIES: BOOK TWO

MARY STONE
BELLA CROSS

❀ Created with Vellum

Mary Stone

To my husband.
Thank you for taking care of our home and its many inhabitants while I follow this silly dream of mine.

Bella Cross

To my family. Thank you for your unending support, love, and patience while I navigate this exciting new world of publishing.

DESCRIPTION

Family is everything...unless they want you dead.

Sweet little Emma Jennings is certain someone is robbing her vast estate, and she wants Kylie Hatfield on the case. Sure, an embezzlement case might be boring—boring and Kylie don't mix—but Kylie feels for the octogenarian and pledges to right the wrong. She's certain that she can. She's just been promoted to Assistant PI of Starr Investigations, after all.

When embezzlement turns to murder, Kylie is once again tossed into a situation she isn't prepared for, and her personal life isn't much better. Sexy Linc Coulter, her Newfoundland's trainer and her friend with benefits, is facing demons of his own.

As her search for answers to Emma Jennings's case grows more dangerous, Kylie is beginning to suspect that she might indeed be a magnet for trouble—and killers. Even worse, she also suspects that she might be Linc Coulter's greatest downfall.

If you like your murder mysteries with a dose of

romance, humor, and a few good dogs, Deadly Lies, the second book of the compelling Kylie Hatfield Series, will tug at your heartstrings even as you pull the covers over your head.

1

The colors weren't right.

Frustrated, Arnold Jennings tossed the pallet of paint onto the long table at his side. They hadn't been right for days. Maybe he needed a rest.

Sighing in frustration, he gingerly sat down on his favorite stool, remembering fondly all the times he and the love of his life, his wife of sixty-one years, had fooled around on that very stool. He felt quite certain that he and Emma had conceived one of their daughters on that very piece of furniture.

The memory made him smile.

He'd been a lucky man.

Well, in the early days.

He'd found the perfect girl, and she'd said yes when he asked for her hand. She'd supported his art. He smiled bigger, settling more comfortably on the worn seat beneath his tired behind. Oh, how Emma had supported him.

"Naughty girl," he'd call her when she'd seduce him from his work.

It hadn't taken much.

It was a wonder that they hadn't had a brood of children, birth control being so unreliable back in those early days.

The smile slid from his face as memories of the miscarriages, one after the next, forced their way into the present. All boys, Arnold was told.

Seven of them, all now lying under their little markers in a row at the Jennings family cemetery.

Each loss made him paint harder. Each painting gave him an escape from the crushing blow.

There'd been no escaping the pain for Emma, so no matter that he'd have preferred a small cabin in the woods, he commissioned this home to give her something to do with her time. To distract her. Allow her to give birth to something that didn't give her sorrow.

The house should have been overlooking some estate in France, grapes growing so near you could reach out the window and pluck them off the vines. Not in some small North Carolina town.

He didn't care.

Emma loved the design, and what Emma wanted, Emma got.

She flew all over the world selecting tapestries and carpeting and stone.

Slowly, she began to smile again.

And three days after they'd moved into their new home, he convinced her to allow him to paint her again. It had been years since she'd felt free enough to do so.

Her body had changed. Four of the pregnancies had lasted up until the child was born, and stretch marks marred the once perfect flesh of her stomach. The breasts that had once sat on her chest so high had fallen from the weight of milk no child would be blessed enough to drink.

She'd never been more beautiful to him.

And he'd painted her with an exhilaration he hadn't felt in so many years.

She'd come to him then, just as she'd done in the earlier years of their marriage. They'd made love on this stool, and weeks later, they learned of another pregnancy.

They dared not hope. They didn't even select a nursery from the vast number of rooms in their stately home. They chose no name. Essentially, they didn't speak of the pregnancy at all.

Until Emma's water broke in the middle of one winter night.

A blizzard had been raging all that day, and their doctor had assured them that the chances of Emma going into labor were slim. They had been three weeks from delivery, after all.

But go into labor, she did.

With more than a foot of snow outside, there was no hope of getting to the hospital or of emergency personnel to get to them. It was good that they hadn't allowed themselves to become excited about the impending birth because, as they spoke of their situation, gathered necessary implements to help them, neither expected a good outcome.

Arnold just hoped he wouldn't also lose his wife.

Emma's pain had been terrible, and it had been the first time Arnold had been witness to any of the births. He thought she would surely die of it. He wanted to run, to drink himself into a stupor.

But he was all she had.

The Christmas holidays had just passed, and all the servants had been given leave to visit with their families. They were well and truly on their own.

And to their amazement, a baby girl had slithered out into Arnold's hands. To their further amazement, the child opened her eyes and then gave a hearty wail.

He hadn't known what to do, but some primal instinct kicked in, and he cleared the baby's mouth and nose before putting the child on her mother's chest. She soon began to suckle. The beauty of the memory played in Arnold's mind in vivid detail. He remembered the color of the first rays of sunlight peeking through the drapes. But most of all, he remembered Emma's smile.

"Noel," Emma said. "Can we name her that?"

Emma could have named her anything. "Yes, my love. Noel Joy."

It had only been a suggestion, but even as it left his mouth, it felt right. Emma beamed at him.

"Yes, Noel Joy."

Three years later, Noel became a big sister, to another girl child who was born in a proper hospital with much less drama, but no less love.

Summer Hope came out screaming and lived life just as loud.

"I'm going to be the first female president when I get older," Summer had declared on her tenth birthday.

At the time, Arnold hadn't doubted it for a second.

His younger daughter had had a plan. Law school. Run for first political office. White House. Exactly in that order and at that speed. When she found a "suitable partner" and got married, it had surprised them all.

His eldest, on the other hand, had one goal…to become a mother.

Her journey to that goal had been as rocky as her own mother's had been. Miscarriages. Stillbirths. Then Nathaniel Gabriel Jennings-Jennings came into their world.

Noel had married a Jennings. No relation, if you please. Her younger sister had insisted she keep her maiden name, as repetitive as it was. Women's independence and all that.

Over the years, Nathaniel became Nate and his surname trimmed down to a single Jennings.

Life had been good.

Until it hadn't.

Until the morning they awoke to a policeman at their door, giving them the terrible news that their daughters were dead, burned alive in a chalet in Maine, where they'd gone on a joint vacation.

Nate had survived, which had been the only glimmer of light left in their world.

But Nate had changed.

No longer the well-loved smiling teenager, this new Nate never smiled and only came out of his room when forced. When he learned that he wouldn't be getting all of his inheritance in one lump sum, he'd been so angry. Scary angry. He'd broken priceless artifacts in their home, ramming his fist through dozens of Arnold's paintings.

Both Emma and Arnold had feared for their very lives.

Sloane, their butler, had called for help, and Nate had been taken away, hospitalized for months.

He'd come home even more different. Not so angry, exactly, just withdrawn.

They hired tutors in which to homeschool him, as he refused to go to school.

They tried therapist after therapist, prescription after prescription.

Eventually, Nate found his own type of drug, and by the time Arnold and Emma learned of what he was doing to his body, it was too late.

They'd lost it all. The babies. The daughters. Now, the beloved grandson was lost in a different, even more brutal fashion.

But they had each other.

"That will be enough," Arnold told Emma one chilly spring morning.

It was just one of the lies they'd told each other.

They had become almost like robots for a while, but slowly...oh so slowly...their steps had grown lighter, their smiles more apt to appear, and Arnold thought that, maybe, just maybe, they would be okay.

Another lie.

Over time, Arnold threw himself back into his painting again, and Emma threw herself into her charitable work. She even hired an assistant to help her, which had pleased Arnold to no end.

Soon after that, Nate reappeared in their lives.

He was clean and sober, he promised. He wanted to be a good grandson again.

And he was. For a while.

A knock on the door startled Arnold from his ruminations, and he pushed to his feet, his knees cracking and popping as his weight left the stool.

"Come in," he called.

The door opened and Arnold smiled as a tray brandishing a pot of tea appeared, along with his favorite cookies. "Thank you, Sloane."

The butler inclined his head. "Anything else, sir?"

Grabbing a cookie, Arnold waved the manservant off. "That will be all."

Arnold was adding milk to his tea, a habit he'd picked up when he and Emma had visited London nearly five decades ago, when a voice startled him.

His heart pounded in his chest. He raised a hand to rub at the spot as he turned and faced his new visitor. "What do you want?"

He hadn't meant to sound so snappish, but he deplored

when people went sneaking about. And he deplored how scared he'd been for those few seconds.

Arnold rubbed at his chest again, willing his heart to quiet its frantic movement.

"I need a loan."

Arnold scoffed. "Another one? Didn't I just give you a loan last month?"

"It wasn't enough."

Shaking his head, Arnold went to pick up his tea again, giving himself time to think.

How had it come to this?

Guilt? Sorrow?

"Please..."

The pleading in the tone had the opposite effect than he was sure was intended. It pissed him off.

"No."

He felt movement behind him more than saw it. He tried not to flinch but wasn't quite successful. "You hateful old man."

Sweat bloomed on his brow, trickled down his back. His chest began to throb, air refusing to fill his lungs.

"Call the doctor," he said, clutching at his chest.

A laugh was his only response.

More panicked now, Arnold knew he had to get downstairs. He had to get to Emma. A phone.

Pushing past his visitor, he stumbled through the door and into the hallway.

Pain seized him, almost taking him to his knees, but he refused to go down so easily.

Making it to the bannister, he flinched as a hand came down on his shoulder. "Give me the loan, and I'll help you."

With as much strength as Arnold could muster, he pulled away, and began his descent down the stairs.

A foot appeared.

He saw it because he'd been watching his own feet as he held on to the railing.

Arnold gasped, and he supposed that he really shouldn't have been that surprised.

While all the world thought how blessed the Jennings were, Arnold knew that was yet another lie.

The Jennings were indeed cursed.

Arnold wanted to warn Emma, tell her that he'd been wrong all along. Tell her to be careful. To be watchful. Their home had been invaded and there was no one they could trust.

But he was falling even as the thoughts crossed over his mind.

It seemed to take a long time to get to the bottom. His paintings flashed across his vision, the colors blurring together.

And as he lay at the bottom, his eyes fastened on Emma. He'd painted that one before their children's deaths. She looked so beautiful. So free. Gazing at her brought him solace.

The pain was incredible but mercifully short as darkness stripped him of even that small comfort.

2

F*ive years later...*

Hunt, peck. Hunt, peck.

Life with one working hand, for lack of a more appropriate word, sucked.

Alone in the office of Starr Investigations, downtown Asheville's premiere full-service private investigations establishment, Kylie pushed back from the typewriter and stretched her aching back. She had a pile of background check chicken-scratch notes she'd taken over the phone that she'd been trying to transfer to some semblance of an orderly report, but her little injury was kind of getting in the way.

Little injury. *Ha.*

She had a gunshot wound in her shoulder. Thirty-eight caliber passed clear through the muscle.

Yeah, she was badass. That's how she rolled.

Except now. Now that Greg Starr, her boss, had resigned

her to office work. Now, in her little cardigan, ponytail, and comfy shoes, she looked about as badass as Big Bird.

Hopefully, that was just temporary.

Not that she wanted to field bullets on a daily basis, but she definitely didn't want to be chained to this desk either, with Greg's easy-listening Muzak piping through his boom box to keep her company. She probably looked like the world's youngest senior citizen now, jamming out to Enya.

Greg had said the exclusive desk work was "until her injury healed," but she worried that he was trying to keep her out of trouble. She frowned. He even made her turn down the robbery case for a sweet little lady who'd called the other day.

That still made her mad.

Weeks ago, Greg promised that he'd train her to be more of a private investigator like him, instead of just his lousy assistant, but one really couldn't be a PI while sitting behind a desk. The fingers of her lame hand itched with the desire to blow this joint and get back into doing some meatier things.

Like, bringing down serial killers. Oh, yeah. That was another badass thing she'd done.

This woman, the Spotlight Killer, had terrorized the entire country, wreaking havoc from Texas to North Carolina, until Kylie Hatfield, badass extraordinaire, stepped in and ended her reign of terror. Or something like that.

Kylie'd actually heard that on an episode of *Nightline*. They'd made her seem so fearless, but…the truth involved a lot more of her cowering and shaking and nearly peeing her pants.

She looked down at Vader, her goofy Newfoundland, and ruffled his fur. She couldn't have done it without him. Him and Lincoln Coulter, her *real* badass of a…

Whatever he was.

She wasn't really sure. He was more than her dog's

trainer, that was for sure, since they were…intimate. Boyfriend sounded so sixth grade. They hadn't really defined it. Fuckbuddy? It definitely seemed like more than that. The last night she'd spent with him, she was pretty sure the "L" word was about to slip out of his mouth. She'd put a stop to that, real fast. Because…love. No thank you. She knew what happened when love and commitment came along. A big ole bunch of nothing.

So, what was he to her?

Significant Other? Man? Man Candy? Male Accessory? What?

Whenever she thought about it too hard, it made her head hurt. Besides, maybe they were nothing now. It'd been three days since she'd last seen him, and she hadn't gotten so much as a text. Of course, he was notoriously awful when it came to texting. Or communicating with anything not a canine.

Still, she smiled, thinking of him. He was so damn… yummy. Yummy and hard and hot and sweet, even though it was a challenge to get him to say more than two words on a good day. He was definitely that strong, silent type.

AKA, the opposite of Kylie.

She, like her mother, could carry on a conversation with a wall. That's what made her and Linc so good together. She was her, and he was the wall. Seriously. The man didn't have an ounce of fat on him.

Just then, Vader licked her hand, reminding her to stop grinning goofily and get back to work on the nightmare of notes she had before her. The hunting-and-pecking was definitely taking its toll. Her eyes crossed.

She'd been working on reports all morning and only completed three of the fifteen she had to do. Her doctor had told her that she should have a full recovery, but that she should take it easy and keep her arm in the sling, but she wasn't exactly good at listening to him. She would never win any awards for patience.

As she was sitting there, floating away on another daydream that involved Linc—their most recent foray into his barn had been particularly hot, even though she still had the scratches on her butt from the hay to show for it—the door opened and her boss walked in, holding a big bouquet of irises.

"For me?" she asked, patting her chest and batting her eyelashes.

Greg grunted a, "Yes," and laid them on her desk.

Really? She'd only been kidding. Her boss wasn't exactly the bright ray of sunshine and liked her only about fifty percent of the time. But he did have a soft side. She smiled and leaned over to sniff the flowers.

"Aww…they're beautiful, thank you! What's the occasion?"

He shrugged as she winked at him and went to get a vase in the kitchenette. "Thought your desk needed some brightening up."

That was bunk. Her desk was plenty bright, what with the photos of her mom and Vader, a funky, hot pink modern-art balloon-dog sculpture, a little African violet plant, and her big smiley-face mug. It was the rest of the place that looked morbid. He was just feeling guilty that she'd ended up shot, even though more than two weeks had gone by. He was blameless, though. She'd told him that, a million times.

Told him that she had a knack for getting in trouble and it had nothing to do with him, since he hadn't even wanted her on the case to begin with. But Kylie could tell Greg still felt bad about it. He didn't say as much, but she had a suspicion he thought of her as the daughter he never had. Though, maybe he did have daughters? Greg was a little tight-lipped about his personal life. She'd been trying for weeks to set him up with her mom, but it was like lassoing a mountain and bringing it downtown.

"You finish those reports?" he grumbled when she started to arrange the flowers in the vase.

"My five fingers are working as fast as they can," she said brightly, wiggling them for him. "Everything seems to be taking twice as long. Can't imagine why."

He gave her his droopy bloodhound frown. "Well. Just stick with it. You finish the report on the Spotlight Killer case?"

She nodded. "On your desk."

He went around and opened the file, reading it over. "What the hell is this? 'Lincoln Coulter heroically burst into the shed, growling fiercely, with no regard to his own personal safety?'"

She nodded. "What's wrong with that?"

"It sounds like you're trying to write a romance novel. Just the facts, Kylie. I know that man of yours is dreamy, as you kids call it, but keep your personal feelings out of it."

Dreamy? She wasn't a member of the Brady Bunch.

She shrugged and slunk down in her chair. "Too much? I thought I *was* keeping my feelings out of it. I refrained from calling the killer a total psycho bitch, didn't I?"

"Great. But your objectivity still needs a little work. *Coulter arrived on the scene*. That's it." He motioned to the file folders behind her. "When you're not busy, take a look at some of the ones I've written. God knows, after decades in the business, I have enough of them. Learn, short stuff."

Kylie sighed. Well, there went her idea of spicing the job up a little by adding flair to the reports. "Fine."

He sat down in his chair and leaned back, yawning. "Any messages?"

She shook her head.

He sighed. "Any messages you're hiding from me because you want to meddle in the case first?"

She gave him an innocent look. "Who do you think I am?"

He smirked at her. "A pain in the ass?"

Okay, so he had her number. Kylie'd been hired at the end of the spring as his secretary, but she wasn't really good at sticking within that role. She'd already gotten herself embroiled in two cases which had started out as messages for *him*. It was all her fault. She was just too curious. Too excited. Too itchy for adventure to sit behind a desk, typing a bunch of crap and doing what voicemail could easily do, when there were actual wrongs out there that needed to be righted.

"Really. No messages. I haven't even gotten a phone call since that sweet little Emma Jennings called the other evening, needing our help."

She still couldn't believe he wouldn't let her take that case. Her shoulder was practically one-hundred-percent better now. She shrugged, hiding the wince. Okay, maybe seventy percent better.

"All right," he said with a suspicious lilt to his voice, sitting down in his chair and fishing out an orange to peel.

She finished arranging the flowers and sat back down at the typewriter, wondering if Greg would ever step into the present and get a computer for this place. He'd told her the day before that he'd just gotten a fax machine last year. In return, she'd told him she was surprised he could *find* a fax machine since no one used them anymore. It was funny watching him try to use it. Like a Neanderthal trying to work an iPhone.

Ten minutes later, Kylie looked up from the six words she'd had the heart to type and saw him staring at her contemplatively. "What?"

He pointed to the report. "And I quote, 'The killer stalked the young private investigator mercilessly, leaving her no choice but to put an end to the horror.' Really?"

She rolled her eyes. "Okay, okay, I know, just the facts. It may sound a little like a Masterpiece mystery, but you asked for details. And it makes the work fun. It's so dull, otherwise."

"Yeah, yeah. But there are so many things wrong with this, beyond that excessive prose. One: You're *not* a PI. I just made you my assistant. I'm training you. But nearly getting offed by a serial killer doesn't change the fact you don't know what the hell you're doing. And two..." He threw a hand against the report. "This is serious shit, short stuff. She stalked you to this office and she followed you to your apartment." He was dead serious now. "Shit, Kylie. Why didn't you tell me any of that before she tased your ass and shot you in the shoulder?"

Kylie shrugged. "She actually tased my neck."

Greg scowled at her.

She worried her bottom lip. She'd actually forgotten that her boss hadn't been privy to most of what was happening with that case, but she'd kept him in the dark because she'd known he'd strip the case from her quicker than she could blink if she'd told him. "It's okay. I survived, didn't I?"

"Barely," he muttered, dropping the report and closing the folder. "Look, Kylie. Consider this your first warning. I hired you to be my office girl, and I've told you time and time again that that's your first priority. If you feel the need to spice up the reports, spice them up. But don't pull shit like that without telling me."

She frowned. "First warning? What does that mean? Is that like...probation?"

Greg threw up his hands. He was the easiest boss around, really. Maybe too easy. Hated a lot of rules. Expected her to govern herself. She probably wasn't the best employee for that kind of arrangement. She had a knack for getting into sticky situations when left to her own devices.

"Call it what you will, but the fact is, you've been getting your cute little ass in too many jams since you started working here, and I don't want to see you get into one you can't pull yourself out of."

She pouted. Probation. That made her sad, especially since she'd been busting her butt to do well at this career. "You know I do all the filing and answering phones and menial stuff fine. And I can't help it if—"

"You *can*. You choose not to. Your handling of the menial shit around the office is acceptable. It *could* be better."

"It *could* be, if it didn't bore me to freaking tears," she muttered under her breath. Like she really cared that the R-S-T filing cabinet was overflowing while the U-V-W-X-Y-Z cabinet had barely anything in it. She was pretty sure that "filing" was the definition of insanity.

"Even so. It's your job. Your job is not getting shot at by serial killers. I've told you this before, but you don't seem to listen to me. You need to concentrate on *your job*."

His voice was harsh. Harsher than she'd ever heard it. It sounded like he was at the end of his rope. She sat back, stricken. She didn't know what to say.

It was a rare moment for her, not to know what to say, and clearly, Greg felt bad about it. He started to backpedal. "It's not glamorous, but it's essential to the day-to-day operations of this business. I'm out a lot, Kylie. I need this help to keep my little outfit chugging along, shipshape."

Kylie had the urge to give him shit, but then she glanced at the pretty flowers and swallowed that back. He suddenly looked a lot older than his sixty-some years, his salt-and-pepper hair sticking up and baring the receding hairline he usually kept it combed over. She hated to think she was contributing to the graying—or losing—of his hair.

So, she nodded. "Okay. If you say so. Even if the mundane stuff drives me insane, I will stick to it. No life-or-death stuff. I promise."

She crossed her heart for good measure.

"Good." He reached for his old blazer and straightened his tie. "I've got a meeting with Impact again. More workers' comp surveillance crap. See? I have my own shit to wade through. But that's why they call it work. If it was fun, they'd call it…fun. You'll be good?"

She gave him her brightest smile. "Always!"

He rolled his eyes. She swore she saw him lose some hair on the way out the door.

She kept plugging away at the report, feeling uneasy and depressed. She didn't do well with mundane. And this was the first time Greg had really, seriously, slapped her hand. Probation. Meh.

She'd failed at so many career starts in her life, and she didn't want to fail at this one, because this one, she actually *liked*. She'd changed her major half a dozen times before deciding to give up on college for a while and take this summer job. After the summer, she'd decided to keep with it.

This was the first thing she'd ever done in her adult life that felt like it could be her real career. It was more than like. She *loved* investigations. She wanted to keep this going, because she knew she'd be good at it.

And Greg was right. All jobs had bad parts. If she wanted to enjoy the many perks to being a private investigator, she just needed to learn how to stomach the bad moments.

When Greg left, she went to his old boom box and turned the radio off of Smooth Muzak 106, to a pop station, jamming out to some 5 Seconds of Summer as she tried to finish the report. After about a half hour, she'd broken a sweat, but still hadn't finished the damn report.

She draped herself over the typewriter, playing dead, and wondered if Greg would allow her to hire an assistant. This was cruel and unusual.

Her phone started to ring, and she pounced on it, eager to do anything but this infernal report. It was her mom. Kylie answered, ready to have a good, long conversation with her, like she usually did. The two of them were pretty chatty together, even though they spoke nearly every other day.

"Hi, Mom."

"Oh, honey. Did I catch you at a bad time?"

"No. I'm at work, but you know," she leaned back and gave the typewriter the middle finger, "it can wait. What's up?"

"I just miss my little girl. How's the shoulder? I thought you'd want to come to dinner again?"

Kylie smiled. She liked cooking almost as much as she liked filing. Most of the time, her dinners amounted to stale cereal, but it was even worse now. Now, she had less of a reason to want to cook, being mostly one-handed. All these things she'd thought were simple, like brushing her teeth or driving down the street...were pretty hard. She'd pretty much lived at her mom's for two weeks after her injury, and she'd eaten nothing but fast food in the three days she'd been back at her apartment. "Aren't you getting sick of me?"

"My only daughter, the light of my life? Never!" her mother cried in her usual dramatic fashion. "Anyway, I'm making lasagna, your favorite."

Mmmm. Her mother's lasagna. Her mouth started to water, since all she'd had all day was a bag of chips and a Diet Coke. And it wasn't like she had anything else to look forward to. In fact, since that little roll in the hay—literally—three days ago with Mr. Strong and Silent, she'd been pathetically unsocial. All the friends who'd had her phone ringing off the hook, wanting to know the deets about the serial killer, had pretty much gone back into the woodwork. No, for the last few days, it'd been her and Vader against the world.

"Well, I..."

She trailed off when she peered out the window and

glimpsed Linc walking down the sidewalk, toward the building in the dying light of day. Speak of the devil. God, he was a hot devil. He had Storm, his dog, with him and was just kind of loping down the street unassumingly, like he wasn't God's gift to women.

She ignored how her heart picked up speed. "Um. Actually. L—"

"You can bring him too. You know I'd love to see that hot hunk of yours."

That hot hunk had a name, but she wasn't sure her mom remembered it. All she'd ever called him was The Hunk. Her mom was right...he was a hunk. Tall, broad-shouldered, tanned, with chocolate brown eyes Kylie'd drowned in numerous times...his entire body was chiseled and strong and well...intimidating. Where she played at being a badass, Linc was as badass as they came, and he had numerous battle scars all over his body to prove it, every one of them infinitely lickable. He just oozed pure male sexuality, so much that her tummy tightened more with every step he took.

Kylie watched him, entranced, until it finally hit her, just what her mother had said. Had Kylie even finished saying Linc's name? How did her mom do that? Sometimes, her mom's psychic connection to her daughter was completely freaky. Or maybe her mom had a psychic connection to Linc.

The very first time she met him, she'd practically jumped into his arms and proposed on Kylie's behalf. Then she'd proceeded to tell him all about Kylie's lack of love life. Embarrassing? Hell yes.

Hmmm. Would she risk a replay of that embarrassment for epic lasagna? It was a close call.

"I've got to go," Kylie murmured as he started to open the door, pulling the phone from her ear.

"Is that a yes or a no?" rushed out of her mom's mouth before Kylie could end the call.

"It's an, 'I'll call you back,'" Kylie said, hanging up and wiping her chin discretely to make sure it was dry. She fluffed her hair, sat up straight, and tried to act as if the movement didn't cause her a little twinge of pain.

"Why, hello stranger," she said when he appeared, cringing as she realized all her efforts to sound sexy just made her sound like a goober.

But him? With his muscles bulging beneath the arms of his rolled-up denim shirt, which was open at the throat a little to reveal a flash of his hard pecs... He was sex. Pure, blatant sex.

God, how the hell did he do that to her? How the hell did he get better and better looking every day?

3

Linc had made a massive mistake.

He'd known it three days ago, the very moment he made his confession to Kylie in the throes of postcoital stupidity that he shouldn't have said it. One minute, she was looking smoky and satisfied and happy as hell after a good hot round of sex on a bale of hay, and the next…she'd been terrified.

And why? Because he'd stupidly told her that he wanted to make her a more permanent fixture in his life.

Also why?

He wasn't good with relationships. In fact, he was shit at them. Hadn't had a real serious girlfriend since college, and things hadn't changed. There was a reason he'd spent the past few years since Syria in the company of dogs. He had a hard time relating to humans. Female humans, especially, unless it was a quick one-night stand.

He only had one excuse for himself. After they'd had sex in his barn, Kylie had been so cute, confessing all these little things to him, and it'd only felt natural to confess something of his own.

But did he have to drop such a massive bomb and spook her like that?

Hell, he'd spooked himself. Badly.

So badly he hadn't spoken to her in three days. Which just made him an asshole. He knew it, but since he was shit at communicating his feelings—outside of postcoital stupidity apparently—he'd found it easier to just work from dawn to dusk and not think about much else.

Except he hadn't been able to get her off his mind.

He didn't know why he'd expected her to jump into his arms and share a happily-ever-after kiss with him. He'd gotten it in his head that she was into mating, into forever, and that she was just waiting for him to declare it.

But he'd been wrong.

And now it was time to right that wrong.

As he drove to town, hoping to catch her before she left work, his hands tightened on the steering wheel. He'd reel it back. If she wanted just sex, then fine. That's what this would be. He could do just sex. It was better that way. She was good in bed. Even better in the hay. He could get what he needed and give her what she needed, no strings. Perfect.

When Linc drove past the Starr Investigations office, he saw the light on and caught a glimpse of her through the storefront windows, sitting at her desk. He quickly found a parking space down the street and jumped out, motioning Storm, his German Shepherd, to follow.

He had it in his head that he'd just stop by to ask her how her shoulder was, but when he went inside and saw her, sitting there with a skirt riding high on her shapely legs, her blouse partially unbuttoned to reveal a hint of cleavage, and her dark hair spilling sexily over one eye, he didn't want to talk. She'd made changes in the last few days. Good ones. Ones that made him want her all the more.

"Well, hello, stranger," she said in a low, sexy voice. "Where have you been?"

He shrugged, trying to be cool and noncommittal. "Where I've always been. Why?"

She gave him a small smile. "Why do you think? I've missed you."

Linc walked over to her, wrapped a hand around her small waist and pulled her out of the chair. Being careful of her shoulder, he dragged her against him. He cupped her face in both hands, and nipped at her lips, feeling her pulse fluttering under her skin.

When she moaned, he smiled. Yes, this would be fine. Just sex. Fine.

Linc tore himself away before he turned her over her desk. "I like the outfit. The shoes."

She twirled, looking delighted with herself. "Well, I figured I should start acting the part, so I spent a whole week's pay on clothes that make me look like an actual adult."

He fingered the soft material of the cardigan. "You look *very* adult. But you were supposed to be resting, like your doctor said. Not shopping."

"Shopping is my relaxation," she said with a wink.

His eyes caught on her heaving chest. "You still not wearing a bra?"

She gave him a saucy wink. "Can't. The strap hits exactly on the sore spot."

He growled low in his throat. He'd missed this. Missed her.

"Come over to my house when you get off," he said, kissing the tip of her nose. "For pizza. And dessert."

She shook her head, playing with the buttons of his shirt. "Can't. I have to finish this report, and then I promised my mother I'd go to dinner at her house."

Damn. That threw a little wrench in his plans.

"You can come with me?" she suggested, sitting down at her desk and petting Storm. "She made her lasagna again. I'll be done in fifteen minutes."

His mind whirled, trying to make sense of this. She didn't like the idea of always, but she wanted to bring him home to mom. She wanted just sex, and yet she was fine letting him get closer to her family. Why did she have to be so difficult to read? Why did it feel like a game?

Game or not, there was only one answer to her question as far as he was concerned…

Hell yes.

A home-cooked meal took precedence over just about everything.

She sat down and started to type, very slowly with one hand. He frowned. "Is your shoulder still hurting?"

She shook her head. "Not bad. It's just with this stupid typewriter sitting up so high, the angle is awkward, so it's just easier to hunt and peck."

He glanced at the paper stuck between the rollers. "What are you working on?"

"Boring," she said, yawning. "Background checks. Companies will hire Starr Investigations to do their pre-employment screening, especially for jobs that require handling sensitive information. So, Greg will go and interview the people, and I need to make it into a pretty report."

"Ah. Interesting."

She gave him a *you've got to be kidding me* look. "Under no circumstances is *this* interesting. I promise you."

She was right. He hadn't been paying attention to that as much as he was paying attention to her curves in that tight skirt, and the way her nipples kept pressing up against her cardigan every time she breathed. "Well, I sure think it beats you getting shot at. Need help?"

She looked up, hope in her pretty eyes. "Can you type?"

He nodded. "I can, but I'm not sure how I'll do on that ancient thing."

She practically leapt from the chair and motioned for him to sit. He sat down and began taking dictation from her.

A few minutes later, he was finished, although his knuckles had begun to hurt. You had to use a lot of force with that stupid thing.

She pulled the paper out of the typewriter, then placed it on her boss's desk. "Thanks. That wasn't so terrible. I think it means I was meant to be the boss. I shouldn't be typing piddly little reports like this. I'm wasting my abilities."

She looked at him, clearly waiting for him to agree, so he nodded. He knew enough that when Kylie Hatfield went on a tear about something, it was best to just agree with her. She should've been a lawyer, because she could win any debate.

"I mean, seriously. There's got to be a happy medium. Because I swear, I might go brain-dead if I have to do forty hours a week of this for the rest of my life." She reached for her purse. "Ready? Should we take your truck?"

"Yeah."

They got the dogs into the back seat of Linc's truck and drove in comfortable silence to her mother's small townhouse, parallel parking down the street. Her mother wasn't a dog person, so they had to leave their pets outside, tied to the front porch.

Her dislike for dogs aside, Linc liked Ms. Hatfield. She was bubbly and warm like her daughter, and looked like an older, blonde version of Kylie. She'd made him feel right at home from the first moment he'd met her. He didn't get along with many humans these days, but Ms. Hatfield was, like her daughter, hard to dislike. He thought he might've liked her so much because she was the only person he knew who could make Kylie blush.

When they climbed the stairs, she was already waiting for them, wine glass in hand. "Oh! What a surprise!" she said.

"Mom. I texted you we were on our way," Kylie muttered, rolling her eyes at Linc.

She ignored her daughter, linking an arm through his, leading him down the hall. "Linc, I swear, you're just the most handsome dollop of whipped cream I ever did see. Gosh, I just want to eat you up! How have you been?"

Kylie groaned.

Linc could feel himself turning a shade or two darker himself. "I've been great. Thank you, ma'am. And yourself?"

She sat him down in the living room, which had been set up like a shrine to Kylie. There were pictures of her on almost every surface. She'd been blonde as a kid, with pigtails, a big space between her teeth, and glasses. But she'd grown out of all of that. His eyes caught on a picture of a much younger Kylie. In this one, she was wearing a long silver gown and stood beaming beside a tall, lanky kid with acne. She was wearing a crown and sash that said Prom Queen. This didn't surprise him.

Ms. Hatfield noticed him looking and smiled. "Oh, yes. Kylie was Homecoming Queen, Prom Queen, Student Council President, Pep Squad President…" She glanced over at Kylie, who was standing there, the very definition of mortified. "Weren't you, sweetie?"

"Go me," she said, less than enthusiastically, grabbing something off the fireplace mantel and hiding it behind her back.

"Oh, show him!" Ms. Hatfield said, motioning to the item she was doing such a bad job of concealing.

Kylie was shaking her head furiously.

Now, Linc was curious.

"Mom, it's humiliating enough that you have pictures from every year of my life in this room. I should be able to pick and choose what I show our guests. And this one is not fit for public viewing. He might turn to stone."

"Oh, come on. You're obviously quite lovely now, so none of these pictures really matter. You should be able to look at them and laugh," Ms. Hatfield said, motioning Kylie forward before looking at Linc. "Kylie had a…um, how shall we say it? She had a rough period during her tweens."

Kylie's nostrils flared, and she made a *ha-ha-ha* sound that was rather scary. "See, I'm laughing."

Now, he really wanted to see. So much that he dared to hold out a hand. "Hey, I had it rough all through high school. I promise, I won't laugh."

"Fine," she sighed, pulling the frame from behind her back and placing it on the coffee table in front of him. "Behold. Yoda."

The version of Kylie in the picture wasn't so bad. Yes, she had an unfortunate, too-short haircut, freckles, a mouth full of metal…but she was still cute.

"What's wrong with that? You're adorable."

"Liar." She snorted and grabbed it from him, doing her best Yoda impersonation as she said, "Eyesight you must have lost." Then she promptly tossed it into the little trashcan sitting at the end of the sofa.

"You wouldn't know it looking at her now, but Kylie was kind of a late bloomer," Ms. Hatfield said, retrieving the picture and dusting it off. It seemed to Linc that she'd done this very thing once or twice before. "She was flat as a board until she was about fifteen."

Kylie shouted, "Mom!" her face turning even redder. "Isn't it time we had dinner?"

She waved her daughter away. "Don't rush me! Let me enjoy some conversation first."

Kylie scowled, and Linc could almost see her in those pigtails. He smiled, amused.

"Now, Linc...I've been meaning to ask you, what do you think of Kylie's job?"

He wasn't sure what she meant. "Well, clearly Kylie—"

"I mean, it's awful, isn't it? Getting herself shot like that!"

"Mom...it's just a flesh wound, in and out."

Ms. Hatfield narrowed her eyes. "Darling, your shoulder contains the subclavian artery, which happens to feed the brachial artery, the main artery of your arm. The subclavian artery also feeds the brachial plexus, the large nerve bundle that controls the function of your entire arm. You could have lost function or even had to have it amputated. It could have been very serious."

Kylie just stared at her. "Did you get a nursing degree in the past couple weeks or what?"

Ms. Hatfield smiled indulgently at her daughter. "And what would be wrong with that? I keep nudging my sweet child to go back to school. She really would only have to put in another year to get her degree. But she keeps fighting me on that. Seems to think that this job is her calling." She paused and took a sip of her wine. "So, what do you think? Truthfully?"

Linc looked over at Kylie, who was wincing as if in physical pain. "I think she's very good in investigations, and it's rare for a person to find a job she likes. She could go back to school nights, if it's that important to her. But—"

Kylie smiled at him as her mother waved a hand at her daughter's arm. "But she got shot!"

"Kylie has probably told you that was just an anomaly. Not every case will be so dangerous. In fact, she spends a lot of time behind a desk."

Kylie nodded, even though she couldn't keep her nose from wrinkling just a bit. "I do tell her that. She just chooses to forget it. And my loans are already bigger than my butt,

Mom. I don't want them to be any bigger. Time for dinner yet?"

Her mother frowned, her eyes a mixture of pleading and reproach. "Nothing is so important as your education, sweetheart. And you were so close."

"I'm getting more of an education on the job than I ever did at school, Mom." Linc was surprised that she didn't stomp her foot. "Besides, if I remember correctly, it was you who told me to call Starr Investigations in the first place. Take a break from school, were your words, right?"

Rhonda Hatfield snapped her mouth shut, and Linc was relieved when the conversation turned innocuous for a few moments. But even though the topics were innocent, he could tell that Kylie sat on the edge of her seat, cringing in anticipation of more embarrassment.

Finally, her mother announced that it was time to eat. They went out to the dining room, where the table was once again set for royalty, complete with fancy china and crystal goblets. Ms. Hatfield sat at the head of the table while Linc sat across from Kylie. It was a perfect vantage point to gaze at the nipples he planned to be feasting on later.

To think, those babies had been flat as a board just a decade ago. Kylie was gorgeous, but the sexiest thing was that she didn't know how gorgeous she was. She was sweet and self-deprecating, funny and bubbly, and he wanted her more than he'd ever wanted anything in his life.

Which still surprised the hell out of him.

"Well," Kylie said to him as her mother served the lasagna, "I'm waiting for my mother to break out the old photo albums of me in the tub. Those are always a good time."

"We could," Ms. Hatfield said thoughtfully. "I know just where they are."

"I'm game," he said, giving Kylie a wink.

"I hate you both." She glowered, pouring herself a glass of wine. "Deeply."

"Hey, how about this? Maybe I'll take you to meet my parents one day. Then we can be even," he said to Kylie, mostly as a joke. "All right?"

She blinked. "I don't know if that'd make us even. Is your house a shrine to you? Does your mother live to humiliate you every chance she gets?"

Kylie's mother snorted. "All out of love, dear."

Kylie rolled her eyes and looked at him expectantly, waiting for an answer.

"Not exactly. But dinner with my family is a...production." That was the most civil way he could think to describe it in present company. Most of the time, he just called it hell.

Ms. Hatfield patted her daughter's hand absently and said to him, "Do your parents live in the area? What do they do?"

Linc nodded. "My father is the founding partner of Coulter and Associates, the big legal firm downtown. You can't miss the building. It has the gold eagle on the front. My brothers work there with him."

"Oh! Of course, I know that building. An attorney, hmmm?" The elder Hatfield gave him an assessing look. "That's impressive. So, your brothers are in law too?" At his nod, she plowed on, "You never wanted to follow in your father's footsteps too?"

That was the question he usually got after people found out what his family was into. The answer was a firm *hell no.* "No, ma'am. Started down that trail then decided it wasn't for me. Went into the service directly after that."

Rhonda Hatfield narrowed her eyes, and he could almost see her scrolling through her memory banks. "Right. Kylie mentioned that you were overseas. Marines?"

"Army. Military Police K-9 Squad."

"Oh, I see. Where were you stationed?"

Her mother was definitely like Kylie. They had a way of making him feel talkative. He didn't think he'd ever said so much at one time. He shifted in his seat. "I did two tours in Syria. Well, one and a half. I was injured during the last one and sent home, honorably discharged."

Her eyes grew wide, and those wide eyes scanned him for an obvious injury. She, thankfully, didn't ask. "I can't imagine. You're so brave."

He dove into the lasagna, stuffing his mouth until he could think of a change of subject. He didn't like to think too much about Syria. Whenever he got talking about it, it usually haunted him with a suffocating, claustrophobic feeling that got him right in the chest.

Then it filled his nightmares.

Shit.

In the past couple weeks, it seemed those dreams had been getting worse. He didn't want to think of that now.

Linc forced thoughts of it out of his head. But, of course, the more he wanted to not think about it, the more it started to invade, like spilled water, seeping in all the cracks in his head, making it impossible to pull out. He needed to change the subject, and quick.

"This is great lasagna," he said as Kylie eyed him curiously. By now, she'd probably guessed he didn't like talking about his time overseas.

"Yes, Mom. It is," she agreed. "You've done it again."

Ms. Hatfield gave them coconut cake for dessert and sent her daughter home with an entire shopping bag full of leftovers, so she wouldn't have to "starve because of her injury." She hugged her mom and said thanks, and then Ms. Hatfield reached up and hugged Linc tight.

"Kylie," she said, still holding his hand. She grabbed her daughter's hand and joined their hands together. "Hold on to this one. He's a keeper."

Kylie's face turned bright red. "Mom!" She looked at him, that cute little pink flush crawling over her cheeks. "Don't listen to her."

Yeah. Right. Just sex.

Leashes in hand, they walked down the street to his truck. She leaned heavily against the side while Vader sniffed the tires and Storm sat like the good girl she was.

"Just another awesome, embarrassing dinner with my mom." She was still embarrassed, but Linc could see the love fighting for domination.

"I like her," he said, opening the back door and letting the dogs in.

"You would." She frowned up at him as he closed the door. She looked damn good in the moonlight, like something he would want to keep. But she'd made it clear. This was just about sex.

Which was all he wanted too, he reminded himself.

Linc pushed a lock of her hair behind her ear. "You're beautiful."

A smile appeared on her pink marshmallow lips. "You still think that, even after seeing that picture?"

He rubbed a thumb over that bottom lip. "I think that *especially* after seeing that picture. Because you're so damn cute when your mom puts you off-balance like that." He pressed his mouth to her ear. "Let's go to bed."

She pressed her warm body against his, killing him slowly. He kissed the bare curve between her neck and collarbone, and she cupped his jaw tenderly. "Yes. That sounds about perfect."

When she pressed her lips to his, he decided that tonight would indeed be perfect.

And it would be enough.

It would just have to be.

4

The tension was thick on the ride up to Linc's house. He had his hand on Kylie's bare thigh the whole way, drawing little circles. She liked this side of him, the man who was just thinking physical, because at this point, she was too tired to think of anything else.

He told her he'd take her back to her car later, that he didn't want her driving on the curvy mountain too late. So, she sat back and tried not to get carsick as they looped their way to his farm.

When they got to his house, the dogs were doing their familiar greeting, yipping and barking to the top of their lungs. The farm animals joined in, and she was pretty sure the llamas were giving her the stink eye for being the cause of so much noise.

Linc opened the back of the truck and motioned for Storm to exit. Vader lumbered out, following the German Shepherd into the fenced-in yard to join all their friends. Kylie climbed the stairs to the porch, waiting for Linc. A moment later, he climbed the stairs two at a time, strode straight to her, and took her face in his hands, kissing her until she was breathless.

Yes. The physical side of this man was very, very good.

A low groan of pleasure rose from her throat. He'd always been delicious, but now he was a man on a mission. What had gotten into him?

Whatever it was, it was quickly getting into her too.

The touch of his hand on her skin made heat prickle through her body. Wanting to touch him freely, she ripped at the Velcro on her sling she'd worn for her mother's benefit, letting it fall to the porch.

"Don't hurt yourself."

She ignored the twinge of pain as she lifted her hands to his chest, freeing his buttons. Aside from her mother's dramatics on how badly her injury could have gone, Kylie had been very lucky. The bullet had barely nicked the muscle, and even though it still hurt, she hated the sling and simply didn't want to wear it anymore. Especially not now.

When Linc reached for her shirt to return the favor, she hesitated after the first two buttons were freed. Kylie had a feeling he wasn't going to stop until he had her naked for him. Right then and there.

"Linc," she murmured as she turned to look out into the darkness. She shivered, thinking of the terrible night she'd been shot. The cabin to which she'd been taken lay just beyond those trees. "I don't want to be on display. Let's go inside."

"On display for whom?" he asked, then froze, understanding seeming to settle in.

Sophia DuBois, the psychopath who'd shot her, had taken great pleasure in recounting how she'd so stealthily stalked Kylie, going so far as to spy on her with Linc, watching them during their most intimate moments.

Kylie had felt so violated. In truth, she still did.

Linc ran his fingers down her cheek. "Shit. Sorry, I forgot."

She didn't know how he could have forgotten such a thing but chalked it up to the differences between how men and women felt about nudity and sex.

Or maybe she was just a prude. A cold fish, as a past boyfriend had called her.

She wasn't sure.

"Can we go inside?" she asked, ridiculously close to tears.

Her doctor told her that she might suffer some symptoms of post-traumatic stress, and until that moment, she'd thought he was wrong.

She didn't think he was wrong now.

Was this how Linc felt when he thought about the war he didn't want to talk about? Her exposure to the stressor had only been for a few hours. How much worse would his be considering he'd been exposed to stressors for months?

She wanted to ask him about it, but he kissed her again before taking her hand. "Let's go inside."

She smiled past the embarrassment her nerves caused her, but she couldn't stop from looking out at the darkness as Linc closed the door behind them, sliding the lock in place. Lifting her in his arms, he carried her up the stairs, not stopping until that door was closed too.

He turned to her. "Better?"

She nodded and leaned forward to press her lips to his chest. "Thank you."

He made love to her then. No, that wasn't right. He actually had sex with her until she was hoarse from screaming and felt like a boneless heap underneath him.

Looking pretty boneless himself, he collapsed onto his back, chest heaving from the exertion and the constant stress on his arms in his attempt to keep his weight from hurting her injury.

He laughed. "Just sex, right?"

She laughed too, still splayed out like a starfish. "Right." With great effort, she found enough energy to turn on her side and press her lips to his sweaty shoulder. "Perfect."

Linc frowned, and Kylie thought she knew exactly what he was thinking. *If this is so perfect, then why are you so afraid?*

She didn't know. Maybe because things were so good just as they were. Maybe because she'd seen her mother go through a hell of a lot of heartache for a man who wasn't worth it. Maybe because she'd always been the type of girl who was distracted by bright, shiny objects and didn't want to hurt him by going off on her crazy whims.

Linc was solid, steady. The last thing he needed was crazy old her ruffling up his quiet, predictable life.

She sighed. She didn't want to think about that.

When unexpected tears burned up her sinuses and wet her eyes, she turned onto her other side, prepared to tell him that her shoulder hurt if he asked her the inevitable "what's wrong" question. Instead, he turned until his front was spooned against her back, a hand snaking around until it was firmly on her breast.

The position offered so much comfort, she didn't want to leave.

But it was getting late, and her car was still parked downtown.

"We should probably go," she murmured, snuggling deeper against his chest.

"Uh-huh," he replied, sounding equally sleepy.

Just a few more moments, she thought. Just a few more moments in the safety and comfort of this man's arms.

The last thing she thought before she could think of nothing else was, *exactly what am I afraid of, anyway?*

❄

SHE WOKE WITH A START, pain digging into her arm. Her eyes flashed open, and she looked around, almost expecting to be back in the shed with the Spotlight Killer.

Instead, she was still in Linc's bed, pressed against his warm body. But he was no longer holding her, keeping her safe.

His face was shining and slick with sweat, and his voice tore through the darkness like a tornado. "*No! Watch out! No!*"

Pain and pressure increased on her arm. Kylie looked down to the source of the pain, and through the minimal moonlight streaming through the windows, saw Linc's big hand clamped upon her bicep, fingers like claws digging into the skin. It was an alien feeling. He'd touched her roughly, but never like that.

Her heart hammered as she caught a glimpse of his face. It was twisted in desperation and agony.

A dream. He was having a dream. No, a nightmare.

Kylie touched the side of his beautiful face, his stubble-crusted chin, his square jaw, his eyelids closed into two half-moons. She tried to pull her arm from his grip, but that only made him tighten it.

"Linc…" She was getting frightened now as he started to jerk her in his grip. He was so strong, he could snap her arm like a twig. She forced her voice to grow louder. "Linc!"

His face twisted into an agony of pain, and he shouted, "Stop! Nooooo!"

Kylie screamed when he sat straight up, his other arm coming around at full power, hand clenched into a fist.

All she could do was close her eyes, waiting for the punch she knew was coming.

5

It was hot. So damn hot in Raqqa. Linc's imaginings of the place before he ever set foot there was that it was a desert wasteland, but that wasn't true. A lot of the time, the weather wasn't different from back home.

But it was a wasteland. Sometimes, it was a struggle to find a building that hadn't gotten bombed out. The air was always thick with dust from the rubble, and it caught in his throat like he imagined desert sand would.

It was late summer now, and he'd been there since April. He'd gotten used to sweating his balls off in full uniform, carrying all his gear on his back. Storm hated it. She didn't like the heat and panted at his feet, using his shadow for shade.

The guys had found some local kids outside the marketplace while they were doing their usual recon, scouting for jihad. These little boys were rough and crazy and knew their way around a soccer ball, that was for sure. The commanding officer had told them to cut it out, to relax and not call attention to themselves, but no one had seen the enemy in weeks, and they all wanted something to ease the tension. Kids didn't care. Especially the little kid with the shaggy hair and the baseball cap who was hounding them, wanting to play.

One of Linc's best friends, Austin, who outranked him by a couple levels, started to kick the ball around with the kid. Linc couldn't really blame him, knowing Austin probably missed his own son back home.

"Hey, Colt," Austin had said to Linc, using Lincoln Coulter's nickname that had both born and died during his time in service. "Here." He passed him the ball.

Soccer wasn't Linc's favorite sport, but he'd always been naturally athletic, and was happy to kick the ball around with the kid. The three of them passed it around until some of the other guys on Linc's squad showed up, wanting to get in on the game. Then, a few of the little kids, who'd been watching, started to join in too.

Looking back, Linc knew they shouldn't have been making a spectacle of themselves like that. They were unwelcome, even among those little kids. But the guys were laughing, having fun, and they meant the kids no harm.

Then he saw her. Grenades strapped to her chest.

The fear in her eyes, the determination on her face told him everything he needed to know.

He ran, gripped her arm holding the detonation device. "Stop!" he shouted. "Nooooo!"

The woman was shouting too.

"Linc!!"

With the word ringing in his ear, everything changed.

One moment, he was in the desert. The next, he was in his bedroom.

One moment, his hand was wrapped around the arm of a suicide bomber. The next, it was wrapped around a terrified Kylie.

The woman was screaming at him, trying to wrench her arm away.

Kylie was screaming too, shouting his name, over and over.

He wanted to cover his ears against the explosion of sound.

His body was drenched in a cold sweat. He blinked and blinked, sure that at any moment this illusion of his quaint bedroom would disappear, and he'd find himself back in the rubble of Raqqa.

Instead, the farmhouse became clearer. Memories of last night began to click in place...dinner with Kylie's mom, the amazing sex, and...Kylie.

Linc's gaze fell on the woman he cared for so much. She was sitting in bed beside him, cringing against the headboard, her eyes still wide with fear. Her chest was heaving with every breath.

His eyes drifted down to his closed fist, and he realized what was scaring her.

Him.

Still breathing hard, Linc lowered his fist, and his eyes darted to his other hand. It was wrapped tightly around Kylie's upper arm.

What had he done?

Linc quickly loosened it, then wiped his hand on the sheets. He was bathed in sweat. He opened his mouth to apologize, but nothing came out. He scrubbed both hands over his face.

"Jesus. Kylie. I'm so damn sorry."

He hadn't meant to fall asleep. He'd meant to just rest his eyes for a few minutes before driving her back to her car. Dammit. He should have known better.

"You were having a nightmare," she said quietly, reaching over to turn on the bedside lamp. In the light, she looked afraid. She had a good reason to be.

That had been more than a nightmare. It'd felt so real, his

pulse was still pounding in his head. He realized his hands were trembling as he ran his fingers through his hair. "Yeah."

"Are you okay?" she asked, rubbing her sore arm. Any higher, and he would've been grabbing on to her injured shoulder.

Damn. He hated himself.

Linc nodded, but he still wasn't sure. It felt too real to be a dream.

"Does that happen often?"

No. At least he didn't think so. Normally, his nightmares seemed real, appeared absolutely vivid, but he'd never hurt anyone because of them. Of course, that was because there was normally never anyone around when his subconscious assaulted him in his sleep.

In fact, the last woman to spend the night with him had been over two years ago, not long after his return from Syria. Shouldn't the nightmares have been lessening in intensity by now?

"Linc?"

He realized Kylie had asked him a question. Unable to answer verbally, he shook his head, his eyes scanning over her, her beautiful breasts heaving out of control as she rubbed her arm. At first, he thought she was massaging goose bumps from her skin because she was cold, but then she flinched when he tried to touch her.

That's when he saw the red welts on her pale skin, right where his hand had been.

A new wave of adrenalin shot through his system, and he jumped from the bed. "Jesus, Kylie. Did I...why didn't you—"

"I tried," she said, her voice a little steadier now. "You were hell-bent on...I don't know. I don't know what you were doing. You were so dead asleep, I couldn't wake you. You almost..."

Jesus. His hand had been clenched in a fist and aimed

right for her face. If he hadn't woken in time, he could've killed her.

"Dammit," Linc growled, reaching for a pair of drawstring pajama pants and slipping into them. "Yeah. I sometimes have dreams. Really vivid dreams."

"About Syria?"

He nodded. She still looked so scared, and now there *were* goose bumps popping up all over her skin. Linc slammed the windows closed and went to her, gathering her into his arms, careful of her sore shoulder.

He lifted her arm, and sure enough, he could see where three bruises the size of his fingers were already beginning to show. They would be much, much worse in a few hours.

"I didn't mean to hurt you. I really didn't."

She ran a finger down his cheek. "I know. It's okay, Linc. I know you wouldn't hurt me."

Not intentionally, at least. But he *had* hurt her, and he'd die before he went and did it again. He grabbed his pillow. "I'm sorry. Go to sleep. I won't bother you. I'll sleep in another room. Or...I can drive you to your car like I was supposed to do."

She grabbed his arm, shaking her head vigorously. "No. Please don't. Please sleep with me. I don't want to leave you." The look in her eyes was desperate, pleading.

Linc stared at the space next to her, afraid to fill it, but at the same time, wanting it more than anything. He loved the feeling of her body next to his, so warm and sweet-smelling and soft. She knew he couldn't deny her, any more than he could deny himself.

"I don't want to hurt..." He couldn't finish it.

She reached for Linc's hand, pulling him onto the bed. "You won't. Tonight, I learned an important lesson."

That the man you only have sex with is insane?

He ran both hands through his hair, but before he could

speak, she added, "If you dream again, I won't touch you. It was the wrong thing to do, I know that now. I won't do it again."

So great was his relief at her understanding, his sinuses began to burn. He forced the emotion away. Forced everything away. He'd deal with his messed up mind later.

Right now, he needed to take care of her.

Very carefully, he put his pillow down and stretched out next to her. She immediately curled her body around him. She kissed the scar on his shoulder, trailing a finger lightly over his lips, repeating, "It's okay," over and over again. "You're still trembling," she whispered.

He was. He tensed, willing his muscles to solidify.

"Come up here," Linc told her, lifting her onto him until she straddled his waist. He thickened under her. She rubbed herself on him, then pulled at the drawstring of his pants to slide them down over his hips.

Linc had a plan. If they had sex, they wouldn't sleep. If they didn't sleep, he couldn't dream. If he couldn't dream, he wouldn't scare the shit out of her.

And for a little longer, he could forget Syria. The destruction. The blood. The death.

It wouldn't last.

After they were finished, and Kylie was snuggled up next to him again, he knew all those terrible things waited for him in the shadows, ready to pounce on him, devour him the second he slipped out of consciousness.

Linc stared at the ceiling, listening to Kylie breathe, for the rest of the night.

6

Light was just spilling into the room when Kylie woke, warm and toasty from lying next to a human oven all night.

She smiled, turning her head to watch Linc sleep. He'd only surrendered to that oblivion a short time ago, she knew. Even in the dark, she'd been able to feel his alertness. She was glad he was sleeping now.

He needed the rest. And it also gave her a few moments to simply enjoy the beauty of his naked body tangled in the sheets. He was all man. So much man, it made her giddy to touch and be touched by him. She shivered at the delicious curve of his ass, dimpled and firm, the sweep of his spine, up to his broad, muscular shoulders. The scars didn't detract from his perfection at all.

The shiver became a shudder when she thought of last night. The rage in his face when he'd nearly hit her.

The contradiction between the two sides of the man beside her was disconcerting.

She slipped out of bed and went to his bathroom. He had the funniest house for a badass bachelor—flowery wallpaper and doilies and farmhouse quilts. It'd belonged to his grandparents, and he hadn't wanted to change it because he loved them that much. Proof of what a sweet guy Linc was beneath the scar-riddled, gruff exterior.

He didn't hurt women. That much was clear. He'd been beside himself with anger and guilt over last night. He'd been someone else entirely, *somewhere* else.

Kylie poured herself a cup of water, needing to down a couple Tylenol, and as she closed the medicine cabinet and swallowed, her attention was caught by the bruises on her upper arm. They were in the exact shape of Linc's fingers.

Every nerve ending stood at attention as she touched the sore spots. He'd been trained as a warrior and could've done a lot worse. He would have, if he hadn't woken in time.

He hadn't meant to do it.

Kylie knew that, remembering the way the rage had given way to guilt and regret. All she'd wanted to do was pull him close and take care of him, soothe him, ease his mind.

They'd had sex, but that time, it had been different. It had been more like desperation. Like he was afraid of falling asleep and hurting her again.

She smiled into the mirror. He had hurt her again. In that wonderful, feel it the next morning way that only really good sex could do.

Then she frowned as she examined herself closer. She looked like death.

Her eyes were bloodshot from lack of sleep, and her hair was a sweat-tangled mess. She'd be dead on her feet at work, for sure, and those boring reports wouldn't help keep her awake. She quickly swooshed some Listerine in her mouth and wiped the sleep from her eyes. Pulling her hair on top of her head, she winced as her shoulder twinged.

She didn't wear a bandage any longer, so nothing hid the

mostly healed wound. It was easily the worst injury she'd ever had. She'd have that scar forever, just like Linc had his.

Had *them*.

Linc had so many, yet he'd never spoken about how he'd gotten them. But last night…

Her frown grew deeper. Last night had given her a closer glimpse of just how terrible his time in Syria had been.

Usually, Kylie was good at drawing people out, getting them to talk, but they had never spoken about what caused the crisscrossing of scars on his back and chest. He had circular wounds too, just like hers, but it looked like, in places, his skin had almost melted.

A lot of his scars, though, were buried deep under the surface. And maybe the anger that went with them was buried too. Festering. Just waiting to come out.

Kylie slipped out the door and watched him sleep, watched the rise and fall of his perfect chest. Despite being so sore and sexed-out, she ached for him again. She loved his strong legs, the way they curved up to his rock-hard ass. Loved every gorgeous part of him.

Instead of crawling back into bed like she wanted to, she found one of his black army t-shirts in his armoire and slipped it on. She swam in it; it easily fell to just above her knees. She went downstairs, into the cool September morning, and fed the dogs their kibble. Then she went back inside and looked through Linc's stocked fridge.

He was quite the foodie—he had a veggie drawer filled with exotic things she didn't like to look at, much less put in her mouth. Kylie was the worst cook in the world, but she did know how to make pancakes. Well, in theory at least. She'd made them exactly once. That counted.

He had a mix for instant batter, so she followed the directions, easy as could be. She found a griddle and set it on the stove, then turned it on. Then she found a bowl, stirred in the mix and some water, and got it ready to showcase her inner Rachel Ray.

It all went so well, up until she poured the batter.

The stuff started to smoke immediately. Angry, black smoke that hissed like a snake. She burned her finger on the griddle and unleashed a string of curses as the pancakes were quickly turned to cinders.

"What are you up to?"

Kylie jumped as Linc strode into the kitchen in just his pajama pants. God, he looked good, and she looked like a total moron.

"Clearly burning down your kitchen!" Kylie shouted in despair as she opened drawers, looking for oven mitts or a dish towel in which to grab the thing.

She groaned as the fire alarm began screaming its alert.

Calm as ever, he opened a drawer and used the mitt to grab the griddle and toss it into the sink. Then, just as calmly, he waved a dish towel in front of the alarm until he stopped its annoying blare.

"I told you I suck in the kitchen," she pouted when she could once again hear herself think.

He put his thumb and index finger on her chin, gently lifting her face to his, giving her a chaste kiss that reeked of pity. "I like it when you suck. And you can do it anywhere you want."

Kylie fake-glowered at him, but the expression wouldn't hold. He looked delicious, even though his eyes were definitely red-rimmed and bleary from the lack of sleep. "Ha, ha."

"You had the burner on too high. You want me to show you?"

She pouted some more. "I hate me."

He kissed her again, this time on the forehead. "Well, I *like* you. Go sit," he said, running the griddle under the tap. He smacked her butt as she did what he said, still sulking as he got to work, moving around the kitchen like a pro. Five minutes later, he presented Kylie with a stack of about ten perfectly round and golden pancakes, with a square dollop of butter on the top. It could've been on a magazine cover, it was so lovely.

"Show off," she muttered, resting her head in her hands. "I will never be able to eat all these."

"I know. They're to share," he said, sitting down next to her and grabbing the syrup before patting his knee.

Kylie smiled, scooted to the edge of the seat, and then perched in his lap as he poured the syrup over the pancakes. Even with her epic kitchen failure, she was happy.

Right here. Right now. With him. She was happy.

When she realized that she was eating more than he was, she glanced over at him, a huge bite of pancake in her mouth. Her cheeks immediately heated as she realized he was simply watching her with dark, tortured eyes.

Her heart squeezed, and she turned in his lap, placing her free hand on his face, her thumb rubbing down the middle of his eyebrows, hoping to ease that worry line away.

Her mouth was still full, and she was forced to chew and swallow before she could ask the question to which she thought she already knew the answer. "What's wrong?"

"I'm sorry about last night," he said, his voice fractured. "I'll make sure that it never happens again. I never want to hurt you, Kylie. Ever."

Kylie rose until she could straddle him, face him completely. Even though her shoulder ached with the effort, she cupped his beautiful face in both hands and kissed the very tip of his nose.

"Like I told you last night, I learned a lesson too. You can't control what your subconscious does, but I can control what I do when I notice you dreaming again."

He nodded, still looking tortured. "You walk away."

"Just a foot away, maybe two. Just out of arm's reach until you wake up." She leaned forward and kissed his lips. "And when the nightmare is over, I walk right back into your arms, and we talk about it…" he stiffened, and she immediately added, "if you want to."

He pulled her close, and she nestled her head under his chin. Of all the sexual things they'd done with and to each other, this felt the most intimate.

"We need to go, get you to work, don't you think?"

She lifted her head just enough to look at the clock, then practically leapt from his lap. "Shit. Yes. Let's go!"

Linc took Kylie to her apartment and waited for her to shower and change, and she was glad for that. Ever since she'd had that run-in with the Spotlight Killer, she didn't really like being alone in the apartment anymore, even with Vader.

When she was ready, Linc drove her and the gigantic mutt to the office. It would've been nice to share some long, lingering goodbye kisses, but she was already late. Settling on a simple peck, she ran up the sidewalk, only realizing after she left him that they'd never made plans to meet up again.

Rushing into the office, she rammed into the door.

It was locked.

She smiled. That meant Greg Starr was late too. Unless he'd already come and gone? As late as she was, that was a real possibility.

Digging in the bottom of her purse, she frowned against the September morning drizzle. Fall was her favorite time of year, especially living in the mountains. While it was still a bit too early for the leaves to begin to turn, the crisp mornings let her know that day was growing close.

Finally inside, she glanced around the space. Everything in the office was the same as the day prior. Perfect. Greg usually left a mess, even when he was only there for a few minutes.

Vader went to his familiar spot by the window and curled up in the murky daylight. Slumping down in her chair, Kylie looked at the pile of reports she had waiting from the previous day and sighed. They hadn't grown wings and flown off overnight as she'd hoped.

She loaded paper into the typewriter so she could start the next report, but her mind soon drifted to Linc. Her heart hurt for him. There was something inside him, torturing him, something she knew nothing about. Horrible things had happened to him in Syria. She wanted to know more but didn't want to pry. She wished he'd just tell her.

Or maybe he'd never told anyone? Maybe he'd kept that all bottled up because he believed that strong military men weren't supposed to have emotions or feelings, and it was eating away at him like a cancer from the inside.

Kylie'd heard about this before, about men from overseas not being able to forget the horrors of war. Or even firefighters and policemen from 9/11 who'd been so affected by what they'd witnessed, their lives were never the same. Some horrors were so awful, they reduced even the strongest men to homelessness or suicide, believing the world was better off without their presence. And to top it all off, they were expected to deal with it in secret, because men weren't supposed to show weakness.

Screw that. In her mind, there was no weakness in seeking help when a person needed it.

Kylie pushed away from the typewriter and found her phone. She typed in *PTSD resources Asheville veterans*. A long list came up. She clicked on one and read: *Western North Carolina is a good place for veterans seeking help with PTSD, in terms of available resources, a strong veteran community and a receptive VA Hospital. But it's also a great place for people to hide from their problems. The nature of the mountains provides isolation and anonymity for many.*

Escaping to the mountains for isolation and anonymity? That was, essentially, Lincoln Coulter.

She read a little more about the symptoms of PTSD, and everything just pointed to Linc: Withdrawn. Antisocial. Tendency to have mood swings. Then she read about treatment options, including group and individual therapy, and wondered if Linc had ever been to anything like that. If he had, he'd never said so. Something told her he might not be the most open person to trying things like that. He was just so macho and tough, talking about his feelings was probably the last thing he'd want to do.

Knowing how tight-lipped Linc was with her, she figured she already had her answer.

Maybe she could look into it for him. If she presented the evidence to him and made a good, solid case, so that all he'd have to do was make the phone call to the therapist, he might go for it. She started to write a few things down on a pad when she was jolted from her seat by the loud sound of the phone ringing.

Annoyed that it was interfering with her research, she lifted the receiver to her ear. "Starr Investigations. This is Kylie. What can I help you investigate today?"

"Hello, Kylie."

The voice sounded creaky, fragile, and old. And very familiar.

Just a few nights ago, Kylie had listened to this same voice after a very spectacular roll in the hay—literally—after her mother had finally allowed her to be discharged from her tender loving care.

She'd left her mother's home and had driven straight up the mountain, determined to retrieve Vader and give Linc the cold shoulder, just like he'd been doing her while she'd convalesced in her childhood bedroom.

But things had shifted quickly, almost from the moment their eyes met, and less than ten minutes later, they had been rolling in the hay, literally. Very, very literally.

Then this same woman had called. Emma Jenkins. No, Jennings, Kylie remembered.

She remembered so clearly because her boss had absolutely refused to let her take the case, and it had broken Kylie's heart to call the sweet elderly lady back, telling her the bad news.

"Mrs. Jennings," Kylie blurted. "How are you today?"

"How do you think?" the woman scolded. "I'm being robbed, and I need someone to do something about it."

Did the sweet little woman have dementia? Alzheimer's?

"Um, Mrs. Jennings. Do you remember that I called you back and told you I couldn't take your case?"

The woman hrmphed her. She'd never been hrmphed quite so loudly before. "Of course I remember. I'm being robbed, not going senile."

Kylie licked her lips. "Then I'm not sure why you're calling. I'm not able to take your—"

"I'll pay double."

Kylie's mouth fell open. It took several beats for her to be able to close it again. "Why?"

The woman's tone softened. "Because you actually listened to me the other night. Really listened."

Kylie's heart gave a little squeeze. "Well...you deserved to have someone listen to you, and I'm still so sorry that I had to tell you no."

"Like I said, I'll pay you double."

Here was where she should tell this woman that she needed to take a message and not get her stupid ass involved. She'd promised Greg. Promised Linc. Promised her mother.

Promised she'd be a good little message-taker and consult with Greg at all turns. Kylie sucked in a breath.

"Can you give me all the details again? And has anything new occurred since we last talked?"

She wasn't officially taking the case. She wasn't. But it wouldn't hurt to be a good listener again.

"Well, like I told you the other night, I think somebody has been stealing from me. But I can't be sure. I'm a wealthy woman, and I get the feeling that one of the people I've put my trust in to handle my estate is not being one-hundred-percent aboveboard with me. So, I'd like you to look into it for me."

Kylie tried to think of the questions she was supposed to ask, things she hadn't thought to ask while she and Linc were naked in a barn.

"Have you spoken to the police about your suspicions?"

"I'd rather not get the police involved," the caller said, tittering a little. "In fact, I'm just so embarrassed about this whole situation. That people in this world can be so heartless and cruel. I trust all the people I keep near me with my heart and soul, and if it's true one of them is stealing from me, I will be devastated. But I simply must know. So..."

Kylie worried her lip. "Mr. Starr isn't available right now, and he is the person who approves where my time is allocated." She gave the typewriter the middle finger again. "I'll need to speak to him again, see what we might be able to do."

There. That sounded professional enough.

And honest. Mostly.

"All right, dear. And be sure to tell him that I'll pay double."

Kylie smiled. "I will. Can you please give me your contact information again?"

She jotted the information down, though the previous note was probably somewhere on Greg's desk.

"Thank you, dear."

"You're welcome. I'll get back to you as soon as I can."

Once they said their goodbyes and she'd disconnected the call, Kylie stared at the message. Who'd want to steal from a sweet old lady? Kylie already felt her acute sense of justice lathering up. She wanted to kick someone's ass on the woman's behalf.

But no. That was for Greg to do, not her. She had reports to tend to, papers to file. She'd promised she would change her ways, and she was going to stick to it.

Kylie jammed another piece of paper in the antiquated typewriter. She'd be a good little note-taking assistant, just like Greg and Linc and her mother wanted her to be.

So, why did it make her feel like a big, fat loser?

7

Linc wanted to kill someone as he walked through the pelting drizzle to the barn and started to feed the animals. The llamas, Dolly and Carl, hummed softly as he approached. As always, they were happy to see him, Carl even more so than Dolly, who could sometimes be grumpy enough to spit.

The farm had changed a great deal since his grandparents' early days. There used to be horses and many additional head of cattle, but the elder Coulters had downsized as they grew older. Linc had added the llamas and smaller farm animals, with the goal of humanely breeding them.

Just spreading the feed calmed him down. Usually, being with animals of any kind had a soothing effect on Linc, and brushing their coats was all it took to calm him, help him find his Zen.

Not today.

Today, he only stood there, feeling impatient, muscles tight.

Linc didn't feel much like a man. He felt like a failure.

He'd wanted to give Kylie what she wanted. Just sex. She asked, he delivered.

And it had started out fine. Great, in fact.

Until he went and had that batshit nightmare and showed her what a grade-A pussy he was. He'd hurt her. Now, something dangerous and hot surged through his veins. Linc hated himself. He couldn't even look at himself in the bathroom mirror without wanting to punch his fist through it. Now, Kylie was sporting bruises that matched his fingerprints. What kind of asshole touched a woman like that?

And the worst part? She'd been so damn understanding. Linc thought he would've felt better about the whole damn thing if she'd yelled at him. Told him what an asshole he was. But no, Kylie had to hold him and cuddle him and tell him it was okay and…why the hell didn't she want a relationship, again?

Oh, right. Because he was freaking batshit, and she knew it.

No wonder she had doubts about getting involved with him. He wasn't giving her a reason to have a lot of confidence in him or a long-term relationship.

Linc sucked in a big breath of air and wiped his face with a handkerchief, pushing away thoughts of how damn good they'd been together last night.

Because maybe even "just sex" was too much to hope for.

Dammit. This shit had to happen just when he was finally getting into a groove with a woman, feeling like maybe he wouldn't spend the rest of his days isolated in his mountain home, just him and his dogs. He'd always wanted that, but since Kylie came along, he'd been thinking of the things his mother wanted for him. Thinking that his mother may have had a point, that having a woman up here might not have been such a bad thing.

Now, it seemed like the worst thing he could possibly think of.

It was his own damn fault. He'd volunteered to go to Syria. He'd protected his country. But he couldn't have known then that it'd destroy everything in his life that came afterwards. Linc was proud of what he'd done. He'd made a difference. He'd do it again in a heartbeat.

But maybe he wasn't meant to live a normal life. Not anymore. Maybe he'd given that up when he enlisted. Maybe he was doomed to having one-night stands with women for the rest of his life.

His balls shrank into his body at the thought of going out and picking up women, especially as vampy and vain as the ones were who seemed to be into the idea of a single night of sex.

Besides, Linc was beyond that. Too old for that shit. Clubbing didn't interest him in the least.

Kylie? She interested him for reasons he still couldn't completely comprehend.

But he couldn't risk hurting her again. Hell no.

As Linc finished feeding the animals, he squeezed his eyes closed, willing those thoughts of Syria to get the hell out of his head. He saw his buddies kicking the soccer ball around in crisp detail, almost as if he were still there. Saw the little boy. Breathed dusty air into his lungs that tasted like metal and gasoline. And after that…

After that…

"Hey, loser!" a voice called from the doors of the barn.

Fear gripped him, squeezing his heart. He jumped almost clear to the rafters, dropping the bucket and staggering back against the stall. "Dammit!"

The animals started to sidestep, their fear and confusion clearly visible.

"Whoa!" It was Jacob Dean, Linc's oldest friend in the world. He eyed Linc suspiciously. "You okay?"

Linc went to Dolly and rubbed her nose, calming her

down. Her black eyes scanned him cautiously, like even she was trying to determine if he was sane. "Yeah. Hell. You just…I didn't hear your truck pull up." He took a deep breath and forced a smile. "What's up?"

Jacob laughed, but he was still clearly concerned. "You seriously didn't hear my truck pull up? What, is this serene mountain wonderland getting to you?" He leaned against the wall of the barn, grinning at him. The big, old red-headed teddy bear was rarely in a bad mood. "Nice greeting."

Linc stalked toward him, feeling tense and pissed off at himself for not being in control. "I have a lot going on. I had to take Kylie to work, and I'm running behind." He rubbed the back of his neck. "Let me guess. You're about to make me even more behind?"

Jacob nodded. "I've been calling your cell all morning. What's really going on?"

Linc shook his head. It wasn't worth talking about. And from the way Jacob was looking at him, he knew the visit wasn't purely social. Did it mean there was new news regarding the Spotlight Killer case? Or maybe there was a search and rescue that needed his and Storm's help. Jacob was a Buncombe County detective, and because of his busy schedule, he rarely made daylight visits up here just to shoot the shit. This had to be business.

"My cell's in the house, charging. Anything new with Kylie's case?"

"No. SAR." Jacob reached into his pocket and pulled out a notepad. "Missing child named Bethany Akers. Disappeared from a trailer park near the Rocky Bluff campground. She's only five. Down syndrome. When they woke this morning, the girl was gone. So was their new puppy. They think she might have followed the dog and gotten lost."

That wasn't good. The girl could have been missing for an hour or for most of the night.

Rocky Bluff wasn't far away. Linc could be to the campground within the hour. It was a chilly, wet morning so the trails had to be slippery, and there were a lot of places where the kid could fall and injure herself if she didn't know better. That poor kid had to be scared out of her mind.

"All right. Let me round up Storm and I'll meet you there."

Jacob's radio crackled with the voice of the dispatcher. He listened, but then waved it off. "Nah. Just come with me. I'll drop you and Storm off when it's over."

All right. Purpose replaced the despondency he'd been feeling since his nightmare. This was Linc's passion. He felt for sure that once he filled his head with SAR work, it'd help him put Syria far into the back of his mind. He went inside to get his gear, then pulled the rest of what he needed from his truck.

When he returned with Storm, Jacob slapped him on the back, and they jumped into his truck. Linc tried to pretend like this was just another day, like he wasn't completely about to lose his shit.

"So…things with Kylie are still good?"

Jacob was just making conversation, but that was the last thing Linc wanted to talk about. The second he heard her name, he thought of those bruises on her arm. "Yeah. She's good."

Him? He was another story.

As they drove down the driveway, Linc thought about all the times that he and Jacob had gone out to the bars, searching for meaningless one-night stands. Jacob was still into that. Hell, he was still into grabbing any hot piece of ass he could find. But that had lost its allure for Linc after Syria.

He closed his eyes. A lot of things had.

8

Kylie felt so bad about what had happened with Linc the night before that she wanted to cheer him up. She was a glutton for punishment when she picked up her phone for the tenth time that morning. She knew better. Linc was an awfully terse communicator via text; every single word he wrote sounded like she was annoying him.

Still, she wanted to try. This time, instead of setting the phone back down as she had the previous nine times, she was determined to send something off. Something happy and cute. If she was lucky, he would respond in kind. At the very least, he would still know that everything between them was okay.

Her thumbs made short work of the message: *Last night was amazing. Can't stop thinking about you.* For good measure, she added a heart and a suggestively winking emoticon.

By lunchtime, still no response.

Dammit.

Why did she do this to herself? Why did she have to get herself involved with men who blew both hot and cold? Hot, when he wanted sex, and cold all the rest of the time.

She leaned forward until her forehead struck the desk.

Actually, Kylie's love life had never afforded her many choices of men. Her mother'd told her that they were intimidated by her bubbly personality, but Kylie was certain it must be something else. Until Linc came along, she'd had the longest, driest dry spell when it came to men that one could possibly imagine for someone her age. Even so, Linc was a total winner when it came to Kylie's pathetic list of past lovers.

Kylie gritted her teeth as she looked at his name in her phone for the hundredth time that day and wondered why he had to tangle her stomach in knots like that. He'd read the message. He had just decided she wasn't worth replying to.

In the hopes of knocking some sense into herself, Kylie lifted her head a few inches and let it fall with a thunk again.

As Kylie was having her mini mental breakdown, Greg walked in, his sparse hair flattened against his forehead from the rain. He wiped at his face and groaned. "What now?"

Straightening quickly, Kylie grabbed for a folder. She came up empty because she'd already finished every last project on her to-do list. "Oh, nothing."

He eyed her suspiciously. "It's always something with you."

She'd tried talking to Greg about her pathetic love life with Linc before, and his stellar advice at that time had been, "Screw him." Kylie figured he'd probably impart the same wisdom to her in this situation, and he would have been right. She probably should've just given Linc the double middle-finger and moved on.

Kylie turned her phone over and forced herself to be her regular, cheery self. "I'm great. Did you have a big case you were working on?"

"Same old shit." He collapsed into his chair and started to

go through the reports she'd stacked neatly on his desk. "Any messages?"

Kylie nodded, trying for a nonchalance she didn't feel. "One. It's on your desk. From Emma Jennings. Remember her? She still thinks one of the people who manages her vast fortune is stealing her blind."

He stared at it, then hooked a finger at Kylie. "All right. Give me the rest."

She'd been so sure that he'd blow it off that it took a moment to register the request. "The what?"

"The rest. I'm sure you've probably been researching the crap out of this case already, looking up this Emma woman on your goggle or whatever it's called. So, what else do you know?"

She held up her hands, her innocence not feigned this time. "Google. And I haven't. Really."

His eyes were still narrowed in suspicion. "Are you serious?"

"I am!" Kylie pointed at the reports on his desk. "I've been a busy little well-behaved beaver. I finished all of them."

He still looked cautious, as if he thought she was trying to pull one over on him. He studied the message again, scratching his nose. "What? Embezzling scumbags aren't your thing? It's only serial killers you care about?"

"No," she said pointedly. "I had work to do. Remember? The reports. So, I did them. I didn't look up this Emma Jennings or anything of the sort."

He crossed his arms and frowned at her. "Well, why not?" he boomed. "What good are you?"

Kylie's eyes lifted in surprise. "Well…it's not my job. You mean…you want me to?"

He shrugged. "I'll admit, your goggling hasn't been entirely unhelpful, short stuff."

She grinned at him. "Googling. Really? So, are you

saying that I've actually been doing a good job? Because I thought you just thought of me as a meddling little nuisance."

Lord help her, but a tear threatened to leak from her eye.

"Relax. You *do* meddle. And you are a nuisance. But every now and again you come up with something good from that internet thing you got going on there. So...why don't you look up Emma Jennings and tell me what you come up with before I give her a call?"

Yes. Yes. Yes.

She hadn't even had to bribe him with Mrs. Jennings's promise of double payment.

Kylie reached for her phone and opened it up, noting with only a bit of sadness this time that Linc still hadn't texted. Then she typed *Emma Jennings Asheville* into the web browser. She scrolled through the many results. "Emma Jennings. Says here she's eighty-four years old. Oooh, lives on Browntown Road in Biltmore Forest. Swanky!"

He gave Kylie a look. "And?"

"And I once had a girlfriend who lived down there. Her house was pretty much a mini Biltmore mansion. She had a pool and a tennis court inside her freaking house. It was—"

"I mean, what else about Emma Jennings?" he grumbled, rolling his eyes.

Greg and his impatience. Kylie bit her tongue and scrolled through a little more. "Looks like she's a wealthy philanthropist. She's given a lot of money away to causes around town. Mostly art foundations and things."

"Jennings," he repeated. "Hmm. Yeah. The name sounds familiar. I think her husband was Arnold Jennings? The artist?"

"Yeah?" Kylie typed in Arnold Jennings. When she did, it brought up a slew of images, mostly of art pieces. Kylie wasn't an expert, but she guessed they were interesting. She pulled up the Wikipedia page on him. "Yes. He's the artist. Married to Emma. But he died about five years ago."

Greg nodded. "I've seen it happen before. Rich, elderly people being abused by those who should be taking care of their fortunes for them. It's a sad state."

Kylie's heart squeezed. That poor old woman. She'd sounded at her wit's end. She should be enjoying her fortune, not worrying about this. Kylie had never known her grandparents, but she'd always wished she had. She seriously hated when people preyed on those who were weaker than them. What was wrong with this world?

Kylie sighed and put her phone down. "That's about all there is."

Greg surveyed the neat pile of completed reports Kylie had centered on his desk. "I'm swamped. How about this? You want to give the woman a call and arrange to meet her? Take the lead and get some information about this missing money for me?"

Kylie's heart soared in her chest. "You mean it?"

He nodded. "You're good at asking the right questions, prying people open. And I doubt this Emma woman is packing heat, so I don't have to worry about you getting shot again."

Kylie couldn't believe it. While her inner Kylie was clapping excitedly, spinning in her chair, the outer Kylie could barely move.

Greg raised a bushy eyebrow. "You okay?"

His concerned look had her practically leaping from her seat. She didn't want to go all catatonic and have him change his mind. "Oh, yes. Absolutely. I can't wait." She went over to shake his hand. She nearly dislocated it, she was so happy. "Thank you. Thank you. I won't let you down."

"I know, short stuff," he muttered. "Calm down."

But she couldn't. Just yesterday, she'd thought she was on

the verge of typing for the rest of her life. And now, he was complimenting her. Telling her she'd done well. Giving her her very own case!

All right, it wasn't a serial killer and would probably be dull. Financial stuff usually was. But Kylie didn't care. It was hers. Her very first Greg-approved case.

Kylie picked up the phone to call Mrs. Jennings and arrange to meet with her, barely able to contain her excitement. She thought for a second about texting Linc to let him know, but the jerkface still hadn't texted her back yet. Other than him, she realized there wasn't anyone else she cared to tell. Her mother would just warn her not to get shot again, and then nag her about starting classes again.

There wasn't anyone else who'd be happy for her. No one else would understand just what this meant. The thought made her sad.

Damn, Linc. All it'd take was three words: *Miss you too.* Was that so hard? What would that take, thirty insignificant seconds of his time?

Refusing to let thoughts like that intrude, Kylie quickly called Emma Jennings back and arranged to meet her that day. Even with the Linc thing dampening her mood, she couldn't stop from smiling. Her first, real, Greg-sanctioned client appointment. She could probably even file an expense report on the mileage for this.

A half-hour before the arranged time, she grabbed her jacket and purse, clipped a leash onto Vader's collar, and said to Greg, "Off to do business! Hold my calls! Wish me luck!"

"Don't get shot," he muttered as Kylie headed for the door, Vader trotting behind her.

A thought struck her. She turned around and said, "You know, if I'm going to be doing important client meetings like this, it might behoove me to get some actual business cards?

You know, with my name and the Starr Investigations logo on them?"

He stared at her, then pointed at the door. "*Behoove* your little ass right out of here."

All right. Well, it was worth a shot.

Kylie shrugged, then lifted her purse onto her shoulder and headed for her car. She was so jazzed, she practically skipped the whole way, even in new heels she could barely walk in. "Vader, this is it! I'm going places." The big dog smiled at her, his tongue lolling out as she stared at him in the rearview mirror. "Want my autograph? You can say you knew me when."

He gave her a droopy yawn and rested his chin on the chewed-up headrest in front of him. She'd interrupted his afternoon nap.

Kylie drove south, to an area called Biltmore Forest, which used to be part of the Biltmore Estate years ago. It was known for its mansions, and Emma Jennings's house didn't disappoint. She gaped as she pulled up a long cobblestone driveway, to an elegant whitewashed stone French chateau that was easily twice the size of her whole apartment building. There was a split staircase going up to two massive doors, so for a minute, she stood there, at the base of it, just marveling and thinking of that house in *The Sound of Music*.

As she did, Vader barked, pulling her attention back to business. "Stay here," Kylie said, using her alpha voice with him. "Remember? Stay! I know you won't do it for me, but just pretend Linc, your best friend, is me."

He tilted his head at her.

"And please...don't eat any more of my headrest. Driving in my car is already uncomfortable enough as it is."

He gave Kylie a sad look and stuck his head out the window, already trying to get out.

"Really? Stay!" Taking a deep breath, Kylie tried to

remember everything she'd learned in Vader's training. She wagged a stern finger at the big dog. "This doesn't look like the type of place that will put up with your shenanigans, dude."

Vader's ears perked up, just before a yipping sound registered in Kylie's brain. Oh no. There was another dog in the near vicinity. She whirled around, her mouth open to shout another "no," but Vader had already managed to wiggle his large frame through the, clearly, too wide-open window.

He took off like a shot, claws scrabbling on the sidewalk as he raced up the stairs and right toward a...

Oh no!

Kylie leapt forward, sure the Newfoundland was about to have the tiny puffball of an orange dog for a snack.

"Vader, no!"

Out of breath, Kylie made it to the top stair, preparing her mind for the bloody mess she'd probably be sued over.

To her surprise, the little dog had Vader cowering in the corner, its frantic yapping like a drill in her eardrums.

"It's quite all right, dear," a woman said, picking up the little dog. She wore a bright teal jogging suit, and her silver hair was tied up in a flowery scarf. She was, in a word, adorable. "Coco likes to visit with friends."

"Um. Mrs. Jennings?"

"Please call me Emma," she said, motioning her forward as she put the little dog back on its feet. "Are you Kylie?"

"Uh. Yes."

Vader, more confident now, came out of the corner and promptly began playing, acting as if Coco was his personal hacky sack. Coco squealed and went airborne. Kylie dove and caught the dog before the little thing hit the ground. Cuddling the furball in her arms, she inspected the five-pound ball of fluff carefully before giving Vader an expression that should have had him obeying any command she deigned to give.

Emma Jennings didn't look the least bit concerned. "Nonsense, Coco's fine. She's a bit of a daredevil, that one. Not a shy or scared bone in her little Pomeranian body."

Pushing to her feet, for the first time it struck Kylie just how small Emma was. At just under five-four, Kylie was used to being called short, but Emma was several inches smaller than her. But for an eighty-four-year-old lady, she didn't look frail in the least. In fact, she largely resembled a pear. She patted her leg and whistled to her little dog, who jumped into her arms as she moved with as much spunk as someone half her age into the house.

And what a house it was. The foyer was at least three stories high, circular, and framed in windows that went from floor to ceiling. Kylie gasped at the enormous chandelier dangling over their heads. The place looked like a museum. "Wow, this is lovely, Mrs. Jennings."

"Emma, dear. And thank you, you're too kind," she said, wrapping an arm around Kylie's waist and leading her to another enormous room featuring a piano, a massive stone fireplace, and framed paintings on every vertical surface. Emma sat her down on a big leather sofa and motioned to a fancy silver tea service like she'd seen in movies, but never thought people actually used in real life. "Tea?"

Kylie nodded. "Thank you."

Emma dropped Coco to the ground and reached for the silver teapot as the two dogs came together again. Kylie winced, waiting for Vader to do something awful, but he simply nosed Coco gently.

Paying no attention to the canines, Emma took the dainty teacup and added a few cubes of sugar with the tiny tongs. "This place was my dream. My husband always wanted a smaller place in the mountains, but I had such a collection of his beautiful works, I insisted on a home that would adequately display them all. We were married for over sixty years before his death. I've always been his greatest fan."

Kylie looked around at the work. She'd been an art history minor…for about three weeks, until she realized art didn't interest her in the least. She couldn't tell what time period they were. Modern? Deco? Pop? They looked kind of creepy, truthfully—people with weird, googly eyes and funnily shaped bodies. But what did she know?

"They're beautiful paintings," Kylie fibbed, sipping her tea.

Emma nodded. "These are only a small sampling. I'll take you to the gallery if you'd like. Arnold was quite prolific. Unfortunately, he really didn't come into his own until several years after his death. He's been gone nearly five years, but I'd say only in the last two or so have his paintings started to become truly priceless."

Kylie gave her a sad smile. "I guess the saying 'an artist is only appreciated after he is dead' is true."

Emma sighed. "In this case, yes. Both mine and Arnold's families were quite wealthy prior to our marriage, and Arnold invested wisely, even before his artwork began selling well. I don't need it all. I'm an old woman and I have no living children, just a grandson I do my best to take care of."

She sighed again, suddenly looking her age.

Kylie reached over and grasped her hand. "What happened to your children?" Kylie asked gently, even though she already knew. The headlines had covered every newspaper on the East Coast, at least.

"There was a fire at our lodge in Maine, I'm afraid. Both my daughters and their husbands were killed. Little Nate barely made it out alive."

The sadness was so deep, that Kylie felt it spread into her hand and enter her cells. She swallowed. "I'm so sorry."

Emma's smile looked weary. "Thank you, dear. But Nate is grown and on his own now, and well…he hasn't always made the wisest of decisions."

That caught Kylie's interest. "How so?"

Emma waved a hand in front of her face, like she was swatting away bad memories. "Oh, just foolish behavior. Acting out, as his therapist called it."

Kylie wanted to dig deeper into Nate's foolish behavior, but she sensed this wasn't the time.

"Do you see him often?"

That brought a small smile back to Emma's face. "Yes, every few weeks, at least. At first, he was very angry that we changed his trust so that the money only trickled out each quarter, but I think he better understands now, why the arrangement was necessary."

Does he now?

KYLIE GLANCED over to see Vader curled up on the lacquered floor as Coco buzzed around his ear. *Good boy,* she thought. "Why don't you start from the beginning and tell me what led you to believe your money is being stolen?"

"Well, like I said, I have a number of people in my employ, and I trust them with everything that I am. Perhaps I'm a little too trustworthy. People think I'm an old lady. That I don't realize when I'm being taken advantage of. But I do. They think I'm weak, that I won't fight back. But I intend to. I intend to string the bastard up. And you, dear girl, are going to help me."

Kylie leaned forward, listening. The woman was feisty. Kylie had a feeling the two of them were going to get along perfectly.

❄

Some might say that I was anal, as if that description was an insult.

Not to me.

I called it a compliment because being overly cautious had always been my friend.

And considering the way the tides were turning in my life, it might be the only friend I had left when it was all said and done.

That was okay. Really. At least that was what I kept telling myself.

From a young child, I knew I had no one to rely on but myself.

I wasn't abused nor ignored nor any of those heart-squeezing abuses so many children face on the six o'clock news. I was loved, adored even. But no one understood me, or even tried to.

When I said I didn't want to share with the others, I meant it.

I simply wanted what was mine.

But the adults would make me, and if I didn't do it willingly, they'd take my precious possessions and let others dirty them with sticky, nose-picking hands.

I was still angry about that, if truth be told.

My favorites would then be allocated to the toy chest, or trash can—if I could get away with it. When what was mine had been touched by others, it no longer brought joy.

I craved joy.

And the others would simply strip it away, without a thought.

As I watched the crusty old crow slurping at her tea like she was a queen sitting high on a dais, it took all my inner willpower not to punch the screen. She was using the delicate fine-bone china that was a favorite of mine, her lipstick leaving a smudge on the thousand-dollar rim.

Even worse, beside her, a girl with clearly no taste clattered the delicate cup on its equally delicate saucer. Couldn't she see the value she held in her hands?

No. She wouldn't. Couldn't.

I should feel sympathy for her lack of taste and manners, but even the lowliest of society could do better, if they simply willed themselves.

That was the problem with society. Instant gratification had become the crutch and the need for willpower disappeared.

Willpower was also my friend. I wielded it well.

Five years ago, all of this could have been mine. The house. The fortune. The teacup that just clattered again. Not that I wanted these old things, but they would have brought a nice penny to go toward things more of my taste.

But I'd implored my willpower. I acted, then I waited.

And I'd been right. An artist was never truly appreciated during their time. It'd been a test, really.

Question: If an artist dies, how quickly does his art increase in value?

Answer: Very quickly.

More quickly than I'd expected, really. Especially considering the paintings themselves were only adequate at best.

I could have done better.

I actually did do better. As I replicated dear old Arnold's paintings, I had to force myself to decrease my skills, force myself to not add the shading and details that would have made the artwork really special.

Taking in a lung full of air, I forced myself to focus on the conversation taking place on the computer screen in front of me.

Not the girl. Not the crow. Not the china.

The words.

I frowned, realizing I'd made a mistake. The crow was

hiring a private investigator, this mite of a girl, because I'd done something wrong.

No. Not me.

My planning had been beyond exceptional. I didn't make mistakes. I didn't.

But…D?

Had D done something stupid again?

That was the problem when you relied on others.

It was a mistake I needed to immediately correct.

Still listening to the conversation on my computer monitor, I picked up my phone and opened the messaging app.

Me: *We have a problem.*

The reply was almost immediate.

D: *What's wrong?*

Me: *The crow has hired a PI. She suspects something. What have you done?*

My thumb hovered over the send button, then I tapped the backspace key instead, erasing the last four words. I didn't want to accuse over the phone.

D: *Don't worry. She won't find anything.*

I narrowed my eyes. I wished I felt such confidence.

Me: *We need to talk.*

The reply took a little longer.

D: *Okay. When? Where?*

Desire stirred low in my belly. I could have my cake and eat it too.

Me: *I'll get the room. You bring the wine.*

D: :-)

I sighed. So juvenile.

But the ends justified the means. It was just logic, really.

And logic was my friend too.

9

As Jacob drove them toward Rocky Bluff, Linc's phone buzzed with a message from Kylie. He read it over and over again: *Last night was amazing. Can't wait to see you again.*

It reeked of Kylie. He felt Kylie's smile in every word, in all those stupid little emoticons she littered it with. All sunshine and rainbows and happiness. In Kylie's world, there was only one emotion: Deliriously ecstatic. That was who she was. It made a smile tug at his lips.

He bit it back.

Linc thought of lying there with her, spooned against her. Her body was so warm, so inviting. He'd wanted to pull her to him, wrap her in his protection, never let anything happen to her again.

Then Linc thought of those bruises on her arm, and he gritted his teeth.

"You okay, man?" Jacob asked him.

Linc wiped the sleep out of his eye. "Yeah. Long night last night. That's all."

"Yeah. Kylie was over, huh?" Jacob gave him a suggestive wink.

Linc nodded and didn't say more. Jacob knew about his relationship with Kylie. Had been through the thick of it with them as they dealt with the Spotlight Killer. But he and Jacob, as a rule, didn't discuss women. Linc had nothing to discuss with him, anyway, since Jacob was still firmly in the one-night stand pool.

Dread pooled in Linc's stomach, tightening his chest as he surveyed the thick forest out the window. "You still going out to the bars with your boys?"

"Hell yes. Met this one girl the other night. Huge tits. She was like a blonde version of Kylie."

Linc gritted his teeth. It was no secret Jacob liked what he saw when he looked at Kylie. Hell, few men could say they didn't like what they saw with Kylie. She was every man's wet dream. "Oh, yeah?"

He nodded. "Hell yes." Jacob raised his eyebrows suggestively. That was the extent of their girl talk.

"So…she going in your book?"

"Nah."

Jacob had been writing the Great American Novel for forever, and he always put people he found interesting inside. Linc was a character in it, and he'd put Kylie in after knowing her for about an hour. "You going to see her again?"

Jacob laughed. "Hell no. What would be the fun in that? She might've looked like Kylie, but she was dumb as a stump. I'm telling you. You lucked out with your girl. She's the total package."

Right. The total package. Linc couldn't agree more. He looked down at the message from Kylie.

He knew what he should text back. *I don't know if we should see each other again.*

He put his thumbs on the screen, began typing the sentence. With a silent curse, he backspaced and pocketed the phone before he grew so aggravated that he threw it out the window.

Reaching out, he turned up the radio, hoping the volume would shut his friend's conversation down. Jacob mercifully stayed silent, just sang along, tapping his fingers on the steering wheel in time with the song.

But every few minutes, he could feel Jacob's eyes turn toward him, filled with concern.

Linc ignored it.

After another tormenting half hour, they reached the trailer park where the boy's family lived. Both stepped out of the truck to see a few police officers already there. At the family's trailer, Linc left Storm outside and went in, where a young mother and father were sitting around a gleaming kitchenette table. In fact, the entire home gleamed it was so clean and tastefully decorated.

"Ma'am," Jacob said to the young blonde woman who appeared to be in her mid-twenties. She was wearing a UNC sweatshirt and chewing on her thumbnail, her eyes puffy and red from crying. "This is Lincoln Coulter, Buncombe County's number one search and rescue guy. He and his dog, Storm, are here to find and bring back your daughter."

Bloodshot eyes turned toward Linc. "Thank you. I'm Stephanie, and this is my husband, Eddy." She swallowed and looked at her husband, who dragged a hand down his weary face.

The father's hands shook as he spoke. "Bethany always wakes up early and goes and gets herself breakfast. We found her bowl of cereal on the sofa, only half eaten. We just got her a puppy and have been talking about how to take care of the dog and..."

The man's throat seemed to close, and his face turned an even deeper shade of red as emotion washed over him.

Stephanie covered her husband's hand, tears spilling from

her eyes. "We think she may have wandered off while walking Scooby. That's the dog's name. The door was open when we woke up."

Eddy cleared his throat, taking the story back. "Bethany's gone out on her own before, but never very far. I kept meaning to put a lock up on the door, high, so she couldn't reach it, but…" he choked up again, "never got around to it."

He hung his head with guilt and his wife moved her hand to his back, rubbing his shoulder. "Bethany has Down syndrome, you see." The smallest smile played on her lips. "We think she's very bright, and she's just a little butterfly socially once she warms up to you."

Linc smiled. "She seems like a wonderful little girl. Is she able to communicate well?"

Stephanie frowned. "Not well. We can usually understand her, and she's working with a speech therapist at school, but most people might find her speech difficult to understand."

Linc nodded, and something that Kylie had once said to him reappeared in his thoughts. She'd said that while Linc might have been good at saving people, he wasn't very friendly about it. She told him that he could be an asshole when it came to his rescues. And she was right. He needed to have more of a bedside manner. Have more compassion to the fear individuals and family were facing.

Dammit, Kylie was in his head now. Breaking things off with her would be easier said than done.

Gently, Linc said, "When was the last time you saw her?"

Stephanie blew her nose. "Not since I checked in on her at about midnight last night before I turned in myself."

"And what time does Bethany usually get up?" Linc asked, equally gently.

Eddy took this question. "Around six, normally. She's an early riser."

Linc checked his phone. It was after eleven. If the little

girl had indeed gotten up at her usual time, then she could have been wandering around for five hours. That'd give them a huge search radius to cover. That wasn't good, especially considering that the rain was picking up. He did his best not to let on, though. "Okay. What kind of pup does she have?"

The father shrugged. "Just a mutt. Beagle mixed with who knows what else. We'll know more as he grows older"

"All right. So, do you think Bethany is wearing pajamas?"

The mother nodded. "Yes. Purple with owls on them." She sniffed. "Purple is her favorite color." She tittered nervously, then buried her face in her hands, her shoulders shaking on a sob.

"Hey. We'll do everything we can to bring her back," Linc said, looking at them both. "Can I borrow something that belongs to her that I can use to have my dog scent?"

The mother handed Linc the girl's purple blanket. It must have been a favorite because the ends were tattered, and it was threadbare in spots.

Linc stood up. "All right." He went outside with Jacob, zipped his hood up over his head, and took the radio Jacob offered him. "I'll be back."

Jacob nodded. "I'm going to walk around and talk to some of the neighbors. See if they saw or noticed anything, just in case this is more than a lost kid situation."

Linc gritted his teeth. He hoped the girl was simply missing instead of having been taken by a human predator, who would do things he didn't have the heart to think about.

As Linc approached, Storm watched him seriously, sure that her work would soon begin.

"Ready to work, girl?"

Storm barked once, her flanks beginning to tremble. Yeah, she was ready.

Linc bent down and replaced the leash with a long line

before making sure her vest and bell were properly secured. Holding out the blanket for Storm to scent, she gave him a "got it" look, and he said what he hoped would be the result of their search. "Find."

Storm took off, nose on the ground. It took a few minutes for her to separate new scents from old, and Linc was forced to guide the dog back from a couple false starts before she caught a scent trail heading into the woods.

Running with her, Linc kept his head up, looking ahead, searching for footprints or any other sign that the girl had come this way.

The outdoors had always brought him calm. Even when they were in a battle with the clock and nature's elements, there was nowhere else Linc would rather be.

The rain fell harder, and he cursed Mother Nature, knowing the clock they were already working against would speed up faster. Even the breeze was working against him, causing Storm to stop and start as the wind took the scent with it.

This was what he was good at. This was the way he could make a difference in the world. But, seriously, couldn't they catch a damn break with this case?

When a half hour passed and Storm stopped, frustration clear on her face, he began to lose hope.

Linc climbed down a ridge, letting Storm lead him, the dog keeping her nose to the ground for the scent.

After about ten minutes of walking, Linc spotted what could've been a small child's footprint on the path. Storm seemed set on this direction, so Linc followed along, until they came to an area littered with a lot of broken glass, cigarettes, and an old fire pit. It was obvious that kids had been out here, having parties.

He crouched down to Storm's level. "Is this what you

were scenting out, girl? This isn't right." Linc offered up the blanket again. Sometimes, competing scents and rain and even the direction of the wind could confuse any search and rescue dog. He heard a noise off the main path that could've been a dog barking, or possibly a puppy, and decided to go in that direction. "Come on, girl. Let's go this way."

He led her into the woods, through piles of fallen leaves, too damp to crunch underfoot. The leaves were slick, so he spent a lot of time sliding on them, even with the traction of his hiking boots. A little girl in pajamas would have it a lot worse.

They descended a rocky hillside, where it got even more treacherous, until Linc could glimpse a narrow stream through the trees. The rain had really swelled it up, and the water was white, flowing rapidly, picking up leaves and bark and whatever else was on the bottom of the forest floor.

Something like this could mean trouble. Especially with a kid that young and with a learning disability.

Linc went down to the edge of the water and searched as far as he could downstream, to where it bent around some fallen black tree branches.

No sign of the girl, or the puppy.

Linc's heart started to thrum in his chest. He was drenched, cold, and shivering, and if that was how he was feeling, the kid was probably a lot worse. Linc was already in a bad mood, and a bad ending to this case would only fuck things up more.

No, it wouldn't just fuck things up. It would give him more fodder for his nightmares.

There was plenty of daylight left. That wasn't the problem. The problem was, it was getting colder, and the rain was picking up. A little girl in her pajamas didn't have much protection from the elements. If Linc didn't get to her soon, death from hypothermia was a definite possibility.

Fighting off the dread that threatened to seep in, Linc yanked Storm's collar and pulled her downstream, blinking back the rain as it fell steadily against his face. He'd bring this child home, if it was the last thing he did.

He was not going to let this case end badly. He wouldn't be able to live with himself if it did.

10

Kylie smiled at Emma as she talked. She was effervescent and full of life and seemed fond of peppering the conversation with rather risqué stories of her past with her husband, Arnold. She told her she'd once been his model—his nude model—decades ago, and he'd seduced her when she was a young girl of only twenty.

He'd been her sex machine, she'd said, always leaving her notes and performing romantic gestures. That was what had kept their passion alive, she said, for all those years. As Emma gave her the sordid details, Kylie blushed, and couldn't stop thinking of Linc.

Her own personal sex machine.

Kylie managed a look at her phone when Emma stopped to pour more tea, but...no. No text.

So much for her sex machine.

Kylie smiled as Emma started to get very graphic about the first time they'd had sex. It was outdoors, in the garden, and she'd been lying on a lounge, letting him paint her, and suddenly he'd become so amorous that he pulled off his clothes and—

"Okay! I think I've got the point!" Kylie said before Emma could go further.

Emma patted her hand. "Don't be afraid of sex. It's a natural thing, sweetheart. All I'm saying is that the relationship between an artist and his model is such a sensuous one. Which is why I never let him paint another woman after me."

"Okay. Now, getting back to the missing funds," Kylie said, realizing that if she was going to get anywhere with this woman, she had to take the rudder on this conversation. Emma was almost as distracted by bright, shiny objects as Kylie was. She seemed sharp, and had a great memory for, uh, details, especially sexual ones, but her obsession with recalling the old days was a little overwhelming. "How did you notice they were missing?"

"Well, you see. I don't go out much anymore. And my lawyer handles all of my donation requests these days, since, as you can imagine, I get a lot of them. But I contribute to quite a few causes and have done so for several years."

Kylie nodded. She was constantly getting donation requests from UNC and hadn't a spare penny to her name.

"Anyway, I have a good friend named Marge, who actually was a nude model herself back in the day. That's how we met. I think she was a bit of competition for Arnold, if you know what I mean. But Arnold always said that my body was the most perfect one he'd ever had a chance to lay his eyes up—"

Kylie looked up from her notepad. "So, this Marge noticed the funds were missing?"

Emma paused. "No. Not exactly. Marge is quite well-off herself, having married an artist too, no one nearly as successful as my husband, though. She's a bit of a moneygrubber, that one, and has a little bit of a competitive streak. Oh, she and I used to fight over Arnold like you would not believe. One day, I saw her standing in front of his door, completely nude, singing to him, and—"

"All right. But how did she notice the money was missing?"

"Oh! Well, she and I were once the top donors to the Asheville Modern Art Society. But she told me recently while we were playing mah-jongg and having tea—which we do every Tuesday at ten—that they'd recently sent her a bulletin with the top donors, and my name was no longer on it. So, she asked around and learned they were sorry to lose my support. But I knew nothing of it!"

Ah. Now they were getting somewhere. "Really?"

"Yes! I was floored. Of course, old Marge thought that I might have been running into some hard times, but I told her that couldn't be further from the truth. I explained that Arnold's paintings have never been doing better. I told her that one of them sold at an auction in Paris for over a million dollars just last month."

She had to be kidding. "So, you never made any changes to the charities you support?"

"No, I did not. I never authorized discontinuing my contributions. Well, I asked my lawyer, but he told me that, as far as he knew, nothing had changed. He said the money was being funneled just as it always had been, and it had to be an accounting error on someone's part. I've been with my lawyer for quite some time, and I think he just assumes I'm being a batty old nutcase. But that's not true."

"That is odd," Kylie said, scribbling down some notes. "How did your lawyer leave it with you? Is he going to look into it or not?"

"He said he would, but I think he's just being dismissive of me. People often are, when you get to be my age. They're condescending and treat me like a child. And yes, my mind is scattered. It might not be what it once was, but I do know what I'm talking about." Emma banged her fists on her thighs. "Most certainly."

Kylie sympathized with the elderly woman's frustration and reached over to squeeze her hand. "You seem exceedingly sharp to me." Emma beamed, and Kylie smiled as she went on. "I'm wondering if it might just be a miscommunication. A technical glitch on the part of the foundation. I'm sure I can get to the bottom of it."

Emma leaned over and patted Kylie's knee. "Sharp girl like you. You're a little firecracker, I can tell that much already. I'm sure you can too. Are there papers I need to sign to retain you?"

Kylie nearly hugged the woman. Greg would be happy. "Yes." Kylie pulled them out of her bag. "I have them right here."

"Wonderful. Let me get my bifocals." Emma stood up and Coco jumped from her lap. "Would you like to take a look at my husband's main gallery? It has been months and months since I've had the heart to go back in the gallery, but there are some lovely paintings of me in there. And other ones too. Though the ones of me are obviously the best." She whispered the last part as if her husband was listening and gave Kylie a sly wink.

Kylie nodded. "Oh yes. I really do love his art."

Kylie stood and followed Emma across a magnificent, gilded hall, which reminded her of photographs she'd seen of Versailles, to a long ballroom. Here were hundreds upon hundreds of paintings of all sizes. There was a huge one at the very center of a young woman, naked, in front of a dressing table, giving a come-hither look.

"That's me," Emma said proudly.

Kylie averted her eyes, but not before she got a whole

eyeful of Emma's…assets. She'd been quite attractive in her younger days, with long blonde hair, rosy cheeks, and massive boobs. Emma gazed at it appreciatively.

"Your husband certainly was talented," Kylie said, focusing on a painting of a little boy playing with a dog. "How many paintings did he do?"

"Oh. Thousands." Emma directed her over to some other paintings but stopped so short Kylie nearly ran into her from behind. "That's strange."

She followed Emma's gaze to an empty space on the wall. There was a small square there, and a hanging hook, as if a painting had been removed. "Is something wrong?"

"Well, yes. *Madonna in Mourning* is missing," Emma said, a troubled crease appearing over her nose. "That was one of my favorite paintings. And one of Arnie's most valuable."

Kylie walked farther into the room and froze. She noticed right away that two more paintings were missing.

"That's very odd," Emma said, her brow wrinkling.

"You're missing three?" Kylie asked, surveying the open spaces. "Is it possible you lent them out to a gallery?"

Emma tapped on her chin. "I don't…my mind isn't what it was. I would remember doing so, wouldn't I?"

Kylie didn't know. Emma seemed pretty sharp. Or maybe that was only in recalling all the details of her love life with Arnold.

"Well," Emma said, striding to the corner of the room and pulling on a large woven bell rope. "I'll just ask Sloane. He's my right-hand man these days. Has all the answers, he does."

A moment later, a balding man who could've been just as old as Emma arrived, dressed formally in a dark suit. "Madam?"

"Good afternoon, Sloane. I was just giving my friend Kylie a tour of our gallery, and I noticed just now that some pieces are missing. Do you know what happened to *Madonna in Mourning, Autumn Sunrise,* and *The Belle in Evening*?

"Why, yes, Madam," Sloane said, surveying the wall. "You asked them to be reframed, did you not?"

Emma stared at the man blankly. "When did I do this?"

He appeared deep in thought for a moment. "Two months ago, I'd say. A man in a white van came to take them away."

She sighed and tapped her temple. "I'm losing my memory. I'm sorry. Thank you, Sloane. That'll be all." Even as she dismissed the man, she studied the empty spaces, concern on her features. As Kylie watched her, she wondered what it would be like to have a butler, someone to call to her for her every whim and then dismiss with a wave of the hand.

No, thanks. She thought she'd rather have her place to herself, even if it meant doing everything herself. Well, except for the cooking. And toilets. And dusting.

Hmm...maybe a housekeeper would be nice. And a chef.

Emma turned to Kylie, still looking troubled. "I can't seem to recall what was wrong with the frames to begin with. They were lovely paintings. Three of my most favorite."

Hmm. That sounded like a part of the mystery to her.

Kylie followed Emma out of the gallery and said, "Would you be able to make me out a list of people close to you, staff members, anyone who might be able to shed some light on the missing funds?"

Emma clapped her hands together. "I thought you might ask for that, so I took the liberty of preparing just such a list for you." She stopped at what looked like a thousand-year-old desk and pulled out a large envelope, handing it to Kylie. "Names and phone numbers, should you wish to get in touch with them."

She opened the clasp and read the first page. Emma had

shaky handwriting. The first was Nate Jennings. "Is this your grandson?"

Emma smiled. "Oh, yes. My sweet grandson. He's a little older than you, nearly thirty. He comes around to help me out with odd jobs now and then. He's quite handsome. And... single, last I heard." Her eyes drifted down to Kylie's hand. "Are *you* seeing anyone, dear?"

"Well, um..." She flashed to Linc, her good old non-texting sex partner. *Was* she seeing him?

Kylie stuffed the envelop in her bag, eager to get back to the office to research the contacts better. Then, she'd interview Emma again. Right now, the elderly woman was looking very tired.

To prove her point, Emma yawned, patting her mouth.

Kylie reached into her purse and pulled out a copy of the retainer paperwork. "All that's left to do right now is for you to sign this, giving me permission to research this case on your behalf. Obviously, you won't want to run this past your attorney, since he'll be part of my investigations, but if you'd like to read it over and let me know if you have any—"

"Oh, no." Emma took the pen from her hand and signed right there. "I have faith in you, Kylie. I know you are the woman for the job. Although I probably should be warier, considering my current state, I can just tell, you're a good egg. I trust you implicitly."

"Well, thank you," Kylie said, shaking Emma's hand. "I appreciate the confidence. I won't let you down."

She took Vader by the collar and led him down the stairs, through the drizzle that was now falling, smiling and waving at her new friend as she pulled out of the driveway. She really didn't think her first client meeting could've gone any better. Kylie was excited again, raring to take off and start working, following these leads.

But she also wanted to tell someone about her success.

Someone who'd care. Who'd be as happy for her as she was for herself.

She wanted to talk to Linc.

Before she pulled out onto the main road, she checked her phone again. No text from him. From anyone.

Kylie sighed and hit the gas. She guessed she'd just have to keep it to herself, for now.

11

Storm and Linc walked streamside for at least another mile, and all the while, the dread inside Linc's chest was growing and tightening. The rain was coming down harder now, filtering through the leaves that were just beginning to spot with autumn color overhead. The air was definitely growing colder too, the rain making the mid-fifty temperature feel even chillier.

The stream was swollen from all the rainfall, rushing fast and furious down the ravine. It may have been narrow, but it was fierce and fast-moving. If the girl'd come this way, she would've had a hard time crossing safely. Linc kept his eyes ahead of him, scanning the banks, full of muddy leaves.

Purple. He was looking for purple.

Storm stiffened beside him, her nose working more furiously than before. Hope bloomed, but Linc kept a tight hold on it. Storm had a good nose, for both the living and the dead.

Storm rushed forward, and Linc fed her more of the long line, picking up his pace to keep up. Soon, he'd have to let her roam on her own if he started to slow her down. But as she ran faster, he didn't think they'd have to resort to that.

This was how she got when she was sure of something. It was a good sign. He broke into a run, sticking close to her side.

Then he saw it. Purple. Just a flash of the color.

As he got closer, he realized it wasn't moving.

Bracing himself, he started to run again, not stopping until he came to a bend in the stream. Linc spotted a foot, pale as milk, poking out from where the bottom of her pajamas had torn away.

That little foot nearly broke his heart.

"Please be alive," he prayed.

The child was curled in a fetal position, holding the puppy to her chest, the roaring stream just inches away.

"Hey, sweetheart," Linc said, sliding down the embankment toward the small pair. With a gentle hand, he touched the girl's face. It was cold. So very cold.

More urgently now, he felt for a pulse, his other hand moving to beneath her nose, praying for any small sign of life.

It was there.

The child's breathing was shallow, her pulse slower than he liked. Pale and clammy. She was in shock. He needed to treat her quickly.

Her eyelids fluttered as he began to strip her from the sodden clothes, pulling the mylar rescue blanket from his pack. He needed to get her warm. That was his first priority.

All the while he was doing so, he spoke to the child, telling her how glad he was to see her, how much her mommy and daddy couldn't wait to see her again. He pulled a second blanket out and wrapped the puppy in its warmth. The little thing didn't look good, but he could only care for one of them at a time.

Then it happened. The eyelids opened, and blue eyes stared up at him in confusion. Fear. The girl blinked several times, looking around.

"Hi, Bethany," he said in a gentle voice. He knew very little about Down syndrome on a personal level and wasn't sure how cognitive the girl would be. Wasn't sure how well she could communicate or understand direction.

Then a miracle happened...she smiled. Just a little.

It was beautiful. Precious. Tinged in blue, but he was working on that. Linc squeezed her a little tighter against him.

The smile faded away, and he released his hold, taking his cues from her. Trusting that the little girl would be able to communicate enough.

"Scoo-beeee."

Link smiled. Yeah, she could communicate enough.

"Scooby is in his own blanket, getting warmed up too." He was worried about the little dog, but now wasn't the time to exude that concern. "I'm going to call for someone to come help us get you and him back. Your mommy and daddy are sure missing you."

Bethany brightened and started shivering hard. Good. Shivering was good. "Mom-my? Dad-dy? See 'em."

Her voice was slurred, like her tongue was a bit too big for her mouth, but he knew exactly what she was saying.

"You sure are going to see them. Hold on a second while I call in our position." Linc reached for the radio. "Jacob. I've got her. Shock but stable at the moment. Get the EMTs over here."

Linc gave Jacob his precise location and waited with his arms around the little girl, keeping her warm while he massaged the puppy with the blanket, hoping to stir him a little.

The EMT team was a welcome site, and Bethany was

starting to look much better as they took control. Linc turned to the dog. Storm had laid down beside the little thing, licking its head and using her own body to help save him. She was totally ignoring the toy he'd tossed to her to celebrate the find, which was unusual.

He patted the Shepherd's head. "Good girl."

Like Bethany's father had said, the little mutt was a beagle mix, no more than a couple months old. It was still breathing, just suffering from signs of hypothermia too. Linc wrapped it tighter and picked it up, holding the dog close as Storm trotted at his side, toy in her mouth. They followed closely behind the stretcher, ready to help if the muddy hillside caused the emergency workers any trouble.

Midway through the walk back to Bethany's home, the puppy began to twitch and yip a little. It was almost back to its old self as he made his way back to the trailer park.

Jacob gave him a high-five as he came back up the ridge. "Well, you did it again," Jacob said, grinning as Linc lifted the edge of the blanket and showed him the puppy. Jacob tickled its belly. "Cute thing."

"Yeah. He'll be okay. Tough little fighter."

The corner of Jacob's mouth turned up in amusement. "The kid, or the dog?"

"Both."

Linc watched as Bethany's parents ran up to the stretcher, tears of relief pouring down their faces while the EMTs began the process of transferring her to a proper stretcher.

"Warms the heart, doesn't it?" Jacob asked, patting Linc on the back. "You made that possible."

Linc frowned and looked down at the puppy. He was no hero. No hero hurt a woman. He closed his eyes against the reminder of the fear in Kylie's eyes.

As Bethany was being loaded into the back of the ambulance, her parents turned toward Linc. Stephanie ran up and hugged him. "I don't know how to thank you."

"No need, ma'am," Linc said, hugging her stiffly back while holding on to the pup. "It's my job. Go and be with your daughter."

Eddy shook his hand and looked at the puppy in his arms. "He gonna be okay?" Eddy asked, rubbing the back of his neck.

"Should be, but he should be taken to the vet, just to be sure."

Linc offered the puppy to him, but Eddy shook his head. "Well, you see..." His face began to grow red. "Believe it or not, my wife and I both have really good jobs, but we had to move here..." he raised a hand to indicate the trailer park, "after Bethany was born. The bills, even with insurance." He rubbed at his jaw and looked down at the ground. "I—"

"Listen," Linc broke in. "Take him to Asheville Veterinary and ask for Dr. Evans, tell her to put it on Linc Coulter's account." Linc stroked the puppy's floppy ears. "He'll be okay, but he does need to be looked at."

Relief flooded Eddy's features. Relief mixed with embarrassment. "Are you sure? That's mighty nice of you. I'll drop him off on the way to the hospital. That should be okay, shouldn't it? Under the circumstances?"

Linc nodded and handed the pup over. If the man had said no, Linc would have kept Scooby for himself. He had a hard time coming across a stray he didn't want to take in. When you had as many dogs as he had, one more wasn't that much of a difference.

"Not a problem," Linc said, turning toward Jacob's truck. "Take care of your family."

Jacob was waiting there for him, his hat pulled down low over his eyes. "Linc Coulter. Friend to man and beast alike."

Linc gave him a playful shove in the chest. "Shut up."

By the time Storm and Linc got back into Jacob's truck, they were both soaked to the skin and shivering. Jacob turned the heat up high and played some country music at top volume and Linc felt better. Finding that little girl and knowing she was going to be all right had done a lot for his mood, and his ego. He didn't feel like such a worthless sack of shit anymore.

Almost.

Linc told himself it was a good thing he hadn't called Kylie. He was exhausted as hell, especially after last night's lack of sleep, but he was back to his old way of thinking.

Search and rescue was what he was good at. This was what he needed to concentrate on. Screw everything else.

That thinking lasted up until Jacob pulled in his driveway, and Linc saw Kylie's little Mazda in the driveway.

"Well, it looks like you got company," Jacob said with a grin.

Linc's body tensed. His cock pulsed. His lips involuntarily mumbled, "Shit."

"What?" Jacob said, giving Linc a look like he was insane. "I thought everything was good in Kylie Land. Damn girl's a damned peach. Don't think you can do any better, man. Because I'll tell you right now. You can't."

"Wasn't thinking that at all," Linc said as they got closer and he spied Kylie sitting cross-legged on the porch swing. She stood up as they approached, holding a little red umbrella and shaking raindrops from her hair.

Dammit. He was happy to see her.

She was wearing this little red flowered dress that reminded him of something a farmgirl would wear. Her legs were bare. Her dark hair was hanging long and wavy in her face. Linc could bet money she wasn't wearing a bra.

Hot damn, he thought, just as Jacob leaned in close to the

window and murmured, "*Hot damn.*" Linc squinted at him. Jacob shrugged. "What?"

No one could deny it. Kylie Hatfield was damn beautiful. And Jacob ogling her like that made Linc feel suddenly possessive. He'd just gotten done deciding he needed to concentrate on SAR and the things he could do right. He shouldn't have been glad to see her. Sitting on his porch. Waiting for him.

But he was. Hell yes, he was.

12

Kylie grinned as Jacob jumped out of the truck, running around the side of it. His arms were wide-open, ready for a hug, his mouth spread in a big, infectious grin. The detective was his normal giant teddy bear self, exuding warmth while giving her a hug that was a little too tight.

"If you ever get tired of the old ball and chain, I'll be waiting for you," he said in a fake whisper so loud she was sure the llamas could hear him.

She grinned back. Jacob was the typical ladies' man, a real player if ever she'd met one. And as charming as the day was long.

But Linc? He looked a little like death warmed over.

It scared Kylie, how dark his eyes were. His normally sun-kissed face was pale, his hair and clothes were wet, and his eyes were rimmed in purple. He looked like he was recovering from some horrible plague. He shivered a little as he slipped almost lifelessly out of the truck, pulling off his jacket to reveal an equally wet plaid flannel shirt, open to expose a thermal that was probably also soaked. Poor thing.

Jacob pointed over his shoulder at Linc. "Your ever-so-dreamy boyfriend is a real hero."

Kylie smiled. She wasn't sure he was her boyfriend, but she was still proud. Dying of the plague or not, he was still super-tasty. "Really? What happened?"

"Little girl with Down syndrome wandered away from home with her puppy. Found them both, like a boss."

They both looked at Linc, who freed his gear from the back of the truck and stared into the distance darkly, quietly, like he was thinking some really heavy thoughts.

Jacob waved at him dismissively. "Ah, you know him. Can't accept praise. All in a day's work for him, anyway. How's the injury, killer?" Jacob teased Kylie, pointing to her shoulder.

She shrugged off her jean jacket and moved aside the collar of her dress to show him her still healing scar. "Much better. I'm supposed to still be wearing the sling, but I hate it, so…" She shrugged and winced a little. "You okay?"

Jacob shrugged too. "Ah, same old thing. Haven't heard of any more serial killings we need to bring our top gun in for yet, or else I'd have been calling your number."

Kylie wrinkled her nose. "And I'd be running in the other direction, thanks very much!"

They both laughed. Of course, Jacob was kidding, but Linc stared at the ground, his face turning darker yet. What the hell had bitten his butt?

As if his dark mood had descended on the mountain top, the smiles fell from both Kylie and Jacob's faces. Jacob rubbed his jaw, eyeing Linc warily. "Ah, well. Better be going now. Take care, you two."

She waved at the detective as he pulled away, but Linc didn't say a word. He just let Storm into the yard, where Vader welcomed the Shepherd with a running tackle. Still not saying a word, Linc turned and went inside. He might have grunted something, but she wasn't sure as the screen closed behind him with a bang.

She turned toward her car. Maybe she should just leave. He clearly didn't want her here. But then she thought of his face, how haggard, haunted, he'd looked.

Taking a deep breath, she followed him into the little mudroom and leaned one hip on a cabinet. "Want to talk about it?"

He didn't answer. Hanging his jacket on a hook, he tore off his flannel, tossing it on the floor, then lifted off his thermal shirt, which was so soaked it fell to the floor with a resounding splat. He kicked off his shoes, his movements clipped, and went into the kitchen, opening up the fridge and ducking to peer inside.

Refusing to give up, Kylie followed him. "So, who are you pissed at? Me or Jacob?"

He gave her a sour look. "Why don't you throw your arms around him and press your tits up against him a little more? In fact, why don't you just screw him right in front of me?"

Her jaw dropped. She'd hugged Jacob, but no differently than she hugged all her friends. She was a touchy-feely hugger. Was Linc really angry about that? If so, they'd never get along.

"So, *me*, huh?"

"Oh, no. I'm plenty pissed off at him too, copping feels of your ass like that. Right while I was watching."

Kylie crossed her arms. Had Jacob grabbed her ass? No! It had been the most innocent of hugs. "Oh. So, you're jealous."

He grabbed a quart of milk from the fridge and turned his gorgeous back on her. His hair was wet, and water dripped from it, down the curved, defined muscles, over his sloped spine, to the rise of the perfect ass covered in wet jeans. "Hell yes. I'm jealous."

The admission startled a laugh out of her. She quickly clamped her lips shut. "Jacob would never—"

"Yeah, he would."

"No, he wouldn't."

He turned on her, milk still in his hand. "Trust me. He thinks you're hot as hell, and you're just his type. He wants you."

"But he's your best friend, so, he'd never—"

Linc took a long step in her direction. "Hell yes, he would, and not just because I know my best friend. I'm a man, and I know men. I know what other men are thinking when they're looking at you. And believe me, the things he wants to do to you, *I* haven't even done to you yet."

Damn, he was sexy when he was angry. She took a step closer to him. She wanted to change the direction of this conversation. Make him understand that he was the only one she wanted. "Really? Like what? Can you show me?"

His eyes drifted down her body, as various emotions flitted over his handsome face. It settled back into pissed. "I don't know. Are you just going to go and show them to Jacob when I get done with you?"

Was he serious?

Kylie stared at him. Surely not, but she couldn't fully tell.

What was she doing?

Why had she skipped her lunch hour so she could leave work early and drive up the winding mountain just to be spoken to in this way? Was she really so pathetic?

"Maybe it's time I leave." Her heart was pounding in her chest as she spoke the words.

He stared at her, his face rigid, chest heaving. He uncapped the milk and didn't take his eyes from hers as he tossed his head back and started to drink. He gulped half the container down, holding her gaze. When he finished, he wiped his mouth. "That might be for the best."

Sadness mixed with anger flooded her system as she turned for the door, hardly able to breathe.

It was over.

Really over.

Maybe it was for the best.

If so, why didn't it feel that way?

Before she reached for the handle, his hands were on her arms. In a blink, he turned her, pulling her to him. "Don't—"

Her shoulder protested the movements, protested being held so tightly, but she nuzzled her face in his chest anyway, ignoring the pain.

"I'm sorry, Kylie." His voice broke on her name. "Don't go."

The angry part of her wanted to pull away. The sad part of her wanted to never leave. And there was another part of her, that part of her was filled with…what? Hope? She wasn't sure.

"Why did you come here?"

The question had her pulling away. She needed to not be touching him. She needed space to think.

"I came because I missed you, Linc. And I was worried about you. I texted you, but you obviously don't have the decency to even let me know you're alive."

"Yeah. I know." He ran his hands through his wet hair, leaving them tangled there as he looked at anything but her.

No apology. No anything. First, he accused her of flirting with his best friend, and then he didn't have the decency to apologize for blowing her off?

What a dick. She had to leave here, and now.

But her damn legs were rooted to the spot. Might have been something about his bare chest, glistening in the orange glow of the lights, all wet and defined and muscular like that. His jeans hung dangerously low on his hips, baring the waistband of his boxer briefs, showing the top of the sexy V that led to his…

God, what was wrong with her? Doing her own Linc impersonation, she looked anywhere but at him.

"I'm with you, Linc. I don't know what we are, but I know one thing…I'm with *you*. Unless you think otherwise?" She couldn't stop herself, she looked at his face, and when he didn't meet her eyes she moved until he had no choice but to meet her gaze. "And if you think otherwise, tell me."

His hands reached for her even as he stepped away. "I don't know, Kylie. I just don't know anymore." His voice was full of grit, his eyes full of pain.

She inhaled deeply, blew the air out slowly. "Do you see how confusing this is for me? You're possessive one second, pushing me away the next. I don't understand. I—"

Like a whip, his hand closed on her arm. He pushed up her sleeve, bringing the bruises to light. His voice was rough, but his touch was soft. "*This* is what happens when I touch you."

Kylie didn't try to pull away. She didn't move. Full circle, they were back to this.

His nightmares.

His fears.

Her three seconds of psychology classes hadn't prepared her for this. She'd never known someone who carried so much pain and responsibility on his shoulders.

Moving with deliberate slowness, she peeled his fingers from her arm, but instead of pushing him away, she threaded her fingers with his.

"No, it isn't." She lifted her arm to show him the goose bumps that had appeared. "This is."

His gaze never left hers. His jaw clenched and worked, his body so tense it shuddered.

With one hand, Kylie slowly unbuttoned the top two

buttons of her dress. She guided his fingertips to her breast, which had hardened to a little bead. "This is."

He took in a labored breath, still holding her gaze.

"What happened last night isn't you, Linc." She ran her hand through his damp hair. "The man who saved that little girl today is you. The man who makes my heart pound in my chest is you. The good man. The decent man. Take me to bed and let me show you how much I trust being with you."

His gaze moved over her face before landing on her lips. She watched his thoughts play over his expression. She'd never witnessed a person war with themselves this much.

"I want you, but you can't stay."

She blinked, unsure exactly what he meant. Did she have to leave now? Was he sending her away forever?

She could change his mind. Trailing her fingers down his chest, she reached for the button of his damp jeans.

He grabbed her wrist. With the other hand, he gripped her face, forcing her head up until she was looking into his eyes. "If this is all you want from me, Kylie, I'll give it to you." He backed her up until she was against the wall, his sex pressing into hers. "Then you have to leave."

She wrapped a hand around his neck, pulled his head down until their lips almost touched, and said, "No."

He tried to pull away, but she held on tight, damning the injured shoulder that wouldn't allow her to hold on with both arms.

"Listen to me, Linc. I don't know what this is between us, but I do know what this isn't. I'm not your booty call. You don't have sex with me and then send me packing."

He pressed his forehead to hers, his breath warm on her face. When his hand trailed down to her skirt, pulling it up, she almost smiled, but she didn't. She had one more thing she needed to say.

"I'm not afraid of you." When his hand stopped its movement, she went on. "You're a good man, and we'll work this out…together."

She watched the emotion play over his face, watched passion war with his fear. She wished she were wise. She wished she knew the exact perfect words to say.

She didn't.

But she knew of other ways to express her longing for him. Her trust. Her need.

Pulling his head down, she kissed him, sinking all the emotion she didn't understand into the gesture, hoping he would understand.

He kissed her back, then grappled with his jeans while pushing her panties to the floor. The movements were fumbling, hectic, and she could feel his heart pounding under her fingers.

She inhaled sharply as he pushed inside.

Linc froze, and Kylie was about to ask him what was wrong when she heard it too. The dogs were going crazy in the yard. Over their cacophony of sound, she barely heard the sound of tires crunching on the gravel.

Linc pressed his forehead to Kylie's before he pulled away, then bent and picked up her panties, handing them to her.

His jeans still open, she watched him stalk to the window. Watched him freeze. Watched him unfreeze and begin zipping up in frantic movements.

"Who is it?" she asked.

As he stalked to the dryer to grab a fresh shirt from its depths, he growled out, "My mother."

Every cell inside Kylie's body froze. His mother? Holy shit!

As Linc pulled a shirt over his head, he looked purposefully down at the panties she still held. "You might want to do something with those."

She went from frozen to a flurry of movement in an instant. Panties on. Dress straight. Fingers brushing through her hair.

"You're buttoning your shirt wrong," she said to Linc when she glanced his way. She groaned. He also had lipstick all over his face. Which meant...

She ran to the metal toaster and looked at her reflection. Yes. Her damned smear proof lip gloss was smeared everywhere.

Kylie groaned as a car door slammed. She rushed to the sink, grabbing a hand full of paper towels. She wet a few and tossed them into Linc's direction. "Lipstick," was all she had time to say before she was scrubbing her face too.

Another glance at the toaster told her that the lip gloss was gone. In its place was pink skin that was in competition with the rest of her flushed face and...she was sweating.

Groaning, she wiped the paper towels under her arms. Oh, shit. Oh, shit. Oh, shit.

This was not how she'd envisioned meeting his mother. Or anyone.

"Kylie..."

She glanced over at Linc, and he had a "sorry" expression on his face.

"What?"

He pointed at the skirt of her dress. There was a stain. *That* kind of stain. The DNA kind that got Bill Clinton in big time trouble.

"Oh, holy hell," she breathed as she raced for the sink again, grabbing more paper towels as she dabbed furiously at herself.

Did she smell like sex?

She inhaled deeply. Yes. That was a definite yes.

Groaning hard, she opened the cabinet where she'd spotted a bottle of vanilla on her failed pancake attempt just that morning. Opening the bottle, she poured some in her hands, rubbing them together before patting them on her neck, her chest, her arms, and her legs.

Great. Now, she smelled like a cake. Better than cu—

The screen door slammed as Linc headed outside to greet his mother, giving her a few extra minutes to fret.

She heard a woman's ridiculously chipper voice talking a mile a minute. It was hard to believe Linc could be related to that.

Kylie heard him say, "Mom, why'd you come all the way up here?"

She couldn't make out the answer. Only the sound of heels clicking on the wooden steps as the voice continued to chirp excitedly.

Linc opened the door and a woman with carefully coiffed, burgundy-red hair stepped in, saying, "I didn't catch you at a bad..." She froze when her gaze landed on Kylie. "Oh." Her eyes traveled down to Kylie's feet and back up again.

Kylie struggled to keep her hands by her sides and the smile on her lips. "Hi." The sound made even her own ears cringe.

"My." Mrs. Coulter turned to her son. "So, this *is* a bad time?"

Oh, god. She knew about the sex. Kylie dropped her eyes to her cleavage. It was covered, but she suddenly felt buck naked.

Deciding that if she didn't introduce herself, it would only make her look guiltier, Kylie strode forward, striving for a confidence she didn't feel. "Mrs. Coulter. Hi, how are you? It's so nice to meet you. I'm Kylie. Linc is training my dog."

Kylie's eyes shifted over to him. He looked like he wished he could slip between the floorboards. She would happily slide in beside him.

Mrs. Coulter stared at Kylie, an astonished expression on her face. "Kylie?" She glared at her son reproachfully, who suddenly looked smaller, more bashful, his hands dug into the back pockets of his jeans. "I'm sorry. My son has told me nothing about you."

Forcing the smile to stay in place, Kylie said, "I can believe it. He doesn't talk much at all, does he? Mimes talk more."

A miracle happened. Mrs. Coulter laughed, turning to her son to cup his face in both of her hands. "Isn't that the truth?" Linc flinched the same way a little kid would from a mother trying to clean up a milk moustache. "My littlest has always been one of few words. Even more so now."

Kylie nearly laughed. Linc was many things, but "little" sure wasn't one of them.

Linc looked appalled, but still didn't say anything, just rocked back and forth on his bare feet like a little boy. The little boy look kind of made him even sexier, like he needed any help with that.

Linc's mother was nothing like Kylie'd expected. She was wearing a bright yellow suit and matching pumps and seemed more like a senator's wife. Her bright gold jewelry was tasteful, and her purse was designer, clearly expensive. She exuded wealth and sophistication. Next to her, Kylie felt underdressed and dowdy.

Or maybe it was just the fact that, not five minutes ago, her "littlest" had been about to do some pretty raunchy things to Kylie's body.

Mrs. Coulter's gaze flitted around Linc's house, and Kylie's heart skipped a beat as she scanned the wall where they'd just been...intimate. If her butt print had been shining from the beige paint, Kylie would have run for the hills.

"I just stopped by to invite Linc to dinner tomorrow

evening, but as long as you're here, I might as well invite you too."

"Thank you," Kylie said as Linc cleared his throat. He looked about as excited for the invitation as one would be for an invitation to clean toilets. Knowing she was about to say the exact wrong thing, but unable to stop herself, she added, "Linc told me he'd bring me to meet you someday soon. I've been looking forward to it. I'll put it on my calendar right now."

His mom's smile widened. "Oh, Linky Dink, you shouldn't have kept this one a secret."

Kylie giggled before she could stop herself. Linky Dink?

In return, Linc gave Kylie the look of death. In the light of the kitchen, she could see a vein bulging on his temple and forced her lips back into a straight line.

His mom shrugged. "But he always does," she went on. "He had a few girlfriends in college, but since then? No one serious. We were beginning to wonder if—"

Linc held up his hand and cleared his throat...loudly. "And I always tell you not to." Kylie nearly groaned as he reached down and picked up the wet shirts still scattered on the floor. "Mom, I hope you didn't come out just for—"

"Well. I was hoping we could visit a little?" she said, coming up close to him and swiping a too long shard of wet brown hair off his forehead. He wiped it back down and stepped away.

Each pore on his face practically groaned. "All right."

For a moment, Kylie felt very sorry for his mother. The grump needed to try a little harder. On the other hand, it was kind of nice to know that he didn't just act that way with Kylie. This seemed to be his normal personality with most people.

So why did she like him so much again?

His beautiful eyes turned to her, and Kylie melted a little

under his gaze. Oh yeah. That was it. Dickwad personality or not, this man did something to her that no man ever had.

But more than the physical, the pain hiding beneath the gruff personality drew her to him in a way she couldn't explain.

She wanted to be the balm that healed him. If a man like him could be healed.

And she had to believe that he could be.

When the silence stretched, Kylie was the one to break it. Smiling at Linc, she made her feet move toward her purse, made her hands pull the strap onto her shoulder, made herself head over toward the door.

"I'll just be going," she said, looking between mother and son. She met Linc's gaze again. "See you tomorrow? You can text me, let me know what time you'll be picking me up?"

Linc blinked, like he was snapping out of some trance. He resembled a big ball of dread. "Sure. I'll text you."

Kylie faced Mrs. Coulter, giving the woman her most charming smile. "Thank you so much for the invitation. I look forward to it."

"I'm glad you're coming." She stepped closer to her son, linking her arm around his. The movement screamed possessive. "See you then."

"Bye, Kylie."

That was it. Cold and clinical. Not even a smile to warm the dismissal.

The door clacked closed behind her.

In the fenced in yard, Vader was jumping and barking, deliriously happy at her appearance. She buried her face in his soft fur, refusing to cry.

As she loaded the big dog in her car, accepting the smelly dog kisses, she was glad someone was happy to see her.

13

Kylie didn't understand.

As much as Linc wanted her with him, it wasn't going to work.

Not now. Not until he could get this—whatever this was going on in his head—sorted out. A few days ago, he thought they might have a chance. Clearly, his subconscious disagreed.

And he sure as hell didn't want her to meet his family. His ridiculous, stick-up-their-butts family, with whom he had absolutely nothing in common. She'd already gotten a small taste of it when she met his mother.

Linky Dink? Really? His mother just had to go there?

But that was just the beginning of his humiliation, he knew.

Dammit. Why had he ever mentioned his family to Kylie in the first place?

But he already knew the answer. He'd mentioned the Coulter clan before he'd damn near punched her in the face following his nightmare. He'd mentioned them when he felt hope for them as a couple…for himself, for that matter.

His raised fist had changed all of that.

Then why the hell was he sitting outside her apartment building, sweat dripping down his temples as anxiety twisted his guts. Why didn't he just tell her that it was over? Why?

He knew the answer to that too.

As exasperating as Kylie was, she made him feel alive. She made him laugh. She made him hope. Which was a problem.

Dammit. His mind was going in circles, like one of the lost kids he tried to find.

He was already fifteen minutes late and had been avoiding Kylie's texts all day. She'd sent him pictures of a couple outfits she was unsure about, and when he went to text her back, his fingers seemed frozen.

He didn't know what was wrong with him. He didn't understand how his mind was working…or not working…whatever.

Part of him wanted her to hate him. It would've been easier that way. He didn't want to hurt her, but he seemed unable to stop himself from doing just that.

Taking a deep breath, he reached for the door handle of his truck, then jumped like a sissy when the passenger door swung open and Kylie jumped into the seat.

She gave him a cynical look, but it didn't hold any heat. "You sure do know how to make a girl feel adored and special." She reached for his phone sitting in the middle console and tapped the power button. The screen came to life. "Oh look, your phone works." She tossed it back down. "Imagine that."

The comment made him laugh, and with that little sound, some of the tension drained from his shoulders.

She was wearing one of her professional skirts, high heels, and a long sweater-looking coat, the deep purple doing something amazing to her skin. She looked damn good, and once again, Linc was struck with that familiar dichotomy of both wanting her and wanting to push her away.

"Hi." As if he was being pulled by a magnet, he leaned over and kissed her.

She blushed and whispered against his mouth, "Hi."

He brushed a lose strand of hair from her cheek. "Sure you want to subject yourself to this?"

She worried her lower lip between her teeth, and he wanted to lean in and bite it. "You make it sound like we're heading to a torture chamber."

He snorted. "Close enough."

She snorted right back. "Maybe if you weren't so cynical, you'd enjoy it."

He just stared at her. She was unbelievable. She was the one who'd said that she didn't want a relationship. After what had happened the other night, he'd come to agree with her. And yet she wanted cutesy texts? To meet his parents?

He wasn't the only one to run hot and cold, he realized.

"Don't do this, Kylie," Linc muttered, putting the truck in gear. "I'm a little wound up right now. I don't have the energy. I have enough in my head as it is."

She was quiet for a moment. "Bad day?"

Linc thought about the question. As far as he was concerned, it'd been a good day. He'd slept well, nightmare-free, and woken up late. No SAR calls had come in. He'd had one training class that went well. He should've been relaxed.

"No," he admitted. "Not bad, just dreading this."

"Will you tell me why?"

His family simply drained his energy, and right now, he didn't have the willpower to explain. "Not important. Let's… just make this quick so we can leave." Then something came to him. "Where's Vader?"

Kylie groaned. "I'm paying my dopehead neighbor to

doggy sit. Vader will probably be high as a kite when I get home."

Linc snorted. "We might need to pick him up a snack on the way back to your place. He'll have the munchies."

Kylie giggled, and the joy-filled sound did something to release some of the tension that had been building inside him all day. Miracle upon miracle, she stayed quiet after that, seemingly content to watch the scenery pass by as they made the journey in silence.

When he made the last turn, Kylie exclaimed, "Oh, Biltmore Forest! The woman whose case I'm working on lives here."

Linc glanced over at her, and it occurred to him that he'd been so wrapped up in his own shit that he hadn't asked her about her day. Her life. Her feelings.

Shit.

The last they'd talked about her job, she was in the midst of typing all those shitty reports. "A case?"

She nodded. "Remember the woman who called while we were in the barn?" She bobbed her eyebrows at him, making him smile.

"Yeah, I remember."

"Well, at first, Greg told me I couldn't take the case, but when she called back again, he agreed that I, Kylie Hatfield, should take the lead."

Linc gave her a skeptical glance.

Kylie huffed, but she was still smiling. "Seriously this time. It's nothing too crazy, just embezzlement, but I went to the elderly woman's home and we went through the reasons she believed someone was stealing from her. She has a case and I agreed to take it on. So..." she held her hands to her chest, practically beaming, "I officially have my first client, with Greg's blessing. I'm excited."

As she spoke, Linc felt like the biggest asshole on earth.

Whether or not he and Kylie could ever be together as a couple, they were friends. And friends didn't treat friends the way he'd been treating her.

"Wow. Kylie, that's great. Sounds like your boss is really starting to appreciate you." He reached over and stroked the back of her neck gently. "Look at you. You've been right all along. Investigation is your calling."

She smiled, looking deeply pleased at the compliment. "Yeah. I have a long list of names to investigate, so I'm going to be pretty busy. But I'm dying to get started and—"

Linc held up a hand. "Don't say 'dying.'"

Kylie laughed, which made him laugh, even though he'd been very serious. Maybe the reason he was having nightmares was because Kylie with her rumbustious nature was giving him PTSD on top of his PTSD.

Not that he had PTSD, he corrected himself. He didn't. Absolutely not.

The smile slid from his face. He didn't like to think that he was screwed up in the head. What soldier did, he supposed.

He didn't have time to think about it more because Kylie was chattering on about art and thieves and little orange dogs, and before he knew it, he was pulling into his parents' driveway.

Kylie grew quiet as he stopped behind Erik's BMW. Or maybe it was Craig's? The two should have been twins. Killing the engine, he didn't move to open the door.

Kylie's hand came to rest on his arm. "It will be okay," she said softly.

He exhaled a breath that had grown stagnate in his lungs, then turned in his seat so he could look at her full-on. She deserved his full attention for this. "I'm glad you're here."

The very tip of her nose turned pink, and her eyes grew glassy with tears she blinked away. She squeezed his arm.

"I'm glad I'm here too." Clearing her throat, she looked away first, scanning the huge expanse of green lawn and colorful gardens. "You grew up here? This place looks like the castle at Disney World."

Linc gritted his teeth as he looked up at the Spanish-style mansion. Every window in the place was ablaze with light. "You think it's ostentatious now, wait until you see the inside."

He got out, walked around to the other side, and attempted to open her door, although she was already hopping down herself. She smoothed out her skirt, looking worried. "I feel underdressed. I might even feel underdressed in a ball gown. I should've asked the mice to help dress me since you were no help."

Linc leaned over, inhaling her sweet scent as he planted a kiss on the shell of her ear. "You look incredible," he told her, fixing his hand on the small of her back. She was wearing these high heels that buckled around her ankles, and her hair fell around her shoulders in lose waves. "In fact," he pushed her against the truck, "how about we spend a minute or two relaxing each other before we face the clan."

She laughed. "Not after yesterday!" She rested her forehead against his chest. "I'm so sure your mother knew *exactly* what we'd been up to. That was mortifying."

"Nah," he lied. "She didn't have a clue."

Kylie raised her head, gnawing her lower lip. She was damned adorable. He was suddenly very glad to have her by his side.

"Did she stay long?"

Linc shook his head. "She left just a few minutes after you left."

Kylie ran a hand down the front of his shirt. "In that case, I wish I'd stayed."

Looking at her now, it was hard to believe he'd found the resolve to ever let her go.

Instead of answering her, he took her hand and led her up the long sidewalk. Not hesitating, he rang the doorbell. *Might as well get this over with.*

Mason, his parents' long-time butler, answered with a nod. "Master Lincoln."

Kylie giggled so low under her breath that he didn't think anyone could have heard it but him. He inclined his head. "Mason, good to see you again."

The door went wide. "And you as well, sir."

Stepping inside, Linc watched Kylie take everything in. Her eyes were huge as they swung up to meet his. Linc could tell exactly what was going through her mind: *You grew up here, in this museum?*

Smiling slightly, he led her into the living room, where the members of his family were gathered around like a mosaic, watching Erik's twelve-year-old daughter, Ellory, play some extremely complex-sounding Chopin piece on the piano.

The music stopped as his mother exclaimed, "Lincoln!"

All heads swung in their direction. Linc's oldest brother, who was closest to the door, swung the rest of his body around, hand extended. "Well, if it isn't our baby brother," Craig said, his eyes flashing over to Kylie. "We were wondering if you were ever going to show up at one of these, or if you'd forgotten us completely."

Linc forced himself to ignore the jab. "Good to see you too."

He was about to introduce Kylie when Ellory shouted his name. "Linc!" The girl scooted out from the piano and ran to hug him. He was tackled from behind by Erik's youngest, six-year-old Jackson.

"Hey, guys," Linc said, grinning as he grabbed them up in

big hugs. This was the way family dinners usually went. Linc would go off and play with the kids while the "adults" conversed about adult things. He looked over to the couch where Craig's two kids sat, teenagers Bailey and Martin, noses buried in their smartphones. They both half-waved. "What's up, Uncle Linc?" Martin said. Even *they* were too adult for him.

But Linc guessed he couldn't leave Kylie alone with the vultures so he could play with the kids this time.

He waved to Addison and Melanie, his brothers' blonde trophy wives, who seemed to forever be in a competition to see who could be thinner. Now, they were practically invisible. His brothers, too, were in a constant competition to one-up each other, professionally, personally, materialistically… in just about every facet of their lives. Kylie shook hands all around and didn't seem to mind too much that they were all staring at her like a space invader.

Then his father came up, swirling his tumbler of scotch, patting Linc on the arm. "Good to see you, son." He turned his attention to Kylie. "Nice to meet you too, young lady. Can I get you something to drink? Wine? Scotch?" Linc's father was always the bartender at things like these.

"Wine, thank you," Kylie said, smiling at Linc's mother. "Your home is gorgeous, Mrs. Coulter."

"Why, thank you, my dear," she said as Linc deposited little Jackson on the sofa, headfirst.

Kylie sat down stiffly on a different sofa, staring at the formal tray of fancy hors d' oeuvres that his mother always had the kitchen staff set out during their family meals, though no one ever ate them. Kylie's back was so straight, Linc wondered if she'd maybe sat on a pole by accident. If Kylie was looking for some down-home family fun, she was mistaken. His family never let their hair down. Never.

He looked down at Jackson, who was playing with his

mother's Limoges like they were action figures. At least they had the boy to lighten the mood.

Linc's mother pointed at Kylie's arm, a look of concern on her face. "Are you injured, dear?" Linc was immediately concerned too because Kylie was holding her injured arm close to her chest. Had he hurt her and not realized it?

Kylie dropped the arm, and Linc could tell from her expression that she hadn't realized she'd been holding it so closely to her body. A self-soothing motion, he realized. He could understand why.

"No. I mean yes. I…injured my shoulder at work." She glanced up at him, clearly worried that she'd say the wrong thing.

Linc accepted the scotch his father poured him. "She got shot by a serial killer a couple weeks ago. Kylie's a private investigator."

It had the desired effect. His brothers all turned to look at his little badass of a companion, the wives gasped, and his mother started to fan herself, her eyebrows shooting straight up to the sky.

Ellory's face lit up. "A gunshot wound? Cool! Can I see?"

Linc's father tapped a finger on his chin. "Wait. Are you that woman who's been in the news? With the Spotlight Killer?"

Kylie nodded, a blush climbing over her cheeks.

His father's face turned impressed. "Well, I'll be damned. If I remember correctly, that psychopath kidnapped you, then shot you in cold blood."

His mother looked horrified. "A serial killer? I can't even read about such things, they upset me so much."

"*You* weren't involved in that, were you, Lincoln?" his father said to him.

"I should hope not!" his mother said, fanning herself harder.

Linc could sense Kylie staring at him. She probably wondered if he ever communicated with his family at all. The answer: No. Not really.

Linc lifted a shoulder. "A bit."

"Well. So, your girlfriend's a hero!" his dad said, raising his glass. "Way to go. We have a celebrity with us. I'll drink to that."

Kylie took a demure sip of her wine. "Thank you, but I really didn't do very much. It was—"

"Nonsense. I read the paper. Don't be modest. That killer was brutal. The news said you were responsible for bringing her down, and without you, she'd still be at large." His dad sounded more enthusiastic about Kylie's accomplishment than he ever had about Linc's. "You probably know that Linc just plays with dogs all day, huh? And you still want to date him?"

Kylie's face turned troubled, and her gaze shot to Linc. Probably wondering why he didn't set the record straight. But he'd heard this shit for years. There was no setting the record straight where his father was concerned. "No, I—"

"Yeah." Erik, sitting on an ottoman in his buttoned-up three-piece suit, downed the rest of his drink. From the hazy look on his face, Linc could tell he was already half drunk. He put on his most charming air as he addressed Kylie. "Sweet, pretty, and brave…what the hell are you doing with *that*?"

He hooked a thumb at Linc.

Craig guffawed behind him, ogling Kylie like a steak he wanted to take a bite of. "Yeah, really. Baby brother, you lucked out. Your girl's a little firecracker."

He'd meant what he'd said the previous day. Most men couldn't seem to get enough of Kylie. She was all curves, long dark hair, sexy eyes…she walked into the room and made every other woman in the place invisible. Linc's brothers, though happily married, were no exception. They were fucking her with their eyes, right in front of their wives and kids.

Kylie opened her mouth, but before she said anything, the butler rang that dinner was ready. Like good little puppets, all the Coulters stood in unison and paired off to walked to the formal dining room.

Kylie just stood there, looking a little lost and something else. Pissed? He couldn't blame her.

After giving her a formal bow to lighten the mood, Linc offered her his arm. She took it and they trailed behind his family. As they walked, Kylie's head swiveled, looking from one wall to the next. "I still can't believe you grew up here. Never in a million years would I imagine you coming from a place like this."

He felt the same. Even growing up, he'd never felt at home here. Too ornate. Too gold. Too…everything his grandparents' farmhouse wasn't. "Well, I had fun sliding down the banister, at least."

Kylie's eyes followed the railing all the way up to the third floor. "You're lucky you didn't kill yourself."

He laughed. He'd had a few close calls indeed.

She hugged his arm tighter against her. "I'm trying to picture little Linc playing ball or Legos in this place, and I have to admit…I'm failing."

She suddenly looked sad.

"Hey," he said, cupping her chin, looking into her beautiful eyes, which seemed clouded, not as bright as usual. "We can leave. If you want, I can tell them—"

"No." She smiled, but he could tell it was forced. "It's fine. It's…different, yes. But it's nice that you have a big family, and that you all get together for dinners. It's sweet. I wish I had a family like this, but it's always just been Mom and me."

And just like that, Linc felt like an asshole again.

Thinking back, he remembered that he hadn't been the only one risking his life on the bannister. Or climbing the big trees in the backyard. Or having rock fights in the expansive gardens. Those days with his brothers, he missed.

"They aren't very nice to you," Kylie said, stopping to study an enormous family portrait, commissioned when Linc had been about two. It was surrounded by a gaudy frame of gold and black. Everyone in the painting looked miserable.

Linc shrugged. "They call it brotherly ribbing."

Kylie narrowed her eyes. "More like brotherly bullying."

He couldn't disagree but agreeing made him seem like a victim. He didn't like that either.

"Well…" Kylie said, drawing the word out, "I don't like it. They are too refined to be so mean."

Linc laughed and pulled her closer to him. "I can handle it."

She scowled, but her voice was as soft and light as a feather as she pulled his head down so she could whisper in his ear. "If you want me to throat-punch them for you, let me know."

Then she turned and walked slowly toward the dining room, hips swaying, giving him a view of her perfect ass.

Linc grinned and followed after her, like a puppet on a string.

14

Looking at Linc, unassuming, down-to-earth, no-nonsense Linc, who wore rumpled t-shirts and worn hiking boots, who lived for the outdoors, who liked to play with dogs and didn't give a shit about what his hair looked like…Kylie never would have thought he'd grown up in that house. A mansion, with crystal chandeliers and gilded walls and so much pretention it should have been on an episode of *Lifestyles of the Rich and Famous.*

No wonder he didn't get along with his family.

When Kylie'd walked in there, she'd thought they stumbled into the wrong house. No, the wrong dimension. Aside from his father's eyes and strong chin, it was clear that Lincoln Coulter shared nothing with his family at all. Definitely the black sheep.

A very sexy black sheep.

Dressed up more than she'd ever seen him, he wore a button-down plaid shirt and khaki pants with a brown pair of Wolverine boots that made her realize the man did have a bit of good taste.

Still, he was nowhere near as dressed as his brothers and

father, who in their dark suits, could be guests at a fancy wedding. Their wives looked like elegant models. Even the kids were dressed well. The little boy was actually wearing a bow tie.

She felt like she'd walked onto a magazine cover shoot. Kylie's mother liked to put on airs, but she wasn't anywhere near as classy as these people.

And as dinner began, it became pretty clear to Kylie why Linc didn't like to speak. His father and brothers commanded the conversation, talking about their cases that they had going on like it was the only thing worth conversing about. They blustered on, as the women sat there, quietly discussing domestic matters, like housewares and the children's private-school education.

Across from Kylie, on the "men's side" of the giant dining table, Linc didn't add a single comment. Apparently resigned to their current circumstances, he simply nodded when the situation warranted and focused on the food on his plate.

He was lucky. Kylie was forced to pretend to be fascinated as his mother and the two wives chatted in low voices about the weather in Fiji, the construction of a new mansion down the street, and whether the house should be done up in gold or white lights for Christmas.

Dinner was the carcass of a little bird sitting primly on Kylie's plate among a few peas and carrots and some white mush she couldn't place. Bleh. How did one eat such a thing? She'd been tempted to pick it up with her fingers and chomp down like she would a buffalo wing, wondering how many of the wives she could make faint if she sucked on the bone.

But she was determined to be on her best behavior, taking tiny little slices from the tiny little bird and delicately placing each sliver in her mouth before chewing, making sure her jaw didn't move too much.

She was bored to tears.

Tuning out the boring talk, she studied the paintings on the wall across from her, not saying a word. Which wasn't like her. She usually was able to insert herself into any crowd. But she was out of place, except the tiny little fluttering in her chest every time she caught Linc's gaze on her.

"Those are lovely paintings, Mrs. Coulter," Kylie said when there was a break in the conversation. The art had actually made her think of sweet Emma Jennings just down the road. "Are you the collector, or is Mr. Coulter?"

They all stared at her for one uncomfortable beat. Maybe they *had* forgotten she was there.

Mrs. Coulter smiled at the paintings. "I suppose we both are. My husband's always bringing home little trinkets he thinks I'll like. That one, over there, is new." She pointed to a scene of trees, the bright gold, red, and oranges reflecting on the still waters of a glassy brook. Next to the water was a googly eyed boy and his dog.

It had a very familiar style to it, but after looking at all the art that Emma had shown her, all the paintings she saw seemed to bleed together into one runny palette. That was what she'd been doing all day, helping Emma go through the inventory, trying to see what else might be missing. They'd only gotten through a fraction of what was there.

"It's very, um, pretty."

"Kylie, dear," one of the wives, she wasn't sure which one, said to her. The two of them, Addison and Melanie, were so skinny, Kylie was sure they shopped in the Barbie department of whatever uber-expensive store they went to. They wore painfully large diamond wedding rings too, and Kylie figured that was where most of their weight came from. It sure didn't come from food. Neither woman had eaten more than a spoonful from their entire plate. "Have you and Lincoln been dating long?"

Kylie looked over at him. For once, his eyes weren't on

her. He was busy listening to something his pretentious brother was saying. Kylie lowered her voice. "Not long. And...we're just friends. He's training my dog, actually."

The women's eyes widened. The other said, "Well, it has to be more than business if he brought you here."

They all nodded in agreement, then, in unison, eyed Kylie expectantly.

She wasn't sure how to respond. She sat there, twisting her napkin on her lap while trying to choose her words.

As she opened her mouth, Mr. Coulter's booming voice drew her attention. "Son, I understand the concept of busy very well. Down here, in the real world, busy must be much different than it is up in the mountain, with your head in the clouds."

Kylie swung her head to him. Before she'd really thought it through, her mouth was open, and words were flying out. "I'm sorry, sir. But Linc does a lot. He trains those dogs, which is no easy feat."

His father laughed. "Our son, the Dog Man. It's hard to believe he wasn't raised by wolves."

Kylie's heart pounded in her chest, and her cheeks grew warm as her temper raised by rapid degrees. "Linc runs one of the most successful search and rescue operations in the state. Just yesterday, he saved a little girl with Down syndrome who got lost." She leaned forward, glaring at the man. "Your son is a hero. I'd like to know the last time you saved someone's life at your law firm. Don't you just suck blood for a living?"

Aside from a few sharp gasps from the ladies, the room went deadly silent.

Had she just called the men of Linc's family bloodsuckers?

Oh, yes. She had.

Linc shot her a look which was the equivalent of swiping

a hand across his throat. *Shut up,* the look said. But there was something else behind it...gratitude?

Mrs. Coulter spoke suddenly from the head of the table. "It's true. I've always thought of Lincoln as a hero." She pushed her slight body away from the fine china at her place setting and disappeared from the room. A moment later, she was back, handing a leather scrapbook to Kylie. "Every time I see an article about Lincoln, I always clip it out and put it in here."

Kylie turned the pages, her mind whirling as she read bits of news articles. There were so many of them, hundreds of people he'd saved.

When Kylie noticed how interested the wives had become, she turned the book so they could see it too, pride filling her heart. They gazed at the articles as if they'd never seen them before, with obvious interest. What? Had no one ever brought up Linc's occupation to them? Of course, his mother knew. His father had to have known. Then why was he being such an ass?

Kylie glanced at the elder Coulter, who was staring at her intently. Even if he was an ass, this was his house. And she'd just met him. Calling him out on his assholeness probably wasn't the best of manners.

Kylie cleared her throat and addressed Mr. Coulter. "I'm sure you do very important work as well. But you shouldn't discount what Linc does just because it's not what you want him to do."

He stroked his chin thoughtfully. "Kylie, sweetheart, with all due respect," he said, his voice dripping condescension, "I appreciate you defending my son like a good girlfriend should, but you don't know a thing about what we do. Or about our family."

Both brothers raised their fists to their mouths, covering

what she was sure were supposed to be discreet chuckles. She wanted to punch them all.

They'd not only struck a nerve, they'd busted it wide open. She didn't let injustices like that go. Couldn't. She clenched her fists, ready to unleash upon them.

"All right, time's up," Linc said, jumping to his feet like a bomb had gone off in his pants. "Mom, thanks for a great time. Everyone else, nice to see you. We've got to go."

Kylie stared at him, her rage quickly giving way to confusion. Linc held out his hand, and Kylie popped to her feet as well. Mrs. Coulter began to protest, asking them not to miss the, "Divine baked Alaska."

"Probably just a thimble full," Kylie muttered as she linked her fingers through Linc's.

"What?" he asked, leading her toward the door where the butler was already waiting with their coats.

She thrust her arms in her duster, thanking the butler for his assistance. Linc just tossed his jacket over his arm and headed into the cool night air, inhaling deeply.

Neither of them spoke as he helped her into his truck. Kylie sighed, suddenly feeling exhausted.

It didn't take a genius to figure out. He was angry at her. Again. Hmm. This was starting to form a pattern.

And it all started the night he had that nightmare.

15

Just another fun-filled, awesome family dinner.

Linc drove Kylie back to her apartment, his hands tight on the wheel, his senses spiraling as he silently cursed his father.

His asshole of a father, and those two goons he called brothers.

There had been kids at the table, but the thoughts Linc was thinking and the things he wanted to say to those idiots were completely R-rated. He'd had to get out of there before his fists went flying, and he really gave them something to talk about.

Or before Kylie did.

Which, from the fire in her eyes, had been looking like the more likely option. He'd known it would happen. Known she'd see through their bullshit and call them out on it, jumping to his defense like a true warrior. Her sense of right and wrong and her desire to correct all the injustices in the world didn't just extend to serial killers and thieves. It was like she simply couldn't just stand by and let the bad guys win.

Maybe that was why letting her go was easier said than done. She was the only person Linc had in this world who was willing to stand by him and fight.

Linc was halfway to her apartment, seething about his father, when he realized she hadn't said a word.

"I'm sorry," she suddenly said, the words barely over a whisper. "I shouldn't have said what I did."

He looked over at her. "What? Oh, hell. It's not you." He should've known she would interpret his silence as being angry at her. He put a hand on her knee. "It's fine. I'm just angry at them, for being their normal selves. *I'm* sorry you had to deal with that."

He felt her gaze bore into the side of his face. "You're not mad at me?"

He squeezed her knee. "Not at all. My father is an asshole while my brothers were practically fucking you with their eyes. Their wives are like plastic bitches, and my mother works so damned hard to make everyone happy. It's like a fucking torture chamber."

Her gaze was still on him. He could feel it. "It wasn't that bad. Wait…your brothers were *what*?"

Linc shook his head. "Forget it. I appreciate you going to bat for me, but it's not worth it. They've been doing this shit for years and nothing's going to change their minds about me. I'm not a hero, either. Just a guy." He cleared his throat. "The disappointment."

Her hand covered his, and when he glanced over at her, she looked pale in the dashboard lights. "They're wrong. You aren't a disappointment. They're just pissed that you didn't fall into step like a good Stepford son and fellow bloodsucker."

Linc let out a bitter laugh. "I actually liked that part."

Her thumb stroked along his fingers. "Well. I may have meant it, but I still shouldn't have said it. I don't know when to keep my mouth shut. It's my worst quality." She lifted his hand to her lips, pressed a kiss to the back of it. "And I'm telling it like it is right now. You *are* a hero, Linc Coulter. You're amazing. You have to believe that."

Right. He was so amazing, she was wearing his bruises on her arm. Yeah, he was a regular stand-up guy. A hero?

Hey, hero!

The little boys scrabbled for the old, half-deflated soccer ball. The little one with the shaggy hair and the baseball cap jogged up to him. "Hey, hero," he called. "Look! My sister!" Linc followed his outstretched finger to a woman standing in the center of the marketplace. She was wearing a military vest over her traditional garments. Her eyes were bulging with fear, her body trembling. She was holding something in her hand...

He blinked as a car laid on the horn behind him and realized he was going only thirty-five in a fifty. He picked up speed, ignoring Kylie's curious look.

The woman in the marketplace...who was she? She'd been in his nightmare the other night, and it seemed like he should have known who she was, but he couldn't remember.

"Are you okay?" Kylie asked.

Okay?

His pulse was throbbing in his neck. Cool sweat bathed his forehead. Linc shook away the fear, but it clung to him like it had tentacles.

The woman in a vest. The fear in her eyes.

He tried to remember her even while he didn't want to remember.

"Yeah," he choked out and cleared his throat. "I'm good."

Her voice was soothing, but Linc needed more than a soothing voice right then. A hell of a lot more. Sex. No. She'd work him up, and he'd end up nearly punching her again. Maybe a lobotomy.

"Want me to come over to your place? We can watch movies or something?"

He looked over at her and managed a smile, pushing away the memories assaulting him. "What kind of movies do you watch?"

"Oh, you know. The ones that are generally hell to men and have them counting the moments until they're over. Rom-Coms. Dramas. Family sagas where someone dies of cancer at the end."

He raised his eyebrow. "Wow. That sounds…awful."

"Actually," she laughed, "I like thrillers. Raunchy comedy too. Um, actually, I like all movies. What about you?"

Linc scratched at his chin. "Can't say I watch them much."

"You…don't? So, you don't have any movies at your house?"

"Have you ever seen a television at my house?"

Her jaw dropped. "Come to think of it…oh my *god*. How do you survive?"

He shrugged. They pulled off at the exit for her place.

"You could come to watch movies with me. I have hundreds. Have you ever seen *The Shawshank Redemption*?"

"No."

"What?" She made a few sputtering sounds. "Okay. We must correct that egregious error right away, Lincoln Coulter." Her voice was teasing.

He shook his head. The second he paused from conversation with her, he thought of the dark, fear-filled eyes of the woman across the dusty road. "You know. That sounds good, but…" he couldn't think of an excuse, "raincheck, okay?"

He could practically feel her deflate. "All right."

Linc walked her up to her apartment building, and she asked him to come in, just to make sure that everything was okay. She'd definitely gotten spooked since her run-in with the Spotlight Killer.

On the way up the stairs, she knocked on a neighbor's door, and Vader began to bark incessantly. The door opened and Newfoundland bounded out, followed closely by a cloud of marijuana smoke.

Kylie coughed, waving a hand in front of her face as she thanked the long-haired dude smiling from the doorway. "No problemo, man," he said after Kylie handed him a twenty.

Before Linc could complain about the quality of dog-sitters Kylie hired, Vader burst up the steps and was jumping at Kylie's door by the time they reached the top step. Linc stroked his ears and gave the command to calm him down. It only sort of worked. The dog was too excited.

"Hey, boy," Linc said, crouching down to hold his big head in his hands while Kylie fished out her keys. "You been holding down the fort?"

Vader was his normal crazy, so that was good. He calmed down and followed Linc through the little studio apartment as he made sure nothing was amiss. After she unbuckled and slipped off her shoes, Kylie trailed after him.

Linc checked the closet and bathroom, then all the locks on the windows. "All looks good."

"Except one thing," she said, her bottom lip poked out in an exaggerated pout.

"What's that?" He looked away. He knew what she was going to say. Before she could open her mouth, he held out a hand. "Come here."

He motioned to her. She wiggled against him and he engulfed her in his arms, feeling a sense of calmness that overtook him only when she was near. If only he could let that carry over into his subconscious, and he didn't have to worry about hurting her. Linc cupped her smooth cheeks, bringing her mouth to his. He kissed the seam of her lips lightly.

"I need to go" he said, dipping his head to her neck and inhaling her scent, letting it seep into his senses. Not too much. He couldn't risk losing control. "I'll see you soon. Promise."

A tiny crease appeared between her eyes. "If this has to do with—"

He kissed her lightly again, closing off the words he didn't want to hear. "Have a good night."

Linc forced himself to leave without looking back. He got into his truck and drove back up the mountain, all the time jamming the heels of his hands against the steering wheel. He allowed himself to be angry about the shit he was going through with Kylie, the way his family had been…because when he focused on that, he didn't see the fear-filled eyes of that woman in the marketplace.

Linc went home and got himself a beer, then sat on the steps heading down to the yard, watching the dogs play. Try as he might, his mind kept going back to the woman in the market, a tug-of-war ensuing in his head.

Who was she?

What happened next?

But something told him he'd blocked everything out for a reason.

Before he knew it, he'd drained the entire beer.

He went inside the house for another, but instead found himself picking up his phone. His good buddy, Austin Burke, had been there that day. Maybe he could fill him in on what happened. It'd been awhile since they'd talked, but the bond they'd made in war meant that time was insignificant. He was due a call.

Linc went into his old address book and found his number, then punched it in on the landline. It rang twice before someone answered. "Hello?" The female voice sounded sleepy.

Shit. What time was it? He checked the clock on the microwave. It was after ten. That was probably too late. "Hi. I'm sorry if I'm calling too late. Can I speak to Austin?"

There was a long pause. "Who is this?"

"It's Linc Coulter. Uh, Colt. Is this Lissa Burke, Austin's wife?"

Her voice cracked. "Ye-es. Colt?"

"Yeah. I served with your husband over in Syria. It's been awhile and I wanted to check in on him. I realize it's late but—"

He stopped when he heard what sounded like a sob.

"Lissa?" he asked, the back of his neck prickling.

He heard it again. She was sobbing.

"Of course I know you, Colt. But don't you remember?" There was worry in her voice now.

His mouth went dry. "Remember what?"

She was crying again, and something told him to hang up the phone before she said something that very well might destroy his world. He was too late. "Austin was killed in a suicide bombing in Syria, a week before he was due to come home. They all were."

They all were.

It all came rushing back.

They all were. Except him.

The phone nearly slipped from his numb fingers. How had he forgotten? The woman. The blood. The death.

"I'm...sorry," Linc stammered. It took him three tries to hang up the phone. After that, he stumbled to the fridge, got himself another beer, and went outside, trying to get his brain to tell him what it needed to remember. But he couldn't think of anything. It was just a big black hole.

Rage surging through his veins, Linc wound up and hurled the beer bottle into the woods. Storm watched him and whimpered. She knew. She'd been there. If only she could tell him.

But if it had ended with all of them dead, maybe he didn't want to know.

Maybe his brain was doing him a favor.

Linc sank to the ground and ran his hands down his face, then stared into the dark woods behind his house for a very, very long time.

16

Kylie walked into work the following day, feeling well-rested and…like crap.

After a pretty disastrous dinner with his family, she could tell Linc hadn't been happy. He was tense and moodier than usual. Something told her it wasn't just his family that had brought this on. That night with her had spooked him.

So, yes. She was worried. She'd wanted to broach the subject of PTSD with him, but in the mood he was in, she didn't know how. And what did she know about it? She'd just read some articles about it online. That didn't make her the expert.

But if she knew Linc, if he was dealing with something like that, he was the type to bury it. Bury all his emotion. Male emotion was not acceptable. He'd been beaten down by the males in his family for so long, taught to keep that stiff upper lip. Seeking help wasn't in their blood.

Greg was in the office that morning, which was unusual for him, finishing some paperwork that he'd likely have her type up later. He said, "Well, short stuff, why the long face?"

Kylie forced a smile. "Nothing. I'm good!" she said cheerily, tucking her leftover lasagna lunch into the little fridge in the back. "How are you?"

He eyed her suspiciously. "Fine. How did things go with that old broad?"

Pure delight spilled over the worry. "She signed us! I have my first client. It's going pretty well. I have a list of names I need to check into today."

Greg laughed. "What? You don't already have the scumbag under the jail."

She thought about Linc, his haunted eyes. "Not yet. I've been a little…distracted."

He squinted at her. Then he dropped his pen and folded his hands in front of him. "All right. Spill."

"What?"

"You have your first solo case. I expected you to go in, all guns blazing, and have it solved by now. That's just you. I didn't expect to hear that you're *distracted*. What's the deal?"

"I'm not. I mean…" Kylie sighed and planted her elbows on the desk, propping her chin in her hands. "Do you know anything about PTSD?"

It was a long shot, she knew.

He let out a bitter laugh. "Sweetheart, I was in Vietnam. Yeah. I do."

"You…were?" Of course. She could just see a younger version of Greg in uniform. He and Linc were a lot more similar than Linc and his dad, that was for sure. This was better than she'd expected. "So, you experienced, like…nightmares? Of the trauma you went through there?"

"No. I was on the tail end of the war so I didn't see much action, but my buddies sure did. A lot of them had a hard time getting back into regular life after they came home. There weren't services for PTSD sufferers back then. Not like there is now."

Kylie leaned forward, feeling better. If this was Linc's

problem, he wasn't alone. "Is it possible that someone can be home from deployment for years and then suddenly be affected by it?"

He nodded. "Yeah. I have one buddy who went home, had a family and a high-paying job on Wall Street. He was the model for getting back into the swing of things after the war. People looked at him and said, 'See, it can be done.' Then he started having nightmares and blew his brains out ten years later."

She swallowed. Okay, nix on the feeling better. "Seriously?" Now she felt kind of sick. "Um, so…there are services around for people?"

"If they want it. That's the big hurdle, most of the time. Wanting it. Most of us guys deal with it in other, probably less effective ways. Self-medicating, you know."

She bobbed her head in agreement. Wanting it definitely was a big hurdle in Linc's case.

He tilted his head as he studied her. "Let me guess? That dreamy boyfriend of yours?"

"He's *not* my boyfriend. And no. I was just curious," she lied, reaching into her bag and pulling out the envelope with the list of people she needed to interview for the embezzlement case. She pointed at the paper. "I have work to do. Conversation over."

"Uh-huh," Greg muttered. He didn't believe her, obviously, since she never willingly ended a conversation. Whatever, dude.

Since Emma had a doctor's appointment that day, Kylie had decided to work from the office, saving the remainder of the inventory evaluation for another day.

Kylie opened up the envelope Emma had given her and started going through it, making notes. Emma Jennings had neat script, like a schoolteacher's, though her hand was shaky. She went down the list, slowly, her mind flashing to the crazed look in Linc's eyes that night when they'd been in bed together, his big hand clasped so hard around her arm she thought he might break it. Then she thought of the way she'd laid into his father and those asshole brothers of his and shuddered a little in embarrassment.

She'd really called them all bloodsuckers.

Oh, yes, Kylie, you sure know how to win friends and influence people.

They'd deserved it. She was like her mother in that way. Sweet as pie, but if someone played the asshole card? She sure as hell was going to call them out for it. It was only fair.

And they were bona fide assholes. How could they treat one of their own like that? It was hard to believe that a guy like Linc could come from that stable of self-absorbed douches.

Of course, Kylie knew a little bit about fathers who treated their family like crap. Her own father, for one. She was actually blessed that he'd gotten out of her life when she was young, before she could form an attachment to him. If she had, maybe she'd be spending her life feeling guilty for not being able to keep him from leaving. Kylie wondered if part of Linc's problem was that he never could live up to his father's unrealistic expectations.

Then she realized she wasn't concentrating on the case.

Case, Kylie. Concentrate on the case. Forget Linc for one freaking second, can't you?

She made a few more notes as her eyes drifted down the page, thinking she'd probably have better luck contacting these people in the evening, when they were home from their jobs. As she was deciding to order in Chinese and do that, her eyes hit upon the name of Emma Jennings's lawyer, the one she had been concerned might be embezzling her funds.

Oh, for all that was good and holy.

It said, Jonathan Coulter.

Jonathan bloodsucker Coulter.

So, basically, Kylie was in the process of investigating an embezzlement accusation involving the lead vampire.

Linc's father.

She buried her face in her hands. As she did, she thought of their house. Of all that expensive and exclusive artwork. Of course he was Emma Jennings's lawyer. Linc had said his father was one of the most respected and well-known lawyers in the state. Of course, she'd have to be dealing with him.

This would make her investigation just peachy. Kylie couldn't wait to deal with the elder Coulter again. She could almost already feel his love and open-mindedness.

And what would Linc say when he found out she was investigating his dad? What if Linc's dad was embezzling funds, and she uncovered it? That could completely rip apart his family…and wouldn't exactly make her feel welcome at future family dinners.

Crap.

Well, she simply couldn't tell Linc that now. He had enough on his mind. Besides, there was no reason to worry until his father gave her something to worry about. Sure, money was missing. But it could've gone anywhere. She may have thought Linc's dad was a bloodsucker, but it didn't mean he was a thief too.

Kylie decided that her first course of action, since it was easiest, would be to research the names of the people on the list. She did so, starting first with Nate Jennings, the dear grandson that Emma was trying to set her up with. When she typed in his name, she wasn't prepared for all the juiciness that appeared.

Nate Jennings was twenty-nine years old and had graduated from Wake Forest just a few years ago. Of course, she couldn't fault him for that. Kylie herself had been taking a tiny bit longer than the normal four years to get all her studies in.

But she wouldn't think about that.

From what she could tell, Emma's "dear grandson" had an arrest record for petty theft. There'd been an article in the paper a few years back that had him stealing a number of items from a fraternity house. She found a Facebook page that wasn't set to private, and as she scrolled through it, she didn't really find a lot that made her think she'd have a love connection with the guy.

In fact, he seemed like a bigger douche than Linc's dad.

He was big on flaunting his money. There were at least three selfies of him wearing expensive-looking sunglasses. He was posed with a fan of hundred-dollar bills, looking like a pimp. He had a hot red Porsche, a different girl on his arm every two days, and he got around the party scene. He also appeared stoned or strung out in most of the pictures. Acne-faced, skinny, and kind of gross, "handsome" wasn't the word she'd use to describe him. Kylie had to wonder if Emma Jennings *was* losing her mind.

He had a record, lived beyond his means, and his grandmother had said he'd been "helping" her around the house. Emma Jennings thought he could do no wrong, so she probably gave him a lot of liberties. Plus, he just looked like a thug.

He could be her man.

Well, it was definitely an easier line of inquiry than going after Jonathan Coulter, big-deal lawyer.

Maybe she'd find out Nate was behind it, all along, and wouldn't have to bother with the lawyer.

Yes. That was the plan.

Please please please, Nate...be responsible for stealing from your sweet old grandma. And confess it to me the second you're interviewed so I don't have to dig any deeper into this case.

Because...wow. What a way to make her first official case about a thousand times less exciting. In fact, as she glumly stared at Jonathan Coulter's name on the paper for the thousandth time, willing it to change to any other name on the face of the earth, she realized she'd probably rather be typing those reports from hell.

Kylie jabbed in the number for Nate that Emma Jennings had given her. It went right to voicemail. "Hi, Nate? This is Kylie Hatfield, and I'm working with your grandmother. I was wondering if you wouldn't mind answering a few questions for me. Please call me back." She rattled off the number.

Hanging up, she wondered if he'd even call. He didn't look like the most responsible guy on earth. Of course, his last Facebook post was a number of years ago. People changed.

She got to work on the other names, finding very little, until she entered in the name Jonathan Coulter.

She clicked on pictures of a much younger man—almost like the spitting image of Linc, though he was dressed in a suit. She scrolled through hundreds of articles about cases he'd tried and won. All of his awards came up. All of his philanthropic activities. Yes, he may have been a lawyer, but he had done good around the city. So, he wasn't a total bloodsucking scumbag.

Was he an embezzler too?

God. She didn't want to touch that with a thousand-foot pole.

But something told her she might have to.

17

He dreamed of fire. Of death and burning buildings. Of people screaming.

But nothing made any sense.

In the pre-dawn hours of morning, Linc woke, sweating and breathing hard. He was surprised to find himself in his own bed.

He got out and stumbled downstairs, then went to go feed the dogs. After he did, he checked his phone. He had one message from Caryn, Dr. Evans' vet assistant: "Hello, Linc. I have the bill for the little beagle that was brought in with possible hypothermia the other day. It's two-hundred and ten dollars even. If you'd like to put this on your credit—"

Linc deleted the message and made a mental note to contact them later. He was sure he probably had a bunch of other bills to settle with them since he was there almost every week.

Deciding the best thing for him was to stay busy, he got to work, doing everything he needed to do to winterize the house. He changed out all the screens to storm windows.

Checked to make sure the radiators were working. And planted bulbs for the following year in his grandma's garden.

Every time a thought of Syria threatened to invade, he pushed it away, repeating, *I'm not crazy, I'm not crazy, I'm not crazy* over and over again in his head until he *felt* crazy.

How had he forgotten that Austin had died? That they all had? Every single one of his brothers? Why hadn't he ever wondered why they never called him to catch up? Had he learned all this, and just blocked it out?

Thinking hard, he remembered riding home on the plane to Asheville after months in the hospital. Men and women in the airport thanked him for his service, and a little kid handed him a homemade card. He remembered his mother and father welcoming him at the gate.

But he remembered nothing else about his brothers. Nothing about them coming home with him. Had they come home in boxes?

Linc was sure, though, that the woman he kept remembering was from that day. The day of the suicide bombing he couldn't remember. All he could remember was Austin, looking up at him with that crooked grin as he kicked about the soccer ball.

Then the little boys, scuffling for the ball.

Then one of them, shouting happily about his sister.

The sister, cowering in fear.

And then…

And then…

"You're busy, huh?"

Linc jumped nearly out of his skin, falling back on his ass with the garden trowel in his hand.

Jacob crouched down in front of him. "Jesus. What the hell, man? Didn't you see me coming? Storm and the other dogs have been barking their heads off. I thought you saw me."

Twice. This had happened to him twice now.

Linc shook his head. "I was thinking of something."

"Of…what, man?"

He pulled off his gloves and scrubbed his hands over his face, sitting there in the dirt. "Nothing. Don't tell me there's another rescue."

"Nah. I just came to see how you were. You looked a little…weird the other night?"

Linc couldn't even remember back to when that was. Oh, right. When he'd been pissed that Kylie and his best friend were getting too close. What the hell was wrong with him? Why was he acting like such an asshole these days?

"I'm good. I'm fine."

"Are you sure, because—"

"Yes!" he snarled. "Dammit, yes. I'm *fine*. Now, just leave it."

Jacob stepped back, his face filled with concern. He lifted his hands in a "meant no harm" gesture. "Whoa. I was just…I guess I caught you at a bad time. I'll just…" He started to walk back to his truck.

Linc pushed himself to his feet. "Hey. Wait. I didn't mean that." He ran both hands through his hair. "Come on in and have a beer."

Still looking wary, Jacob agreed, and they went out onto the back porch, popping the tops off two beers Linc retrieved from the kitchen.

Jacob took control of the conversation. "Little Bethany Akers is doing great, and so is the pup." That got a smile out of Linc. The topics turned to where they always did…sports, bars, women. Before he could stop his thoughts, Linc wondered if Jacob compared every girl he met to Kylie.

After a while, though, Linc felt tired. Empty. Beat to shit. The nights alternating between sleeplessness and nightmares were starting to pile up on one another.

Jacob acted like his usual jovial self, but Linc'd known him since kindergarten. They used to talk about all kinds of crazy shit, no holds barred, and rib each other incessantly. Today, it was almost like he was being too nice. Linc could tell Jacob was on edge, almost walking on eggshells. He didn't want that.

He wanted…normal.

Whatever that was.

And if anyone could understand, it was Jacob. He'd been in the Marines, one tour in Afghanistan, right out of high school.

"Have you…ever had nightmares?" Linc ventured when they'd fallen to silence, staring out at the thick woods behind his house. The dogs were at their feet, and as they rocked in the rocking chairs, Linc felt another headache coming on. "About your time? Overseas?"

Jacob gave him a surprised look, then shook his head. "I didn't see the action a lot of guys did though." He took a swig of his beer. "Not like you. Why? Is that what this is about?"

Linc looked up at the eave overhead and rocked back on the chair. "Yeah. No." He laughed, the sound as exhausted as he felt. "I don't know. I don't know what the hell is going on in my head anymore."

Jacob was quiet for a moment. "If you're having problems, go to the VA. That's what they're there for. They have medication. Therapy."

That all sounded like a bunch of new-age shit that wouldn't work. Besides, this was mind over matter. It was just a matter of showing his brain who was boss. He was strong. He should've been able to handle this himself.

"Nah. It's not bad. Just a few dreams." Linc shrugged and laughed, playing it off. "I just don't know why the hell I'm having them now when I haven't been in Syria in over two years."

Jacob snorted. "Maybe it's because you've been forced to save your girlfriend's pretty ass a couple times lately." He sobered, turned to look at Linc more directly. "You witnessed some pretty intense shit a few weeks ago, Linc. That would mess with anyone's mind."

Linc didn't close his eyes because, if he did, he would see damned Sophia DuBois holding a gun to Kylie's head. That was one thing he hadn't forgotten. Nor had he forgotten how loud that gun had been when it went off. He also hadn't forgotten the fear. The blood. The moments that ticked by before he knew Kylie hadn't been fatally injured.

"You should get it checked out, though, if it gets worse," Jacob advised. "The brain works in really weird ways."

No, shit.

Jacob stayed for close to another hour, still keeping up most of the conversation. They shared another beer, but Jacob turned down a third on account that he was driving. When Jacob finally pushed to his feet, Linc followed him to the truck, both relieved and sad to see him go in equal degrees.

He wanted to apologize for acting like an asshole, but he couldn't think of how to form the words. He wanted to tell Jacob he'd been an idiot for thinking he'd screw around with Kylie behind his back, but he didn't want the detective to know how paranoid and out of control he'd become. So Linc told him that he'd see him later, and that was the end of that.

They were best friends. Always would be.

Well, if Linc didn't push him away too.

18

Kylie sighed and threw herself over her desk, wanting to bang her head on the wood repeatedly, her frustration was so great.

Greg walked in and found her there. He didn't say anything for about ten minutes, which was when he came over, kicked her foot, and said, "Are you dead? Because I don't pay the deceased."

"Just about," she muttered into her arm. With all the energy she could muster, she sat up.

He pointed to her arm. "You in pain?"

Kylie frowned down at her shoulder and shook her head before sighing deeply.

"Okay." Greg scratched at his chin. "That sigh means something is wrong."

Oh, there were plenty of things that were wrong. Linc hadn't been in touch with her since the disastrous dinner at his parents' house. She wasn't sad about that—she was damn near irate—but was determined to stick to her guns and not call or text him at all. As someone who texted just as often as she spoke, it was damn near impossible.

So, Linc? Top of her shit list. The very top. In her estimation, the Spotlight Killer ranked lower.

Then, to top it all off, she'd gotten nowhere in the Emma Jennings case. Nate never called her back, nor had any of the other people on the list. Kylie felt like she was running up against a brick wall. She kept looking at Linc's dad's name, wondering if she should bite the bullet, call him, tell him he's not just a bloodsucker, he's an embezzler, *plus* he raised a son with absolutely no manners, and *shame on him*.

She didn't think Greg would want to hear her love-life rantings, since god knew she'd terrorized him with those enough, so she stuck to the professional stuff.

"I'll have you know that I've been very thorough, trying to research everyone on this godforsaken list Emma gave me for the embezzlement case," she said, stabbing it with her pen. "But no one is getting back to me. I think they all think I have cooties. Do I have cooties, Greg?"

"You may," he said, still rubbing his scraggly jaw. "Which is why I keep you on the other side of the office. Have you called everyone?"

She nodded, hoping he wouldn't see the lie on her face.

"What have you been telling them? Sometimes people won't call back because they think you're a telemarketer. You have to get creative."

Creative? Hmmm. Creative was her middle name. "What do you mean?"

"I mean that you should go right now and talk to Mrs. Jennings. Tell her that you're attempting to interview the people on the list, but you're worried they aren't answering because they're suspicious as to why you called. Then ask her if she could make the introductions. Tell people you're an…I don't know…auditor or something. That way, they'll be more forthcoming with information for you."

Kylie blinked at her boss in awe. "Greg, that's brilliant. Did anyone tell you you're brilliant?"

"Yep. Every day." She grabbed her coat and purse, clipped on Vader's leash, and practically skipped over to Greg. She was about to give him a big hug from behind when he held up a finger. "Uh-uh. Cooties."

"Ha ha." She kissed the balding top of his head. "I'll be back!"

"Go get 'em, short stuff," he muttered after her.

She was still excited as she rang the ornate bell of Emma Jennings's mansion. It wasn't Emma who greeted her this time. It was the butler.

"Hello, Mr. Sloane."

The man inclined his head but still managed to look down his nose at her. "Miss Hatfield. Did I miss an appointment on the calendar?"

It was the politest rebuke she'd ever heard. She blushed. "No. I'm sorry for dropping by unexpectedly. I was hoping—"

"Kylie, dear."

Kylie blew out a relieved breath as Emma appeared at the top of a sweeping marble staircase. "Come in, come in."

Face carefully blank, Sloane opened the door farther, and Kylie stepped through, then waited patiently at the bottom of the steps for Emma to make her way down. By the time she was at the bottom, she looked exhausted…and sad. Lifting her hand to her lips, Emma kissed her palm and then the bottom banister.

It hit her. Kylie had read that the late Mr. Jennings had fallen down a set of steps. She shivered. That very set of steps?

Emma sighed and a smile brightened her face. "I'm happy to see you. Do you have any information?"

Since the elderly woman seemed a bit out of breath, Kylie

offered her an arm. "How about we sit, and I'll give you an update?"

Emma linked arms with hers, and after instructing Sloane to bring them tea, they slowly walked to the parlor. The pace worried Kylie. Emma seemed much more frail today than when she'd last seen her. She wanted to ask her about her doctor's appointment but wasn't sure if she should.

When they were seated, Kylie confessed. "I don't have much of an update, actually. I've been running into issues getting the people on your list to respond to me. But I wanted to run something by you that I think could help."

Emma looked troubled by the news. "Oh?"

"I think it may help if I pose as your new assistant, hunting down this information for a tax audit so that they don't question my inquiries or resist answering. Do you think that would be okay?"

The elderly lady brightened. "Yes, I see. Of course. I think that makes perfect sense. I had to let my assistant go a couple months ago."

Kylie frowned. "You had an assistant? Is his name on the list?"

Emma tapped her bottom lip, clearly thinking. "*Her,* dear. Denise is a her, and I can't quite remember if I thought to write it down."

Biting back an exhale, Kylie opened her notepad. "What's Denise's last name?"

"Summers. Denise Summers."

"And how long did Denise work for you?"

The lip tapping continued. "For years, dear. Absolute years. At least two before my Arnold passed."

Kylie wrote down *seven*.

"And why did she leave?"

Emma sighed. "Because of Nate."

Kylie's ears perked up. "Your grandson? What happened?"

Emma lowered her voice. "Nate was a cheat."

Kylie shook her head, trying to make the dots align. "What?"

"On Denise, dear. Nate cheated on Denise."

"So, your grandson and your assistant were in a relationship?"

"Yes. That's what I just told you."

Kylie refrained from running her hand down her face. "I understand now. Were they dating before you hired her?"

"Oh no. Denise was in her late thirties, dear. Quite the cougar, if you get my drift."

Kylie did, indeed.

"How did you feel about them dating?"

Emma rolled her eyes. "I'm no prude, as you know, but I didn't approve of the relationship in the least."

"Because of the age difference?

The older woman's hand waved in a pish-posh manner that made Kylie smile. "Love is love, dear…unless it's not."

Kylie wanted to thunk her head against a wall. "Can you explain that to me please?"

"Well, my Nate was heads over heels in love with Denise, but I could see from a hundred miles away that she was just using the dear boy…" she leaned forward conspiratorially, "for sex."

Kylie cringed. Grandmas just didn't need to know such things.

"How long did they date?"

"I learned of their affair in a most unexpected way this summer."

Kylie was afraid to ask.

She didn't need to. "Walked in on them making love on my Arnold's favorite stool. I was livid."

Kylie's stomach churned a bit. "I'm sure."

Emma's cheeks turned a bright pink as she glowered at

the memory. "No one had even sat on that stool since Arnold's passing, and there her fat ass cheeks were smearing all about."

Kylie slapped a hand over her eyes, trying to unsee the image that flashed through her mind. "Oh no. That's simply terrible. In every way possible."

"Indeed. It. Was. And that tramp was screwing my grandson on company time, to add insult to injury."

"So, you fired her?"

"On the spot." Emma glowered, and Kylie could glimpse the formidable woman she once was. "And had that stool disinfected every day for a week."

Kylie looked at her notes. "But you said Nate was a cheat. If he was so in love with Denise, why cheat?"

Emma nodded, her brow still furrowed in anger. "He was in love with her, but rumor has it that he was also in a relationship with his ex-roommate, a boy he knew from college."

Kylie blinked. "So, Nate is bi-sexual?"

Another pish-posh wave of the hand. "Love is love, dear."

"Unless it's not," Kylie concluded and got a beaming smile from the elderly woman.

"Yes, indeed."

"Do you recall the ex-roommate's name?"

The furrow returned, and Emma stared at Kylie's chin in deep concentration. "Derrick? David? I'm quite certain it starts with a D, but those don't sound quite right." She pressed her fingers to her temples. "Oh, this memory."

Kylie laid a hand on the woman's arm, about to tell her to not worry herself when Sloane arrived with the familiar silver service tray, which he placed on the coffee table. After he left, Kylie said, "Do you mind if I interview some of the employees right now?"

"Not at all." Emma was busy pouring creamer and scooping sugar. Kylie was impressed that the octogenarian remembered that she liked hers extra sweet and milky. "Of course, Sloane is the only one available at the moment. I'm sure he'll tell you everything you want to know. He knows all and sees all. Very reliable and trustworthy. He's been in my family for almost sixty years, can you believe that? Was my mother's butler before mine."

"I'm sure he'll be helpful," Kylie said as she sipped her tea, which tasted so much better than when she tried making it at home. She drank it hurriedly, excited to finally make some tracks on this case.

They chatted a little more, and then Emma led her to the servants' quarters in another wing of the house. There, she found Sloane relaxing with the paper while finishing his lunch. He looked appalled to have someone enter his domain, especially while he wasn't in full uniform, but he set aside his paper and moved some books on the chair across from him to the floor to let Kylie sit.

As she sat down, she peeked around. It looked like an old widower's home, dark and dreary and sparse, and smelled vaguely of Bengay.

"I'm sorry to bother you right now, Mr. Sloane." Kylie motioned toward his mostly empty plate. "Please finish your lunch, and after that, I have a few questions to ask on behalf of Mrs. Jennings if that's all right."

"I'm quite finished," he said in a gravelly voice, scanning her carefully as he pushed a pair of glasses up onto his nose. "May I ask why a *friend* would need to ask me questions?"

Confused for a moment, Kylie thought back to her first visit to the house. Emma had indeed introduced her as a friend.

"Mrs. Emma has asked me to be her assistant." When Sloane only raised an eyebrow, she went on, "As I'm sure you know, she has a great deal of paperwork to handle on a weekly basis, and she's worried that her mind isn't as sharp as it once was, so she hired me to keep track of things." Kylie pulled her notepad from her purse. "In order to help her best, I thought it vital that I understand the inventory, and I'm specifically interested in the three paintings that appear to be missing from the gallery. You said they were sent out to be reframed a few months ago?"

He nodded. "Yes. A place downtown. The name escapes me. Her grandson called to tell me that they were to be picked up and delivered there for new frames and cleaning."

That sounded all sorts of suspicious. "Her grandson? You mean, Nate?"

He nodded, keeping his neck stiff. "He was always doing things for his grandmother. Very handy boy. Haven't seen him around here much in the past few months. Not since the...incident."

He sniffed, and Kylie felt sure she knew of which incident he was speaking. She needed to be certain, though.

"The stool incident?"

Sloane sniffed again, looking thoroughly disgusted. "Indeed."

Kylie nodded. "Before the stool incident, would you have assessed Nate as someone who was trustworthy?"

Sloane held the last of an egg salad sandwich in his hand and was about to take a bite, but he stopped. "I would like to believe so. He's Emma's grandson. I've known him all his life. My daughter was Nate's nanny after Nate's parents passed away. So, he was raised right, I tell you." He glowered. "Until he was led astray."

Kylie bit her tongue. "Of course."

He popped a bite of the sandwich into his mouth and started to chew, his dentures clicking together in a way that made Kylie pledge to increase her flossing schedule dramatically. "Artful Frames. Downtown. That was the place. Mr. Jennings always used their services."

"Ah." She scribbled the name down. It sounded legit, she guessed. "Did Emma specifically tell you she wanted the portraits reframed?"

He narrowed his eyes. "I thought we went over that."

"You said Nate called and told you they were going to be taken away and reframed. But did you ever hear Emma say herself that she wanted them reframed?"

His brow knitted, and he frowned deeply. "I…I see what you mean. I suppose not. Nate told me over the phone that Emma wanted them reframed, so I just assumed…oh, dear."

The poor old man. She put a hand on his, patting his tissue-paper skin. "It's all right. I'm sure she just told Nate, and he was carrying out her orders. Considering you know him so well."

But what she didn't tell Sloane was that in her book, this boy he'd known forever was looking more and more like a dirty rat.

And then there was this Denise…

"What do you know about Denise Summers?"

Sloane's nostrils flared, and he looked like he'd smelled something bad. "Up until…"

"…the stool incident," Kylie filled in when he paused longer than she had patience for.

"Yes. Until then, I would have told you that Ms. Summers was a capable assistant. Timely and all that."

"Did you know of her and Nate's affair?"

The nostrils flared again. "Only when I was forced to bleach Mr. Jennings's favorite seating implement a number of times."

Seating implement? Kylie smiled.

"One other thing. You said that Nate called you about taking the paintings for reframing. How sure are you that it was Nate you were speaking to?"

His bushy white eyebrows knitted together. "Quite sure. He said it was."

"Yes, but how do you know it wasn't someone pretending to be him?"

"Oh." He picked up a pickle and then set it back down. "Oh. No, I don't believe that could happen. I know Nate's voice well, having practically raised him. And whenever he calls, he's very sociable. We talk for a while about many things. I think I would know if someone was pretending to be him. Besides, who would do such a thing?"

She shrugged. "You've been very helpful."

Kylie thanked him and decided to head downtown to this Artful Frames shop, just to see if she could find the whereabouts of the paintings. She parked outside the tiny shop and went in.

A bald, middle-aged man with glasses was standing behind the counter of the empty place, walls littered with frames of every shape and size. "Hello!" he called cheerily. "May I help you?"

"Yes." She beamed back at him. "Are you the owner of this place?"

"Indeed, I am. Jeffry Gaines, at your service."

"Thank you, Mr. Gaines. I'd like to talk to you about some reframing you're working on for Emma Jennings?"

He frowned thoughtfully, his lips silently repeating the name. "Jennings?"

Uh-oh.

"You don't know the name?"

His nostrils flared a little. "And you are?"

Kylie stuck out a hand, thinking that not having business cards would be the bane of her existence. "Kylie, Mrs. Jennings's new assistant. We're doing an audit of her gallery."

He looked mildly more impressed. "Well, in that case, of course I know who Mrs. Jennings is. Her husband was the famed artist, Arnold Jennings. Magnificent work." He clasped both hands to his chest, seemingly enthralled by some memory. "Just magnificent."

Kylie supposed she'd never understand art, but now wasn't the time to try. "Do you remember the last time you were commissioned to frame one of his works?"

The glow faded into another frown. "They have used us in the past, but I'm afraid not recently." Moving to a desk in the back of the room, he flipped through a file. "Yes, it's been over five years."

When Arnold Jennings passed away.

"Are you sure? I have three paintings that were sent out for reframing a couple months ago, and I've been trying to locate them for her." Kylie leaned over the counter to see what he was digging through. "It would have been, oh, over two months ago?"

"Three paintings?" He paged through his files some more. "I'm sorry, they were never brought here. I have no record of them whatsoever. And even if they were, we wouldn't have kept them two months, for certain. Our normal turnaround time is two weeks. Customer service is our priority."

"Oh. Well. Thank you."

He pulled out a pen and paper and started to scribble something down for her. He handed her a paper with the words, BAKER FRAMING, printed on it. "Maybe she had them sent there? We always have people confusing us."

Kylie took it. "Maybe. I hope so. Thank you."

He called a "good luck" after her as she left and went out to her car, finding the number for Baker Framing on her phone. She called them right away and asked them if they happened to have an order from an Emma or Nate Jennings there. The salesclerk told her that they had nothing fitting the description of the three paintings at all.

Kylie thanked her and ended the call, then let out a big breath of air.

She definitely smelled a rat in Nate Jennings. She called his number again and left yet another voicemail message. And she was totally going to smoke him out.

Denise Summers too.

As Kylie headed back toward the office, she passed a well-kept, stately brick building with golden eagles on the front, and read the sign. *Coulter and Associates.*

But it wasn't the bloodsucking lawyers she ended up thinking about.

No, she was thinking of the *other* Coulter, the black sheep of the family.

Taking a deep breath, Kylie punched in a call to Jacob, wondering if Linc would be angry at her for talking to him. He'd been so off the other night, which was completely out of left field.

He answered with his typical, "Yello?"

"Hi, Jacob. It's Kylie."

"Kylie! And what has you calling me on this fine day?"

"I was just...." She paused, trying to decide how to approach this. "I was just wondering if you'd noticed anything different about Linc lately."

"Different. Hell yeah. He's moody as hell. Moodier than his normal, bad-boy brooding. You caught that too?"

"Yeah. I haven't talked to him in a couple days, and I'm worried about him."

"Listen," he said after a long sigh. "I get the feeling he's going through some stuff right now, and as hard as it is to hear, he needs some space. That's Linc. He was always the loner type. When he was dealing with shit, he did it on his own."

"Maybe. But is that healthy?"

"It's what he does. What he knows. What he's comfortable

with. If you try to tell him otherwise, Kylie, he may end up pushing you away for good. He does that, sometimes. He's not the easiest guy to get to know."

She bristled at the thought of pushing him so hard that he removed himself completely from her life. Maybe she'd done that already?

Kylie gnashed her teeth together. She wasn't sure she could bear that.

"Well. Thanks, Jacob. I'll take that under consideration," she said, ending the call and throwing her phone down on the passenger seat.

As much as she tried to convince herself that she was angry at Linc for what he'd done, when she thought really hard and long about it, she *was* sad.

Because she got the feeling he was keeping away from her for one reason only, and it wasn't because he didn't care about her, or didn't want her around.

No. It was the opposite. He was trying to keep her safe.

From him.

19

Linc leaned back in his chair after spending hours staring at his laptop and groaned. His back was stiff. He stretched, then scrolled through the SAR website he was in the midst of creating.

It looked like shit.

He wasn't helpless when it came to web design; he'd taken classes in college. He'd had an idea of what he wanted to create for his new site, advertising his services. But this wasn't it. It reeked of amateurism. Not to mention the five-hundred photos he'd uploaded with hopes he'd have some good ones to use on the site had nearly crashed his computer, and now it was running slow.

It was not his day.

Not his week.

It didn't even feel like his life anymore. It felt like someone else was in control, and he was just along for the ride.

Linc'd tried to keep busy. He really had. But the flash-backs were coming full force now, not just hitting him at night, but all the time, while he did the most innocuous things. He'd be going into the fridge to get breakfast, only to be rocked by an explosion of fear, right in his heart. It had nearly knocked him off his feet. He'd ruined a whole sleeve of eggs that way. His body was tense and wound tighter than a spring. It felt like *he* was the bomb, like he wasn't safe anymore, with anyone, no matter what he did.

When he flashed back, it was always to that same day, in the marketplace. That woman with the fear-filled eyes. Austin's face, smiling at Linc as he kicked around the soccer ball. The blistering heat. That dusty air, heavy with the smell of machine oil and gasoline. Kids' shrieks of laughter dissolving to screams of terror.

And Linc knew Kylie was probably wondering what was up with him. She hadn't called or texted since he'd seen her last on the night of the dinner; he figured that was just her, being stubborn, since she'd warned him enough. She was a little firecracker. Linc could almost feel the flare of her hot temper aimed right at him, even from all the way up on the mountain.

The only thing that had made him smile in the past few days was thinking about his father's face when she laid into him. No one ever did that to his father. It was pretty hilarious to see the wide-eyed shock on his face. Even if it hadn't put him in his place totally, it had, for about five seconds, which was more than anyone had ever done.

And Linc wanted to call her. Wanted to ask her to come over and beg her to have patience with him. But as shitty as he felt about it, as much as he wanted her—in his bed and in his life—he couldn't do it.

She hadn't signed up for this shit, and she sure as hell didn't deserve it.

Powering down his computer, Linc got up and stretched. Storm did too, from her comfortable place under his feet. Even she seemed to know something was going on with him, or maybe it was his imagination that she seemed to hang back a little more, a look of concern on her face. He put on his boots and his flannel. They went downstairs, and he grabbed a beer from the fridge and sat down on the couch with his phone.

He opened up a text to her.

But he didn't know what to say. *Hi, sorry I've been such an asshole. But I think I'm going insane.*

Yeah, that would work out really well. Way to make her go running for the hills.

The worst part about it was that Linc didn't think that would make Kylie run. In fact, he thought that would just make her hold him closer. She was that type of girl. Nurturing. Caring. If someone was hurt, she tried to fix it. She'd probably do a bang-up job of understanding just what he was going through. She'd take him in her arms and try to comfort him, and she'd put her entire heart and soul into it.

And she wouldn't admit it, but he'd be a total drag on her.

That's not what Linc did. He didn't rely on anyone. He'd spent most of his life alone mostly because he'd realized that he was his own best company. After Syria, he'd adopted a few mottos…

If you want something done your way, you do it yourself.

Prepare for the worst.

Do or die.

Linc healed his own hurts. He'd gotten his brain sick, and he was responsible for getting it well. Or living with it the best he could.

Alone.

Because he could control alone.

Linc dropped his phone to his chest and took another swig of beer, then slid down on the couch, propping his head up on his arm as he stared at the ceiling.

Commanding himself to relax, he deliberately slowed his

breathing, and the edges of the room went hazy before he drifted into a sense of peace.

When he opened his eyes, Kylie was there, wearing that red farmgirl dress again. "Miss me?" she said, biting on her lip seductively.

And all those thoughts about not needing her went right out the window.

Linc tried to sit up, but Kylie clearly had other ideas. She leaned over, hovering over him, and placed a finger on his lips.

When she straddled him, he ran both hands up her back until they fisted in her hair. She leaned forward, pressing her breasts against his chest. "I missed you," she said, her voice just a breath before she pressed her lips to his.

Dropping his hands to his sides, he lay there as she undressed him, letting her do as she pleased. As she stripped her panties down her legs, she smiled. "Did you miss me too?"

Linc let out a hard breath of air. "Yeah. I did miss you. I'm sorry, Kylie. I didn't mean to…but I'm glad you're here now."

She kissed him again. The tip of his nose, his cheeks, his jawline, making her way to his ear. "Make love to me, Linc."

Moving her into position, he raised up to meet her as she sank onto him, joining their bodies.

Heat exploded in his brain, their connection searing every part of him.

Flame. Fire. Starting where they joined, it radiated outward until the rest of his body turned to red-hot embers.

He heard a scream. And another and another. Then an explosion so loud it rocked his entire world.

Kylie!

He grabbed her arms and rolled them both until he was on top of her. He had to keep her safe.

Kylie started screaming. Screaming. Screaming.

When he looked down, pushed her hair from her face, it wasn't Kylie at all.

It was the woman from the marketplace, her eyes wide with fear. Her voice was old, creaky. "You left them," she wailed as flames tore at her face, melting her skin until she was nothing but a burning skeleton. "You killed them all. You know it should be you."

Linc jumped to his feet, then fell to his ass, the jolt running all the way up his spine.

The woman was gone. The flames were gone. The night-mare was gone.

It was only him and Storm that remained.

And the guilt. The sorrow. The grief.

Rain fell like marching soldiers upon the roof, competing with the only other sound. His harsh breathing.

You know it should be you.

Rubbing his eyes and looking around in the dim blue light from the clock on the radio across the room, Linc reminded himself that he was safe. That he was in his house, in his living room, where he'd fallen asleep. Alone. Even though he could still smell her, feel her, Kylie wasn't, hadn't been here.

He jumped when the phone buzzed on the wood floor beside him.

He stood up and stepped onto something sharp. His phone buzzed again, its display illuminating the bottle of the beer he'd been drinking. It now lay shattered, pieces both big and small littering the space around him. His feet were bare. His soles began to sting.

"Shit," Linc ground out, collapsing back onto the couch and wiping the glass from his feet. He'd sliced his toe. Blood trickled from the wound. He needed a bandage.

Ripping off his sweat-soaked t-shirt, he wrapped it

around his foot, applying pressure as his phone buzzed again.

Cursing a long line of filthy words, he reached for the phone and checked the display. He had five missed calls from an unfamiliar number in Spartanburg, South Carolina.

And it was two in the morning.

There was only one reason he'd be getting a call from a number out of state like that, at this hour. And it was definitely not something he was equipped to deal with right now.

Shit.

As Linc stared at the phone, his chest still heaving, his mind still reeling with thoughts of fire and damnation, a sixth call came in from that same number. He answered it this time, his voice thick and gravelly. "Yeah?"

"Is this Mr. Coulter? Mr. Linc Coulter from search and rescue?"

That was how these things usually started out. He swabbed at his toe again. The bleeding was stopping. "Yeah. How can I help you?"

"There's been a terrible accident at the college down here in Spartanburg, South Carolina. A parking garage collapse. We have SAR on it right now, but we need another to come right away, and you were highly recommended by your peers."

Right. Linc had many peers all over the area who had him in mind for disasters like this, and usually, he'd be all for it. In fact, a week ago, this would have been a no-brainer. He'd already be on the road, ready to help. But now he had no idea of what he was capable of. What he could handle. What might set him off. He felt like a ticking time bomb, with no idea what his body would do.

Linc gritted his teeth. He had to push through it. This was his job. His *life*. And he wasn't about to lend any more truth to his father's assertions that he didn't do anything but play with dogs high on the mountain.

"Yeah. I'm on it." Linc reached for the pull-string for the lamp and turned it on. "Text me the address."

Wide awake now, he checked how long the drive would take, and told them he'd be there in a little over an hour. The glass would have to wait. Every damn thing else would have to wait.

He changed quickly and grabbed his go-bag, checking he had everything he needed.

He did.

This part of his life he was good at. Competent. In control.

After leaving a message with his veterinary clinic to watch his dogs, which they were usually on call to do when he was going to be away for an uncertain amount of time, he called to Storm and they both jumped in his truck.

Ready.

But as he headed down the mountain, the dark, fearful eyes of the woman still seemed to bore into the back of his head.

This time, she was laughing.

What makes you think you can be a hero after what you did?

20

Kylie stopped at the local McDonald's on the way to her meeting with Nate Jennings and ordered a super huge of just about everything on the menu.

Other people, when they were depressed or bothered about something, couldn't eat. Kylie had the opposite problem. When stressed, her stomach became a black hole, constantly grumbling for anything she could put in it: the greasier, the better.

As she popped a handful of ketchup laden fries into her mouth, she realized she was very stressed…about Lincoln Coulter.

Which made her even more angry and stressed.

Taking a long sip of sweet tea, she tried to force her mind in more productive directions, namely the case she was supposed to be working on. Sweet little Emma Jennings.

She'd spent the entire day going through the rest of Arnold Jennings's entire inventory of paintings, thinking if three were missing, how many more? It turned out…at least another dozen, and Kylie wasn't even finished yet. The paperwork was a mess. Paintings, both finished and unfinished, were stashed in the attic, under beds, in closets. In a word...everywhere.

Emma had been horrified.

Denise Summers hadn't just been shagging her grandson, she was a terrible assistant to boot.

"How long did it take Mr. Jennings to complete a painting?" Kylie had asked the sweet old woman.

Emma had just waved her hand. "Anywhere from hours to twenty-five years."

Kylie hadn't understood. "How's that?"

Emma sorted through the newly sorted stack and pulled out a painting of a lopsided little boy and his...bear? Wooley mammoth? No, a dog. A hideously ugly dog that seemed very close to eating the child.

"My dear Arnold finished this one in a single morning."

Kylie tried to look impressed, but she secretly thought dear Arnold had needed to spend another couple decades on that one before making it presentable.

Art and couture fashion...Kylie didn't understand it.

Emma leafed through the stack and pulled out another one. Kylie almost jumped. The woman in the portrait very closely resembled the nun in one of the horror movies she'd watched not long ago.

"This one, Arnold worked on for over five years, off and on." Emma looked at the horrifying thing with abject admiration. Maybe the woman was a touch demented. "He was never quite satisfied, so he'd bring it out and dabble every once in a while."

With a loving look, Emma ran a finger over the nun-woman's mouth, and Kylie tensed, waiting for the thing to come alive and chomp off half of Emma's arm.

She'd definitely been watching too many scary movies.

Nevertheless, she'd been glad when Emma set the painting back down, and when the old woman turned her back, Kylie pulled a sheet over the canvas, hating how the eyes seemed to watch her.

Actually, all the eyes seemed to watch her.

Shuddering at the memory, Kylie took a huge bite of burger and chased it with a few more fries.

Vader whined beside her, begging her with big, pitiful eyes. She glanced over at him. "No. This is mine."

He whined again, and she softened and tore him off a chunk.

He gobbled it up just as a new update hit the radio.

She turned the volume up. The radio was full of live coverage of a horrific national tragedy—a parking garage collapse in South Carolina. She didn't need any more awful news to bring her spirits down, so she flipped off the dial and sighed, licking the salt from her fingers as she drove to her appointment.

It turned out that Nate Jennings's Facebook profile was a little out of date. He wasn't as much of a thug as she'd originally thought. He'd actually graduated from Wake Forest, had a decent job as an IT professional downtown, and even mentioned a girl named Ava who he'd said "had masterful taste" as he described her. Kylie assumed it was a girlfriend Emma knew nothing about.

She couldn't help wondering about Denise, though.

Where was she now?

And Nate's ex-roommate? Was he still in the picture?

What a complicated relationship web.

Nate had called Kylie back after her last message, apologizing profusely for not responding because he'd been so busy with work, and invited her over to his apartment in North Asheville to discuss the information she was looking for.

Arriving ten minutes before their four o'clock appointment, Kylie wiped her mouth and wondered if she smelled like hamburger grease. Nate's apartment building was rather swanky, too, located above a bank, and looked newly renovated. She rang the bell at the door, and he answered via the intercom and buzzed her up.

When he opened his apartment door, Kylie was floored. "Nate?"

He raised an eyebrow. "You were expecting someone else?"

"Oh. No. I just…the only photos I saw of you were from your Facebook page," she said, taking in his khaki pants and dress shirt. Emma was right; he was handsome. "You look different now."

"Yeah, being an adult will do that to a person," he said, waving her into a homey little apartment. Either he had a flair for decorating, or this was Ava and her masterful taste he'd mentioned. "Had to grow up and take responsibility."

Kylie nodded, though really, she wouldn't know.

Would this grown-up and responsible grandson be stealing from his grandmother?

Well, he hadn't shown a great deal of responsibility this past summer, having an affair with Emma's assistant…in Emma's home…in broad daylight.

Sex made people stupid.

Before she could go down that rabbit hole, thinking about Linc, Kylie sat down on the sofa, hoping Nate Jennings would do the same.

He didn't. He remained standing. No, actually, he was fidgeting, shifting from one foot to another. She wanted to shout at him to stay still.

Nate had been gracious on the phone, but now she felt like an infiltrator. Was he always this nervous? "I'm sorry. You said you were my grandmother's assistant? She's retired. Why does she need an assistant?"

Because you screwed the other one out of a job?

"She may be at the age of retirement, but Mrs. Jennings is very active and enjoys handling your late grandfather's business. And since she, um, lost..." Kylie eyed Nate closely, keeping her expression carefully neutral, "her last assistant, she has missed having someone help her keep track of her estate dealings and charitable donations and things like that."

Nate colored a little at the mention of the assistant, but he didn't give any other reaction except to ask, "Doesn't her lawyer do that?"

"In part, but she wanted someone to tie it all together," she said vaguely, hoping he wouldn't ask any more questions. To that end, she pushed on. "So, I've been auditing all of her possessions and dealings, and I had a few questions for you that I hoped you could help me with."

He started to drum his fingers nervously on the back of a chair. God, the guy did not know how to stay still. Was he guilty after all? "I doubt it. But okay. Shoot."

"Thank you." Kylie pulled out her notebook and scanned the questions she'd had planned. "Do you—"

"Hey. Why do you look familiar? Do I know you from somewhere?"

She inhaled a deep breath. Her face had been plastered all over the news after the Spotlight Killer takedown, but with the passage of time, Kylie had hoped fewer and fewer people would remember her.

"I get that all the time," Kylie said quickly, wondering if she should start wearing a wig when in her "Emma's assistant" ruse. "I've been told I have a face that's very memorable. I create feelings of déjà vu in a lot of people."

He continued to eye her closely but nodded after a moment.

She didn't give him time to question her further. "Anyway." She tapped on her list of questions to get him to refocus. "When was the last time you saw your grandmother?"

"Honestly?" He started to pace. "It's been months."

"Really? And why is that? You live so close, after all."

He stopped. Stared at her. She looked into his eyes, and he quickly looked away. Interesting. The body language was definitely of a man who had something to hide. And Greg had said she was good at getting people to open up. So, it would be her mission, she decided, to get him to.

He shook his head. "Well, to be honest, she's going a little insane. Acting really crazy. Accusing people of all sorts of things and acting paranoid. I think she has dementia or something."

Was he denying the stool incident?

Kylie bristled at the description of the sweet elderly woman. "Did she accuse you of anything you didn't do?"

He lifted a shoulder in jerky little movements. "I don't want to talk about personal matters. It has nothing to do with so-called missing paintings."

That was true. Would a lowly assistant be digging into personal matters? Kylie jumped at the segue he'd given her. "Okay, let's discuss those paintings then. Your grandmother brought that to your attention then?" He nodded and Kylie scanned her list. "The butler, Sloane, told us that you called and had them taken away to be reframed?"

He looked genuinely surprised. "Paintings reframed? No." He finally…finally…sank down into the chair. "Jesus. Sloane said that? I can't say that old man's much better." He swirled a finger around his ear, indicating that the elderly butler was also a bit demented. "I didn't touch any of her paintings. I swear, I haven't been there in months."

"You didn't call and have a service come out?"

He shook his head. "Definitely not. I could give a shit about any of those paintings."

She wrote that down and scanned the apartment, her eyes landing on a scene over the mantle of a large stone fireplace.

It looked like Arnold Jennings's style, with the creepy vibe and the googly eyes of a blonde woman, semi-nude, looking out over a stone balcony. And come to think of it, it used similar colors to the painting hanging in the Coulters' dining room.

"My grandmother gave me that," he snapped, following her line of vision. "A long time ago. It was a gift. If she's missing paintings from her gallery, that's not one of them."

Kylie stared at it. She wasn't sure she'd want her grandmother giving her anything with nude people in it, but okay.

Wait! Was that young Emma Jennings in the buff?

She stared at the grandson, her skin starting to crawl. The way he was staring back at her was unnerving. Her spidey-senses were doing backflips in her head.

"Who are you again?" he asked, pushing back to his feet, eyeing her as he once again began to pace.

"Your grandmother's assistant," Kylie said and looked back at her notepad. "And I'm here to help her track down missing inventory. Would—"

"No one's cheating her," he barked, "if that's what she's thinking. She was always really worried about that. But most of the people who handle those things for her have been doing it for years. She's probably being paranoid."

"There are at least three missing paintings. She's not being paranoid about that. Do you have any idea of—"

"Look." Annoyance crept into his voice. "I don't know what kind of stuff you're trying to uncover as my grandmother's *assistant*, but like I said, I can't help you very much. I haven't been in her life in months."

"Okay." She kept her voice calm. "But aren't you the least bit concerned about these missing paintings?"

He barked out a laugh. "Three? Out of a thousand? No. She probably just moved them for dusting or something and forgot where she put them." He sat down, grabbed a cigarette out of the pocket of his shirt, and lit it. "You mind?"

She did, but she shook her head.

"Look. You don't sound much like an assistant. You sound like an investigator."

Kylie blinked. Was it that obvious? A part of her was proud, but she needed to dial that part down. "Why would you say that?"

Nate snorted. "I'd never put it past that paranoid old lady to sic a PI on her own flesh and blood."

Kylie bristled at his description of his grandmother but stayed in her seat, wondering where this rant would lead.

He threw up his hand. "And I don't know what stuff you dug up on me, but like I said, I've changed. Yeah. I still have a lot of debt. And yes, when I was in college I did some dumb things. Who didn't? But I'm working through the debt the old-fashioned way. With an actual job. I didn't take those paintings, and if Grandma thinks I did, she's wrong. Tell her I don't know anything about it."

On the last word, he sucked on his cigarette until almost half the thing was in ash. Much more slowly, he blew out the smoke.

Kylie forced herself not to cough while she studied him, unsure of what to believe. Wanting to keep him talking, though, she tried a different direction. "Can you think of anyone who might be trying to swindle her?"

His shoulders slumped a little bit, and she could tell he was relieved to have the focus off him. "Jesus. Who knows? She has people going in and out of that house all day. Probably half the service people in the city have been there to fix something or other. The house is old. If you ask me, those paintings are gone for good."

"What about Denise Summers?"

The man jerked at the name, then took another deep drag from the cancer stick. "What about her?"

"When was the last time you saw her?"

He turned to face her, eyeing her suspiciously. "That's none of your business."

"Then could you please give me the name of your former college roommate?"

Ash fell to the floor. Nate Jennings's face turned a purply kind of red.

"Get out."

Kylie's eyes widened at the vehemence in his tone. "I—"

"I said to get out."

Very slowly, Kylie rose to her feet, the hair on the back of her neck standing on end. "Thank you for your time."

He said nothing, just opened the door and closed it with a loud click once she'd passed the threshold. Almost feeling his gaze bore into the back of her head through the peephole, she moved away, heading to the fresh air outdoors.

She shivered. The look in Nate's eyes had been…murderous.

As she walked outside, she thought through his reaction. Was Nate a closet bi-sexual? Was that why he'd reacted so violently to the question about his ex-roommate?

It made sense.

Just because he tossed her out of his apartment didn't mean he was a thief. He was still high on her list of suspects, but from her criminal justice classes, she knew she couldn't get tunnel vision when working a case.

She scanned the list of names. If Nate didn't take those paintings, then…she had to face the very real but very awful possibility that Jonathan Coulter might have something to do with it.

The thought made her head hurt.

Of course, as Kylie shoved aside thoughts of the father,

they were quickly replaced by thoughts of the son. Vader, delirious to see her reappear, jumped and barked from where she'd tied him under a shady tree.

At least someone was happy to see her. Vader and her mother. She guessed it could be worse.

After letting the big dog do clean up duty, hoovering down the fallen fries and crumbs from her lunch, she finally got him settled in the back seat. The very fact that the dog obeyed her made her think of the sexy trainer.

Gah. She needed to get him out of her head.

It felt like forever since she'd last seen him, and after what Jacob said, she was worried. Sure, Linc might need his space, but how much space was that? A week? A year? She needed to know.

Kylie looked down at her purse. She'd just gotten paid the day before, and Link had been floating her on her obedience lessons for Vader. That would be a good excuse for going up to the farm, right? Just settling their tab?

She was already heading toward his mountain, even as she argued with herself on the wisdom of going. At a traffic light, she even checked her makeup and smoothed her hair.

She was primping.

"Stop it," she berated herself when she slicked a layer of gloss over her lips.

Business. She was only going there for business.

Yeah, right. The last time she'd done that, she'd ended up naked on the hay in his barn.

"Not this time," she told her reflection. This time, she wasn't going to let Mr. Hard Body with the sweet cocoa eyes charm his way into her pants. She would keep them firmly where they belonged.

Although, the way Linc had looked at her the last time she saw him, when he'd left her apartment? She'd practically offered herself up to him on a silver platter, and he'd turned her down, flat.

So maybe he just wasn't into her anymore. Maybe the Kylie ship had sailed.

The thought made her sadder than she thought was possible.

"You'll be okay," she pep talked herself. It wasn't like she didn't have lots of experience watching men walk away.

Well, she'd been too young to understand why her father was leaving her, but she'd felt his loss off and on her entire life. That pissed her off. And concerned her.

If she missed a man she didn't remember, how badly would she miss the man she couldn't forget? The man who seemed to understand and tolerate her more than anyone ever had?

Was that it? Had his tolerance for her and her personality come to an end, and he used the nightmares as a convenient excuse to make her go?

After all, underneath his gruff exterior, Lincoln Coulter had a heart of gold. He wouldn't want to hurt her unnecessarily. At least she didn't think so.

Plus...it had been Kylie who'd been putting the brakes on their relationship, trying to slow down and just enjoy each other sexually.

Gah. Just thinking of it made her head hurt.

"Which was exactly why I'm not supposed to be thinking about it," she grouched to herself. "Pay for the obedience lessons. That's the focus. The only focus."

Mind made up, Kylie drove as quickly as she could on the horribly curvy road, and pulled into his long drive, not quite knowing what she'd find when her car came to a stop. Would he welcome her? Send her away?

Pull her into the barn for round two?

"Stop it," she muttered to herself.

When she got closer to the house, though, she didn't see his truck in its regular spot or anywhere else. Instead, there was a sporty red Kia SUV she'd never seen before. Pulling up behind it, she wondered if he'd gone through a mid-life crisis so terrible he'd decided to give up his badass truck and become a soccer mom.

Kylie blinked when a girl with long, blonde hair stepped out of the front door, her hands in the back pockets of her jeans. She eyed Kylie as closely as Kylie was eyeing her.

Jealousy spiked inside Kylie, and the junk food she ate earlier made her feel bloated and fat.

She reminded herself to chill. There could've been any one of a million completely innocent explanations for this attractive woman standing on his front porch. To have access to his home.

As rattled as she was by this beautiful, nature loving looking woman, Kylie took a deep breath and stepped out of her car. "Hi," she said in a businesslike fashion. "Is Linc not here right now?"

The blonde shook her head. She had a deep southern accent, which just added to her nature loving appeal. "No. He probably won't be back for a while."

Cute as a button.

Kylie hated her.

Still, Kylie did a good job of keeping the smile plastered on her face. "Oh. Well. I just came to drop off payment for the obedience lessons he's been giving my dog," she said, picking through her purse and pulling out a hundred dollars. "Will you be able to make sure he gets it?"

"Well, I'm not sure that's the best idea," the blonde said, eyeing the money. "I might not see him. I'm just here to give his dogs a workout and make sure they're fed. I'm from the vet."

"Oh?" Oh! She was from the veterinary clinic? Kylie

instantly relaxed, even though she didn't remember seeing her there before. "Did Linc go somewhere?"

"Yes. You probably heard about it, since it's all over the news. They needed someone with his experience on the scene of the parking garage collapse in Spartanburg."

Kylie's eyes widened. "He's there? With Storm?"

The blonde nodded. "Of course! He's the first name people in the area think about when they need a SAR guy. Left in the middle of the night to get down there. I don't think he'll be back for a couple days." She looked at the money in Kylie's hand and wrinkled her cute-as-a-button nose. "So maybe you'd better hold on to that and drop it off when he's home. I'd hate for it to get lost."

"Okay," Kylie said, tucking it away. Of course they'd call Linc. They'd want the best. But that sounded like dangerous work.

The last she'd heard, several people were still missing and buried under the rubble of a total collapse, most of them college students. Two people had already been found dead. Officials said that it was one of the worst building disasters in the nation's history, and that search and recovery work was very detailed, intricate, and dangerous.

He'd be gone for days. And he hadn't felt the need to call her?

Her heart was getting a stomachache.

Kylie didn't know what she'd been expecting, but she knew she shouldn't be surprised to not hear from him. Of course, he was in the middle of a very serious situation. He had other things on his mind.

She only wished that somewhere, even way in the back of that gorgeous head of his, there was still a little place for her too.

21

Linc had been on scene of the Spartanburg collapse since four o'clock that morning.

The place was a zoo, just another thing to put him on edge. As if he hadn't already been teetering there to begin with.

The entire block had been swarming with reporters, distraught family, emergency personnel, and curious onlookers since long before the sun rose, revealing the extent of the damages.

It turned out that the garage had been deemed structurally unsound and was under repair, but some moron thought it'd be safe enough to continue to use, when the collapse occurred. One bright spot was that it occurred late at night. Otherwise, it would've been packed with hundreds of students on their way to class. As it was, when the accident happened, the garage was being used by a small number of young men and women attending a party at a bar nearby.

The sun hadn't risen yet when Storm and Linc hit the rubble, which had flattened cars into layers that reached several stories high. It could take months to go through the mess, but they all knew that after a few days, rescue would change to retrieval. Several SAR dogs were already on-site, but none had the experience Storm possessed. There were hundreds of rescue personnel standing around, waiting for survivors to be pulled out. So far, there'd only been three.

The problem was, they had no idea who they were looking for, or even how many people were trapped.

Linc'd been in building collapses since returning from Syria, though never anything this massive. Once, part of a warehouse roof in Asheville had caved in, trapping some workers inside. Another time, an apartment building under construction had given out. Both times, they knew exactly what they were up against, and he'd never felt the least bit worried. Now, he had to ball his hands into fists at his sides to keep them from shaking.

It had taken most of the day for construction vehicles to move away some of the concrete and structural specialists to give them the all-clear to rescue. During that time, Linc and Storm had circled the collapse, Storm's nose on high alert as they attempted to better understand what they were facing.

It wasn't until well into the afternoon before they'd determined the safest way in, although the word "safe" was an operative word under these conditions.

Making sure Storm's harness was secure and her bell was attached, Linc carried her into the claw of a yellow backhoe. Storm's flanks quivered in anticipation as the machine lifted the pair to the top floor.

The top floor itself was in near perfect condition, easily traversable on a good section of it, but about halfway through he saw the entry point, a crack in the asphalt where the rescuers had gone. According to the police, this area was closest to the little college bar and where most of the survivors likely were located.

His head hurt as he reached the opening, where a couple

of men were working with axes and chainsaws to break through the debris. After pushing his hard hat down on his head and affixing his safety mask and glasses, he ensured Storm's safety gear was secured as well.

With a "Let's get to work," he and the Shepherd climbed down into the hole.

The man with the chainsaw stopped his work so they could pass. He gave a double take. "Hey. You're Linc Coulter, right?"

Linc looked at the guy. He was a Spartanburg firefighter but didn't appear familiar to him. "Yeah."

He shook Linc's hand. "Seth Gruver. I was at that conference where you were the speaker. It's an honor to be working beside you."

"Honor's all mine. Nice to meet you."

Storm, eager as ever, attacked the challenge with her usual excitement. Her willingness to embrace this task spurred Linc on. If after all the shit she'd been through, she could do it, then so could he. He went forward with her, over the piles, letting her guide him. It was a cloudless day, making sighting easier, and temperatures rose as they carefully navigated deeper into the hole.

And Storm continued to search.

Sweat coursed into Linc's eyes and trickled down his torso. That wasn't like him. Usually, he was calm during these things. He'd been through enough stressful situations, that was for sure.

He didn't know what it was. He, like Storm, lived for this. But the deeper he got into the collapsed building, the more his pulse began to pound in his temples. The more he felt like the walls were closing in on him, getting ready to collapse around him. And then he heard the words:

You're no hero. You killed them all. You know it should be you.

Linc's heart skipped several beats, echoing in his ears, and the world tilted to the left. He reached for the crumbling wall of stone to brace himself, thinking the building had shifted under his feet.

He jumped as someone shouted. It was Seth, calling him over. "Hey, Linc. What about here?"

Linc turned back. There was a door buried under the rubble. He hadn't seen it. Shit. He was thorough. He usually never missed opportunities like that.

Seth was using bolt cutters to cut through a lock. He ripped off the chain, and Linc climbed over the chunks of giant concrete bigger than he was to get back to him. Working together, they managed to lift the door up a bit.

They both stared down into a gaping, dark hole.

"Anyone down there?" Seth called, shining a flashlight in the empty space. He let out a growl. "I don't see shit."

Linc guided Storm over to scent it, but she merely sniffed without interest and circled around to continue forward. He shook his head at Seth.

"Dammit. Been at this more than twelve hours and haven't found shit," Seth said, tilting his helmet back and reaching into his pack for some water. His face was covered in dust, and for a second, Linc saw Austin's blue eyes.

Linc blinked and looked away, and only noticed Seth was offering his bottle of water to him when he shook the bottle and said, "You okay, man?"

Fuck. Could people tell?

Yeah, they could. Linc felt it. Felt like his inferiority was oozing off him in waves, hitting everyone it came across. He not only looked batshit...he was batshit. He was the person people avoided.

"Fine." Linc took the water from Seth and downed a few thirsty gulps. Not that it helped at all. He shoved it back into the firefighter's hands and gritted out, "Let's keep going."

They pressed on, over entire cars that had been flattened

into complete pancakes. Storm sniffed around them but didn't alert.

"There's got to be someone here," Seth said, shaking his head. "That bar's always packed, and it was last call, so all the people were spilling out into the street and going to their cars."

They stopped every few seconds to listen for any noises. But there was nothing. When there was work like this to do, Linc tried not to think of the victims. Too much of that got in the way of making reasonable decisions and interfered with judgement. That was one of the main things he taught in his seminars.

But as he walked, he thought of these unwitting young people lying in a tomb of concrete. They'd gone out for a night of fun and had ended up here. Dead, or dying.

You killed them all. You know it should be you.

Linc sagged against a wall.

Seth came up to him. "Hell, man. You came down here in the middle of the night and probably haven't eaten all day, huh?" he said, the corner of his mouth quirking into a smile. He was young, probably just over drinking age. "You want to go back up and have a donut? We usually have more hospitality than we do. But this has rattled us. Things like this don't happen here."

That was the problem. Bad things happened everywhere. You couldn't escape them.

"I'm good." Whatever was ailing him, a donut sure as hell wouldn't cure it.

They pressed on, and meanwhile, Seth told Linc in whispers a little about how he'd been in the fire department since he was sixteen. His father was captain. He said he felt like he was born to do this, to save lives. Then he went on to say that Linc'd been an inspiration to him. That he had a few dogs of his own and had always thought about going into SAR work.

He asked Linc if he would give him some more pointers about the job.

Linc was glad Seth was doing all the talking, because he could barely breathe. But the kid clearly looked up to him, and he felt like he was the shittiest role model a person could've picked. Every so often, Seth paused to listen for sounds. He was respectful to a fault, and Linc could tell he thought he was in the presence of greatness.

Linc hated to disappoint him, but he wasn't great. Maybe once, but that'd ended long ago.

Suddenly, Storm's ears perked up, and she ran to the end of the pathway, stopping at a wall of rubble. She barked, then ran back to Linc, lifting her front feet to bump him in the chest.

She'd found something.

They pushed forward, over to where Storm'd returned, looking back at them with a clear "come on, idiots" on her face. Their two legs took more work to get them there, but when they made it, he gave Storm a treat and her toy, although she had little room to fully enjoy it.

"Good girl," he said, rubbing her head. No matter how tired he was, no matter how messed up he was, he had to make sure Storm knew she'd done a good job.

And she had.

It took a while to cut their way through the rubble. As they did, they slowly unearthed what used to be a small, silver sports car, mangled so badly Linc couldn't tell which part of it he was looking at.

"There's one here," Seth said, but Linc had already seen her.

He'd seen the pretty blonde hair first, splayed out of the flattened car window. The glass had been shattered, as had the woman's skull. There was brain matter everywhere, but her eyes were closed, peaceful, as if in sleep. An arm, graceful and slender, with equally slender fingers dangled out. She wore a silver bangle bracelet with charms all over it. Blood trailed down her hand like a snake.

His heart drummed in his chest. Breathing became impossible.

Linc flattened himself against a wall and closed his eyes as Seth radioed in the find. Beside him, Storm nuzzled his hand, clearly worried.

He needed to move. He needed to check the rest of the crushed car. He needed to start the process of clearing the rubble, cutting away the barrier so the body of this young woman could be freed.

He couldn't move.

"Hey, Mr. Coulter, sir," Seth said, but his vision was bending, and the words sounded like they were being spoken underwater.

Linc sunk to a crouch, only partly aware that he was shaking. His heart was squeezing in his chest, the pain radiating out to his fingers and toes. Storm's warm tongue licked at his nose, trying to comfort him, but he was powerless to move, to stroke her. All he could do was shake.

And then he leaned over, his head against the concrete, and vomited the nothing inside his stomach.

22

After Kylie's run-in with the peppy little vet assistant, she decided to take it a little easier on Linc. Yes, he may have been MIA, but he'd had a good reason, and a stressful job. It couldn't have been very easy doing what he did. No matter how many times he said otherwise, and no matter how many times he neglected to call her, one thing would always be true. In her book, he *was* a hero.

So, Kylie decided to do what Jacob had advised her and give Linc the space he needed. It made sense. Besides, she had other things on her mind. The Jennings case was more perplexing than ever. She'd gone down the list of all the potential interviewees and come up with a big zilch. No one seemed to know where any of those paintings were.

Well, she'd interviewed everyone...except one person.

She needed to put on her big girl panties and do what needed to be done.

The problem was, when she imagined going head-to-head with Jonathan Coulter, it always dissolved into an all-out screaming match.

Ugh.

So, she decided on a little workaround, putting off Jonathan Coulter for the moment.

First, she'd see what his wife knew.

It was the most logical thing to do, anyway. Women always knew more than their husbands. Linda Coulter was a smart woman, and she very well might be able to shed some light on her husband's activities. Late afternoon, when Kylie knew he'd be at work, was perfect timing. At the dinner the other night, all the men had boasted how they were never home until seven o'clock, at the earliest, and always worked on Saturdays. Always.

She really hoped they hadn't been lying.

Dressed in her nicest sweater and slacks combo, complete with heels and what she hoped was tasteful jewelry, Kylie stopped by the flower shop at the end of the street to get a bouquet of lilies. Then, she made the drive to Biltmore Forest with Vader in tow. She had one thing on her mind: to get a better look at that painting in the dining room of the Coulter house.

The place looked bigger and even more spectacular in the daylight. They must've had not just a gardener, but a team of gardeners manicuring the perfect lawn and landscaping. The house was so sparkling white in the sunlight, it almost hurt to look at it.

She parked in the long driveway, feeling a bit like an intruder. She didn't even have to ask. They were most definitely anti-dog. "Look," Kylie said to Vader, pulling her key out of the ignition, "be goo…" She gasped. "What are you doing?"

The big dog tilted his head at her, the lily between his teeth twitching at the movement.

"Vader…" She used her most alpha tone as she pointed a finger at him. "Bad dog. Bad."

Vader looked perilously close to bursting into tears as he

gently placed the flower on her lap.

Aww…now she felt like a rat.

She petted his head. "It's okay. I just hope lilies aren't poisonous to dogs."

She pulled out the destroyed stems and arranged the flowers a bit, and voila. Not as impressive as before, but not terrible. She wagged a finger at Vader. "Stay. No chewing. On…anything. Got it?"

He really didn't get it. As usual. Unless Linc was around, he generally did as he pleased because she was still trying to get up the heart to assert her alpha self.

Kylie climbed the stairs to the beautiful Coulter home, still trying to imagine a young Linc playing and growing up there, and rang the doorbell.

Their butler answered. "May I help you?"

"Hi," she said brightly. Mason's expression was like a blank mask, but she didn't let that stop her. "I'd like to visit Mrs. Coulter, please."

He lifted an eyebrow. "And you are?"

Did he really not remember her?

"Kylie Hatfield. I was here with Linc for dinner a few nights ago."

The eyebrow hadn't moved. She swore it said, *If you say so.*

"Anyway," she babbled on. "I have flowers as a thank you for a lovely dinner. Is Mrs. Coulter available?"

He opened the door wider and stepped aside. "Right this way, miss."

Kylie followed him inside and found herself once again ogling all the expensive-looking things hanging on walls and sitting on little ornate tables. In her lifetime, she didn't think she'd make enough money to buy even one of the vases gleaming beneath its individually placed spotlight.

When they passed the dining room, Kylie briefly

wondered where they were going, but paused long enough to catch another look at the googly eyed painting.

She shivered. Why did anyone want the thing staring at them while they were eating?

"Miss?"

Kylie snapped back to attention, realizing that Mason was waiting for her at the end of the hall.

"Where are we going?"

He totally ignored the question, just continued walking. Kylie shrugged, hoping he wasn't leading her to some dungeon where all the other peasants were taken.

Trying to orient herself, she realized they were at the very back of the house. Was this his idea of a joke, showing her out of the servants' entrance?

Then she spotted Mrs. Coulter, lounging under an umbrella in tennis whites, a racket by her side. She tilted her visor up when she saw Kylie. "Oh…?"

Oh, god. Linc's mother didn't recognize her either.

"Hi," Kylie said. "Mrs. Coulter. I'm—"

"Kylie," she finished, to Kylie's relief. "So nice to see you. What brings you here so unexpectedly?"

The rich really did know how to offer a rebuke with style.

Kylie walked out into a veritable wonderland of a fairy garden. The Coulter's backyard was a masterpiece, complete with trellises, gazebos, and a long, rectangular pool full of dark water that didn't look suitable for swimming in.

"Oh, this is lovely, Mrs. Coulter," she said, looking around, then motioned to the lame flowers in her hands. "Just wanted to thank you for dinner the other evening."

Mrs. Coulter motioned to the chair across from her. The wrought-iron chair scraped against the stones as Kylie pulled it out and sat. "Please, call me Linda. You're very thoughtful, Kylie," she said and glanced at the butler, who still hovered at the door. "Mason, please put those in water and bring Kylie a beverage."

He looked at Kylie. "Yes, madam. What would you like?"

She was tempted to ask for a glass of wine, extra large, but settled on ice water instead. He nodded and retreated back into the house.

Kylie smiled at the older woman. "You play tennis?"

She could have slapped herself for the obvious question, but instead of offering a sarcastic comment in return, Linda Coulter simply smiled. "I usually play with my sons' wives. You just missed Addison, I'm afraid. Do you play as well?"

"No, I'm afraid not." Just another reason why she'd never fit into Linc's family. She didn't even know how to hold a racket correctly, as her high school gym teacher had reminded her each year.

Linda's smile didn't waver. "We all play. Well, except Lincoln. He's always been the oddball. He hates tennis. Most of the time, he just liked getting his hands dirty."

Kylie was about to jump to Linc's defense, but Linda hadn't said the words with any contempt. She clearly loved her son, even if she didn't understand him and his ways.

"I must say," Linda went on, "it was such a shock to everyone but me when he decided not to go into law. I could tell it was making him miserable, but my husband took it for granted that that was what he'd do. You have to admire a person who follows his calling, especially against such strong opposition."

Kylie smiled. It was good to know Linc had at least one ally in his family. "Did they fight him on it every step of the way?"

"Oh, yes, every step. I fought him, too, but for a different reason. No mother wants to see their child put in danger. I'd hoped that if he was going to do something else, it wouldn't have been something dangerous. But that isn't Lincoln. He has his own mind and has always taken his own path in life. And he should. He should follow what brings him joy."

At that moment, Kylie missed him so much she nearly shook. It wasn't right for her to feel that way, since he obviously hadn't missed her, so she cursed herself and got down to the business of why she was there.

"I wanted to tell you that I was sorry if I said anything at dinner that offended you. Sometimes, I just don't know when to shut up."

Linc's mom waved a manicured hand at her. "Nonsense. My husband needs to be put in his place every now and again. And you were right. Plus, I think Lincoln needs a woman who speaks up for him because he usually just sits there and takes everything his father shells out."

Kylie leaned forward. "Why do you suppose Linc does that? Takes it, I mean."

Linda seemed to consider the question. "Well, he was always a quiet child, happiest when playing alone." She smiled wistfully. "We would tell him what to do, and he'd never argue about it. Instead, he'd just do whatever he wanted anyway. A man of action instead of words. Always has been."

Kylie smiled, thinking of a headstrong little Linc, but she also wondered how much of being in the military had hampered his ability to speak up for himself as well. After joining the military, soldiers learned very quickly not to argue with authority. From what Kylie understood, they basically did as they were told, no thinking about it. After so many years living in those conditions, when did a soldier simply stop arguing?

"Plus," Linda went on, "you really can't win an argument with my husband. He's in the business of arguing, after all." She met Kylie's gaze. "It worries me for Lincoln. When a person bottles things up for so long, there has to be a breaking point. That's what I worry about with him. He became even more reserved when he left the military. Now, he's so quiet, you'd never know if he was in trouble."

Kylie stared out into the garden. She worried about that too. "Have you spoken to him since then?"

"No. Where my other sons call me almost daily, with Lincoln, I'm lucky if I hear from him once a month. Usually, I have to hunt him down."

Kylie barely stopped herself from snorting. *Well, that makes two of us.*

A cloud covered the sun and Linda shivered. "My, it's definitely getting chillier," she said, scooting off her chair. "Let's go inside. Would you like to stay for tea? Dinner won't be ready for another couple hours. Jonathan works so late, I normally prefer to dine with him. Of course, you're welcome to stay for dinner as well."

As repulsed as she was by the idea, Kylie gave it some consideration. Dinner meant dining room. With one particular piece of artwork staring down from the wall. Was tea served there too? Her stomach rumbled at the thought. Though they weren't in Europe, Kylie hoped there'd be some little sandwiches and biscuits to snack on. But looking at the pencil-thin woman, she seriously doubted it.

"That'd be lovely. I might do that."

They went inside and through to another parlor-looking room, and though she was kind of turned around, Kylie spotted the flowered wallpaper in an adjoining room that looked familiar…her heart leapt. Was that the dining room?

She kept sneaking furtive looks. Meanwhile, Linc's mother went on about how the décor wasn't exactly what she liked, asking Kylie what she thought of seafoam green for the palette. Kylie had no clue.

Her apartment's walls were as naked as a baby's backside, mostly because it was an apartment and she wasn't allowed to mess with the walls too much, but also because she wasn't sure she had much of a domestic touch. Linc had more of one than she did. Or maybe not. His farmhouse did closely resemble Auntie Em's home on *The Wizard of Oz*.

Mrs. Coulter frowned at Kylie's lilies on the coffee table, looking pretty in an ornate vase. "Not the crystal," she tutted. "Never the Waterford for lilies. It must be the Tiffany vase. I have no idea what Mason was thinking." She lifted the vase, shaking her head like it was a sin against humanity. "Go ahead and sit, Kylie. I'll be right back. I'll have Mason set the table in the sunroom for two."

The table in the *sunroom*? Crap.

Kylie beamed at the woman. "That sounds lovely."

As Linda Coulter carried the offending vase down the hallway, Kylie's gaze drifted around the room. There was a spindly little coffee table and a high-backed Victorian sofa, and what appeared to be antique paintings of people who apparently thought smiling was a sin.

Turning away from the creepy faces, Kylie's eyes drifted to the other room. That *was* the dining room. From her current position, she could see the corner of that massive table.

Before she could second-guess herself, Kylie crept into the room. The dining table was clear of place settings now, and sun streamed in, bouncing off the rich walnut surfaces. The painting in question was on the wall next to it, in a small alcove, surrounded by other artwork. She leaned forward, studying the details more closely. One of Arnold Jennings's trademarks was how he enjoyed hiding his signature within the scene.

Where was it?

Feeling rushed, Kylie grabbed her phone, figuring she'd snap a picture to examine more closely later. She focused and pressed her finger.

"Miss?"

She whirled to find Mason standing in the doorway, her water on an elegant silver tray. "I love art!" Kylie blurted, pocketing her phone. "I was an art history minor, actually. When did you get this painting? It's so…unusual."

The old butler narrowed his eyes. Maybe he thought she was sizing things up to steal. Moments passed before he said, "Just recently, miss. Mr. Coulter has an eye for art. Local artist, I believe."

She believed that too.

Kylie followed him back to the other room and took a seat on the uncomfortable little sofa. Holding her pinky out, she sipped at her drink as Mason's shoes clapped a rhythm back down the hall.

When the footfalls were gone, she fished her phone from her purse. It was a bit blurry, but the photo would do. Was that one of the missing paintings? And how had Jonathan Coulter come by it?

More and more, it was looking like she'd have to ask him.

Talk about intimidating.

Or…maybe Linda knew. Maybe Kylie could just ask her.

Yes, that was the plan.

Linda Coulter came back with the lilies in a vase that looked no different to Kylie than the other one. She set it on the table and smiled. "Now, that's better."

"You have such an eye for detail," Kylie said. "Could you tell me a bit more where you find such lovely paintings?"

For the next twenty minutes, Kylie was in artistic hell as Linda Coulter walked her from one piece to the next, talking about its meaning and where she or Mr. Coulter picked it up.

Kylie steered her toward the dining room. "What about in here?"

Another few minutes of artistic hell ensued before they reached the one in the alcove. Kylie perked up.

"This is an original. I don't know where my husband got it."

She moved past the target painting, but Kylie laid a gentle hand on her arm. "Who is the artist?"

Linda tapped her chin with her index finger. "I believe the artist is one of his clients. I could ask and put you in touch with him, if you'd—"

Kylie felt a moment of panic. "Oh, no. That's okay. I was just curious." She tried desperately for something nice to say. "I just love those nature scenes."

Linda smiled, and the expression was almost maternal. "No wonder you and Lincoln get along. That boy would probably rather live in a cave than a house. He used to sleep in a tent out back all summer long, rather than spend time in his bedroom. How did you wind up meeting him, again? You said he's your dog trainer?"

Kylie didn't bother explaining that she wasn't a fan of *real* nature. "I met him in front of the veterinarian. I'd just found a giant Newfoundland mix on the side of the road who'd been hit by a car and was trying to bring him in to be checked out."

Linda laughed a little. "Well, that sounds just like Lincoln. Would you believe we never let him have pets of any kind? I don't like them myself, but Lincoln started volunteering at the animal shelter when he was a boy. He'd go missing for long chunks of time and I'd never have to worry he was doing drugs or hanging out with the wrong crowd. He was always at the shelter."

Kylie tried to imagine Linc as an awkward teenage boy. She couldn't. "You wouldn't happen to have pictures?"

The older woman giggled, the first really joyous sound Kylie'd heard her make. *"Do I?"* She hurried from the room and returned a moment later with about ten professionally bound albums. "Where do you want to start?"

Kylie stared, excited. He'd seen her worst photos. She thought it only fair that she look at a few of his. She lifted up the first one, opening it to a picture of Linc, sitting alone in front of a Christmas tree. He was probably about ten. He was blond, all skin and bones, wearing flannel pajamas, but other than that…not weird looking in the least. He was cute.

Kylie flipped a few more pages. There were pictures of him with his family at weddings, in front of a giant European castle, posed with his brothers in front of the house…but not in one, not in a single picture, did he look like a gangly dork with growing pains.

"Did he ever have an awkward phase?"

His mom tapped her chin. "Not Linc. He managed pretty well. He was always comfortable in his own skin," she said as Kylie flipped through some pictures of him in his football uniform. He looked tanned, handsome, just a skinnier version of himself now, like the type of guy who would have a zillion friends and be elected Student Council President, Prom King, and everything…but there was no photo of him at prom. "Didn't he go to prom?"

"Oh, no," Mrs. Coulter said. "He didn't even talk to girls in high school."

Kylie smiled at that as she flipped another page. "I get it. He barely talks to them now."

Linda rubbed a smudge off one of the pages with her thumb. "True. He had a serious girlfriend in college, but they broke up when he went into the service."

Kylie's phone buzzed in her pocket, making her jump. She was about to reach for it but realized how rude that would be. As tempted as she was to peek anyway, she ignored it and kept flipping through the photo album pages.

Just as her phone started buzzing again, Mason appeared at the doorway and cleared his throat.

Linda glanced up. "Yes?"

The butler looked a bit distressed. "Apologies for the interruption, ma'am, but you have what I'm told is an urgent call."

Startled, Linda Coulter flashed a worried look at Kylie. "Excuse me, dear."

Kylie's own phone buzzed again. Since she was now alone, she pulled it from her pocket.

Nate Jennings.

She rushed to hit the answer button. "Hello."

"Hi, is this Kylie? It's Nate Jennings. Emma's grandson."

He sounded rushed, and Kylie frowned at the empty doorway through which Mrs. Coulter had disappeared. Was there a connection?

"Hello, Mr. Jennings. How are—"

"I have something to tell you." He sounded even more agitated now.

Kylie held her breath. "Go on."

"I was thinking a little about the painting you were interested in, and it suddenly occurred to me to check it out. A good friend of mine is an art dealer, so he dropped over after work, and well…"

He paused for so long that Kylie thought she'd explode. "Well, what?"

Nate sighed. "Do you think we can meet?"

Oh, sure, keep her hanging. "Yes, of course. When?"

"Tomorrow night, after I get off work. Can we meet at the Perky Coffee Shop downtown?"

She held in a sigh of disappointment. "What about tonight? I can meet you anytime, anywhere."

He paused. "I have…plans. It would be late. Like ten tonight."

Her heart sped up. That felt like forever. She wanted to ask him to spill it now, because Kylie'd seen enough mysteries to know that the guy who called the detective with "important information" usually ended up murdered or thwacked on the head before he could impart the damning information.

Thank goodness this wasn't a murder case.

But she was standing in the living room belonging to the man who might be one of her prime suspects, so…

"Yes. I can be there at ten."

"Great. See you then."

What in the world could he be talking about?

Wracking her brain at the mystery, Kylie tucked the phone back into her pocket and nearly jumped out of her skin when she turned to see Mrs. Coulter behind her. She'd floated into the room without a sound.

"Oh, you scared me. I—"

Kylie hushed, taking in the woman's now fragile appearance. Linda Coulter's face was paler than her tennis whites.

"What's wrong?"

Linda pressed her fingers to her trembling lips, her eyes brimming with tears. Adrenaline spiked in Kylie's system as she waited for a reply.

"That was the Spartanburg Hospital. Linc was admitted there a little bit ago."

Kylie forgot how to breathe. "What happened?" she asked on a gulp of air.

"He apparently was there for a search and rescue operation, and—"

Kylie immediately thought of the worse.

"Did the building collapse on him? Did they say how bad he is? Is he alive?"

Linda took Kylie's hand in her own. "He's alive, yes, and I don't know any more than I just told you. They're doing tests." She looked at the cell in her other hand. "I'm going to call, see if he'll answer."

Kylie nodded as Linc's mother tapped at her screen.

Please be okay. Please be okay. Please be okay.

Linda Coulter's eyes closed, and she let out a long breath just as Kylie heard a tinny voice say something on the other line.

"Lincoln? Oh, thank goodness."

Kylie's knees felt like they were going to give out, but Linc's mother looked to be in worse shape. Putting her arm around the older woman, Kylie led her to the overly embroidered sofa.

"Fine?" Linda said, her voice stronger. "Don't give me that *fine* business. You're in the hospital, and I want to know why."

Tears welled in Linda's eyes, then spilled down her cheeks. Kylie tried her very best to understand what Linc was saying. Tried her very best not to yank the phone from his mother's hand. Learn what was making her so very upset.

"I'm coming down there, Lincoln. I—"

She glanced at Kylie, shaking her head.

"But Lincoln, I can't just let—" She worried her lower lip as she listened. Taking a deep breath, she finally said, "Fine, honey. If that's what you want. I love," she closed her eyes again, and Kylie saw the screen go black, "you." Lowering the phone to her lap, she stared at it for a few moments. "He was always the most stubborn of my sons."

"What did he say?" Kylie prodded, desperate for information.

"He said that he was fine and then he made me promise not to go down there."

Kylie wanted to throttle the woman. "Did he say what happened exactly?"

"No." Linda frowned. "They're running a scan or something on his heart."

Heart?

Kylie was sure either she'd heard the woman wrong, or the woman had heard her son wrong.

She swallowed. "His…heart? But he's so healthy. He doesn't have a heart condition, does he?" But even as she said it, she realized they'd never really talked about stuff like that.

"He was having chest pains," Mrs. Coulter explained, then stood to pace back and forth. She threw up her hands. "He really is the most stubborn person. Says he's fine and not to worry about him. Like I could ever not!"

Kylie pulled out her cell phone. "Well, you may have promised not to go down there, but *I* never promised the same," she said to her, holding her phone at the ready. "Give me your number. I'll call you when I see him."

Linda's eyes brightened. "You will?"

Kylie nodded and took down her number. "Of course. Spartanburg Hospital, here I come. I'll have to take a raincheck on tea." She patted Linc's mom's fragile, bony shoulder. "And please don't worry, Mrs. Coulter. Linda. It'll be fine. I'll keep him in line."

"I'm sure you will," she said, wiping at her cheeks.

Kylie went outside to find Vader asleep in the back seat of her car. He was comfy on a pile of laundry she'd been meaning to take to the dry cleaners. At least he wasn't chewing on anything. She decided to let him sleep as she pulled out of the driveway and headed south.

23

This was for shit.

The damn hospital was filled with people who'd been near the collapse, or in the collapse, or had breathed the dust from the collapse. The medical staff was running around like mad.

The last thing they needed was to have to cater to some asshole with a few chest pains. "I'm fine, really," Linc said to the nurse when she came in to check on him for the tenth time. "Don't worry about me."

"That's our job," she said brightly, checking his vitals. "The doctor will be in to see you in a moment."

Linc scrubbed his hands over his face. He'd been poked and prodded for going on two hours now. It was all he could do not to rip out the IV and these monitors and leave. He'd come close a few times.

He needed to get back to the site.

He needed to pull his head out of his ass, find Storm, and get back to work.

But he knew he wouldn't be able to do that without an "all clear" from the doctor.

So, he was stuck.

And he was embarrassed. He hadn't been having a heart attack, he knew.

Sure, at first, when he'd been looking at the mangled corpse of that woman, he felt as if he might be dying. Visions of the mangled bodies in Syria kept swirling through his head, the dusty ground, black with blood, those little soccer playing kids blown to pieces.

But the second he was in the ambulance, speeding toward the hospital, the pain in his chest had lessened. How damned embarrassing. Linc was sure Seth and the other guys *really* looked up to him now. He couldn't even hold his shit together for the first recovery.

A panic attack.

That's what it had to have been. His heart felt fine now. And he was in shape. It wasn't a heart attack, or any of the other serious things they were testing him for. It was just him, being in his damn head too much. A little air, a little space, that was all he needed. He was fine. That's what he kept telling everyone, including his mother.

He groaned, thinking of how worried she'd sounded.

Guilt piled on top of guilt. Did it ever stop?

Linc had no doubt she'd probably make the trip anyway. In fact, he expected her to come bursting through the door at any moment.

He needed to be gone before that happened. Not that he didn't love his mother. He just didn't love her hovering. Especially right then, when he should be helping instead of being a drain on an already overwhelmed health system.

Though, truthfully, his heart squeezed a little when he thought of going back to the site.

Truth be told, he just wanted to get home.

He closed his eyes, thinking of his farmhouse...his dogs...Kylie.

When he opened his eyes again, he thought he'd summoned her in his dreams. Because there she stood just inside the door, her fingers twisting in front of her.

"Hey," she said. She sounded so incredibly real. She stepped closer, and her scent hit him even before her fingers curled around his hand.

So warm. So real.

It took several more moments to realize Kylie really was in the room. His heartrate spiked, and the monitor beside him began to alarm, giving him away.

"Why are you here?"

He hadn't meant for the words to come out so gruff, but he could tell by her expression that he'd sounded like his usual asshole self.

But he didn't want her to see him this way. How much more was his ego supposed to take?

"I was worried," she said, her eyes weighted with concern. "Are you okay?"

Linc sat up straighter in the bed. "How did you know I was here?"

"Your mother. I was at your house when the hospital called."

"You were…what?" He closed his eyes, trying to get it through his head. She certainly hadn't gone back because she'd felt so welcomed the first time. That had been a disaster. "Why?"

"It's not important." She sat on the edge of his bed, and her nearness made his pulse thrum even harder, his monitors beeping in response. She looked at the display, alarmed, then patted the sheet covering his abdomen. "What's important is that you get better."

"I'm better. I'm fine. It was just…" He didn't want to talk about it. And he didn't want her seeing him in this stupid hospital gown. "Nothing. Really."

"Well, it must be something if you're here. What happened?"

Linc frowned and exhaled slowly. She didn't know when to give up.

She must have sensed his unease because she smiled, walked her fingers up the crisp white sheet to his arm. She gave him a sexy wink. "Want me to play doctor?"

The question startled a smile from him.

Maybe that would be fun, if they were anywhere but there. He'd love to take her on his lap, and he was sure she could fix what ailed him. Before he could make a mistake and pull her closer to him, the doctor burst in.

"Good news, Mr. Coulter. Your blood work and EKG are all normal, and there are no signs of any other distress. After learning about the situation that was occurring just prior to your admission, I feel safe in saying that you experienced a panic attack."

Linc gave Kylie a sideways glance, then glared at the doctor. Wasn't this a HIPPA violation or something?

The harried doctor didn't even notice his unease, just studied Linc's records closer. "You've been in search and rescue for some time, though. You ever had one before?"

"No," Linc grumbled. "And I won't have one again. Like I said, I'm fine. Didn't get much sleep last night. Didn't eat. I know you have other patients to deal with. Can I go?"

The doctor gave Linc a stern look. "In a moment. I'm having the nurses finish up your discharge paperwork now, but it says you're a veteran. I want to make sure that you're fully aware there are resources for dealing with any stress you might be experiencing."

Kylie straightened beside him, but Linc just wanted the doctor gone.

"I know of them, thanks," he said dismissively, pulling at the edges of the tape holding the IV in his arm. He was itching to get out, like worms were crawling all over his body.

The doctor looked ready to dig in his heels, but a nurse opened the door, telling him he was needed in the next room, "Stat."

Linc exhaled a breath of relief at the reprieve and instantly felt like an ass for doing so. The person next door was in bad shape, probably fighting for his or her life, and Linc and his fucking panic attacks were taking up much needed space.

Kylie blinked at Linc curiously and slapped his hand away when he started pulling at the tape again. "Talk to me, Linc."

He looked her dead in the eye. "Blah, blah, blah, blah, blah. The end."

For a second, he thought she might seriously punch him in the face, then the corners of her mouth quirked into a smile. "Ha ha, you're hilarious."

He started pulling the tape again, and Kylie looked ready to tackle him when a nurse came in and started doing it herself. As she pulled the needle out, he felt a little bit freer.

After what felt like an hour, he'd signed the millions of pages of paperwork and retrieved his clothes so that he could get out of the damn gown after the nurse pulled every hair out of his body removing the electrodes that were evidence to what a pussy he was.

"Where's Storm?" Kylie asked.

"With one of my SAR buddies."

"Can I drive you home?"

Linc shook his head. "My truck's down here. I'll drive myself."

"You should have your buddies bring it up later. You shouldn't drive yourself."

He raised an eyebrow. Shouldn't drive himself, really? What was he, an invalid?

"I can drive myself just fine," he said through gritted teeth.

The second his boots were back on, he strode to the door, but Kylie stopped him, one hand on his chest, the other holding his discharge papers.

"Ah-ha!" Kylie said triumphantly. "I told you that you shouldn't drive yourself."

"What?"

She pointed at the discharge paper. Sure enough, number twelve on the list said he should be careful when operating heavy machinery since they'd given him a sedative when he arrived.

"I feel fine. But whatever." Truth be told, Linc was a little relieved. "We have to get Storm, though. I'll have some of the SAR guys drive my truck up tomorrow."

Kylie smiled, looking relieved herself. "I'll drive you to Storm." She pulled her phone from her pocket and began texting.

"What are you doing?"

"I…" she held up the phone for him to see, practically waving it in his face, "am communicating, namely with your mother."

He groaned. "My mother. How—"

"Don't worry, I'm relieving her mind, letting her know that you're really okay so she doesn't have to worry herself sick like you were most likely going to let her do."

Linc grunted. She wasn't entirely wrong.

It wasn't that he wanted to hurt his mother. It was more that he didn't know what to say or how to respond when she mothered him so intensely.

Linc threw on his jacket, checked around the room to make sure he wasn't leaving anything behind, and stepped into the hall, ripping the plastic identification bracelet off his wrist. A number of emergency personnel began running toward the doors, and he wondered if it was another victim of the collapse that he hadn't been able to save.

His heart squeezed in his chest for a split-second. He took a calming breath, but the feeling only drained away a little.

Vader was waiting in her car. His tail wagged happily, and he barked as Linc approached. Linc calmed him down and nudged him into the back seat.

When Kylie slid in and closed the door, she fixed him with a stare. "So, let's get this over with. You're not happy to see me."

Linc stared straight ahead. "I *am* happy to see you." His voice was low, controlled.

"But?"

"But I don't know if it's *good* that I see you." He shook his head. "I've got a lot on my mind."

"Is that what caused the panic attack?"

"It wasn't a panic attack."

"But the doc—"

"I don't care what the doctor said," he growled. "It wasn't. I'm fine. It was too little sleep and not enough food and water. Plus, I just need people to leave me alone."

Her voice was so soft. "Me?"

"Yeah."

"Because you don't want to hurt me again."

He nodded slowly, not meeting her eyes. "Right. I don't want to hurt you again."

"I missed you, Linc." Her voice sounded softer, fragile. "What if I'd *rather* be hurt than not be with you?"

Linc almost laughed. "No. That won't work."

She didn't respond. He ventured a look at her. She *looked* fragile too.

"Come here," he said, sliding a hand around the nape of her neck, pulling her across the console and meeting her halfway. He felt her trembling as he brought her to him, forehead to forehead, nose to nose. He inhaled her scent, wanting to dive into it. "I missed you too."

Linc kissed her lightly, and she sighed. "Don't shut me out, Linc. If you don't want me to stay the night with you, I don't have to. But I want to be in your life."

"All right."

She drove him to his friend's house, where they picked up Storm, and then with the two dogs in tow, they headed back home. Linc held her hand the whole way up. It was the best apology he knew how to offer, and probably the most inadequate thank you he could give.

24

With each mile they got closer to home, Linc seemed to relax a little. To her immense relief, he actually smiled once. Almost twice, but the movement faded before it could actually curve his lips.

"I'm curious. How did you happen to be at my parents' house?"

Kylie shrugged, her fingers tight around the steering wheel. "I brought your mom some flowers to thank her for dinner. I thought it was only right."

He snorted. "And, you were also apologizing for what you said to my father, huh? Admit it."

With an embarrassed grin, she nodded. It was actually nice to hide behind the fib. It was far better than telling him the real reason she'd gone over there. Kylie wasn't sure she wanted to tell him, ever, that she suspected his dad of theft and embezzlement. She might have to, eventually, but he'd had a hard enough day as it was.

"You don't have to, Lee," he said, and she glanced over at him, smiling at the use of the nickname. She'd never had a nickname before. She kind of liked it. "You have nothing to feel bad about. He deserved it."

She slowed for a sharp curve. "Your mom said the same. I like her."

"Yeah. Well. I like her too. I actually love her, even though she can be more than a little overbearing." He scrubbed his hands down his face. "My father, on the other hand…"

He didn't need to finish because she understood. Well, kind of.

"Well, my dad was a douche too. So, I feel you. It's a sad thing when you get more fatherly advice from your boss than you ever did from your dad."

"Yeah? Speaking of bosses, how is your new case going?"

Kylie nearly bit her tongue. "Slow. Unearthing details bit by bit. It's dull, but not as dull as sitting behind a desk all day. So, it's fine. Which reminds me. I owe you for some lessons, and Vader hasn't had a good one in a while. He pretty much ate my thank-you gift to your mom before I could give it to her."

"Oh, yeah?" He turned around in the seat and gave Vader a stern look. "What did I teach you, boy?"

Vader immediately gave him a "rar-ee" whimper. It made Kylie smile.

"I actually came up to pay earlier today, but a girl from the vet was there and told me you'd left for Spartanburg."

He raised an eyebrow. "Caryn?"

"Is that her name? I don't know…blonde. Gorgeous. Very earthy." Kylie glanced over, trying to gauge his expression. She waited for a lovesick look to appear on his face.

But his mouth was twisted in amusement. "Are you jealous?"

She blew out a breath so hard her lips fluttered. "No. Not me. Of course not."

"Caryn's a friend. Just a friend. The vet's office takes care of the animals when I'm out of town. Well, them or Jacob."

"Hmm."

"What? You don't believe me?"

She narrowed her eyes but didn't say anything, unsure if it was worse to be jealous or not care at all.

She was still pondering on that thought when she pulled into his driveway. As soon as she turned off the car, she hopped out of the door, shouting, "Stay there," to Link.

He was giving her a confused look as she opened the door for him. Then she reached in to help him out. "Come on, old man," she said. "Up you go."

"Old man?" Without warning, he wrapped an arm around her waist and pulled her onto his lap. She shrieked as he started to tickle her. "Take that back."

"Okay. Ancient man?" Kylie suggested, and he tickled her harder. When she winced, he stopped immediately, turning serious.

"Sorry, I forgot about your shoulder."

"It's okay. I forget about it all the time. One minute it feels completely healed, then the next it reminds me that it still has a little ways to go."

Which pissed her off because the twinge of pain had wiped all the amusement from his face.

The sour Linc was back.

But he seemed steady on his feet as he got out of the car and walked up the steps to the porch.

She scurried inside and fluffed the pillows on the couch, lifting up one of the comfy afghans for him to snuggle underneath. He watched her with a look on his face that was borderline predatory. "What do you think you're doing?" he asked.

"I'm getting you all set up. You should rest here until you're ready for bed. Or did you want to go to bed now?"

He wrapped a hand around her wrist. "I don't want to rest."

A thrill raced through her, but the discharge papers said that he needed to rest.

Sex was not resting.

"You have to." She pointed to the crumpled square of pink discharge papers in his front pocket. "It says so. For your old ticker."

His lips twisted up in amusement. "My…old ticker?"

Kylie nodded, shaking the blanket a little to get him to climb under it. "I'll make you dinner. Please tell me you have canned soup."

He moved forward, spanning the distance between them, and at first, she thought he was going to sit down like she'd asked, but instead he reached for her hand and placed it on his chest. "Does this feel like an old ticker to you?"

Her own heart rate kicked up at how close to him she was. *No sex. No sex. No sex.* The two words played like a mantra in her head.

"Hmm," she said, very clinically and professionally. "I'd have to do some more research."

Okay, maybe a little sex. But just a little.

Kylie unbuttoned his waffle-knit Henley and reached inside, her fingers touching warm skin, his strong heart beating underneath. He peered down at her, as if waiting for her assessment.

"Maybe only semi-old," Kylie said.

"Semi?"

Before she could say anything in response, he was crushing her to him, his mouth on hers.

"God, you feel good," he growled into her mouth. "Show me how much you missed me."

"I don't know if I should," Kylie countered. "Are you just going to show Caryn?"

He snorted out a laugh. "Touché."

He went to kiss her again, but she pressed her hand to his chest. "We shouldn't be doing this. You're sick."

It was the exact wrong word to say.

"Sick? I'll show you sick."

Bending down, he hauled her up and over his shoulder, and began carrying her up the steps.

In the bedroom, he was like a man possessed, on a definite mission.

A mission to make sure no one—especially her—ever called him sick again.

"You're not sleeping with me," he said as she lay sated in his arms.

Kylie played with the hair on his chest. "You don't have to worry about me."

He didn't say anything in response, but she felt him stiffen. He did worry, she knew. He worried so much that he'd landed himself in the hospital.

"Was it terrible?" she asked.

It took him a moment to answer. "What?"

It was telling that he needed for her to clarify which terrible situation she was talking about. How many terrible situations had he faced?

Since meeting him at the vet that day, she knew of several...mostly because of her.

"The parking garage collapse," she clarified. She wanted to talk about them all, but they'd start there, she reasoned.

He was quiet for so long that she thought he might have fallen asleep. Then he sighed, a long exhalation of breath. "Yeah. It was bad."

Goose bumps raised on her arms and she tried not to

imagine what he'd seen. The news footage had been terrible from afar, the concrete sections of the parking garage collapsed onto each other.

As she'd been going through Emma Jennings's files that afternoon, the *Friends* re-runs she'd had playing in the background had been interrupted each time a new body had been discovered.

She sat bolt upright.

"Shit."

Linc sat up beside her. "What's wrong?"

She'd forgotten.

She'd made an appointment with Nate Jennings for a late-night meeting. There was something he'd had to tell her. Something monumentally important. Crap. Crap. Crap.

"I forgot a meeting." She sprang from the bed. "I've got to go!"

Linc picked up his phone. "It's nearly ten at night? You have a meeting this late?"

"Yes! I made an appointment to meet with someone about the embezzlement case tonight. He told me he had something important to tell me, but he couldn't get with me any earlier."

She stuffed her legs into her pants, wishing she had time to shower, but she was already going to be terribly late as it was.

Running into the bathroom, she washed her hands, ran a finger over her teeth, and splashed water on her face. Threading her fingers through her tangled hair, she curled it into a messy bun on the very top of her head.

Not very professional, but it would have to do. Besides, they were meeting at a coffee shop. How professional did she need to be?

Linc was holding her shoes out when she ran back into

the bedroom. She tucked them under her arm, not even taking the time to slip them on.

At the bottom of the stairs, she stopped in her tracks. Vader was curled up next to Storm, eyeing her with one open eye.

"Crap. Vader." She cursed some more. "Come on, boy. We need to go."

Vader just yawned and laid his head back down on top of Storm's chest.

"He can stay with me," Linc said from midway up the stairs. "Go and be careful. You're already late, so killing yourself on the mountain won't make a difference."

Kylie checked that she had her phone, grabbed her keys from the table, and sprinted for the door.

"Thank you," she called over her shoulder.

Kylie tried calling Nate as soon as she had her car running. No answer.

She tried calling him again once she was at the base of the mountain. Still, no answer.

Kylie pulled into the parking lot behind the Perky Coffee Shop a half hour late, then rushed inside, praying that Nate hadn't given up and left.

Even at that late hour, the little shop was busy, mostly with college students on their laptops. Smooth jazz music played overhead, barely audible over the laughter of some drunk girls in the corner. Were they trying to sober up?

Shaking her head, Kylie scanned all the tables. Being vertically challenged, it took her three trips around the room to see over all the high-top tables and giant stools.

Nate wasn't there.

She tried calling him again. Nothing.

She ordered a latte, thinking he simply might be late as well.

Kylie was clearly not the most punctual person on earth,

but she couldn't stand being kept waiting. Her mind filled up with all the things she could be doing, only one of which was canoodling in bed with Linc. She tapped her foot on the footrest of the stool, wondering where Nate could be.

After another fifteen minutes passed, she watched one of the drunk girls hook up with one of the laptop guys. Hmm... if things with Linc really fell apart, she'd have to remember that coffee shops instead of bars were apparently now the dating scene.

Her stomach curdled at the thought of dating, and she pushed her lukewarm latte away and contemplated purchasing a cinnamon bun. Only the reminder of how her squishy body met Linc's rock-hard one stopped her from doing just that.

But it was tempting. Especially as the clock on her phone ticked off another five minutes.

When the clock hit eleven, she gave into what she already knew. Either he'd given up on her when she'd been late, or he was a no-show.

But why didn't he answer his phone, at least? She tried one more time. No answer.

Sliding off the barstool, she decided to call it a night. She'd track him down tomorrow.

She walked outside, getting hit by a blast of cool night air. Pulling her sweater tighter over her chest, she headed to her car, but she was forced to wait until another car backed from its spot. The headlights of the Acura flashed on something red and shiny. And sporty.

In his Facebook photos, Nate had been in a bright red Porsche a couple of times.

She'd thought it made him even more suspicious...how was he paying for that fancy car?

She marched over to the car, noticed a shadow inside.

Had he been waiting for her in the parking lot all this time? Had he fallen asleep?

Frustrated to her core, she knocked on the top. Nothing.

She knocked harder. Nothing.

Kylie's fingers were trembling as she tapped on her phone, searching for the flashlight app. Her spidey-senses whirred into overdrive.

"Stop it," she grumbled to herself. After all, this wasn't Masterpiece Theatre. This was a freaking boring embezzlement case, as safe as could be. That's what she'd assured Linc and Greg and her mother. It was dull. Boring. There was no reason to have her mind spiral out in all these wild directions.

Taking in a deep breath, she turned the flashlight on.

It was Nate. He was sitting in the driver's seat, his head back, nose to the sky. Eyes open. There was blood on his shoulders, soaking the front of his white starched shirt.

It took Kylie a moment to register what she was looking at.

A dead body.

She'd never seen one before. Even with her run-in with the serial killer last month, she'd been removed from that. This man, Nate...he'd been alive and well just hours ago. And now, he was most definitely not.

Because of her?

Nausea gripped her, and she staggered back against another car, nearly dropping her phone.

What should she do?

Call 9-1-1.

No. She headed to her car, needing to get away. Inside of the safety of the little Mazda, she scrolled through her contacts. She knew exactly who she needed to call first.

25

I didn't want it to be this way.

I love him. *Loved* him.

As best as I could, anyway.

But he left me with little choice. Even as he kissed me goodbye after our hours of lovemaking this evening, I felt the sadness and guilt inside him as he left.

No. If I looked back, I'd known he was going to betray me before then. Wasn't that why I'd joined him in the shower, cleansing every inch of his skin, not wanting to leave a trace of my DNA on his body?

Yes, I'd known instinctively that it would come to this. And my instincts were my friend.

Now, my only friend.

Almost.

I closed my eyes, sadness welling inside me as I remembered how surprised he'd looked when I appeared at the car's window after making sure there were no cameras in the back lot of the coffee house.

Cameras could be such a nuisance. But they could also be quite handy, especially the tiny ones I placed in strategic places, letting me, quite literally, be a fly on the wall to many conversations.

"What are you—" Nate had asked as he rolled the window down.

I fired the gun before another lying word could exit his mouth.

It was guilt, I knew, that had been eating at his insides. From the beginning, I'd known Nate Jennings would be my greatest strength, or my greatest weakness. In fact, he'd been both.

We'd had the same goals. Wealth. Not for the monetary things money could buy. At least not only that. It was the power I sought.

Wealth offered protection. Being vulnerable terrified me in a way I didn't understand.

While Nate had wanted wealth right away, thinking he could simply burn his grandparents' home to the ground, I'd convinced him to wait.

After all, his mother and aunt died in a fire. One of his making. He hadn't meant to kill them, of course. At least that was what he'd told me. He'd just been a boy, he'd said, sobbing on my shoulder. The fire had just gotten away from him, and he didn't let anyone know because he hadn't wanted to get in trouble.

I'd soothed him, assuring him it wasn't his fault.

No…the fault lay at the feet of his grandparents, who had seized control of the fortune young Nate should have received, thinking he needed to be older and wiser before so much money fell into his hands.

Sixteen wasn't too young, in my opinion, but the old crow and her artistic goose had clearly not agreed.

It had been the exact wrong thing to do.

Guilt from the fire and anger from his grandparents' strictness had led young Nate down a treacherous path. They gave him enough money for "essentials," but I was sure it never occurred to them that the most essential thing in his life would go up his nose.

By college, Nate had been a mess, but I straightened him out soon enough.

I gave him a purpose. A plan.

Then...*pop*.

The end hadn't even been so dramatic, the silencer on the gun making Nate's death almost anticlimactic. But it had been for the best.

I knew that now.

Of course, I still had a problem.

Namely, Kylie Hatfield.

As I watched Kylie walk from the coffee house, I almost laughed out loud.

This was perfect.

Two birds, one stone. Well, officially two bullets, but metaphors didn't matter.

Moving from shadow to shadow, I watched her recognize Nate's flashy sportscar. Another purchase I hadn't approved of. I watched her approach it. Watched recognition hit her like a brick.

Little Kylie Hatfield reacted faster than I thought she would. Most girls her age would have screamed and cried or even fainted.

Yes, fainted. That would have been good.

She'd been shocked, yes, but had gone into action sooner than I wished. As she headed to her car, I followed, wondering if she simply planned to drive away.

But instead of starting her car, she pulled out her phone, and began scrolling down the screen.

So close. One shot through the window and this little problem would be done.

She tapped the screen and went to put the phone up to her ear.

I was beside her when the coffee shop doors opened, and a gaggle of giggling girls floated out. Frustration simmered in my every pore as I was forced to back away.

Later.

I would simply have to find her later.

It was okay. I could wait.

After all, patience was my friend.

JACOB CURSED as his phone rang, and he was tempted as all hell to ignore it. He squinted at the clock on the nightstand.

Well, that was embarrassing. It wasn't even eleven p.m.

He was becoming an old man.

Not even looking at the screen, he held the annoying thing to his ear. "Yello?"

"Jacob," a woman breathed into the phone. "Can you come here? There's a *little* problem."

Jacob paused and squinted at the screen. "Kylie?"

"Yes. You really need to come."

Sitting up in his bed, he ran a hand over his face. "Okay. Slow down. Where is here, and what little problem?"

"At the Perky Coffee Shop. I was going to meet someone about an embezzlement case. And he was a no-show. And now I'm out in the parking lot...and he's here, too...dead! I think he was shot."

"Whoa."

Typical Kylie. She was talking so fast he was barely able to register the words.

"Kylie, listen to me. Are you okay? Have you been hurt?"

She let out a shaky breath. "No, I'm fine. I locked myself in my car."

Good. That was good.

"Okay, stay there. Perky Coffee Shop is in city jurisdiction but..."

"So?"

He sighed. They'd had this discussion before. "So, it means it's in the police department's jurisdiction. I'm with the sheriff's department, remember." He stuffed his leg into a pair of trousers he'd tossed over a chair.

"I don't care!" she yelled. "I need your help."

He was already pulling on his shirt. "I know. Have you called 9-1-1?"

"No, I called you first."

Of course she did. Kylie Hatfield didn't follow any rules.

"When we hang up, call them."

"Why?"

He groaned. "Because I said so." Then a thought occurred to him. "Where's Linc?"

"At his house. I had to take him home from the hospital and he left his truck and then I had to leave and—"

"Whoa, whoa, whoa. Back up. Linc was in the hospital?"

"Yes! I was at his parents' house when the call came in."

Why had she been at Linc's parents' house? He shook his head. That was a question for later.

"Is Linc okay? What happened?"

"He was called in to help with that parking garage collapse in Spartanburg and had a panic attack."

Shit.

Linc Coulter panicked? Jacob never thought he'd hear such a thing.

But then the memory of his best friend's face the past two times he'd seen him flashed in his mind...he hadn't looked good.

In fact, Jacob was worried about him.

Very worried.

"People are coming out of the shop," Kylie said. "Heading toward Nate's car."

Shit.

He was going to tell her to stay put, but he already heard her door click open and the ding-ding-ding of where she must still have her keys in the ignition.

"Hey," he heard her yell. "Don't go—"

"Is that dude dead?" someone said. The words were followed by a scream.

Shit. This was going downhill fast.

Jacob forced his concern for Linc away and focused on the current situation.

"Call 9-1-1, and I'll be there as soon as I can."

The police and sheriff departments had a good working relationship. With a phone call, he could be on this case.

Shit. Did he want to be on this case?

Another case involving Kylie Hatfield?

Dammit.

"Okay." Her voice sounded weak. Frightened.

"Sit in your car until the cavalry arrives."

"Okay."

He disconnected the call and placed one of his own.

Two minutes later, he was out the door.

What had Kylie gotten herself in to now?

Kylie shivered as she sat in her car, even though she had her heat on high blast.

The first responder had arrived, a policeman who was taking control of the scene, pushing the onlookers and their cell phones as far away from the Porsche as possible.

Jacob's truck pulled up a few minutes after an ambulance arrived. She opened her car door as he headed straight to the red car. He spoke to the paramedics, but they were talking too low for Kylie to hear.

Minutes passed, and Kylie considered getting back into her car for the third time, when he turned and headed her way.

"Well, shit," he said.

Kylie nodded. "He was shot, wasn't he?"

He watched another police car arrive. "It appears so, but we'll need to wait for the ME to get him on his table."

Kylie shivered. Too many crime novels and movies had told her what would happen to poor Nate Jennings there. Not that he'd feel anything.

Jacob frowned. "Why don't you go wait in my truck?"

She did as he told her, watching the circus of emergency personnel doing their jobs.

Her fingers still trembled as she raised them to her temples.

She couldn't believe this was happening.

Poor Emma. She would be beside herself.

And Linc. Kylie cringed just thinking of his reaction. He was going to be pissed when he learned that she'd gotten herself embroiled in something way beyond her capabilities again. Greg too.

That didn't matter right now.

Right now, she needed to solve the case. And if Nate knew something...and someone shot him for it...that meant that foul things were afoot. It wasn't just Emma's dementia or paranoia. And it surely must be bigger than a few missing paintings.

Someone was cheating the old woman, and whoever it was, they were desperate enough to kill to keep it a secret.

Kylie was scrolling through her phone as Jacob appeared in the window. "Hey, Kylie. Want to tell me what this has to do with the case you're working on?"

She nodded. And told him everything. Well, almost. How Emma had hired her to look into possible embezzling, how she thought some of her paintings had been stolen, and how she'd interviewed Nate regarding the possible theft.

"Then earlier today, he called and said he needed to talk to me about the painting he had in his apartment. We set up this meeting. I was late and he didn't show. When I gave up and headed to my car, I saw him."

Jacob nodded. "And how did he sound when you spoke to him earlier?"

"Really nervous. Worried. I think whatever he knew, someone killed him to keep it a secret."

Jacob let out a big sigh. "Yeah. Maybe. Or it could have nothing to do with you. Nate Jennings was wrapped up in a lot of shady things and deeply in debt. Mostly gambling debt. It's possible that his loan shark just had enough of him."

Kylie shook her head. She didn't believe that for a second. "Whatever it is...please don't tell Linc that I was here."

He raised an eyebrow at her. "You're kidding."

She pleaded with him with her eyes. "He has enough to worry about right now. We don't need to make it any worse."

"Kylie, I don't—"

Kylie laced her fingers in front of her. "Please. He'd freak if he found out I was in a situation like this. And besides, it might not have anything to do with the case, like you said. So why worry him?"

She could tell that Jacob didn't like the idea. At all.

"I'll think about it. Right now, you need to retell your story to one of the city detectives on scene."

Jacob introduced her to a stern-looking woman by the name of Lisa Dalton, and Kylie told her story again.

When she got to the part about Jonathan Coulter being Emma's lawyer, Jacob held up a hand. "Wait. You didn't mention him before."

Kylie gave him an innocent look. "Sorry, it must have slipped my mind."

Jacob narrowed his eyes at her. "And you still don't want to tell Linc?"

She shook her head. "I *especially* don't want to tell Linc about that. He has enough on his mind."

"I don't know if I agree on that, but like I said, I'll think about it."

The police detective stepped in. "I need you to come by the police station tomorrow to give your formal statement."

Kylie stared at her. Wasn't that exactly what she'd been doing? Twice?

But she didn't argue. It was well after midnight by then, and with the day and evening she'd had, she was beyond exhausted.

"You can go home, Ms. Hatfield," Detective Dalton said. "Would you like one of my men to escort you?"

"No. I'm fine," she said, managing a smile.

But she wasn't.

And she wasn't going to her apartment. Hell no.

She was going to go back to Linc's house and beg him to let her spend the night. She'd sleep on the floor or even the porch swing, if she had to.

But she didn't want to be alone.

More than that, she needed Linc.

She just couldn't tell him why.

26

After Kylie left, Linc'd cursed himself.

Had he had sex with her to prove to himself and her that he wasn't slowly going insane?

Wasn't that insane in itself?

He wasn't even sure anymore.

It all had to do with today. He still felt shitty for putting the Spartanburg emergency personnel through that extra level of hell. As if they didn't have enough to worry about without having to take care of his sorry ass.

Linc made himself a late dinner, put some logs in the fire-place, and grabbed a six pack with the full intent of getting drunk. He tried to think more about Kylie's sexy body and less about what had happened earlier. But when he thought about her, it only made him feel guilty. He could give her the sex she wanted, sure. She'd never asked for anything more.

But he wanted more.

And he knew he couldn't have it.

Not with the way his brain was.

Linc tossed back beers, one after another, while Vader

and Storm looked on, both with their ears perked up as if to say, *You're doing this again?*

What else could he do? That was the good thing about drinking. When he did it, he usually woke up in the morning with a hangover, but at least it kept the nightmares at bay. At least he didn't wake up screaming.

Before long, he'd polished off the entire six pack. He went to the fridge, leaving the bottles on the coffee table, and got another. The room swayed as he turned back, and he stumbled to the couch.

He closed his eyes…

It was hot. So fucking hot in Raqqa.

His team was there. The kids. Storm.

Austin passed the ball to the little kid with the shaggy hair and the baseball cap. The boy, cute as hell, shouted, "Hey, hero! Try this."

He kicked the ball to Linc, which he easily blocked. He kicked the ball back, but the boy missed it, and it raced over the dusty road and into a deep ditch.

Linc held up a hand. "I'll get it," he called and jogged over to retrieve the ball. For fun, he twirled it on his finger like he would a basketball.

The little one with the shaggy hair and the baseball cap beamed at him. "Hey, hero," he called. "Look! My sister!" Linc followed his outstretched finger to a woman standing in the center of the marketplace. She was wearing a military vest over her traditional garments. Her eyes were bulging with fear, her body trembling. She was holding something in her hand...

"No!" he screamed.

He began to run, not away from the woman but toward her. He had to stop her.

As she watched him, tears streaming down her face, she held her hand up. Her thumb hovered over the detonator.

Linc shouted for his men to take cover and started to run faster. Beside him, he caught the flash of Storm's fur as she ran by his side.

One step. Two. Then the world exploded.

Bodies fell all around him. His brothers. The kids.

He spotted Austin, his very best friend, and fell to his knees beside him.

Even as he screamed Austin's name, the soldier sat up, his hands going around Linc's throat.

"This is your fault," his best friend said, blood splattering into Linc's face.

Beside him, Tyler sat up. The exposed tendons of his neck creaked as he turned his head to face him. "This is your fault."

One by one, the men he'd fought beside sat up, pointing their finger at him.

"No..." Linc said, trying to explain. "I was too far away. I—"

Fangs sank into his neck, and he felt the blood drain as Austin took his revenge.

Linc screamed, and he sat bolt upright, his fists punching the air.

Storm barked, drawing his attention to her and a scared looking Vader crouching by the dying embers of the fire.

He clutched at his chest, sure that he really was having a heart attack this time, and grabbed his t-shirt bathed in sweat. Nausea gripped him. He stumbled to his feet and made it to the toilet just in time to vomit all the beer and dinner he'd consumed. Again and again, he vomited until he was just dry-heaving, slumped over the toilet.

So much for getting drunk helping to ward off the nightmares.

That one had been the most vivid dream yet, and with its clarity, his memory returned as well.

He'd lost ten men that day, his brothers. He'd almost lost Storm.

The little boy. The other children. The girl who'd been persuaded to do such a terrible thing.

Grabbing a wad of toilet paper, Linc swabbed at his mouth. Vader whined from the bathroom door. Storm sat beside him, eyeing him closely.

"I'm all right, you two," he said

Storm huffed out the softest of barks. It sounded very closely like *liar*.

27

Kylie drove the rest of the way up the mountain, obsessing about Nate Jennings.

Nate, dead.

She couldn't get the scene out of her head. His bloody body. His face, so lifeless and pale.

She bet that when he'd gotten into the car, he'd had no idea he'd never get out alive. She bet that when he woke up in the morning, he didn't realize that this was the day he'd die.

Or maybe he had.

Kylie couldn't help but wonder if the man had turned to suicide as the only way out of his predicament. Jacob had refused to let her get close enough to the scene again to look for a gun, saying that the medical examiner and law enforcement officers would investigate fully.

She kept shaking, she was so wound up, but she forced herself to be calm so that she wouldn't spook Linc. He'd had enough to worry about on his own; he didn't need her sorrows to deal with too. Kylie took deep breaths, trying to channel her inner ray of sunshine so he wouldn't kick her to the curb and tell her to get lost.

Which he probably would do, since he didn't want her spending the night.

As she pulled into his driveway, she wondered if he'd let her sleep on the couch, with the dogs. She'd do that, happily. She just didn't want to go home. Kylie checked the clock. It was so very late. Saying a silent prayer, she pulled to a stop in front of his porch, opened the door, and went inside.

She knew that something wasn't right the moment she stepped through the door. The dogs were in the foyer, waiting there, she assumed to greet her. They wagged their tails as she petted them. She walked in farther, to the living room, and looked around. The place was hot and stuffy. There was a dying fire in the fireplace, and one two three four five six...*seven* empty beer bottles lined up on the coffee table.

Oh, no.

Behind her, the toilet in the powder room flushed. Kylie whirled in time to watch Linc lumber out, looking like he was all kinds of hurting. His eyes were darker than ever and bloodshot, his hair sticking up in all directions, his clothes rumbled. "Linc...are you okay?"

He nodded wordlessly, then went and slumped onto the couch. He dropped his head in his hands. It was almost a full minute later that he mumbled, "Why are you here?"

"I just...wanted to come back."

"But you're not staying."

"Fine." She was getting tired of this. She crossed her arms. "I'm not staying. Are you drunk?"

His eyes fell over the bottles. "Not anymore." He vised his head in his hands again. "My head hurts."

"I don't understand. What happened after I left? What—"

"I took care of things, the only way I knew how. But even that didn't work."

"Took care of things? By drinking? You really think that's going to help anything?" Kylie asked, fisting her hands on her hips. "If you're having some problems, you don't drink. You need to talk to someone. Or—"

"I don't want to talk to anyone. I don't want some stranger to worm their way into my head."

"Then tell me. I'm not a stranger."

"Yeah." His laugh was bitter. "You're the woman who just wants to fuck me."

Kylie stared at him. Was that what he thought?

"I never…I mean, I don't just want you for that. I thought we were more than that, Linc."

He scrubbed at his face so hard she thought his skin might peel off. "It doesn't matter what we are or what we aren't. It has to be over, Lee. Can't you see that? I'm a ticking time bomb."

"No, you're not."

"Yeah. I am. I've been having these nightmares about Syria and they keep getting clearer and clearer. I feel like I'm there again."

She sat on the chair across from him. "Clearer? Do you mean they've been foggy up until lately?"

Another bark of laughter. "Stone cold black is more like it."

She stared at him, willing herself to understand. "You had amnesia?"

He scrubbed his face again, and she wanted to pull his hands away before he hurt himself. "Yeah, amnesia. That's how fucked up I am, Lee. Do you get it now?" He pushed to his feet and began to pace. "I'm so fucked up that I completely forgot that a suicide bomber took out ten of my brothers right in front of me." His hands went to his hair, pulling it from the roots. "I'm so fucked up that I completely forgot that I was the only survivor. That I couldn't save them."

She went to him, tried to pull his hands from his head. "I'm so so—"

He pulled away, his hands still on his head like he was afraid he might touch her. "I'm going upstairs. I need a shower."

Without another word, he stomped up the stairs. A moment later, the water turned on.

Kylie sank onto the couch, petting the dogs and wondering if she should just leave like he clearly wanted her to. But no. She wanted to take care of him. She wanted to be there for him. And if this wasn't just sex, then fine. She cared about him. She might have been scared of it, but deep down, she wanted more too.

Slowly, Kylie climbed the stairs and went into his room. The water was still running as she perched on the edge of his bed. She slipped off her shoes and waited.

What felt like forever later, the door opened, and he stood in the doorway among the steam wafting out, his frame taking up much of the empty space. He was wearing a pair of drawstring lounge pants, his hair slicked back, droplets of water still coating his shoulders and bare chest.

He glared at her, and she braced herself for the onslaught. For him to tell her that she needed to go.

But he didn't. He sat down on the bed beside her. "You didn't leave."

"No," she said quietly. "I'm not leaving you like this."

"Like how?" he said, his voice tense. "Like a sick man? A crazy man? I deserve to be left. Just like I left *them*."

Tears sprang to her eyes. "You didn't leave them, Linc! They died. You didn't. Do you really think that if given the chance, they would want you dead too?"

He stared at her. His mouth moved, but he didn't say a word.

"If the outcome had been reversed, and you died instead of them, would you want them to spend the rest of their lives hating themselves? Or would you want them to enjoy each blessing of a new day?"

He dragged a hand down his face. "Well, the outcome is what it is." He looked at her, finally meeting her eyes. "You should leave."

She shook her head. "No. I'm staying. Even if you try to push me out and make me sleep on the porch or the barn or in my car, I'm staying."

He dragged in a breath, and his nostrils flared. "You don't know what you're getting yourself into, Lee."

"Yeah," she said and got underneath the covers, completely dressed. "That's why I haven't left, Linc. I want to get into it. Even if it's messy. I want to."

He turned to her, looking glorious and perfect, even as fragile as he was.

For a long while, she thought he'd continue to argue, or maybe he would be the one to leave. Then, to her amazement, he moved closer to her on the bed.

"What are you doing to me, Lee? I don't want to hurt you," he said, his voice ragged and tortured.

"You'd hurt me more if you made me leave."

Very slowly, Kylie sat up and wrapped her arms around him, her chin resting on his still damp shoulder.

With a long exhale, he turned and moved beneath the covers, pulling her close to his side.

How could he think this was bad? She felt so safe in his arms.

"I'll call," he whispered in her ear. "The therapist at the VA. I'll call her."

"Okay," she said, snuggling closer, wanting to give him the same comfort he was giving her.

She held him until he closed his eyes and his breathing evened out.

As he slept, her mind wandered through the day, eventually landing back on Nate Jennings, then Emma.

Her heart began to hammer as she thought of the vulnerable older woman. Who was there to protect her?

After a few moments of fretting, Kylie slipped out of bed and padded downstairs, taking her cell phone from her purse. She quickly called Jacob.

"What's wrong now?"

She smiled at the greeting. "Nothing. Not really."

"So…you're calling me at four a.m. why?"

She looked at the clock. Wow, he was right.

"Sorry. Look. I'm here at Linc's, and I just thought of something."

She heard a creaking noise and whipped her head toward the sound as Jacob said, "Yeah?"

Shit, it wouldn't be a good idea for Linc to catch her calling Jacob right now. He'd either think she really was sleeping with the detective or else she'd have to spill the story about Nate Jennings.

She peered into the darkness and spotted two glassy eyes peering back. Vader. Letting out a sigh of relief, she leaned over and petted him. "Yeah. I've been worried about Emma and was wondering if you could get someone to keep an eye on her house. Maybe now that her grandson's out of the way, whoever tried to steal the artwork could come back for the rest."

He let out a tired breath. "Yeah. That's something you couldn't wait for the morning to tell me?"

She gnawed on her lip. Yes. She guessed it could've waited. "Sorry."

"Kylie, girl. I'm growing quite fond of you, but if you're going to work in this business, one thing you've got to learn is how to turn your brain off. You keep it firing on all cylinders like you have been, you're gonna burn it out. Got that?"

Kylie swallowed. He was so right. "Yes. I know. Thanks, Jacob."

She ended the call and climbed the stairs to the bedroom, then changed from her clothes into one of Linc's soft shirts before slipping next to his warm body.

She tried to do what Jacob'd told her to do.

She tried to turn her brain off.

It didn't work.

28

Jacob Dean mourned the concept of sleep, especially now that the grandson of a prominent Asheville family had been murdered.

And it had been murder.

Sick and heartless as it sounded, his job would have been a lot easier if they'd conveniently found a gun in Nate Jennings's palm.

They didn't.

What they found? A great big pile of nothing.

No video camera coverage at the scene.

No witnesses.

No great big sign pointing *bad guy that way*.

What they did have was about a hundred random fingerprints on the car. And they had the bullet, but it would take a few days for ballistics to get a match. If they could get a match.

As much as the crime shows on TV loved to abracadabra DNA and ballistic results, tying crimes up in a neat little bow in the space of an hour, real life didn't work so efficiently.

Those results were important, yes, but in Jacob's experience, nothing did a better job of catching a suspect than good old-fashioned detective work.

But first, the next of kin had to be notified, and although Biltmore Forest had its own police department, Jacob somehow became the one to break the news to Emma Jennings. Maybe because he'd been the one to investigate the death of her husband when he fell down the stairs five years ago.

He hated going back into that house. Hated looking at the staircase, his memory overlaying the image of the broken man at the bottom.

Although the death had been ruled an accident, the ME believed Mr. Jennings had been in the process of experiencing a myocardial infarction at the time. He might have been coming down the steps, seeking help, and lost his balance or even his consciousness. One thing was for sure… the man had been alive when he hit the ground. But not for long.

Jacob hoped that as he lay there, he'd been comforted by the portraits of his family, looking down on him from up above. His wife. His daughters. Even the baby sons who had been lost before they took their first inhalation of air were dancing on what must have been Arnold's depiction of Heaven.

So much loss.

And now the grandson, gone as well.

Just looking at those portraits made Jacob shiver, the cool air of the early morning having nothing to do with the chill.

Something was wrong in this house.

He'd felt it back then, and he'd felt it when he stepped inside the gilded walls after Sloane had opened the door, dressed in his butler attire but looking very sleepy just the same.

Jacob was too logical to believe in ghosts, but if he did…

he'd believe they roamed these halls, staring at him from the hundreds of painted eyes as he told the butler that he had some disturbing news to share with Mrs. Jennings.

"Oh, dear," Sloane said, looking at a loss for what to do. "Should I call Mrs. Jennings's personal physician, have him be with her while you share your news?"

Jacob nodded. "That's a very good idea. And perhaps the chaplain."

Sloane's face fell, but he was too professional to ask for additional details. Instead, he led Jacob to a parlor where he waited until all parties arrived.

Emma Jennings recognized him almost immediately. Looking like a giant ginger teddy bear did hasten introductions. She arrived to the room in a long dressing gown, the matching robe cinched tight at the waist.

"What has happened?" she asked at once.

The doctor took her arm and led her to a chair.

Jacob was of the opinion that it was better to rip the band aid off quickly instead of extending the agonizing moments when breaking bad news.

"It's your grandson, Nate Jennings. He was murdered last night."

Her hand flew to her mouth, and for several terrible minutes, Jacob thought she'd suffered the same heart attack that had felled her late husband. From the doorway, Sloane sagged against the doorframe, and the physician rushed back to care for him.

Seemingly unaware of what was taking place behind her, Emma pressed her trembling lips together and met Jacob's gaze with her devastated one. "What happened?"

Jacob shared what details he could, beginning with the phone call to Kylie and ending with her finding his body.

Emma's lips trembled again. "This is my fault."

Jacob straightened in his seat. "How is that possible?"

"I hired Kylie to investigate the missing portraits. And now this." She shook her head. "How is Kylie? I'm sure she's quite traumatized."

Jacob linked his fingers together. "She's tough, and I think she was most worried about you."

That brought the tiniest of smiles to the elderly woman's face, but the movement didn't last long before grief took its place. "I think I need to lie down now."

Jacob stood. "Of course."

The doctor was still taking care of the stricken butler, so Jacob and the chaplain escorted Emma back to her room. Jacob was relieved to leave the chaplain to his prayers of comfort.

The master suite was at the end of the house, and he was forced to find his way back to the front of the mansion. He shivered again.

This house had eyes. He could feel them on him.

Unable to help himself, he looked over his shoulder, peering down the dark hallway.

He would have to come back. He would have to question Emma Jennings further. The butler too. The rest of the staff.

But that could wait. Besides, he pretty much knew the entire story from one Kylie Hatfield.

Little troublemaker.

He still couldn't believe that she wanted him to keep a secret so deep from his very best friend in the world. Worse, he couldn't believe that he'd actually told her he would keep her deadly lie to himself in the first place.

He was relieved when he stepped outside and breathed in the cool morning air. He wanted to shake himself like a dog, shaking off the feeling of apprehension that wanted to cling to him.

In his truck, he pulled out his phone and dialed her number. Voicemail. He sighed and rubbed his fingers over his eyes.

"You've reached Kylie Hatfield, what can I help you investigate today? Leave me a message and I'll get back as quickly as I can."

At the beep, he said, "Kylie, it's Jacob. Listen…I've thought it through, and I can't in good conscious keep what happened last night from Linc. I'll give you until this afternoon to come clean or I'll do it for you. I'm serious. Starting now."

Noting the time, he headed to Nate Jennings's apartment, where the forensic team was busy picking the place apart. He contacted the IT department to see if they had any luck breaking into the murdered man's phone. Nope.

He spent the next several hours tracking down the pitiful number of leads he had.

By the afternoon, Jacob was both aggravated and worried that he hadn't heard back from the fiery little private investigator in training. Maybe she was on the mountain with Linc. The day had been heavily overcast, which could mean some spotty signals. Plus, she'd had a terrible night. She could simply be sleeping.

Or…

Jacob shook his head. She was fine. He wasn't going to borrow trouble and worry until there was something to worry about.

Pocketing the phone, he grabbed his keys. This conversation was better face to face. Plus, he was still worried about his friend too.

He drove by Starr Investigations first, looking for her car. She wasn't there.

He drove by her apartment building. Nope.

He headed up the mountain, his dread growing with each mile he drove.

LINC'S HEADACHE was finally gone.

It had actually been gone the second he'd crawled into bed with Kylie, pulled her warm body against his, and breathed in her shampoo. He fell asleep…probably the second his head hit the pillow and didn't stir once until the sun started to break through the blinds.

Thankfully, they hadn't had time to "talk" this morning because they'd woken late and she had to get to work. She bounded from the bed, her pink underwear clad ass peeking out from underneath his t-shirt as she hurried for the door. As the shower turned on, he headed downstairs and started a pot of coffee, then let the dogs out before pulling out bacon and eggs.

"You're the best!" Kylie said, taking the bagel sandwich and commuter's mug of coffee from his hands, giving him a lingering kiss on the lips. "You'll be okay?" Even though she was smiling, he could see the worry in her eyes.

He actually felt better than he had in weeks. Maybe the nightmare had been a good thing, letting out all the toxic memories that had been festering inside him for so long.

Maybe he didn't even need the therapist now. The idea made him smile, and he realized he hadn't been using those muscles often enough.

"Yeah. I'm good."

He watched her bustle Vader into her car and drive away before heading outside to take care of all the animals.

Hours later, his phone rang. It was his primary care doctor. Probably one of those message systems to remind him that he was overdue for his yearly appointment. Way overdue. He answered, knowing that if he didn't, they would just call again.

"Mr. Coulter, this is Christine from Dr. Sigler's office."

He was still waiting for the rest of the message to play when he realized he was on the phone with a real human being. "Oh, okay. How can I help you?"

"We received your emergency room report from your visit to Spartanburg Hospital yesterday, and Dr. Sigler wanted me to follow-up with you, make sure you're okay."

Nice customer service. Too bad he didn't like the reminder about yesterday's visit.

"I'm good, thanks."

If he'd been hoping that was the end of it, he was sorely wrong. "I don't see where you've made a follow-up appointment to see Dr. Sigler. Can I do that for you now?"

"No."

"I see." He could sense her disapproval. "What about the therapist the emergency room physician recommended?"

Linc gritted his teeth. "Not yet."

"I'm happy to help you make that appointment, Mr. Coulter. What day of the week works best for you?"

Jesus. He felt like he was being chased by a human bulldozer.

"Um, I can make that appointment myself."

"That's terrific. Do you have a therapist in mind that I can jot down in your file?"

Linc rubbed at his eye, trying to remember the name of the therapist he'd researched the other day.

"Teresa Watts," he blurted, hoping it was right.

"Wonderful. Do you have her number?"

Geez. The woman was like a mosquito buzzing in his ear.

"Yes, I do."

"And you'll be calling to make an appointment today?"

He was very close to tossing his phone into the pond.

"Yes," he gritted out.

"That's perfect. Dr. Sigler will be glad to hear that. He's been very concerned."

Dr. Sigler can kiss my ass.

"Please tell John that I appreciate the concern."

"I'll do that. Have a nice day."

He shot his phone the bird and disconnected the call.

Then he stared at the thing for a good five minutes.

"Dammit."

Dr. John Sigler would just have the pesky nurse call back, he knew. He'd been friends with the man for years and had trained four of his dogs.

Googling the number for Dr. Watts, Linc placed the call before he could change his mind. A couple minutes later, he had an appointment for later that week.

It hadn't even been that bad. Nobody laughed, asked intrusive questions, or accused him of being weak. After he hung up, he felt the opposite of how he thought he'd feel. For the first time in a long time, he felt like he was finally taking control.

Linc went to his office and whipped out the rest of the website he'd been struggling to put together, and went back to his regular, daily chores around the farm. As he did, a strength he hadn't had in a long time pulse through him, and his brain cleared.

He even managed not to jump out of his skin as two of his SAR buddies brought his truck back and stayed long enough to enjoy a couple sandwiches before heading back to Spartanburg. They talked about the garage collapse, but they'd all avoided mentioning anything about Linc's little breakdown.

Which was good.

Of course, both men were former military too. Brothers who intuitively understood.

After they left, he was just finishing repairing the back

door in the barn, something he'd been putting off for months, when he heard the gravel crunching—another truck coming up the driveway. It was Jacob.

Linc slid his toolbox onto the porch, wiped his hands on his jeans, and waved at him, wondering if he'd heard about the snafu in Spartanburg.

Jacob hopped out of his truck and said, "Well, you look better."

"I feel better. Must've been coming down with something before."

"You were down south, right? At that garage collapse?"

"Yeah. But not for long. I was run down. Got sick pretty early in and had to leave," Linc said as vaguely as possible.

"Shit, really?" Jacob knew it wasn't like Linc to turn away from a disaster scene, especially one as big and high-profile as Spartanburg. He could be coughing up a lung, and he'd still go in. But this time, he'd had no choice. "Heard they rescued a few survivors."

He'd purposely been avoiding news of the collapse. Linc shrugged. "Wasn't my doing." Unfortunately. He let out a breath and sat down on the porch steps. "Want to come in? Or are you here to drag me to another rescue?"

Jacob smirked. "No rescue. All's quiet on that front, fortunately." He kicked the bottom stair and scratched at his cinnamon stubble-covered jaw. It looked like there was something he was wrestling with how to put into words.

"Annnnd?" Linc prompted, leaning back on his elbows. Now, he was worried. Linc knew Jacob too well. There was something clearly on his mind.

Jacob took off his hat and dropped it on the post, then ran his hand through his scrubby hair. "Well. Remember when Kylie was on the trail of that killer and she was getting her nose stuck in a lot of places where it didn't technically belong?"

Kylie. Shit. Somehow, Linc should have known that she was at the bottom of this. "What did she do now?"

"She told me not to tell you because she knew you were going through some shit and didn't want to upset you, but…"

She did, did she? What the hell.

"What. Did. She. Do?" Linc asked, digging his hands into the stairs at his sides, so hard he splinters stung his palms.

"It's that new case she's on."

"The embezzlement case?" Or was it a robbery case? Both? He couldn't completely remember.

"Yeah. That one. Started out that way, but it's grown teeth and fangs. There's been a murder."

Linc stared at him. Holy shit. Kylie was a danger magnet. "What murder?"

"This witness that she was looking into. She was going to meet with him last night at this coffee shop downtown. She's inside waiting for him, he never shows. Then she goes outside and finds him in his car. Bullet in the brain."

Linc pinched the bridge of his nose with his fingers. "You're serious?"

Jacob nodded. "I'm guessing she never told you any of this."

"Not a thing."

"Well. It just happened last night. When did you last talk to her?"

Linc shot to his feet and climbed to the porch and started to pace. "This morning. She was here all night. She…" He stopped. He'd been too far gone last night to notice if she'd been agitated, and she'd kept the focus on him. He clenched his fists. "Damnation. She didn't tell me anything."

"She's been worried about you. That's why."

Linc stared at his friend, feeling annoyed. "How is it that you know so much? Why is she telling you everything, and not me?" He slammed his chest. "She's my girl, not yours."

"Whoa." Jacob took a step back. "I know that. We both know that, Linc. Jesus. We're both worried about you."

We. He didn't like there being a "we" between Jacob and Kylie. It rubbed him the wrong way. Linc closed his eyes and shook his head, trying to ward off the dangerous urge building inside to punch his best friend in the world.

Linc raked both hands through his hair. "All right."

"I came up here because I wanted to let you know what was going on, Linc. She means a lot to you, and—"

"Yeah. Got it."

Go the hell away.

He didn't. Jacob stood there, and Linc could almost hear the wheels turning in his head, trying to think of what to say. Finally, Jacob threw up a hand. "See you."

He got into his truck as Linc stalked inside, slamming the door behind him. His life had been calm, relaxed even, before Kylie. But she upended every little thing in his head. She may have been responsible for calming his head last night, but more and more, he had the feeling that she'd been the one who brought the nightmares to the forefront to begin with. She was constantly in close scrapes. And maybe that was what had been stirring up his dangerous but mercifully forgotten past.

But Linc sure as hell wasn't willing to let her go now. She was a tornado, but she was also the calm after the storm. Somehow, she was slowly becoming everything to him.

She couldn't tell him about last night because she'd been walking on eggshells with him. But she'd told Jacob. She had to have been scared. What kind of asshole was he not to notice that? To make it all about him?

He went out to the yard to play with the dogs, feeling like an asshole again. The only reason he didn't trust the two of them now was because he felt shit-poor about himself. But

Jacob had been a stand-out best friend for most of his life, and Kylie had always been there for him.

Linc needed to get his head out of his ass and concentrate on what really mattered.

Namely, keeping Kylie safe.

29

Kylie was exhausted.

She'd just left the police department where she'd given her statement again, after waiting for an eternity in the smelly place. In fact, she'd waited so long that the battery on her phone died just as she was finally beating the bitch level of Candy Crush that had kept her stuck for days.

Truth be told, she'd rather be locked up herself than pushing the doorbell of Emma Jennings's home.

When Emma came to the door, she looked even smaller than before. Her body was hunched, her eyes red-rimmed from crying. Kylie hugged her at once, and her small body felt like it was made of twigs. Meanwhile, Coco yipped at their ankles, wanting a pet.

"I'm so sorry, Emma," Kylie said into her ear as she glanced around the house. Her servants seemed busy, scurrying quietly about. "Is there anything I can do for you?"

"Oh, thank you for asking, but no," Emma said as Coco continued her ear-splitting yapping. "Shush, Coco. It's a friend. Remember Kylie? I'm afraid it's a bit of a zoo around here. I'm having them clean the house top to bottom because I expect I'll be getting a lot of visitors."

Kylie nodded. "I'm sure. It's a shame that it takes a tragedy to bring people together."

Emma led Kylie into the same room where they'd originally discussed the case. As they sat down, Sloane came with tea, almost as if he'd been expecting company.

"I've been through death before. First my lovely daughters, then my Arnold. Now, Nate. It makes no sense. He was in the prime of his life. So young and vibrant. My only grandchild. Who could do such a thing?" Emma reached into her pocket, pulled out a handkerchief, and swabbed at her eyes. It pulled on Kylie's heartstrings.

"I don't know yet, Emma," Kylie said, patting her knee gently. "But I plan to do whatever I can to find out."

Emma had started to pour the tea, but her eyes widened, and she missed the cup. "Oh, no! Oh, no no no! You should let the police handle it."

Kylie took the delicate-looking teapot from the woman's trembling hands. "Nate called me yesterday, saying there was something important he needed to discuss with me regarding the missing paintings. The police aren't sure if that is why he was...attacked or if..."

Kylie froze. She didn't really want to go into what Jacob had told her, about Nate's gambling debts. The woman had enough worries on her mind.

Emma sniffed. "If what, dear?"

Pouring the tea, Kylie cleared her throat. "If it could have been random. But I think he might have been...harmed because of what he was about to tell me. Someone found out that he was suspicious and decided to silence him."

Emma shuddered, lifting her fingers to her lips. "Oh, dear. Then it's far too dangerous for you, Kylie, dear. In fact, I believe we should call off the whole investigation. I'll pay you for your services thus far, of course, but I don't want anyone else to get hurt."

Kylie shook her head. "Emma, with all due respect, I can't just sit by and let this happen. It's obvious someone has done something very wrong, and I personally can't sit still and let it continue. Please don't think you're forcing me into it. I'm compelled to do it. For myself. I want to see this creep behind bars."

"All right," Emma said doubtfully, taking a sip of her tea. "I'm awfully worried. Are you sure you want to get involved in that?"

Kylie forced herself to speak with a confidence she didn't feel. "I'm already involved, Emma. I wish I didn't have to ask you this now, but can you think of anyone who would want to hurt Nate?"

Emma shook her head. "No. I'm sorry. I…I hadn't seen Nate for a couple of weeks."

"Are you certain it's been that soon? Nate seemed to think it had been several months, at least."

She didn't want to bring up the stool incident again.

Emma frowned, and Kylie watched her eyes move, like she was attempting to scan a calendar that only she could see. "I'm not sure." Her lower lip trembled at the admission.

Kylie had printed off the picture of the painting in the Coulter's dining room earlier that day, and she pulled the copy out of her folder and handed it to Emma. "Does this look like one of your missing art pieces?"

She squinted at it, then lifted a pair of reading glasses from the pocket of her pink blazer and slipped them on. "Well, it's certainly one of Arnold's. I can tell by the style."

"You said one of the missing paintings was called *Autumn Sunrise*? I thought it could be this one," Kylie suggested gently.

She wanted a yes. A yes would've told her she was getting

somewhere. Or a no would've been good too, because then maybe she could cross Linc's father off her suspect list.

But she got what she didn't want. What she'd gotten so much of during this case.

Emma simply pressed her lips together and shrugged. "I honestly can't tell. He did so many paintings, they all seemed to run together. It could be one that was sent for reframing. Did you show it to...to Nate?" Her face fell as she said her grandson's name again.

Could be wasn't good enough.

"No. I didn't have a chance. Besides, he told me that he never sent any artwork from your house for reframing. Sloane seemed to think he had, but Nate denied it."

Emma tapped on her chin. "Oh, my. This is awfully strange." She set her cup down on the coffee table, and Coco jumped excitedly onto her lap. She fed him a cookie. "What about my lawyer? Have you spoken to him about the missing funds?"

Kylie shook her head. "I'd been so focused on the missing paintings that I haven't had the chance," she lied. She'd put it off enough. She probably needed to bite the bullet and talk to Jonathan Coulter as much as she dreaded it. "I'm planning to go over there after this. It's on my way home. I'm sure he can shed some light on things."

"Oh. Of course. He's a very good man. Very shrewd. He's been my attorney for many years," she said. "Would you like me to call him and tell him to expect you?"

"Oh. No," Kylie said, standing. She preferred the element of surprise. "It's better if I stop by unannounced but thank you."

She gave Emma another hug, got into her car, and drove up to the Coulter and Associates's imposing brick building. Parking in the lot with all the luxury cars, Kylie felt woefully inadequate. She wondered if they'd tow her hunk of junk for making their sparkling estate look bad. She looked down at herself. Her outfit was a pencil skirt and sweater, but that probably wasn't up to the Coulter and Associates's dress code. She probably needed a suit. As if she'd ever be caught dead in one of those.

Kylie walked inside and to a giant oak reception desk, so massive it came up to her nose. A woman in a severe bun under a pinched face leaned over and peered down at her, making her feel about three inches tall. "You have an appointment?"

"Actually, no. I'm here to see Jonathan Coulter."

The woman laughed, the sound clearly saying, *silly little girl.* "You surely realize that Jonathan Coulter is the senior partner here? His clients must book appointments with him months in advance. He doesn't simply take anyone off the street."

Well, wasn't she all high and mighty? Maybe Kylie should have taken Emma up on the offer to call ahead and announce she was coming.

"Well, I'm working on a case for his client, Emma Jennings, and I was hoping I could have a few moments of his time."

The receptionist eyed Kylie with annoyance but lifted a phone to her ear. Her voice transformed into pleasantness personified as she spoke into the mouthpiece. "Hello, Dustin. How are you? I have a young woman out here who wishes to speak to Mr. Coulter regarding Emma Jennings." She paused, listening, a smirk appearing on her face. "Yes, that's what I told her, extremely busy." Another pause. "Your name?"

Kylie realized she was now addressing her. "Kylie. Kylie Hatfield."

The woman's eyes narrowed. "Kylie? Now, why does that name sound familiar?" Everything she said sounded like an accusation.

Kylie only smiled, letting the woman attempt to figure it out. Since she doubted Jonathan Coulter spent his time around the water cooler, telling his colleagues about what a massive doofus his youngest son's girlfriend was, the secretary could only know her from the press time she received after taking down the Spotlight Killer

The receptionist put her mouth to the mouthpiece. "Kylie Hatfield…I'm not sure…yes. Emma Jennings."

There was a little mint dispenser on the oaken fortress. Kylie tried to press the button to get one out, but it got stuck, and tiny square white candies plinked all over the shiny floor before she figured out how to close it. She popped the one she managed to catch into her mouth.

"Sorry," Kylie said and knelt to scoop them up, hoping she wasn't flashing anyone in her skirt.

When Kylie straightened, looking around for a trash can, the woman was standing, eyeing her with ill-concealed contempt.

"Are you quite finished?"

Kylie tossed the mints into a shiny trash can she spotted. Focusing on conjuring a bright smile, she nodded and said, "Quite," in the poshest voice she could manage.

"Fantastic," the woman returned. "Follow me, and please don't tarry."

Kylie barely refrained from rolling her eyes and rubbed her fingers on her skirt. "No tarrying here."

She was being a smartass, which wasn't the best way to make friends, but the woman was as annoying as the day was long. She even had an annoying walk, with her high heels clattering down the marble hallway.

After an eternity of clack-clack-clack, the secretary stopped at a small conference room with dark oak paneling and an imposing oak conference table. "Dustin Weiss will be with you shortly. He's Mr. Coulter's assistant's assistant."

"Oh? Mr. Coulter isn't available?"

She sighed heavily. "Sorry, you tarried."

The door clicked between them before Kylie could open her mouth to tell the woman to kiss her tarrying ass.

Nice.

"Shortly" must've had a different meaning in the legal world, because there was nothing short about the amount of time Kylie waited. She spent about two minutes of it sitting in that high-backed executive chair. She pulled out her phone, then remembered it was dead, and spent the next minute berating herself for not putting her charger back in her car after riding in Linc's truck.

Bored and restless, she walked around the massive table, checking out the artwork. Nothing of the style of Arnold Jennings so she quickly lost interest in that. She went to the window and looked out onto an unappetizing stone courtyard. When she turned around, she spotted Jonathan Coulter's diploma from Duke University School of Law.

The man was intimidating enough as it was. Did Kylie really need to know he was Ivy League?

Probably not. She usually didn't let people spook her, but since that dinner, she'd elevated Jonathan Coulter in her head to the stuff of horror movie legend. Which was ridiculous. Linc didn't talk about him much, except to imply that he wasn't his favorite person, but Jonathan Coulter was still human. Kylie was sure Linc had plenty of heartwarming stories of playing ball with his dad, or his father watching him play his first game in high school, or Christmases as a family...something. She was sure of it.

Still, even if he might not have all the details she needed, she was damn glad she was meeting with his assistant. Even if he was keeping her waiting, it was better than having to sit across a table from a guy she'd called a bloodsucker and tell him she *also* suspected he might be a thief.

After about twenty minutes, the door opened, and a man wearing a mop of dark curly hair and thick black hipster glasses came in. He was so thin she imagined a stiff wind would knock him over. But huzzah! He wasn't wearing a three-piece suit. Just a spiffy tie and argyle vest. Kylie imagined that without it, he'd probably look about thirteen, although he pegged him as closer to thirty.

"Kylie Hatfield?" he said as she shook his hand. "I'm Dustin Weiss. I'm Mr. Coulter's assistant. I hear you have some questions about Emma Jennings's estate?"

She wanted to correct him since she'd already learned he was the assistant's assistant, but since Kylie had just been through her own assistant to the PI hell, she left it alone.

Kylie figured she couldn't keep the PI thing under wraps since Jonathan Coulter knew what she did for a living, so she said, "Yes. I'm a private investigator handling a case for her. She seems to think that some money and artwork has gone missing from her estate, and I'd like to get to the bottom of it."

"Missing?" He sat back, looking stunned. "Well, I can assure you that we keep a close eye on her estate, along with her financial advisor. We haven't seen anything untoward. What makes her think that's happening?"

"She's lost a number of paintings from her own gallery, and some of the charitable organizations she always supported have not been receiving their funds. She said she spoke to Jonathan Coulter and he advised her just what you're saying to me now. But if that's the case, why is the money not showing up where it belongs?"

"Ah. I see." He lifted a manila file. "Let me call Mrs. Jennings to make sure she allows it, and then I'll be happy to make copies of our records of charitable donations for you. We keep very good records here."

"I'm sure you do. Thank you. I appreciate it."

He left, closing the door behind him, and it was about twenty minutes of Kylie twiddling her thumbs until he returned. "Sorry for the delay," he said, not looking sorry in the least. "I was able to get in touch with Mrs. Jennings and she authorized the copies. But there are quite a lot, dating back nearly twenty years. Here's the first batch."

He dropped a massive, crippling stack of legal-sized paper in front of her. "Oh. Wow."

He laughed. "Yeah. Tell me about it. Generous folk, those Jennings people. The other half is on the way."

"Great. This is amazing. Thank you," she said, lifting the first page and squinting at the tiny writing. These contributions were from the late nineties. "I guess I'm going to be busy tonight."

"Yeah. Can I get you anything while you wait? Coffee? Tea?"

She shook her head. "I'm good. Thanks."

Kylie decided to concentrate on the more recent things, but even so, it took her a while to understand what each entry was. Yes, there were a lot of contributions to art guilds, museums, and societies around the town, but they were all abbreviated, so she had to make sense of the shorthand. About fifteen minutes later, Dustin returned with a second half that was even bigger than the first. "Lots of fun reading material," he quipped.

She started to pack the papers up. "Tell me about it. I really appreciate your help." She paused a moment, meeting his eye. "How do you like working for Mr. Coulter?"

"Mr. Coulter is hard, but he's fair. He's straight as an arrow." He stuffed his hands into his pockets. "You know, I was very surprised that there's a problem. If the books aren't matching up, it's not because of any criminal negligence. It's just got to be a mistake."

A mistake. Right. Tell that to Nate Jennings, Kylie thought.

She stood up and shook his hand. "Thank you, Mr. Weiss."

He didn't drop her hand right away. Instead he looked at her more closely, a smile appearing on his face. "Wait a minute. You're that girl. The one who brought down the Spotlight Killer, aren't you?"

She nodded. "Yep. That's me. I mean, I didn't do it all by—"

"Holy shit!" he shouted. Kylie thought he'd forgotten that he was in the Coulter and Associates building because she doubted anyone here cursed or shouted in glee, ever. He beamed at her. "I'm in awe. Seriously. Wow. Kylie Hatfield. You're like a legend. This is better than meeting Thor. The Spotlight Killer's downfall, right here, shaking my hand."

Yes, he was still shaking her hand, and about to dislocate her shoulder.

Kylie carefully pried herself away, though she was kind of amused by his excitement, her head swelling with pride. He thought she was better than Thor? That was a mighty nice compliment. She controlled herself before she offered to show him her gunshot wound by putting her finger to her lips. "I get the feeling you're probably not supposed to shout around here," she whispered.

He nodded. "Yeah. You're right. But it was an honor to meet you."

"The honor's all mine," Kylie said, smiling at him. He was kind of cute, in a geeky way. She lifted the pile of papers. "And my thanks is all yours. Really. This is fantastic."

"I hope you find what you're looking for," he said, leading her through the doors, into the lobby, where the Bitch On High sat, staring down at them from her throne.

"Were you shouting?" the receptionist said, her voice grating.

He nodded and hooked a thumb at Kylie. "This woman brought down the Spotlight Killer."

The woman looked confused. "The who?"

"The Spotlight Killer," Dustin Weiss said again.

"For the last time, Mr. Weiss. I don't play video games," she said, shaking her head at them both. Kylie could almost hear her thinking, *Damn millennials!*

He opened his mouth to explain but quickly closed it. "Forget it." He shook Kylie's hand again. "Very nice to meet you, Kylie."

She said goodbye and headed for the door. "Miss Hatfield! Miss!"

Kylie turned around, and a professionally dressed older woman came huffing and puffing up to her. "Dustin forgot to give you these."

Kylie almost groaned as the woman laid another couple inches worth of paperwork on top of what she was already carrying. "Thank you very much."

The woman nodded and turned on her heel, hurrying back the way she had come. Kylie rearranged the surprisingly heavy stack of evidence she would soon have the joy of leafing through.

As she walked outside, Kylie found herself smiling. Who knew? She'd never imagined that place would get a smile out of her.

It was probably because she didn't have to come face-to-face with Jonathan Coulter, but so what? She—

"Oh...I'm so sorry."

Kylie looked down in dismay as all the papers she'd been holding fanned out over the floor, then up to the dark-haired woman who'd just run into her, nearly knocking her down. The woman gave her a *sorry* smile from her too red lips, then waved her fingers and hurried away. She wore a dress way to tight for the workplace and heels so high they gave Kylie a nosebleed.

Bitch, Kylie thought as she bent to gather the scattered papers. *Don't even worry about helping.*

Still muttering to herself as she walked to her car in the lot, she groaned when she saw it.

Seriously?

A small sliver of paper was tucked under her windshield wiper.

Kylie picked up the pace and rushed to it. A ticket, really? She was parked in a legal space, or so she thought. Did they give out tickets in this lot if you didn't have a BMW or similar luxury car? Maybe she'd needed to have a special sticker to park there. Muttering a curse under her breath, she lifted it up and turned it over. And realized it wasn't a ticket at all.

It was something much worse.

A single message was scrawled on the paper in black Sharpie: *Stop Meddling or You're Next.*

30

Linc turned off the radio as he drove downtown. The news was all about the miraculous rescue of a pair of sisters who'd been involved in the collapse of the parking lot. As happy as he was that they'd been found, it should've been him and Storm who found them. That brought the total number of people rescued up to twelve. He hadn't been involved in a single one of them.

But he had something else to worry about now.

It was now nearly dinnertime, but if he knew Kylie, she was still at the office, nose-to-the-grindstone. When he drove past the little storefront, sure enough, the lights were on, clearly illuminating her in the window. She was hunched over a large pile of papers and appeared to be going through them one by one.

The first thing Linc felt wasn't anger. It was pride.

But the anger was a close second.

He forced himself to keep that emotion at the forefront as he pulled into a space a few doors down.

Linc went inside, and she looked up. "Hi!" she said, obviously genuinely happy to see him. Vader jumped up from his place at the window and ran to greet him too. With a word, Linc easily calmed him down.

Funny, just months ago, the big dog had been a crazy, disobedient mess, and Linc'd taught him a thing or two. But his owner? She never learned.

He'd planned to unleash on her the second he stepped inside, but then he saw that she had company. Her boss, Greg, was at the sink in the kitchenette in the back, cleaning the coffee maker.

"Hey, Linc," he said, turning off the faucet and shaking Linc's hand with his wet one. "You come to relieve me of this troublemaker?"

That's exactly what she was. They all knew it. Why had he expected different?

She batted her eyelashes at them innocently. "What? Me? Trouble?"

Greg laughed. Linc didn't. His voice was stiff. "Actually, I just came to have a word with Kylie. I can't stay."

Kylie lifted up the stack of papers. "Good. I can't go anywhere anyway. I'm going to be chained to the office for the foreseeable future, until I figure this out."

"Is that your *embezzlement* case?" Linc asked with a hint of sarcasm. Embezzlement, which had just become murder.

She nodded, giving him a curious look.

"To hell with that," Greg said, grabbing his keys. "It'll still be here tomorrow." He had to be the easiest guy to work for because he clearly didn't give a shit.

Kylie shook her head. "But I—"

"Take that pile of papers and work on it at home if you have to. The lights in here are going out."

She sighed. "Fine. Give me five." She stood up and started to pack up her things. "You can go, Greg. I'll close up."

"All right," he said, zipping his jacket up over his beer belly and heading out. "See you all."

Linc watched him leave, the top of his balding head shining in the streetlights as he hurried to his car, this beat-up old boat that he'd left right outside the place. He got in and pulled out, and when he left, Linc turned to see Kylie watching him.

"You're clearly upset at me for something." She pushed some stray hairs back from her face. "What did I do now?"

"It's more like, what *didn't* you do." He crossed his arms. "I had a talk with Jacob, so can you now imagine why I'm here?"

Her eyes widened a little, but then her expression turned mulish.

He didn't let the silence last. "Were you even going to tell me about your little adventure at the coffee shop?"

The glower collapsed, and she covered her face with her hands. He watched her take a deep breath, exhale it, and drop her hands back to her sides, her expression carefully neutral.

"Yes, I was going to tell you when the timing was better." She paused, letting the meaning of that sink in.

"I'm not an invalid," Linc snapped.

She softened a little. "You're the strongest man I know, but you're going through something very difficult right now. What was I supposed to do, Linc? You have PTSD, and while you're still clearly recovering from a violent episode of it, I'm supposed to give you the play-by-play of how the man I was supposed to meet was offed in his shiny red Porsche?"

He wasn't quite sure what to say to that, so of course something stupid slipped from his mouth. "I don't have PTSD."

She rolled her eyes, but it was a gesture loaded with sadness. "Yes, Linc. You do. And I feel strongly that I've contributed to the recent intensity of it. It makes me want to protect you…" She seemed to realize she'd said the absolute wrong thing. "Not protect. I just want you to be better. Be happy."

His head was starting to hurt. "You're right, I don't need protection. I'm fine. What's important now is that we protect *you*."

She rolled her eyes. It only annoyed him. She'd done the same when he warned her about the serial killer.

"Kylie. Don't. Someone murdered that guy, and you could be next. Don't take this lightly."

She stiffened. "I'm not a total idiot," she mumbled, picking up the printout in front of her again. She didn't look at him. "And, for the record, did Jacob also tell you that Nate Jennings was into some shady stuff, so his murder might not have anything to do with me? The timing could be purely coincidental."

Bullshit. He could tell from the way she avoided his eyes that she didn't believe that for a second.

"Yeah, but you can't be too careful. I think…" He stopped. He hadn't planned on bringing this up, but what the hell. It made the most sense. "I think you should move in with me."

She blinked. "What?"

"You heard me."

She sank into her chair, but the mulish expression returned. "I'm not moving in with you so you can put a leash on me like one of your dogs."

He didn't think she could have said anything that would have pissed him off more. "I would never do that. If you want to protect me and I want to protect you, living together makes sense."

She popped back up and walked around the desk, stopping only a foot in front of him. "How does it make sense?

You don't want me sleeping with you, but now you want me to move in? You don't call me for days, but now you want me to move in? You push me away with your words, but you want me to move in? You—"

He held up both hands. "I get it, and yes, I still want you to move in. It's for your protection."

Her eyes shone with defiance. "You don't get to protect me if I'm not allowed to protect you. Those are the rules."

Turning on her heel, she marched away, not stopping until the bathroom door clicked closed behind her.

Dammit. He should've known she'd make this hard. Hell, he should have known that he'd screw up the invitation.

He sat down in her chair, elbows on the desk, head in his hands, over that stack of papers. He couldn't not look at it. It was a stack of financials. Photocopies of checks to various public arts entities. Charitable donations, it appeared. These must have been the financial records for the client she was working for. He knew it was confidential information, so he attempted to look away, but not before he saw a familiar logo on the top of each check copy. He'd seen that elegant, frilly script a million times.

It was the Coulter and Associates logo.

Linc sat up. Rubbed his eyes. Pushed away from the desk and walked to the window. Vader perked up, came over, and licked his hand. Instead of a SAR dog, the big Newfoundland should be trained as a comfort animal. He had the instincts.

He petted his big head, trying to breathe, not turning when the bathroom door opened again. In the reflection of the window, he could see Kylie pulling on her long sweater coat, grab a stack of the papers and force them into the giant purse she was carrying.

After she disconnected her phone from the charging cord, he finally turned to face her. "You mind telling me why my father's company is on those papers?"

She froze. Lifting her gaze to meet his, she pressed her lips together. "I'm going through a number of possibilities, Linc."

"Wait." He dragged a hand down his face and tried to connect the dots. She wasn't saying it, but it was written on her face. "Are you investigating my father's company for something?"

She lifted a shoulder. "Right now, I'm just gathering facts and—"

He snorted. "So, do you think my father killed your client's grandson?" He said it with sarcasm, but he watched her closely for a reaction. Surely she didn't think his father, asshole that he was, would do something like that.

"No! Of course not!" Her face had transformed into a splotchy red. "I'm attempting to follow the money trail, Linc, and the only way I can do that is by looking through financial records...which your father's company possesses." She waved a hand at the pile.

"What have you learned so far?"

She sighed. "Not much. As you can see, there are stacks upon stacks for me to go through."

Linc strode to the desk, picked up a pile.

Kylie narrowed her eyes at him. "What are you doing?"

"I'm going to help you sort through all this."

Her mouth opened. Closed. Opened again, but nothing came out. He'd have to mark the calendar. He'd stunned her into silence.

Or was it something else...?

He leaned his hip against the desk. "What aren't you telling me?"

She opened her mouth again. Silence. Long moments of silence.

"Are you trying to protect me again?" he asked quietly.

She nodded, then quickly shook her head, regaining the power of speech. "No, of course not. I—"

He turned toward the door. "Good, then it's settled, I'll help you."

"Linc!"

He was smiling as he strode outside, Vader on his heels.

The smile fell away when she grabbed his arm, pulling so hard he almost lost his grip on the paperwork. With the cool breeze that had kicked up, it would have sucked trying to chase them down.

"Linc, stop."

He turned to her. "Kylie, listen to me. Your embezzlement case just turned into a murder case, and somehow, big or small, my father is involved. I'll go out of my mind if I don't help you. Do you get that?"

She let out a breath. "But—"

"If you want to protect me, move in with me and let me help you. It's only fair. He's my father."

She nodded, but it was with clear reluctance. "Fine. I guess that makes sense. I just didn't want you finding out something that might hurt you."

He gritted his teeth. Did she really think he was made of glass?

"Jesus, Lee. I'm not twelve. I won't be hurt. I'll be pissed. And if he is doing something, which I highly doubt, I want to be the first to know about it."

"Okay. Well," she held up the pile, "maybe I should go to my apartment and get a couple changes of clothes?"

He took a step closer to her. "That's a good start. But I'm starving. Maybe we could stop in at the Chinese place on the corner and start working through some of this paperwork first?"

She smiled and raised her hand to his cheek. "Chinese sounds good."

He leaned down and kissed her forehead. "Don't worry. I'll protect you."

She pulled his head down until their lips almost touched. "And I'll protect you right back."

31

Kylie felt better, working with Linc.

After the love note she'd gotten on the window of her car, she'd thought about giving up. Once again, she had some criminal stalking her, threatening her, possibly wanting her dead. The first time, she'd ended up shot. So Linc was right. She needed to be careful.

And she felt a thousand times safer with him by her side.

Not to mention, she'd get through all this work faster with his help.

She was calling it a win-win.

Except the whole "move in with me" situation. Was he serious? Was he thinking temporarily or on a more permanent basis? Either way, it was a huge step, one she wasn't sure she'd ever be ready to make. As scared as she sometimes was since the Spotlight Killer broke into her home, she still valued her little solitary corner of the world, a place that was hers and hers alone.

The China Palace was nearly empty when they walked in. It'd just started drizzling, so they shook the raindrops out of their hair as the hostess seated them at a table in the corner. They didn't even look at the menu. They both ordered chicken teriyaki and egg rolls.

Kylie sipped her iced tea and rubbed her hands together, preparing to dig into the load of work in front of them. As she divvied up the stack of papers, she realized Linc was watching her curiously. He tented his hands under his chin and said, "So?"

She smiled. "Are you thinking I'm a mind reader now? So…what?"

"Nothing. I just know you and Jacob have been talking. And clearly, you've been talking to my family too." His lips curved in amusement that seemed genuine. "It's like you're more involved with my friends and family than I am. I figure you can fill me in on what I'm missing, so I won't have to actually interact with anyone ever again."

She laughed. "You'd love that, huh? It's not my fault you're a grouchy old miser!"

He smirked at her. "Would you please stop calling me old."

Her grin grew wider. "Your people aren't half bad. Jacob's great, your mother is a sweetheart, and…"

His eyebrows shot up to his hairline when she paused. "And my dad?"

Kylie cleared her throat. "Well…"

"Still a bloodsucker?" He leaned forward. "Did you talk to him at his office?"

She wrinkled her nose. "No. He was *too important* for me." She made a face like the Bitch on High had made at her.

He let out a snort of disgust. "That's where I would've come in handy. If I told him you were coming, he would've made time for you."

She gave him a suspicious look. "Really? He hates you.

Well, at least he doesn't seem to respect much about your life choices, so it surprises me that he would go out of his way."

He leaned back in his seat, looking a bit surprised. "I'm his son."

"Well, he hates *me*, then. After that dinner." Kylie sighed, thinking of the way he'd looked at her across the dining room table. She'd always believed that no one could make her feel inferior without her consent, but he had a way of making her feel as worthy as an inchworm. "I don't know what it is about him, but when I think of him, I feel…speechless."

"Holy shit. You…speechless? Really? I don't believe it." He winked at her. "Come on, Lee. He's just a guy. He would've been happy to meet with you."

Happy was probably a strong word where Jonathan Coulter was concerned. She didn't even see him getting mildly amused. "Well. It doesn't matter. I did talk to his assistant's assistant, Dustin Weiss. That's where all the print-outs came from."

"Dustin Weiss?" Linc scratched at his jaw. "Must be new."

"He was very helpful. And the best part about it was that I didn't have to deal with your dad."

"Wow. You really have a problem with him, don't you? I never thought I'd see the fearless Kylie Hatfield intimidated by a man."

She felt her cheeks heating. "He's not just a man. I don't know what it is. Maybe that he's your dad, and a successful fixture in this town. Or that we really didn't hit it off during our first meeting. But I'll admit it. He turns me into a pile of nerves."

"Probably doesn't help much that you're investigating him for…" he gestured to the papers, "something."

"Right. That too."

He shook his head. "Well. Next time, as long as he's not

getting cuffs slapped on him, we'll get together and I'll prove to you he isn't a demon. Just a flesh and blood man with a wickedly sharp tongue. How about that?"

Kylie smiled. She was glad Linc had a bit of his sense of humor back. It'd been a while since she'd seen it. "That sounds good. Thanks."

"Great." He checked his phone and pointed to the top paper. "We'd better start looking this stuff over. I have a SAR training session at my house at eight."

She glanced at the clock. That gave them just over an hour.

They each started to go through their piles while also digging into their food. They were mostly silent until Linc straightened and tapped on a paper. "That's interesting."

She perked up. Her eyes were about crossed by then. "What is?"

He was looking at the stack of checks from The Asheville Foundation, an artist's colony for underprivileged young people. "Well, your client has been contributing to this charity since 1999, and every year, the amount she donated grew substantially. Then without warning, about seven months ago, the checks stopped."

"Stopped?"

He nodded. "Yeah. Cold."

She flipped through her stack, looking to see if any of the foundation's paperwork had been misfiled. "That *is* interesting because Emma said she never authorized cutting off contributions to any of the charities she supported."

Linc ran his finger down a column. "The money's been disappearing from her accounts, but it hasn't been going to where it's supposed to be going."

He lifted his cell phone from his pocket and started to punch in a number.

"Who are you calling?" she asked.

"This Asheville Foundation," he mouthed.

She was about to tell him that the place would surely be closed when he held up a finger. "Hello? Yes. This is Mr. Coulter with Coulter and Associates, and I'm working on records for Emma Jennings's charitable donations." He paused and looked up at the ceiling, listening. "Yes…Yes…I did what? Okay."

She watched the confusion dawning on his face and tapped the table. "What?"

He covered the mouthpiece and said, "Supposedly, the checks stopped coming, and when it was questioned, some paperwork from my dad's company was forwarded to them, officially ending the relationship."

"Paperwork? Can they email it to me?"

"They will probably only email an official Coulter and Associates email address."

Kylie tapped her fingers on the table. "Would they fax it to Emma?"

He shrugged. "Yes, thank you." He was speaking into the phone again and motioning for her to write the number down. She flipped through her notepad, found the number and turned the book toward Linc. "Yes. If you could fax it to Mrs. Jennings, that would be helpful." He stared at the notepad. "Yes, that's the correct number."

Once he'd disconnected the call, he looked both excited and dismayed. "Let's go through and find out how many other organizations had their relationship end with Mrs. Jennings about the same time."

They spent the next fifteen minutes putting together a stack of organizations, five in all, whose checks stopped coming in the first quarter of the year. They were some of her smaller charitable donations, but the amount was significant, at least $750,000 in total. To someone like Emma, that was probably a drop in the bucket, but to anyone else…it was big money.

"I wonder if whoever took the money thought she wouldn't notice it was gone?" Kylie asked, finishing up her iced tea.

"That's exactly what this person is thinking," he said with a confidence she agreed with. "Now, we need to get our hands on that fax."

Kylie smiled. "That part is easy. Emma has a fax to email system, and guess who has the password to her email?"

Linc grinned, although he still looked troubled. Pushing to his feet, he pulled his wallet from his pocket and paid for their meal. "Let's go."

As they walked back to her office, Vader started to bark from the storefront window of Starr Investigations, looking highly offended to have been left behind. She hoped he hadn't torn up everything.

She opened up the door again, and he licked and jumped, as if he hadn't just seen them an hour before.

"Whoa, boy," Linc said as he assaulted them, not letting them through the door. "Calm yourself."

Kylie was the one who needed calming. She raced to her laptop, nearly tripping over the trash can in her rush.

Booting it up took forever, and she was ready to scream by the time she logged into Emma's email account.

There it was. She clicked on the attachment and printed it off.

As Linc continued to quiet Vader, he said, "The next thing would be to find out who touched your client's financials. Starting with whoever sent them that notice ending all the contributions. You said she was a little absentminded. Are you sure she didn't just forget?"

"If she did, then where did the money go to?" Kylie reasoned. "Can you get that light? Behind the coffee maker?"

He flipped it on, and Kylie had to blink to get her eyes adjusted to the light. It was a two-page document on Coulter and Associates letterhead. She read over all of the legal mumbo-jumbo, then flipped to the second page to see who'd signed the order.

She gnawed on her lip.

"What?" Linc grumbled, coming over to her side.

She held up the page to him. "I guess the person we have to start with is your dad. *He* signed these papers." She pointed to the second page. "This is his signature, right?"

He stared at it. "Looks like it. Shit." He let out a tired sigh. "*Shit*. What the—"

"Linc..." she started gently.

He waved her off. "I can't deal with this now. If I don't leave now, I'm going to miss my SAR class. Let me take you back to your place to grab a few things."

"No need. My car is just down the block. I can meet you at your place later."

He looked doubtful. "Are you sure?"

"For the last time, yes. I have Vader. I'll be okay. You go ahead."

He nodded, his face drawn, looking ready to argue.

Kylie folded the fax and tucked it in with the rest of the papers. "Look. It doesn't have to mean that he's involved. A number of things could've happened that your father knew nothing about. We just have to figure it out."

He leaned on the edge of the desk and stroked his chin. "Very few things go on under the Coulter and Associates umbrella that my father doesn't know about. I guarantee you he even knows that *you* were there today, even if you didn't see him personally."

She blinked. "Really?"

Linc walked her to the Mazda and gave her a kiss on her

hairline. “I don’t want to lord over you, Lee,” he said gently. “I just want you to be safe.”

“I know.” Kylie stood up onto her tiptoes and gave him an actual lip-to-lip kiss. It was cool outside, but his lips were so warm. She wanted to sink into them. Sink into the rest of him. There may have been a fine line between protection and imprisonment, but at times like these, she didn’t mind either, as long as Linc was doing the keeping.

But when they parted, and she got into her car, she’d barely driven to the end of the block before those familiar nerves returned and she started to worry again.

If Jonathan Coulter knew everything about what happened at his office, did he also write that threatening note and put it under her windshield wiper? If it wasn’t him, did he know who had? With his wealth, did he have a person who cleaned up all of his messes?

And was she a new mess who needed to be dealt with?

Kylie shivered.

If she ever hoped to solve this case, she needed to get over her fear of Jonathan Coulter, and soon.

Eeny, meeny, miny, moe.

Which meddling kid should be the next to go?

I smiled, amused at myself as I watched Kylie Hatfield and Linc Coulter kiss on the sidewalk.

Scooby Doo had been my favorite show as a kid. I’d loved the ghosts. The mystery. And I loved how, even as a young child, I would sit and think about all the ways I wouldn’t have been caught, had I been the villain.

The smile faded as I watched them part ways, neither looking like they had a care in the world.

Which should go first?

Eeny or meeny?

Of course, I could wait until they were next together in that dilapidated farmhouse Linc Coulter called home. A can or two of gasoline, some matches.

Whoosh…Nate Jennings style.

All my problems burned to the ground. Well, except one.

The old crow.

Her old man had proven so easy to eliminate…but Emma Jennings was turning into much more of a challenge. Things had been so perfect as we followed my carefully laid plan.

We just needed to be patient, I'd told D a number of times. But no. D had gotten greedy.

Now, here we were.

On the defensive.

I didn't like it. It wasn't how it was supposed to be.

I should be in bed, making love to my partner instead of sitting in this vehicle I'd bought in cash from the lot in Virginia. Actually, I'd bought two. One never knew when they'd need a covert giveaway.

Another detail of my planning.

Tapping on the screen of my phone, I watched the crow lying in her bed, her shaking hands lifting a teacup to her lips. A man appeared, the doctor, I recognized, and the crow waved him off when he attempted to take her blood pressure.

The crow was no good tonight. Too many people surrounding her.

I looked back up, in time to watch Linc and Kylie part ways.

Eeny. He strode to his truck, a man apparently on a mission.

Meeny. She bounced to her little hatchback, the dog at her side.

Miny. Linc was already in his truck, roaring it to life. He honked once before pulling from the curb.

Moe. As Kylie placed the paperwork in her car, the dog wondered into the grass to pee.

I smiled.

The game had chosen.

32

Heading back toward home, Linc was thinking hard.

He patted the jacket pocket in which he'd snuck the copy of the fax when Kylie wasn't looking. He planned to go down to his dad's place bright and early in the morning, confront him on it. He'd have the answers soon.

Kylie may have been suspicious of his father, but Linc knew his old man couldn't be behind this. He didn't care what the papers showed. His father had too many years in the business to suddenly start skimming other people's money. There was some other explanation.

But what?

Curious, Linc called his dad's cell phone, but it went right to voicemail.

With each mile he drove, the doubt grew. His father was and always had been ambitious, almost to a fault. He could be cutthroat if he wanted to be. More than once, he'd told Linc he had to go out and take what was his because no one would simply give it to him. If his dad had let his ambition overshadow his morals, he wouldn't be the first person. And maybe he had been doing it all his life and this was the first time he'd been caught.

Linc drummed his fingers on the steering wheel, thinking.

He couldn't wait until tomorrow to find out. If he did, he'd go insane.

Pulling to the side of the road, he made a U-turn.

He'd just go talk to him. His dad'd be home by now, and Linc could begin to clear this up. It'd set his mind at ease, if nothing else, to know where he was.

As Linc drove, he picked up his phone and rescheduled the SAR class. It was an online one, anyway, and the producer assured him that enrollment was low because there'd been a glitch in the marketing campaign, so it'd be fine to give it a couple more weeks to gain interest. Relieved about that, he pushed on the gas and drove to Biltmore Forest.

He pulled into his parents' driveway a few minutes later and climbed the steps to their front door. He rang the doorbell, and their butler answered. "Hi, Mason," Linc said to him. Mason reached for Linc's coat, but he shook his head. "Is my father in?"

His mother's hearing was apparently sensitive to his voice. She appeared at the top of the staircase right away, her face lit up by his presence. "Oh, Lincoln, this is such a nice surprise."

"Hi," he said to her as she swept down toward him and took his hand. He gave her cheek a kiss. "Is Dad here?"

She nodded. "In his study. We just finished dinner." She frowned. "Are you…is everything okay?"

"Yeah. Perfect. I just need to talk to him," Linc said, striding toward the back of the house. He'd made sure his study was far removed from the noise of the home, and it was every bit what one would expect from a man's study: mahogany walls, hunting trophies, the faint scent of cigar smoke. As a kid, Linc wasn't allowed there, and he wasn't sure he was much more welcome now. He knocked on the door anyway.

A muffled voice muttered, "Come in." He looked up from a small circle of light created by his banker's lamp and frowned. "Linc?" If his father was happy to see him, he didn't let on.

"Dad."

Jonathan Coulter set down his pen and straightened. "I'm in the middle of something important. What brings you down here now?"

Linc reached into his pocket and unfolded the printed fax. He spread it out and slammed it down on the desk in front of his father. "I think an explanation for this is more important."

Jonathan's eyes drifted to it without much interest before spearing into Linc. "I don't have to explain anything."

"Do you see what it is?" Linc said, tapping the paper. "It's a notice, signed by you, stating that your client would not be contributing any longer to this charitable organization. We've found five organizations so far for which contributions ceased earlier this year."

His dad flipped the page over. "So? This is standard practice."

"The problem is that Mrs. Jennings didn't authorize that these contributions be cancelled, and the money was still withdrawn from her account. It's missing."

"Mrs. Jennings?" He suddenly sounded interested. He lifted the page and stared at it. "Emma Jennings?"

"Yeah. She's concerned. And she hired a private investigator to look into it."

"Ah." His dad put his elbows on the desk and rested his chin on his fingertips. "You mean Kylie Hatfield, your girlfriend? I heard she was snooping about the offices. I told Dustin to give her whatever she was looking for. I have nothing to hide."

"Well, there's clearly something going on. Mrs. Jennings may be elderly, but she's smart or she wouldn't have hired a PI in the first place."

Jonathan rolled his eyes. "I've known Emma for decades. She's a lovely woman, but since Arnold died, she's been acting increasingly odd, and a bit paranoid. Starting a year or so ago, she began calling, concerned someone was after her money. I told her that everything is as it should be, she should stop worrying, and let us take care of her estate. I suppose she found me to be dismissive." He sighed. "Perhaps I was. I'll call her tomorrow and straighten this whole thing out. Satisfied?"

Linc stared at him. Jonathan Coulter could be a lion when he wanted to be, but anytime Linc tried to assert himself, he always made him feel like he was overreacting. Linc's eyes slipped to the paper. "Tell me why you signed those papers."

He let out a loud, booming laugh. "Emma must have asked me to. She's suffering from dementia, boy. She can't remember what she had for breakfast most days. No, I don't recall her asking me to, but she's not my only client. As for the money, I have no idea what she did with it. That's something for her financial advisor to sort out."

Linc sucked on his cheek, thinking. "So, would she ask you directly to do such a thing?"

"No. That's why I have assistants. As you well know, Heather Collins has been my primary assistant since before you were born, and her assistant, Dustin Weiss, is a fine young man. He's been in charge of the administrative work on the account for the past year. He has an impeccable record. In fact, he was recommended to me by Emma. He was her son's roommate in college, I believe she told me."

That caught Linc's attention. "Emma's…son?"

Jonathan waved a dismissive hand. "Grandson, nephew… something like that." His dad sucked in a breath and let it out slowly. "Are we done with this inquisition because I really have to get back to work."

Linc planted his palms on the enormous desk. The thing was huge—his dad's motto was Go Big or Go Home—so the desk took up much of the room. Even so, he kept it immaculately clean. The only things on it were papers, a pen, and his elbows.

When Linc came closer to him, he dropped his elbows off the table as if he thought Linc might strike him. Or as if he couldn't stand to be near his own son.

That made Linc pause.

This was his father, not a monster like Kylie seemed to think. The father no longer scared the son. Linc just had nothing in common with the man and couldn't tolerate the insolence that dripped from his mouth.

Bullies, Linc knew, often barked more than they bit. And they ran with their tails between their legs when threatened in return.

"Look," Linc said. As much as he didn't want to be there, he needed his father's help if he was going to help Kylie. "There's something going on, and I need to get to the bottom of it."

"*You* need to?" Jonathan's lip was curled into a mocking sneer. "I thought it was your girlfriend's case."

"I don't want her getting into it. Nate Jennings, Emma's grandson, was murdered last night. Shot in the head."

For the first time, his dad looked surprised. He lifted off his glasses and rubbed his eyes. "Shot?"

"Yeah. So, this is bigger than missing money."

"How do you know that crime has anything to do with this?" He tapped the fax with his glasses.

Reluctantly, Linc admitted, "I don't. But I don't want to take chances with Kylie's life. If the two are tied together, she could be in trouble."

"Sounds to me like your girlfriend's a tough cookie. She brought down that serial killer, remember?"

"She was almost killed bringing down a serial killer." Linc didn't even bother to share his role in that horrendous night. He didn't want to relive it. And, it wouldn't have mattered.

Linc's father's face transformed into a mask that was all too familiar. This was the face he used when he was going to verbally slaughter someone. "Does your girlfriend even really need you? Or are you just meddling because you want to feel useful?"

Linc let the verbal blow land and slide off. "If Nate is dead and your assistant knows him, you don't think that's too suspicious to be a coincidence?"

"Assistant's assistant," Jonathan corrected. "I know that you must be going insane up there on that mountain alone with your dogs, and you're obviously coming up with wild conspiracy theories."

Linc forced his hands to unclench, his face to relax. "For the last time, Father," he said in the calmest voice he could muster, "I am not some mountain man living away from society and doing nothing with his life. I have a job, and it's a good one. One that I like. One that I'm successful at. I know that you don't think that's possible since I'm not plodding along in your footsteps, but people define success in different ways. I don't need the mansion or the BMW, and I sure as hell don't want them. I'm happy with my life! Why can't you accept that?"

Linc was standing above him, but his dad still managed to look down his nose. "I don't care what you do on that mountain. What I do care about is when you come down here, accusing me of all kinds of ridiculous nonsense like I'm some two-bit criminal! How dare you."

All the fight drained out of Linc's system. "So, you'll believe some 'fine young man' you've known all of a year over your own son? Is that what you're saying?"

His dad pressed his lips together, and his nostrils flared. "I'm not—"

"If you're not going to check him out, I'm going to get the police involved," Linc said, grabbing the fax from the desk, turning on his heel, and heading toward the door.

"Wait," Jonathan boomed. "Don't do anything rash."

"If this has been happening for months, it isn't rash." He turned back to face his father. "What I see is someone who insists on keeping his head in the sand, so go ahead. But don't be surprised if your *assistant's assistant* doesn't show up to work tomorrow. You'll know where to find him. Downtown, being questioned, which is something you should be doing."

Jonathan threw up his hands, his face turning a mottled red. "Linc!"

But Linc pulled open the heavy mahogany door and walked into the hallway, nearly running into his mother, who was staring at him with wide eyes. "What on earth is going on, Lincoln?"

He shook his head and pocketed the fax. He'd get out to the car and call Jacob and ask him what he thought. Jacob wouldn't think he was overreacting. "Nothing for you to worry about." He leaned in and kissed her cheek. "I've got to go."

"But you just got here." She followed him closely, as if she was planning to bar him from stepping out the door.

"I'm sorry, Mom. I'll come another time." His ire softened as he looked into her worried eyes. "I promise. I've got to do something."

As he leaned in to kiss her sweet-smelling cheek again, she said, "I wish you two would just get along."

"Yeah." He squeezed the hand gripping his arm. "Me too."

But as the door closed behind him, he didn't think that would ever be possible.

33

I'm a big girl, Kylie told herself as she pushed open the door to her apartment.

Vader trotted in happily. He had no qualms about going inside, wasn't acting nervous or suspicious. That should've calmed her, but she'd come to learn that while he was a good watchdog in barking at everything that moved, when he was hungry, which he was now, he didn't give a rat's ass about anything else. He ran off for his food dish, then looked highly insulted that it was empty.

Kylie bristled as she turned on the lights. Only a couple months ago, the Spotlight Killer had been waiting for her in the apartment, and Vader hadn't noticed. The killer'd poisoned his food and tased her into unconsciousness before kidnapping her.

She kept trying to remind herself that lightning like that didn't strike twice. She was fine.

It didn't stop her from peeking under her bed, behind the shower curtain, and inside her walk-in closet, expecting a masked stranger at every turn.

But it was fine. No boogeymen to speak of. Sighing, she

poured Vader the food she'd started buying in individually sealed packs and kicked off her heels, her feet singing praise at the freedom. Standing in front of her empty fridge, she wished she had some dessert to wash down her chicken teriyaki. Ice cream. That would've done so nicely.

As usual, her fridge was empty. What a great diet.

Slamming the door, Kylie went to where she'd left the pile of papers. Something odd was definitely going on, and she was determined to solve the puzzle.

For Emma.

The sweet little woman who was being taken advantage of. The sweet little woman who was currently mourning her only grandchild.

And then there were the charities that were stripped of needed support so cruelly.

For one person's greed?

Was that how the Coulter family got so rich? Were they bloodsuckers in a way she hadn't anticipated?

Sifting through the stack, she searched for the fax, hoping to examine Jonathan Coulter's signature more closely. Maybe she could find additional signatures on the world wide web and be able to make a comparison.

Tomorrow, she would call the other charities that had contributions ended around the same time. Even better, she'd visit them personally. For the hundredth time, she mourned the fact that she didn't have business cards.

Brows furrowed, she sifted through the stack again. The fax was missing. She looked a third time, but it was definitely missing. Had it fallen between the seats in the car?

As she reached for her shoes, it suddenly hit her.

What if Linc had taken it? What if he'd gone to confront his father?

Heat shot through her veins. This was her case. Yes, she'd

told him he could help because his father was involved, but that didn't mean commandeering it!

Calm down, she told herself. A missing fax did not a commandeering boyfriend make. Then she snorted at the word "boyfriend," reminding herself that they were not in a relationship.

Whatever he was to her, she needed to give him the benefit of the doubt.

Wiggling out of her skirt, she quickly threw on jeans and a pair of comfy sneakers. "How dare he!" she hissed at the walls as Vader looked on. Just like that, her benefit of the doubt speech was out the window. He'd taken it. She just knew it as sure as she knew she needed to pee.

Heading to the bathroom, she tried to reason with herself.

Okay, so what if he had taken it? He would probably get more intel from his father than she, a virtual stranger, ever could.

But...ohhh!

Grabbing her sweater, she hooked the leash to Vader's collar, still cursing herself.

"Move in with me," she muttered in a deep-voiced Linc imitation.

Now she knew why! So he could insert himself into her business. And her panties.

Speaking of panties, if she'd just pulled her big girl ones on and questioned Jonathan from the get-go, maybe Linc wouldn't have felt the need to do it himself. That's what she got for acting like a scared little girl. Next time, she told herself as she ran down the stairs to her car, she wouldn't let fear control her.

Inside the car, Vader at her side, she couldn't help mumbling to herself. She knew Linc had his SAR meeting, so he probably hadn't spoken to his dad yet. She didn't care if he was in the middle of training a thousand SAR dogs up there.

She would commandeer her little ass right in the middle of his meeting, tackle him to get the fax back, then remind him that this was her case and to back the hell off.

She would be the one to question his father, thank you very much.

As she was working herself into a lather, Kylie didn't realize until the light was shining into her rearview mirror that a car had come up pretty fast on her backside and was now riding her rear end. As she squinted into the mirror, the lights swerved, like the car was trying to go around her.

Great. Just what she needed. Some drunk college kid on the way home from the Asheville bars, taking chances with her life. It was a narrow, two-lane road up the mountain with hardly any shoulder and deep ravines off each side. Even though it wasn't a passing zone, Kylie didn't want him on her tail for the next fifteen minutes. She slowed a little and moved toward the shoulder, rolled down her window, and motioned for him to go around.

The idiot didn't get the picture. He pulled back slightly, then sped up, coming so close she expected to feel the jolt of his car hitting her bumper.

"Holy lord," she breathed when the contact didn't come. Every muscle in her body was on high alert, causing her shoulder to twinge as she gripped the steering wheel for dear life.

Beside her, Vader seemed equally concerned, his front paws splayed in a bracing position.

She had to keep him safe.

Speeding up, Kylie thought through her options. There wasn't a turnoff in which she could safely pull into, but they were reaching a short straightaway a half mile or so ahead. Maybe the asshole would get brave enough to pass when they reached that. As she came out of the curve, she slowed a little, hoping he'd just go ahead.

He didn't. He stayed right on her rear.

Kylie grabbed for her cell phone, grateful that it now had nearly a full battery. She fumbled with the screen, pulling up the phone app.

She managed to tap 9, then her blood pressure spiked higher. The other driver was playing cat and mouse, swerving like he was going to pass, then falling back. Again and again. Once, he did it while another car was coming, almost causing a head-on collision. The car's horn screamed as it passed, mingling with Kylie's yelp of fear.

This wasn't just some road-raged moron, she realized. This was a real threat.

Stop Meddling or You're Next.

Every hair on her body stood on end as the person's bumper kissed hers.

She fumbled with her phone again while holding tight onto the steering wheel, which had jerked a little at the impact. A fresh surge of adrenaline made her heart pound.

"Be calm," she said to Vader, trying to use a voice that wouldn't scare him. Scare her.

The screen of her phone had gone dark, and it was too dark for the device to recognize her face. She blindly pressed her finger on the reader, hoping she was touching the right place.

He tapped her bumper again. Harder this time.

The steering wheel jerked again, and she dropped the phone, needing to put all her attention on the task of staying on the road.

A quick glance at the speedometer told her she was going nearly sixty on this twisty road, and the speed limit was only forty in the straighter places. She'd never gone so fast up this steep incline.

Bright lights grew brighter in her mirrors, and she braced for another hit.

It never came.

Instead, she heard a loud bang just as the steering wheel pulled sharply to the right.

She fought to control the steering wheel, and for a moment, she thought she'd been successful, but the flop flop flop of the burst tire transformed into the skid of the other tires sliding on the gravel shoulder. Then the scream of metal on metal as she careened over the guardrail that might as well have been made from paper.

Then there was nothing.

No yellow lines on the road. No bright lights behind her.

She stared out into the inky darkness just before gravity took the upper hand and her little Mazda fell back to earth.

Poor Vader hit the ceiling before she did, the strap of her seatbelt digging cruelly into her shoulder.

She had to save her dog.

Fighting the momentum of the falling car, Kylie reached for Vader, pulling him to her side.

Kylie screamed as the little car picked up speed, whizzing down the steep mountain, trees blurring in the illumination of her headlights. She held on to Vader, bracing them both the best she could as tree limbs scratched and clawed the windshield. Her vision blurred as her head banged the ceiling a second time as it was lifted, airborne, into the unknown.

34

As Linc pulled out of his parents' development, he put in a call to Jacob. As the phone rang, he knew how pissed Kylie would be at him, but he couldn't worry about that right then.

He needed to help her and keep her safe. Her anger would be worth it.

When Jacob answered, Linc said, "I think I have the answer to Kylie's embezzlement case and Nate Jennings's murder."

"Whoa. Wait one second. How the hell did you get involved in this?"

"Kylie told me."

Jacob laughed. "Did she? Willingly?"

"She had to. She thought my father was involved in some way. So, we started looking into it together, and it turns out that my father, who happens to be Emma's attorney, has a fairly new assistant to his assistant who's been handling a lot of the administrative work. Dustin Weiss. He was also Nate Jennings's college roommate."

Jacob was quick on the uptake. "Kylie told me that Nate's

college roommate was recently back in the picture. Some story about a stool and bisexual affair. I don't remember the details."

Linc scratched his chin. "I'm not sure about the stool, but she told me that Nate cheated on the female cougar assistant with the male college roommate. Or something like that."

"And you think this Dustin Weiss has been skimming off Emma's accounts?"

"Could be."

"And killed Nate Jennings?"

"Possibly."

Jacob cleared his throat. "What does Kylie say? This being her case and all?"

"What does it matter?"

Jacob groaned. "You're playing with fire, man. She finds out you did this on your own, and she'll have your balls for lunch."

Linc had no doubt. "She'll get over it. Anyway, you need to bring Dustin Weiss in for questioning."

"Can you give me a little more to go on than what you have so far? The kid being new to your father's practice doesn't give me much of a leg to stand on."

His friend was right. What hard evidence did they really have?

"He used to be roommates with Nate Jennings in college."

"Sooo..."

Link gritted his teeth. "So, they knew each other. And what if Nate figured out what his old college roomie was doing and was going to blow the whistle?"

"So, you seriously think that this Dustin Weiss killed Nate Jennings because he found out he was embezzling from his grandma?"

"Yeah."

"That's pretty thin, Linc," Jacob said after blowing out a

long breath. "Let me call the city detectives, and we'll put our heads together to see what we can legally do based on what we have so far. That's the best I can do."

Linc felt the disappointment like a punch, but he also knew his friend was right. "Thanks, man. Let me know what you all decide."

As the call disconnected, Linc stared at the screen. He needed to call Kylie and let her know all that he'd just done. She'd be pissed, but she'd also probably appreciate him coming clean...and actually making the effort to call her this time.

Deciding to get it over with, he tapped her number. It went straight to voicemail.

Which was odd.

He'd known Kylie long enough to know that, nine times out of ten, she answered her phone. Even when she was angry as hell at him, she answered the phone and bestowed upon him the most agonizing silent treatment ever. He'd only had it go to voicemail once before.

When she'd been taken by the Spotlight Killer.

Shit. His heart sped up. He warned himself to calm down before that gripping panic took hold again. There was probably a good explanation. Maybe she'd been so tired that she turned her phone off and went to sleep.

That didn't sound like Kylie.

Maybe she was in the shower.

Or maybe she'd been killed by Dustin Weiss. Maybe she'd gotten kidnapped again. Maybe...

For every perfectly innocuous explanation he could come up with for her not answering, Linc's mind came up with twenty bad scenarios.

To calm himself, Linc took the exit for her apartment and parked in front of the old Victorian building. His pulse drummed in his throat as he looked around and didn't see her little car. He went inside the building, climbed the stairs, and knocked on the door. "Kylie," he said through the door. "Open up. It's Linc."

No answer. Not even Vader's excited bark.

This was not good.

Linc tried the knob. Locked, of course.

As he was coming down the stairs, the door to the apartment below opened and a familiar college kid stepped out. Linc'd been introduced to him, but he'd forgotten his name. All he knew was that he had a permanently stoned look on his face and that, every time he opened his door, a cloud of pot smoke wafted out into the air that was so heavy, Linc got high just standing in it.

"Hey, you looking for my girl?"

Linc eyed him warily. "*Your* girl?"

"Ah, you know what I mean," he said, punching Linc on the shoulder. He seemed surprised Linc didn't topple over. "Wow. You are one built dude. Want to come in for a beer?"

He was perilously close to grabbing this dude by the throat. "Do you know where Kylie is?"

"No, but I saw her leave."

"When?"

The dude shrugged. "Not much of a watch man, if you know what I mean, but I'd guess about ten or fifteen minutes ago. I was going to be neighborly and invite her for a beer, but she was in a hurry. Went to her place and presto chango, came out not long after wearing different clothes. Practically ran from the building."

This definitely wasn't good. "You see which way her car went?"

Stoner shook his head. "Not much of a compass man either, man, if you know what I mean."

Linc gritted his teeth. "Thanks. If you see her, will you ask her to call me?"

"Sure. What's your name?"

"Lincoln."

Stoner dude saluted him. "Yes, sir, Mr. President."

Linc swiped a hand down his face. "Go smoke another one."

"Sir, yes, sir."

If Linc hadn't been so worried, he might have actually found some humor in the whole exchange. But as he jogged down the remainder of the stairs, the foreboding that had been haunting him grew even heavier.

He was very worried.

Maybe it was his screwed up brain sprouting new ways to be even more screwed up, but he didn't think it was just paranoia or panic this time.

He tried to track Kylie's movements in his mind.

She'd come home, and after changing into more comfortable clothes, she probably sat down with the papers. And the fax would have been missing.

It might have taken her a few minutes, but she'd have figured out pretty quickly that he'd taken it.

She would have then gone looking for him. Straight to the farm? That seemed reasonable enough, since he'd told her he had a class to teach. But she also knew him pretty well. She would have known that if he'd taken the fax, he wouldn't have been satisfied with waiting to confront his father.

Was that where she was now?

And what if Linc was wrong and his father really was an evil man? Would she be walking into a trap?

His heart began to pound even harder.

He called his mother, who answered on the very first ring. She was worried about him, he knew, but he didn't have time to satisfy her with a long conversation. After learning that Kylie hadn't dropped by or even phoned, he promised his mother that he'd call again soon. He'd damn well do it too.

That left the farm.

Jumping in his truck, he headed toward the mountain, intent on getting there as quickly as he could. As he started up the first steep incline, it began to rain.

Of course.

Cursing under his breath, he drove the winding road, careful of the tricky spots. A lot of people had been known to take the curves too fast and ended up flying into the guardrails, especially during rainy weather like this. The rails were battered in a lot of places, there were sections missing entirely in others.

Having driven this route a thousand times since he turned sixteen, Linc knew the lay of the land, the curves to watch out for, and the places to slow down. He increased the speed on his wipers and turned up the defrost as the rain picked up, squinting in the light of oncoming cars to see the faded center line.

As he drove around a curve, he was forced to slam on his brakes. The truck skidded for a second before pulling up to a dark sedan parked on the side of the road. No hazard lights.

That was taking a chance.

There was only a sliver of a dirt shoulder between the road and the guardrail, so the person had parked with his or her driver's side sticking out into the main road. Anyone going too fast, which people had a tendency to do these days, could've slammed straight into it.

Suspecting trouble, Linc slowed and flipped on his hazard lights, trying to see if the driver was in distress as he passed. But from what he could tell, the vehicle was abandoned. Linc slowed even more when he saw what might have been the issue. There was debris on the road from a blown-out tire. Looking closer, he saw skid marks on the asphalt as well as an area where a car might have gone over the side of the road, taking a section of guardrail with it.

One thing popped into his head: Kylie.

Linc knew there was a turnaround about a hundred yards up ahead where he could safely park his truck. Calling Kylie's number again, he pressed on the gas and got himself there, cursing when her phone went right to voicemail. He pocketed his phone and hopped outside, grabbed his pack from the back of the truck, then jogged back the way he had come.

As he ran, cold rain pelted his face. He grabbed his flashlight from his backpack and shone it in front of him, noting what he'd seen from the truck: the remains of a broken tire and dark skid marks.

The dusty road.

The woman in the military vest.

The children screaming.

Pressing the heels of his hands against his temples, Linc closed his eyes against the images flashing before them, willing himself to breathe. To think. To focus.

He wasn't sure how many seconds-minutes-hours passed before he found some semblance of control. With hands that still shook more than he liked, he forced himself forward, shining the light into the cabin of the car, an old Toyota Corolla. It was empty, so he ran to the top of the embankment and pointed his flashlight into the abyss, blinking away the rain to see if he could make anything out.

Nothing. His heart squeezed, and he started to gasp for air. What if he couldn't get to her in time? What if…?

Stop it!

Linc brought a hand to his chest and told himself to calm down, that he needed to be in control, for Kylie's sake. If she was down there, she needed him.

What makes you think you can be a hero after what you did?

Ignoring the voice in his head, he shouted Kylie's name,

then listened closely for any response. But the only answer was the rain, which started to pour, and the wind blowing off the mountain.

Even if it wasn't Kylie, he had a responsibility to go down there. He called 911 on his phone. When the dispatcher answered, he gave his location. "I'm at the scene of what I think might be an accident. Looks like a car went down into the ravine at the S-curve. I can't see what's going on down below, but I'm headed down. There's also an abandoned silver Toyota Corolla here, no status on the driver. Please send the police and an ambulance."

Linc hung up and scanned the area for a way to get down. It was too steep to walk, so he'd have to find a way to climb.

He flashed his light in an arc in front of him, when he noticed something on the damaged end of the guardrail.

Someone had tied a thick length of rope to the end of the railing. It trailed down into the nothingness of the ravine.

Had someone followed her down?

To help or…

He refused to finish the thought.

Linc had no choice. He threw his backpack in place, snapping it together in the front and adjusting the straps. Pulling on the thick work gloves he always kept in his truck, he tucked his other flashlight in his pocket before stepping over the guardrail and grasping the rope.

What makes you think you can be a hero after what you did?

He began his descent, his heart pounding in his ears.

No. He wasn't a hero.

But he had to try.

35

Vader growled, low and deep in his throat.

Kylie blinked and lifted her head, instantly wishing that she hadn't moved.

What had happened? Where was she?

Then memory hit her like a slap.

The car bumping into her. The explosion of the tire. Tumbling down into nothingness.

The sound of steel being crushed and trees snapping.

Then…nothing. She couldn't remember anything after that.

Vader growled again, and the hair raised on Kylie's arms. She tried to orient herself, to find where her good boy was, but there was only layer upon layer of darkness.

"Vader." His name came out as a rasp, so she licked her dry lips and tried again. "Vader." The sound was louder this time, making her head pound even more.

Warm breath heated her ear, and Vader's wet nose pressed into her cheek.

Another growl…longer, deeper, more intense.

If Kylie hadn't known her dog so well, she would have sworn he'd been replaced by a bear.

"What is it, boy? Are you okay?"

Turning as best as she could in the mangled mess of her car, she put her hands on him, feeling for any injuries. He whined a little when she touched his left shoulder, but the sounds transformed into another growl very quickly.

She held her breath, listening for approaching danger. It was raining harder, filtering through the trees, drumming on the metal of her car. She couldn't hear anything else.

The windshield was shattered, and her jeans and coat were soaked, her hair hanging in wet strands on her cheeks. Her body was sore from the impact of the accident. And her head…god, her head.

She pressed her fingers to her temples, trying to get the pounding to stop.

How long had she been unconscious? She had no idea.

She tried to move her legs, but they wouldn't move. She wasn't paralyzed, she knew, because she could feel the metal pressing into her jeans. She was pinned. Knowing she was trapped sent a surge of panic through her system.

Her phone.

Feeling around in the darkness, she willed the device to appear in her hand. She nearly cried in relief when her hand wrapped around it, and she prayed for service as she attempted to turn it on.

Nothing.

A sob escaped her lips, but she pressed them together, refusing to cry.

She had to stay calm and think if she was going to get herself and Vader out of this mess.

Another growl came from the big dog.

That, more than anything else, was terrifying.

Giving up on the phone, she tried to extract her legs, but stopped when sharp metal pressed into her thigh. She didn't think she had any wounds, but she would if she wasn't careful.

Did blood attract bears in the woods like it did sharks in the water? She didn't know and didn't want to find out.

As she was moving about, her keyring jingled, and she remembered one of the gifts her mother had given her several Christmases ago. Pulling the keys out of the ignition, she held the tiniest, most useless flashlight on earth in her hands.

But it was all she had.

Turning it on, she smiled as the tiny beam of light illuminated the inside of the car. She stopped smiling as she saw just how mangled everything was. Her poor little Mazda. She'd have to mourn the loss of it later.

She turned the spotlight onto Vader, who had his nose pressed to the rear window, his hackles raised as he growled again.

The sound was like ice sliding down her spinal cord.

"What is it, boy?"

But truth be told, she really didn't want to know.

Whatever it was, she wouldn't be able to fight it, trapped as she was.

She needed to extricate herself. That was the number one thing on her to-do list.

Shivering from the cold, she shone the light through the window. The little flashlight was strong enough to show her a small swath of uprooted trees and flattened bushes she'd taken down. Kylie stared at it in disbelief. She'd come down that? It looked like nearly a sixty-degree angle. Was it even possible to climb that without equipment?

Focus.

She wouldn't be climbing anything if she couldn't get herself out of this car. Feeling around the back seat, she found a bag of drive-through trash, several empty paper coffee cups, and a whole bunch of junk she'd forgotten to clean out, but nothing useful. Under the seat she found the little first aid kit she'd bought after her run-in with the snakebite couple. Oh, and her dry cleaning. She made a mental note to never buy anything Dry Clean Only again.

She slumped back into her seat. As if dry cleaning was her only problem.

Kylie nearly laughed at herself. Doom and gloom had never been her thing. She wasn't usually so fatalistic. But her head hurt. Heck, her everything hurt. And she was so very, very tired.

Even with the rain dripping in on her, all she could think about was how nice it would be to have a little nap. Just a little one.

It was nearly bedtime, after all. Yes, she would just settle down here, cover herself with her dirty dry cleaning, and then worry about hiking out of the woods in the morning when she could see better.

Grrrr...

Her own hackles rose at Vader's menacing growl.

Then she heard another sound. And another. Another.

A bear? Or something else? Someone else?

"Vader . . ." she said cautiously, straining to see past the few feet the little flashlight illuminated. "What is it, boy?"

Grrrr...

Vader might not be the genius SAR dog that Storm was, but he had a good sense when it came to these things. If he sensed something was wrong, it was wrong.

And whatever was out there, it wasn't friendly.

And there was something out there. Vader could feel it. She could feel it.

Now, spending tonight in the car didn't seem all that wonderful.

"Vad—"

Grrrr...

He was perfectly still as he stared out the window. She let out an uneasy breath and began working to free her legs again, crying out as a piece of something sharp stabbed her through her jeans.

Then there was another sound. Kylie held her breath, listening hard. It was a scraping sound, almost like someone was scrabbling through some gravel. A branch snapped. Another.

Vader barked, the sound like a gunshot in the little car.

Kylie covered her ears, her head pounding furiously now. She screamed when something hit the side of the Mazda, then something else.

Rocks?

Vader's barking became furious, and he began lunging at the window like he was a battering ram in canine form. She'd never seen him like this. He was terrifying.

Through her fear, one thought immerged. Was someone climbing down, trying to help them? Was Vader simply barking like crazy at a stranger? Would he scare the person off?

Or was it something else? She thought of the driver who'd been behind her. Were they climbing down to finish off the job?

Would someone be that reckless?

What should she do?

"Who's there?" she shouted, scrabbling for the first aid kit she'd tossed into the passenger seat. Bug spray. All she had was bug spray. "I've got a gun," she lied, holding the can like a pistol, "and I'll shoot if you don't identify yourself."

Over the sound of Vader's frantic barking, she heard no answer.

Oh, how she wished she really did have a weapon.

Adrenaline making her stronger, she pushed at the dash, pulled on her legs, ignored the bites of pain as metal ripped into her skin.

She needed out of there.

Friend or foe, she needed to get untrapped to either climb or fight.

Then she smelled it.

There was no mistaking the scent for anything but what it was.

Gasoline.

At first, she thought it was her imagination. Then she thought maybe the gas line had been cut in the accident. But as the smell became overpowering, she fought more furiously to extricate herself.

Someone was dousing the car.

Methodically, deliberating pouring gas all around.

Unable to stop herself, Kylie screamed.

36

Linc wasn't sure how far down the embankment he was when he heard the sound of frantic barking. Then a scream.

He froze.

Kylie. Vader.

And someone else.

The thought spurred him on. Though his grip on the rope in the wet weather wasn't sure, Linc went faster, loosening his gloved hand and sliding down as quickly as he could, trying to be watchful of the craggy rocks and trees that were everywhere.

The ravine was steep, and his feet scrabbled for purchase when they hit the ground. He stumbled but quickly regained his balance.

Vader's barking was fierce, but even over the sound, he heard Kylie scream again.

His flashlight was in his pocket, but he didn't turn it on. Whoever was down there, terrifying Kylie, didn't need to see him coming. Plus, his night vision was excellent. He didn't want it ruined with a flash of light.

Muscle memory kicked into gear, and he began to move in military mode, using the trees and rocks to propel him, avoiding the forest floor with its dried leaves and twigs as much as possible. Silence was his friend.

The barking was closer, and so was something else.

He scented the air as Storm would have done if she'd been by his side.

Gasoline.

Another surge of adrenaline dumped through Linc's system as he crept closer, assessing the situation. The car was a mangled mess, held up by a pair of young trees that had thankfully broken the rest of her fall. Looking down, he knew Kylie wouldn't have survived the rest of the plunge.

In the shadows, Linc saw movement, and he crouched, trying to understand what the man was doing. The man carried a flashlight, which seemed to be tucked under his armpit. He was also holding a large container. When the flashlight slipped to the ground, shining up to illuminate the scene, understanding dawned.

Fury burned through his brain as the man's purpose became clear.

Time was not his friend, and silence was no longer needed since the dog's barking would cover any noise made by his movements.

He needed speed.

Pulling the heavy flashlight from his pocket, he hoped the bastard couldn't hear his heart race as he crept up behind him. As careful as he was being, a twig snapped under his shoe, but before the man could turn around, Linc brought his makeshift weapon down on the man's head. The asshole dropped like his legs had been cut out from beneath him.

He exhaled. Easy enough.

The gas can hit the ground too, then began to roll the rest

of the way down the ravine. He needed to let the emergency crew know of its approximate location.

Later.

Right then, the smell was almost overwhelming, but the rain had picked up again, already diluting the scent a little. Thunder rumbled in the distance.

Terrific.

He needed to hurry.

Scrambling over the hood of the car, Linc turned on his flashlight, using it now for its intended purpose, and caught his first sight of Kylie.

She was alive. Terrified but alive. And she was holding something like it was a weapon.

He laughed in spite of the circumstances. Bug spray.

Leave it to Kylie Hatfield to bring a can bug spray to a gun fight, metaphorically speaking.

"Linc!"

There was a waver in her voice and tears were streaking down her cheeks when she smiled, happy and relieved to see him. Bedraggled as she was, she looked so achingly beautiful it made his heart squeeze.

Vader had stopped his yapping and was now lolling his tongue out, looking exhausted but happy to see him too.

Holding on to a tree, Linc made it to the driver's side of the car, but try as he might, he couldn't get the door to open. Climbing back onto the hood, he cursed when the car moved under his weight.

The two trees holding the car up were bending more sharply now. That, together with the rain, could cause the car to slide.

Time wasn't on his side.

"Are you hurt?"

Her hand went automatically to her head, and a large bump already forming on her forehead. "I'm good enough."

He thought that was a fair statement.

"Grab my hand," he yelled. "I'll help you out."

Kylie pulled at her legs, then cried out as something clearly caused her pain. "I'm stuck."

Shit.

Reaching through the busted window, Linc tossed a piece of clothing over her face. "Cover yourself, face and eyes."

She didn't even question him, which was a miracle unto itself. Opening one of the zippers of his backpack, he pulled out a safety hammer and broke out the rest of the glass, using his gloved hand to remove any sharp pieces.

Ducking inside, he moved the flashlight to where her legs were stuck. There was blood there, from a piece of metal gouging through her jeans, but the injury didn't look too extensive.

Her hand went to his face. "You're here. I can't believe you're here."

Grinning, he leaned over and kissed her hard on the lips. "Of course I'm here."

But they didn't have time to chat. Bracing his feet on the dashboard, he pushed with all his might, Vader licking the side of his face in support.

It gave only a little.

He tried again but couldn't get a good enough angle to make much difference. He needed a different plan.

He moved to climb back out of the window, but Kylie pulled at his clothes, stopping him. "Where are you going?"

"Trying a different way to get you out."

She let him go, nodding vigorously, then pressed her fingers to her head at the movement. Probably a concussion. Her pupils had looked huge and the knot on her forehead seemed painful.

She was probably also in shock or getting very close to it.

Going as fast as he could, he slid from the hood, then

checked on the man he'd knocked out, doing a quick pat down for any weapons, which he should have already done. That, in itself, told him how frantic he'd been to get to Kylie's side.

It had been a stupid thing to forget, and he cursed himself as he checked every pocket. The man groaned when he turned him over onto his back. He shined the light on the bastard's face. He didn't recognize him.

He found a wallet, and as curious as he was to know who the man was, it wasn't pressing. It would have to wait.

Patting him down further, he found a pistol in his jacket and relieved him of the weapon. There was a small knife in the front pocket of his pants but that seemed to be about it.

The man groaned again, and Linc pulled a couple zip ties from his backpack, glad he kept some in there just in case. After binding his hands, he used a third one to secure him to a small tree. The mother wasn't going anywhere.

That job done, he tucked the weapons into a pocket of his backpack and pulled out a small lantern with enough lumens to blind someone who stared too long. Placing the lantern on the hood, he pocketed the flashlight, giving him back the use of both hands, then started moving toward the back of the car, intent on opening the hatchback.

If he could get inside, he could lay Kylie's seat down as far as it would go. From that angle, he might have a better chance of pulling her to safety.

"Hurry," he muttered to the emergency personnel, listening hard for any sound of sirens.

Only thunder rumbled, getting closer.

Dammit.

Vader began clawing at the back window, then barking his fool head off again. Linc's hand was on the trunk, ready to open it, when he heard it...

Ch-chunk. The unmistakable sound of a shotgun being racked.

The big dog went crazy as Linc tried to locate the position of the sound, his mind whirling through the possible options. There weren't many, especially since the shooter had higher ground.

"Raise your hands."

It was a female voice, which surprised him. It shouldn't have since the Spotlight Killer had been female too.

Evil didn't discriminate, it seemed.

Very slowly, Linc raised his hands, but before he did, he finished releasing the latch on the hatchback door. Moving his body so that the door remained closed, he slowly turned to face the enemy.

The light from the lamp illuminated her just enough to get a glimpse of her features. She would have been pretty if not for the bright red lipstick that looked like a bloody slash across her face. Mid-thirties or later, he figured.

Her hands shook in fear even as her face was stiff in resolve.

Her hoodie, for a moment, looked like a traditional hijab.

It was *her*, come back from the dead.

No.

Heart pounding even harder at the tricks his mind wanted to play, Linc forced himself to focus. Focus, dammit. He was a freaking soldier. He had training. He needed to remember that.

What makes you think you can be a hero after what you did?

He willed the voice away.

"What do you want?" he asked, his voice less steady than he would have liked.

The woman raised her chin, the angle of the gun going with it. Good. She didn't appear to be a trained marksman, but with a shotgun, you didn't necessarily have to have good aim.

"Where's Dustin?"

And with the question, a piece of the puzzle clicked into place.

"Here!" Linc's father's assistant's assistant called from where he was zip tied to the tree. "Denise! I'm here."

Linc remembered that name. Denise Summers. Emma Jennings's assistant. The stool incident. But how were she and his father's employee connected? And what about Nate?

Denise kept her gun pointed at Linc as she worked her way over the rugged terrain to where Dustin Weiss was seated. Without the use of her hands, the going was treacherous, and Linc prayed she'd slip and slide down the side of this damn mountain on her ass.

She was careful, though, taking her time. The woman wasn't stupid.

Linc kept his eyes on her, and each time she was forced to look away from him, he dropped his hands an inch or so, all while moving to the side to allow the hatchback to open a little bit more. He wasn't worried about the interior light going on because he'd already noticed that the battery had probably been knocked lose. Not even the little clock on the dash had enough juice to be visible.

He wished it was Storm by his side, but he'd been working with Vader, trying to teach him how to protect Kylie. And now, he could only hope the big dog would cooperate. To his astonishment, Vader obeyed his hand commands.

Down.

Sit.

Wait.

The big dog whined only once, limped a little on his left

front leg. But he stayed in the shadows. Stayed quiet. Stayed alert.

Good boy.

Linc closed the hatchback as softly as he could, not wanting it to spring open, giving away his plan. He gritted his teeth when the latch clicked, sounding like a gunshot to his ears.

But the woman apparently hadn't heard it. She was picking her way over to Dustin Weiss, her focus intent on not sliding down the rocky slope. Eyes still on the woman, Linc waited to make his move. He needed to do it before she cut Weiss loose, but the barrel of the gun hadn't moved from his direction. Although she was distracted, a bullet moved faster than his feet.

"Cut me loose, dammit," Dustin barked when the woman was just a few yards from him. "Hurry up!"

When the woman turned to face the bound man, Linc let the backpack slip from his shoulders, catching it on his elbows. He needed to get to the gun.

"Don't tell me what to do!" Denise shouted, turning the shotgun on the other man. "I'm tired of men telling me what to do! You both were stupid! Stupid! And look at us now!"

This was an interesting development.

Drama. It could sometimes be useful.

Linc hurried up his movements, keeping his eyes on the woman as he pulled the gun from the pocket of the pack he'd slipped it in only moments earlier.

The car beside him shifted, causing Vader to startle and back up a good foot.

At first, Linc thought the trees holding it up were giving, but then he realized that Kylie was moving. He wanted to scream at her to stay still, but he knew that wouldn't do any good.

The car's movement caught Denise's attention, but she only glanced in Kylie's direction. The gun was still pointed at her…what? Accomplice? Boyfriend?

Letting the backpack fall to the ground, Linc inched forward, needing a better angle. Vader crept forward beside him, staying at his feet.

"Did you kill Nate Jennings?" Kylie yelled from the car, and Linc wanted to kick her down the side of this mountain himself. This was not the place or time for an interrogation. How did she not see that?

Denise, apparently emboldened from her power position, just smiled. "No. My lapdog did that for me."

Dustin's eyes grew wide. "You bitch!"

Bam!

The unexpected blast of the shotgun made Linc jump, and Vader whined, cowering beneath the car.

But either the shot had missed badly or had only been meant as a threat.

If it was the latter, it seemed to have worked.

Dustin Weiss was thoroughly shaken, huddling into a ball at her feet.

The woman seemed to enjoy frightening the man because she made a show of ejecting the round and racking the next shell into the chamber. Linc tried to get a closer look at the gun, but the woman was apparently left-handed, and the bulk of the gun was hidden from his view. He had no idea if it held three shells, or five, or eight.

"I know you!"

It was Kylie again, and he wanted to slap a hand over his face.

"You bumped into me at Coulter and Associates," she went on. "Knocked all the records out of my hands."

The woman smiled. "You have a good memory. That part

was tricky. If Jonathan Coulter's meddling assistant hadn't raced out with the incriminating files, all of this could have been avoided."

"What do you mean?"

The woman sighed, loudly. "I needed you to drop the papers so they would all jumble together. Otherwise, the pattern of false payments would have been clear."

"It was clear enough," Kylie said, egging the woman on. "I figured it out, didn't I?"

"Yes." The woman lifted her chin. "You did. Even after my warning."

What warning? So help him god, if Kylie had known that she was in danger and didn't tell him about it, Linc was going to wring her pretty neck.

Something bumped into Linc's side. It was Vader, come out from hiding. In the distance, he thought he heard the first wail of sirens. It didn't matter. They weren't close enough.

Linc gave the dog the signal. *Stay.* He could have sworn the big dog nodded.

Thunder rumbled, getting closer even as the bottom fell out of the sky and it began to rain harder. The ground beneath Linc's feet would soon become more treacherous than it already was.

If he was going to move, he needed to move now, or he'd lose his chance.

"Why did you kill Nate?" Kylie asked, but this time, he was glad for the distraction.

He put his hand on Vader's head, glad he was in the shadows. "Get ready, boy," he murmured, his heart pounding harder in his chest.

What if he timed it wrong?

What if he wasn't fast enough?

What if…

He shut that negative shit off. He didn't have time for his crazy thinking to get in the way.

He had to think.

How many bullets did he have? He checked the magazine of the gun in his hand. It would suck if he made a move and the damn thing wasn't loaded.

Six in the clip, one in the chamber.

That was good. That was more than enough.

"He was your lover," Kylie shouted, and Linc took another step closer. "He loved you. How could you kill him like that?"

His stomach sank as the woman turned the shotgun toward where Kylie sat trapped in the mangled vehicle.

He was out of time.

"Go!" he shouted, and Vader took off like a shot.

Linc only had a second to say a prayer for the dog's safety before sighting his gun and pulling the trigger.

The pistol didn't have the same impressive roar, but the aim was true. Blood bloomed center mass.

As the woman stumbled back, her shotgun went off just as the Newfoundland jumped at her chest, pushing her backward.

The roar of the gun, the screams, the thunder almost took Linc Coulter to his knees.

Within seconds, Denise Summers had disappeared, tumbling down the ravine. He could no longer see her, but he could hear her bone-breaking descent.

Where was Vader?

Heart in his throat, Linc made his way to the other side of the car. And saw the big dog about ten yards down, all four legs splayed as he braced himself with all his might.

"Good boy."

Tucking the gun in the back of his pants, he scrambled down the incline and helped the dog back up to some measure of safety. Vader's entire body was shaking, and he whimpered each time he put his left foot down, but he was a hero.

"Good job, boy."

By the time he had Vader secured, red and blue lights became visible at the top of the hill. Finding his phone, Linc called the emergency line again, giving them an update.

"We need a jaws of life, but send down a steel cable so I can secure the car first."

Making sure the car didn't slide was quickly becoming his most primary concern.

The next hour was a flurry of movement as Kylie was extricated from the little car and was being strapped to the safety basket. It was the first time she'd gotten a good look at the little Mazda.

"My car!" She glared at Dustin, who was now sporting a proper set of handcuffs. "You bastard!"

Leave it to Kylie to be more pissed by the loss of her car than the near loss of her life.

"Let's go," one of the EMTs said.

Kylie grasped at Linc's hand before they could carry her away. "Thank you for saving me."

He kissed her. "No bullet holes this time. It's an improvement."

Vader licked Kylie's cheek in a *what about me* gesture, and Linc pushed his wet fur back from his eyes.

"You, good boy, are the real hero of the night."

Kylie winked. "Told ya he was special." She laughed, then held her head at the sound. Definitely a concussion. He'd put money on it. She'd also need some stitches in her leg. She'd done some damage trying to get out and save him.

"Did my questions help?" she asked, her wet hair framing her pale face.

He smiled. "Leave it to you to provide the perfect distraction." Then he nodded to the paramedics. "Time to go."

They could talk later. Right now, they needed off this mountain.

Vader whined as he was strapped to a basket of his own. They'd determined it was the best way to get him out, considering the conditions.

"Don't worry, boy," Linc told him as the wench that would help pull him to safety was engaged, and the big dog began to panic. "I'll see you at the top."

When both Vader and Kylie were both safely off the mountain, Linc sank onto a rock and put his head in his hands.

"You okay?" Jacob asked, sitting down next to him.

Linc lifted his head. "Yeah. Just needed a minute."

"Dustin Weiss is already singing like a canary," Jacob told him. "And search and rescue has already been called in to find Denise Summers. Want to help?"

Linc snorted. "I think I'll sit that one out." He pulled the gun from the back of his pants. "I'm figuring you'll be needing this." Since his fingerprints were already all over the weapon, he did the honors of ejecting the magazine and the round still seated in the chamber. "One round shot, center mass."

Jacob pulled a plastic evidence bag from his pocket, holding it open for Linc to place the weapon inside. "We'll need to swab your hands and get your statement."

Linc nodded. He'd already expected all that. "Can the statement wait until tomorrow?"

Jacob yawned. "Hell yeah, it can. Let's get the hell off the side of this mountain so you can go see your girl."

Linc was ready, and he happily secured the steel cable to the safety harness he'd slipped into once the emergency personnel had hit the scene.

"Need a basket?" one of the EMTs asked.

Linc pulled his gloves back on and shook his head. He surprised himself when he smiled at the man. "Nah. I'm good."

Kylie was safe. Vader was safe.

He'd done his job, and he'd done it well.

37

"Get it, boy!" Kylie said to a still limping Vader.

He wanted to play fetch, but his sprained leg still needed to rest. So, they were compromising.

She rolled the ball a few yards away, and Vader bounded after it as quickly as he could...which was getting better every day. He came trotting back to her, all proud of himself, then deposited the ball, coated in a heavy layer of drool, into her palm.

She grinned at his droopy face and ruffled his floppy ears. "Okay, this one won't be so easy," she challenged, holding the ball in front of her, ready to give it another roll.

Vader heard it before she did, and he went limping over to the driveway just as Linc's truck appeared from around the curve.

Her heart squeezed in her chest when he smiled at her through the windshield.

Vader rushed over to greet him and Storm, so Kylie dropped the ball and followed. She tried to control her own limp, not wanting Linc to worry, but the slash on her thigh still hurt, and the stitches pulled like a mother.

It was her head that caused the most trouble. A concussion was no joke, and her mother had regaled her with all the bad things that could have happened to her, which were many.

Kylie knew that.

With crystal clarity, she knew how close her call had been. And Vader's. She was still a little mad at Linc for putting the good boy in so much danger, but the big dog had come through like a champ.

Like a hero.

Just like Linc.

She also knew that she'd do it all over again. Just seeing the relief on Emma's face when she visited her earlier was reward enough.

As sad as the elderly woman still was, she'd been soothed when Kylie told her that Nate had planned to come clean in the end. It wasn't a lie, either. Dustin Weiss was pointing fingers in all directions and had confessed that Denise had killed Nate when she became convinced he was going to turn them all in.

It was a tangled web, it turned out. Nate loved both Denise and Dustin, and they both used the troubled man to secure his grandparents' riches.

Denise had even stolen the painting on Nate's wall, replacing it with the forged one she'd painted herself.

"That's how she worked," Dustin had said. "One cautious step at a time. It was maddening."

Apparently, the men had wanted their riches much sooner.

Emma cried when Kylie told her that Denise Summers had caused Arnold Jennings to fall.

She cried harder when Kylie told her about how Nate had been the cause of the fire that had killed her daughters.

"The minute Nate told Denise what he'd done, she had

him by the short hairs, emotionally and figuratively," Dustin had confessed. "He became her lapdog after that."

Dustin was brought into the picture when Denise convinced Nate that a threesome would be fun. "She sucked me into the plans," Dustin accused. "I diverted the charity donations and got a cut. I had student loans coming out my ass, and it became clear that it would take years to march up Coulter and Associate's corporate ladder, so I needed the money."

He'd also accused Denise of being the one to shoot out Kylie's tire.

"I was only going to scare her, not kill her," the man had wailed.

But he had no defense for being caught with the gas can, only to say that he was only trying to scare her with that as well.

Kylie hoped he rotted in jail.

Emma had seemed relieved to know that Denise Summers was dead. The rescue team had found her at the bottom of the ravine, the shotgun still clutched in her hands. The medical examiner had put cause of death from a broken neck from the fall rather than the gunshot to the chest, although that, in itself, would have been fatal soon enough.

She knew that haunted Linc.

Once again, she'd put him in the situation where he'd been forced to save her during very difficult circumstances.

In the three days since, he had refused to let her sleep with him, giving up his own bed and taking the guest room for himself.

Twice, she heard him crying out in the night. It'd broken her heart to see him clutching at his sheets, his face a twisted mask of agony when she went running down the hallway to check on him.

She'd learned, though, not to wake him, so she'd sit and

cry as the nightmare came to whatever conclusion only his subconscious would ever know. When he woke, she'd bring him a fresh t-shirt, so he could change from the soaked one invariably clinging to his skin.

Other than that small bit of comfort, Linc refused to talk about what was going on in his mind.

They'd make love instead. Gently. Urgently. Their bodies communicating what their mouths wouldn't say.

"Hey," Linc said as he closed the truck door, pulling her back into the present.

She pressed her hands to his face, pulling his head down until she could kiss him. "Hey."

She had so many questions, but she only asked one. "You okay?"

He pulled her close, laying his head on her hair. "I guess. Dr. Watts was hell. She wanted me to talk about my feelings and shit."

But Kylie could hear the tinge of humor behind the words, and it made her laugh. She was so relieved that he'd kept his appointment with the therapist that her knees felt weak. "The horror."

"It is for me."

She guessed that was true. "So…you don't think it's going to be helpful?"

One side of his mouth quirked up in a half-smile. "I didn't say that." He smacked her ass.

She laughed and moved away from him. This was good. The best thing she could hope for. Getting him to realize he had a problem and go to the first session was the major hurdle, and he'd jumped that.

Her man. Her strong, sexy, amazing man…being all badass and taking control of his mental health. She just wanted to squeeze him. And…other things too.

He walked around the truck and pulled out a couple of

bags from the back. He'd gone to the store with the plans of making her dinner. She ventured a peek, and he nudged her hand away. "What are you making?"

"Food. And you'll like it," he said mysteriously, giving her a peck on the cheek and heading for the front door.

She followed him inside and watched as he started to pull ingredients out of the bags. Pasta…tomato sauce…garlic…

"Something Italian?" she asked, trying to peer in the other bag. She hadn't eaten since breakfast, since she'd been busy all day, meeting with Emma first, then handling a couple of surveillance reports for Greg at the office. Her mouth was already watering.

He slapped her hand away. "Hey. Nosy. Cut it out." He turned on the little TV he'd just installed on the counter.

The news came on, but she looked away. She'd had enough of the news. Kylie shrugged. "Well, you know me. I'm intrinsically curious."

"I sure as hell know that, but I also know that you're not a little kid, and can wait an hour until it's ready," he said, then raised an eyebrow at her suspiciously. "Actually, I don't know that you can wait. But you're going to have to."

"I can't! I hate surprises," she pouted.

He lifted a bottle of red wine from the last bag. She licked her lips and grabbed it, tearing off the foil.

Linc grabbed it back, knowing to not trust her with the cork since she usually destroyed them, leaving little bits of cork bobbing in the bottle.

He popped it open with an ease that made her jealous. He seemed to do everything that way. But all jealousy was gone by the time she took the first sip.

"Thank you."

He smirked. "You won't be thanking me when I tell you that we've been invited to my parents' for dinner."

Kylie groaned. "When?"

"Friday. It's my dad's birthday, so my mom tries to make a big deal of it."

Kylie bobbed her eyebrows. "Cake?"

"Yep. A big one."

Her smile grew bigger. "That means leftovers for a week since the stick insects you call your sisters-in-law probably won't even take a bite."

He laughed, pouring things into a pot.

In the couple days since Dustin Weiss had been arrested, Kylie'd actually gotten to know Linc's father a little more. He was thankful to her for exposing Dustin as a creep, and so the whole bloodsucker thing had been largely forgiven.

"So, we are going to dinner with them?" she asked, needing the confirmation. "I hope so. It'll be fun."

"Root canals are more fun," he grumbled, reaching under the counter and pulling out another pan.

"Stop grumbling! Anyway..." she drummed her hands on the counter, "I have two bits of amazing news I want to share with you."

He looked at her suspiciously. "And...?"

She reached into her purse sitting on the table and pulled out a tiny white card. It wasn't fancy, because Greg wasn't, but it was all hers. And it was probably the most beautiful thing she'd ever seen. Greg had given them to her that morning. She had five hundred of them, just waiting to decorate downtown Asheville. It said:

Kylie Hatfield
Assistant Private Investigator

He read it and smiled. "Business cards, huh? Good for you, Lee."

She clapped her hands excitedly. "I know! I feel so official.

This morning, Greg told me I'd earned it. I think he's still feeling guilty that my little car got destroyed."

"Forget about the car. He's happy you're alive," Linc said, turning up the heat on the stove. "And your second bit of good news?"

"Oh." She couldn't help bursting with excitement over this one. Because it was truly amazing. The most amazing thing that had ever happened to her.

Well, except for the man standing in front of her, but this was a close second.

She reached into her purse and pulled out the check, written in Emma's careful script. She unfolded it and looked at it again, almost like it was a dream that would evaporate the second she shared it with someone else. She pushed it over to him.

He stared at it, and his eyes widened. "Holy shit."

"I know!" She did a little victory dance, refusing to let the wound on her thigh stop her movements.

She'd finally succeeded in making Linc's eyes bug out. "Holy…wow." He was still staring at the check. "Is that for the whole case?"

"No, it's just for me! She called it my bonus!" She snatched the check to stare at it again. "Fifty freaking thousand dollars! I gave it to Greg, thinking I should split it with him, but he said it was all mine."

He turned to her, pride practically glowing from his expression. "That's amazing, Lee. Really amazing." He got back to work, setting the pans to heat on the stove and pulling out a cutting board. "This is turning into a celebration dinner. What are you going to do with your newfound wealth?"

Kylie smiled. She'd been thinking about it ever since she first got the check in her grubby little hands. She'd never had this much wealth, ever, but it had quickly sunk in how little it was in the grand scheme of things, compared to how much debt she currently had hanging over her head.

"I guess I should be practical and put it toward school loans." She sighed, her bubble deflating a little. "I have a lot of those. Or just put it in the bank for a rainy day?"

She expected Linc to agree with her. He was nothing if not practical. But he shook his head. "To hell with that. It's a bonus. You're supposed to have fun with a bonus. Plus, don't you need a new ride?"

She thought of her poor little Mazda. She had insurance, of course, but she'd also learned that she would only get about three thousand dollars because of its age. That had been a blow.

"What kind of car do you want?" Linc asked as he began chopping vegetables.

"I've always wanted a VW bug, but…"

Linc put down the knife. "But what?"

She worried her lower lip. "Well, since it looks like I'll be making a lot of trips up and down a certain mountain, I'm thinking something with four-wheel drive will be more practical."

He turned to face her again, and although her stomach was rumbling, she wished they weren't having this discussion while he was making them dinner.

"And…" she went on before he could jump to any conclusions. She pulled out a flyer from her purse. She unfolded it, staring at the pictures, and slowly passed it over to him.

He raised an eyebrow. "A townhouse?"

She nodded. "They're brand new. They're building them right in downtown Asheville, so it'll be within walking distance to the office. And they'll have twenty-four-hour security, all the latest amenities, a gym, not that I'll use that, and—"

"Wow. It's nice," he said, turning away from her but not before she saw the look of disappointment on his face.

"I've wanted my own place forever," she explained, "and this money will make a good down payment. I'm not much of a decorator, but I thought with my own walls to paint and my own things, I could actually get into it. Make a little corner of my world that's just my own."

He nodded. "Okay. I get it."

Did he? She wanted him to be happy. She wanted him to give her permission for this. Because his opinion meant everything to her. "You don't think I should?"

He shrugged, the knife chop-chop-chopping away. "It's not that. You should buy whatever you want, but I meant what I said before."

Kylie sucked in a breath. She knew exactly what he meant. He'd mentioned it once, but she thought he'd done that in the heat of the moment, because he was so worried about keeping her safe. She didn't think he'd actually want her around like that, every day. Besides, wouldn't they drive each other crazy, being together like that, all the time? "You did?"

"Yeah. I don't mind sharing, Lee. You know that." He waved a hand, but still didn't face her. "You can change anything you want. Decorate."

Kylie didn't know how to respond. She looked around the house he'd so willingly offered up to her, and tears sprang into her eyes. This place was so much better than any townhouse. And even better, it came with Linc.

But, in reality, they'd only known each other a short while. Plus, it had been all her fault that his PTSD had kicked into high gear.

If she moved in with him, she wouldn't just be risking her own heart, but his.

Her heart seized up. "I…I…"

"Hey. It's all right." He put down the knife and picked up her glass of wine, taking a long drink. "Just know that the offer is out there."

She nodded, relieved to be taken off the spot. "Thanks."

He set the glass down and opened his arms to her. She slipped inside them, and he laced his fingers around her back as she pressed her cheek against his hard chest.

Yes, this felt right.

But Kylie wasn't sure if it felt like forever. Honestly, she'd come from a broken family, where she'd seen a lot of heartbreak, mostly on her mother's side. She didn't know anything about forever.

As Kylie settled in, Vader jumped between them, wanting to get in on the hug. Maybe he was trying to tell her something, but she didn't want to think about that. She just wanted a nice night of relaxation, without having to worry about the future for once.

After the crazy few weeks they had, they'd earned as much.

But just because they earned it, didn't mean it was going to happen. When she looked up at Linc, there was something in his eyes that told her she'd hurt him.

And that was the last thing she wanted.

Why couldn't she jump at this chance? Most other women would. He was perfect, gorgeous, sweet, capable... everything. She should've been sitting in his lap, picking out curtain colors right now to replace the old, sun-bleached gingham ones that had belonged to his grandparents.

Funny...threats from murderers and stalking serial killers didn't seem to scare her.

But this? Moving in with the guy she was crazy about?

Her heart pounded at the thought.

She stood on her tiptoes and kissed his jaw as a little

voice inside her said, *You know you love him. And he won't wait for you forever. Just say yes. Say it, Kylie. Yes. Yes. YES.*

But for once in her life, her tongue betrayed her, and she found it difficult to form any words.

She swallowed, licked her lips. Just say it, she told herself. She opened her mouth.

"...William Hatfield witnessed the account, and officials state that he is cooperating fully."

Kylie pulled back, turning to the little television. A man was walking down the sidewalk, surrounded by other men. His name flashed on the bottom of the screen.

William Hatfield.

"What's wrong?" Linc asked, but she couldn't answer as she peered into the man's face.

She'd only seen one picture of the man. Her mother had put all the others away.

It looked like him.

The man being led into a police department somewhere in New York…could it be?

Could he be her father?

The End

To be continued...

Find all of the Kylie Hatfield books on Amazon.

ACKNOWLEDGMENTS

How does one properly thank everyone involved in taking a dream and making it a reality? Here goes.

In addition to our families, whose unending support provided the foundation for us to find the time and energy to put these thoughts on paper, we want to thank the editors who polished our words and made them shine.

Many thanks to our publisher for risking taking on two newbies and giving us the confidence to become bona fide authors.

More than anyone, we want to thank you, our readers, for clicking on a couple of nobodies and sharing your most important asset, your time, with this book. We hope with all our hearts we made it worthwhile.

Much love,

Mary & Bella

ABOUT THE AUTHOR

Mary Stone lives among the majestic Blue Ridge Mountains of East Tennessee with her two dogs, four cats, a couple of energetic boys, and a very patient husband.

As a young girl, she would go to bed every night, wondering what type of creature might be lurking underneath. It wasn't until she was older that she learned that the creatures she needed to most fear were human.

Today, she creates vivid stories with courageous, strong heroines and dastardly villains. She invites you to enter her world of serial killers, FBI agents but never damsels in distress. Her female characters can handle themselves, going toe-to-toe with any male character, protagonist or antagonist.

Discover more about Mary Stone on her website.
www.authormarystone.com

Bella Cross spent the past fifteen years teaching bored teenagers all about the Dewey Decimal System while inhaling the dust from the library books she loves so much. With each book she read, a little voice in her head would say, "You can do that too." So, she did.

A thousand heart palpitations later, she is thrilled to release her first novel with the support of her husband, twin girls, and the gigantic Newfoundland she rescued warming her feet.

facebook.com/authormarystone
instagram.com/marystone_author
bookbub.com/profile/3378576590
goodreads.com/AuthorMaryStone
pinterest.com/MaryStoneAuthor

Made in the USA
Middletown, DE
25 September 2020